THE HEROES OF EASTBROOKE SERIES

CHRISTIAN ROMANTIC SUSPENSE SERIES

JULIETTE DUNCAN

BOOKS 1 - 4

Cover Design by http://www.StunningBookCovers.com

Copyright © 2022 Juliette Duncan

All rights reserved

The books in THE HEROES OF EASTBROOKE SERIES BOOKS 1-4 are works of fiction. Names, characters, and incidents are all products of the author's imagination or are used for fictional purposes. Any mentioned brand names, places, and trade marks remain the property of their respective owners, bear no association with the author, and are used for fictional purposes only.

THE HOLY BIBLE, NEW INTERNATIONAL VERSION®, NIV® Copyright © 1973, 1978, 1984, 2011 by Biblica, Inc.™ Used by permission. All rights reserved worldwide.

PRAISE FOR JULIETTE DUNCAN

★★★★★ "Juliette Duncan is a very gifted author" - Amazon reviewer about **Under His Watch**

★★★★★ "Another awesome book to lose yourself while reading" - Amazon reviewer about **Under His Watch**

★★★★★ "Juliette writes so well and has become my favorite Christian author." - Amazon reviewer about **Within His Sight**

★★★★★ "Mesmerising. From the first page I couldn't put the book down" - Amazon reviewer about **Within His Sight**

★★★★★ "Great book. What more need I say? - Amazon reviewer about **Within His Sight**

★★★★★ "Loved this book and series. Christian suspense using flawed characters that turn to God for help. I would recommend it! - Amazon reviewer about **Within His Sight**

★★★★★ "Very good read! Clean and wholesome. Good story line!" - Amazon reviewer about **Safe in His Arms**

FOREWORD

Note from the Author:

HELLO! Thank you for choosing to read this book - I hope you enjoy it and are blessed by it! Please note that this story is set in Australia, and Australian spelling and terminology have been used throughout.

Happy reading!
Juliette

SAFE IN HIS ARMS

PROLOGUE

They were trapped.

Panic rose inside Junia as the reality of the situation sunk in. The adrenalin that had kept her going through the crazy events of the last hour had subsided. In its place, terror curled in her stomach.

Below, smoke blanketed the horizon, darkening the sky and thickening the air. Above reared the mountaintop, high and forbidding against an azure sky. She swallowed hard, fighting to keep her cool, but her body began trembling uncontrollably. Their route off the mountain was blocked in every direction except up.

"Junia," Max said, his voice low but urgent, and threaded with pain from his gunshot wound, "Did you hear me? The radio signal isn't coming through...I can't get hold of my brothers."

She sucked in a breath. If only her thighs and hands would stop shaking. "What do we do?" Her voice sounded muffled.

"We have to go higher so we can get around the other side." His mouth was set in a grim line.

She gave a slow nod, trying not to voice her immediate fear. They could only go so high. She was no mountain climber, and if the fire came in their direction, it would catch them in minutes.

"Will we get a signal if we go higher?" She was grasping at any slight hope. If they could get through to Joseph, who worked in Mountain Rescue, to give him their location, the Rescue helicopter could pick them up.

"Maybe. We'll keep trying. Come on."

But she couldn't move. Her ears still rang from the gunshots which had seemed impossibly loud on the quiet mountain. They had no idea where the gang members had gone, if they were looking for Max to finish him off, or if they'd managed to catch Tasha.

Where was she? A fresh wave of panic surged through Junia. The girl was as trapped as they were, but she was alone with no survival skills, and the gang members were after her, intent on dragging her back to the city.

Even worse, she'd fled straight in the direction of the fire.

Junia stared at Max, her lip trembling. "I'm...I'm scared."

He held her gaze, and for a moment she thought he might hug her. But of course, he wouldn't. They'd only known each other a week, and she'd already gleaned that he was far from a touchy-feely person. Instead, he narrowed his gaze. "I'll look after you. We'll be fine." His voice was gruff but held a small amount of compassion. *But how could he be so sure they'd be fine?* He suffered from a gunshot wound and a raging bushfire was hot on their heels.

"We need to pray," she said. Only God could help them out of this mess.

He nodded. They might not see eye to eye on everything,

but they both had faith in God. That was something. Taking her elbow, he led her to a rock where they sat next to each other.

He enclosed her shaking hands with his. This token of empathy was totally out of character for the gruff wilderness guide who'd kept himself at arm's length all week. If they weren't fearing for their very lives, being close to him could have been pleasant. In that moment though, she was simply grateful for his strength.

She swallowed hard, closing her eyes and trying to go within, to reach the peace that was always there, deep down, but terror welled up in her again. Throwing herself on God's mercy, she prayed aloud for them both.

"Lord, lead us through this danger to a place of safety. Guide our steps that we might find rescue and refuge. Calm the fires with Your mighty hand. Heavenly Father, watch over Tasha. Keep her safe from her pursuers. Blind their eyes so they don't find her. In Jesus' name, we pray. Amen."

"Amen," Max echoed.

Raising her head, Junia met his gaze. Pain filled his eyes. She lifted one of her hands from his and placed it gently over the roughly bandaged wound in his shoulder.

"Lord," she prayed again, "send Your healing to Max. Bind his wounds and heal his flesh. Take his pain from him. I beseech You in the name of Your Son. Amen."

He drew a deep breath and released it slowly, as if allowing God's healing presence to touch the injury, before lifting his gaze and nodding. "Thanks. It feels a bit better."

Still seated, with one of her hands in his, Junia sensed something had changed between them. Perhaps because they faced a common enemy. Their gazes held, and she felt her face warm as she suddenly realised how close they were. They both dropped their hands and gazes at the same time, and an awkward silence filled the space between them.

Max coughed and stood, and the moment was gone. "Come on," he said briskly. "We need to move. The further we can get away from that smoke, the better. Even if the fire doesn't reach us, the smoke will kill us."

With his words, Junia was again reminded of how desperate their situation was. They had to go up before they could go down, because there was no way they could traverse the sheer cliffs on either side. They couldn't go back, because that would put them in the direct line of the fire.

As she followed him up the mountain, she tried not to think what would happen if help didn't come soon. They were truly in the wilderness, and right now, there was no escape.

CHAPTER 1

One week earlier

"Okay guys, we're here." Junia stepped down from the minivan and waited for the young people she was responsible for to follow. One by one they climbed out and waited for the driver to get their bags from the luggage hold while she looked around. Eastbrooke Mountain Retreat looked just as the brochures had pictured. A small property at the bottom of a forbidding looking mountain, just two kilometres out of the small town of Eastbrooke, it had seemed the perfect place to bring the teens for a ten-day retreat, where they would learn team building and practical survival skills of a different sort to the ones they were used to. These were kids who knew how to survive on the street, but she wondered how that would translate to the wilderness. Her hope was that this retreat would boost their self-esteem, as well as teach them gratitude for the simple things of life.

Not to mention burn off some of that adolescent energy.

Chuck, an angelic looking blond boy with ADHD and a previous tendency to set things on fire, jostled Gavin, a brooding boy with a prominent gang tattoo on the side of his neck.

These were her kids, not just her work. They were her vocation. After her own struggles in childhood, Junia had always known she'd become a youth worker, and she couldn't imagine doing anything else. She loved her job, as challenging as it sometimes was.

She cast her gaze over the group. Four boys, two girls, all with their own stories to tell, challenges to overcome, and potential to be watered into bloom. As well as Chuck and Gavin, there was Marley, a quiet girl with purple braids, Sonny, the joker of the group, and Kevin, a youth offender who was determined to turn his life around and was the unspoken leader.

And then there was Tasha. With her slight frame, huge green eyes and high cheekbones, the girl was both fragile-looking and beautiful, but her appearance was deceptive. Having run away from an abusive home at the age of twelve, she'd ended up in the midst of gang life. She was as hard as nails and about as forthcoming. Although she'd been with Safe Harbour, the Christian youth charity Junia worked for, for less time than the others, Junia was surprised she'd lasted even this long. Yet, Tasha had seemed excited about this trip. Junia guessed it was the closest thing she'd ever had to a holiday.

"Okay guys, everyone got their bags? Let's go in, shall we?"

She bid goodbye to the minivan driver, who reminded her that he'd be in Eastbrooke for the weekend if they needed to go anywhere. She made a mental note to ask about churches since it was Sunday the next day and it'd be nice to take the guys to a service if possible. Not all of them were Christian, but they all seemed to enjoy the worship sessions Safe Harbour ran each week.

As they walked towards the main building, a slight, fair-haired guy of about thirty came out and greeted them.

"You must be Max," Junia said, stepping forward and smiling, although his voice wasn't as deep as she recalled when they spoke on the phone.

"No, I'm Jay, Max is in there." He indicated behind him and held out his hand.

"Well, I'm Junia. Nice to meet you." She shook his hand.

"I can show the kids to the dorms while you check in if you like," he said, shoving his hands in his pockets.

"Thanks. That'd be great." Junia smiled again and gave the youth cohort a gentle, encouraging push before she followed the signs to reception. Reaching the steps, she glanced over her shoulder before entering the small, log building. The teens didn't need her to hold their hands every moment of the day, but this was new to them. She prayed silently they'd be polite and would show gratitude to the young man, not give him a hard time as they tended to do. She blew out a breath, walked up the steps, and opened the door.

A small bell jingled as she pushed it open. A dark-haired man, who'd been sitting with his head down behind the desk, looked up.

Now, *this* man's looks matched the deep voice on the phone. With dark hair, piercing blue eyes, sensual lips that were at odds with his chiselled face, and a wiry, muscular frame, Junia was momentarily tongue-tied.

He lifted a brow. "Can I help you?"

She felt flustered, almost lost for words. "Yes, sorry. I'm from Safe Harbour. Your worker, Jay, took the young people to their dorms." She extended her hand over the counter. "You must be Max Carlton."

Standing, he nodded and shook her hand, his grip firm and cool. "And you're Junia Fox. How was your trip?" His voice matched his grip and confused her. She'd expected a warmer welcome. After all, they were paying guests.

"Oh, it was fine…" she began, but then her voice trailed off when he began rifling through a drawer as if he wasn't at all interested in her reply.

He looked up moments later with a key in his hand. "We've prepared a separate room for you. It's small and basic, but basic is how we do things here. Or did you want to sleep in the dorm with the girls?"

Junia chewed her lip. She wanted to keep an eye on the youth in her care, but she also wanted them to enjoy the experience and have some time to themselves. It also didn't seem fair that the boys would get to board on their own if the girls didn't.

"I'll take the room. Thank you."

"I'll show you where it is." He stepped from behind the counter and headed for the door. She was surprised when he held it open for her, but once outside, she struggled to keep up with his long, lean stride. He took her to the main building, which was also made from rough-hewn logs, and had a long, covered walkway down the middle. She followed him to a small room opposite the dorms.

He was right. The room was definitely basic, but it had a cosy feel. There was a small single bed with a mattress that looked clean, a wooden chair with a navy-blue chair pad under the window, a sink and a small cupboard. The floor was timber, as were the walls. It was clean, and the view from the window was stunning, the mountain rearing up like a sentinel standing guard.

"It's lovely," she said, setting her bag on the floor and glancing at the clock on the wall. It was already four in the afternoon. It had been a long drive, and she would have loved a short nap, but doubted there'd be time. "Is there a schedule for today?" she asked, swinging her gaze back to him.

He stood in the doorway, arms crossed. He was close enough for her to see the stubble on his face which glinted in the late afternoon sunlight streaming along the verandah. "Dinner's at five-thirty in the hall. Jay's wife Sonia does the cooking. I'll do some fire-building with the group tonight before they head off to bed. There's a schedule in reception. I meant to give you one."

"I'll come back with you and get it," she said.

He shrugged and headed down the steps, leaving her scurrying to catch up with him again. Despite his reticence that bordered on rudeness, there was something about the wilderness guide that made her curious. He seemed to be a man of few words, but there was no harm trying to make conversation.

"It looks like an amazing place. What inspired you to start the retreat?" she asked as they walked across the yard towards the reception cabin. Or rather, he walked, she half jogged.

He shrugged again. "I like the outdoors. The place used to be my father's." He didn't offer any more, and although she burned with curiosity, she sensed he wouldn't appreciate her prying.

Back in reception, he handed her a few copies of the schedule, printed simply on plain paper. As she cast her gaze over one of them, a flicker of excitement coursed through her. She was a city girl, and this was her first wilderness retreat as well, and the schedule looked amazing.

The next day, Sunday, was relatively light. Sonia was scheduled to take them for a short hike in the morning, followed by Sunday lunch and a recreation afternoon, but the week was filled with everything from high ropes, to bush craft, to foraging. For the last few days, they'd venture up the mountain for a three-day hike and camp where they would implement the skills they'd learned over the course of the week.

"It looks great," she said, smiling. "Everything the brochure promised."

"Good," Max replied, retreating behind the counter to sit in front of the computer, effectively dismissing her.

"Right, I'll see you at dinner then," she murmured.

He lifted his gaze momentarily. "I eat in my rooms. I'll see you for the fire-building session."

"Okay, well, bye then." She headed for the door.

He grunted inaudibly, making her wonder why he was a retreat leader when he had such limited people skills. She shrugged. Maybe he was simply having a bad day. She'd learned not to judge people by first impressions in case something had happened to make them act differently to whom they really were. She'd so often seen troubled teens judged for their poor behaviour when they were simply crying out for help, but most people didn't see that.

Reaching the path, she remembered she hadn't asked about a church. She started to head back inside but decided to ask later rather than disturb him again now. She got the impression he'd rather not see her again so soon.

Instead, she headed for the dorms to distribute the schedules. The four boys were lying on their bunk beds listening to music. Their bags were strewn on the floor, half unpacked, and already the room smelled like rotten socks.

The boys sat up when she handed out the schedules. Chuck was excited about the fire-building, although the other boys teased him, albeit in a good-natured way. Even Gavin seemed relaxed.

In the girls' dorm, looking lost amidst six bunk beds, Marley was tutting at her phone while Tasha stood by the window, staring out of it.

"I can't get a signal. This sucks," Marley grumbled.

Junia raised an eyebrow. "You do remember you weren't supposed to bring a phone, right?"

Marley sighed as Junia held her hand out, but she passed her the phone anyway. "I forgot," she mumbled.

"Of course, you did," Junia said with a grin. She walked over to Tasha, who was still staring out the window. "You okay, hon?"

Tasha lifted her shoulder without turning. "Yeah, suppose."

Junia lowered her voice. "You can come and talk to me anytime if you need to, you know. About anything."

"I know," Tasha mumbled, still not looking at her, although her face softened a little.

Junia smiled sadly. Tasha reminded her of herself when she entered foster care at the age of thirteen, desperate for someone to love her but too fearful and distrusting to show it or allow anyone to get close. She'd been lucky. She'd been adopted quickly by a lovely Christian couple she now called Mum and Dad. A lot of children in care never got that opportunity. Not enough people wanted to take on a troubled teen; people wanted cute little kids.

She left the schedules on a spare bunk bed and returned

to her room to unpack and prepare for dinner, wondering just what the next ten days had in store.

∼

THEY WERE GATHERED around the fire pit, a collection of wood stacked on one side. Max studied the faces in front of him. The boys looked curious and ready to learn some skills, the girls less so. That was fairly typical. City girls often had little interest in wilderness pursuits, but if they ever got lost in the wild, the elements were no respecter of gender.

This evening was simply an introduction to fire-building. Later in the week he'd teach them about gathering materials. He'd found that city kids had little idea how to set and light a fire they could cook on and that would last for hours, but he gained great satisfaction from teaching them those basic survival skills.

Junia sat on the ground amongst the group of teens. He was carefully avoiding her gaze, but that was easier said than done. Her sudden appearance in the cabin that afternoon had unnerved him. The group had arrived early, but it wasn't that. He hadn't expected her to be drop-dead gorgeous.

To be honest, he hadn't given any thought to her before she appeared at the door. She was simply a name on an email and a voice on the phone, but the moment she stepped inside, she'd pretty much swept the breath from his chest. She was wearing a white V-necked top paired with faded jeans that accentuated her slim figure, but it was her eyes that captivated him. Deep hazel, brimming with tenderness and compassion.

He'd been short with her. Rude, even, but it had been the only way to control the unexpected, and unwelcome, reaction of his heart.

He was resolutely single and had been for some years. He loved solitude and the freedom that living in the wilderness gave him. If he was ever lonely, his mother and three brothers weren't far away. He didn't need people around him...and he carefully avoided any exploration into why that might be. As a result, he didn't think much about women, or feel the desire for a relationship.

And so, his immediate reaction to Junia had thrown him. Now he had to act professionally and not give any hint that she'd bowled him over. It wasn't just her looks, though. There was a light about her, what his mother would describe as 'spirit'. He found her intriguing, and even felt an urge to get to know her, which was pointless, because she was here as a paying customer with her bunch of teens, and she'd be gone in ten days and he'd never see her again. So, he had the next ten days to get through without making a fool of himself.

He hunkered down in front of the fire pit and began to talk, demonstrating as he did so. "If you're ever lost in the wild or find yourself having to stay outdoors without resources for any reason, then knowing how to build a fire could save your life," he told the group, his serious tone immediately grabbing their attention.

"Fire's your friend in those circumstances, but it can just as easily be your enemy. Up there, on the mountain, you won't have a fire pit like this to contain it, and fires can get out of control fast. You must respect fire, and never take its power for granted." He paused, letting his words sink in, then gave a rare grin. "Right. Who knows anything about building one?"

The lad called Chuck raised his hand eagerly. Judging from the sniggers the others gave, Max gathered that the boy's experiences with fire were less wholesome than a course on survival skills.

He motioned him over. "Okay." He gestured to the pile of firewood. "What would you start with?"

Chuck hesitated, then pointed to one of the bigger logs. "Uh, with that?"

"And what would you light it with?"

"A lighter."

"And what if you didn't have one?"

He shrugged. "Dunno."

His eyes widened when Max pulled a flint from his pocket and demonstrated how to get a spark. "Want to have a go?" Max asked, offering the flint to the lad.

"Sure." He took ten tries, and then frowned. "This isn't going to light that log, is it?"

"No," Max said with a small chuckle, "it isn't." He picked up a handful of bark. "We start with stuff like this. It's less dense and burns easily, especially when it's dry. When we go on the hike, you'll strip it from the trees yourselves, but I'll show you how to do that so you don't take too much and harm the tree. I'll also show you how to use an axe to create kindling, but this evening, this will do just fine."

As Max helped Chuck get the tinder going, a look of achievement grew on the lad's face. Max then took the smaller logs and showed the group how to make a smaller teepee fire. They all had a go at lighting the flint, and then with his help, each built their own teepee fires in smaller, pre-prepared pits. By the time he showed them how to ensure their fire was properly extinguished and how to cover the ground so that no trace was left, the sun was disappearing over the mountains.

"That was great!" Chuck enthused as the group began heading back to the dorms.

Max grinned. Fire-building was always a winner. For someone so resolutely solitary, he was always surprised by how much he enjoyed teaching, especially youth, and how seeing city kids loosen up was so rewarding.

Junia hovered at the back of the group, her hair glowing rose-gold against the sunset. He tried not to think how close she was, or how pretty she looked in the soft evening light.

"They absolutely loved that, thank you so much." Her smile lit up her pixie-like face and sent his heart spinning as he fell into step beside her.

"I'm glad they enjoyed it," he said, swinging his gaze ahead of him, while very conscious of her beside him.

"I wanted to talk to you about tomorrow's schedule."

"Yes. What did you want to ask?"

"We're supposed to be going for a hike in the morning."

"Yes, with Sonia. I'll be at church."

She turned her head and stared at him. "Really? I was going to ask if there was a church in town that I could take the kids to. We normally do a church service on Sundays back at Safe Harbour, but it'd be good for them to go to a proper church for a change. That is, if you're happy for us to tag along. Although we're supposed to be going on the hike. We couldn't change that, could we?"

He blinked. How had this happened? She was intending on bringing the teens to his quiet, little church? *What would everyone think?* But that wasn't the real problem. *She'd be with them.*

He raked his hand across his head and met her gaze. "Ah... I guess it would be okay. We could change the hike to the afternoon."

"That would be great. Thank you." She smiled, then an awkward silence followed as they stared at each other for a moment.

He quickly averted his gaze and breathed a sigh of relief as the dorms came into view. "Good night." He lifted his hand as he veered towards his cabin.

"Oh, okay, then. Goodnight." She sounded miffed.

He didn't blame her. He'd been rude again. But what else could he do? He was way out of his depth. As he walked off, he felt sure she was staring at his back.

CHAPTER 2

After the teens were settled for the night, Junia spent some time praying for them before she, too, turned her light off and tried to sleep, but it didn't come quickly or easily. The bed was narrow and hard, and with no traffic noise, the silence was deafening, broken only by the occasional hoot of an owl.

After half an hour, she put on some quiet praise and worship music and finally drifted off. The following morning, a shard of sunlight beaming through the flimsy curtain woke her. Sighing, she checked the time on her phone. It had just turned five. No wonder it felt like she'd just gone to bed. Hoping for a few minutes more of sleep, she squeezed her eyes shut, but it was useless. She was awake, and her mind was active.

Climbing out of bed, she stretched and slipped on a pair of jeans and a pink T-shirt. According to the schedule, breakfast was at seven, although Max had told her it was self-serve, so there was plenty of time to take a walk and have a quiet time.

After grabbing a light jacket, she headed outside with her Bible in hand and breathed in the crisp, mountain air. It smelled of pine needles, damp moss, and a hint of smoke. Dappled sunlight filtering through the trees cast a gentle light on the sleeping earth. It was such a peaceful time of day, especially when no one else appeared to be up.

The previous afternoon she'd noticed what looked like a bush chapel. It wasn't far, only a two-minute walk from the main centre along a gravel path, so she headed in that direction. Reaching the secluded area encircled by towering eucalypts, she entered reverently and sat on a roughly-hewn timber bench. It was slightly damp, but it didn't worry her. Birds chirped in the surrounding trees, and dappled sunlight made patterns on the leaf-covered ground. A slight breeze started up, rustling the branches above.

She hadn't experienced such peace in a long time. After taking a few moments to enjoy it, she bowed her head and spent some time in prayer before opening her Bible and reading. She was part way through Colossians three when footsteps crunched on the gravel path. She looked up and peered through the trees, quickly hunkering down. It was Max. She didn't want to hide from him, but he wouldn't want to see her, she was certain of it. Not knowing what she'd said or done to upset him, she still had the impression he didn't like her. In fact, he'd been downright rude last night. She had a good mind to respond in kind, but that was at odds with her reading. *Therefore, as God's chosen people, holy and dearly loved, clothe yourselves with compassion, kindness, humility, gentleness and patience.* Although it would be difficult, she needed to treat him with kindness, even if he didn't reciprocate.

When he passed by without seeing her, she bowed her

head and prayed for him. She wasn't sure what his problem was, but he sure had one.

Later, while she and the teens were helping themselves to breakfast, he walked by again. Taking a deep breath, she stepped outside and smiled. "Lovely morning, isn't it?"

He stopped and turned around, looking momentarily stunned.

"Sorry, I didn't mean to interrupt you," she said when he didn't respond. "You're obviously on your way somewhere."

"No. It's fine." His Adam's apple bobbed and a muscle in his jaw twitched. "I've just come back from my morning jog."

He didn't look as if he'd been jogging, but he was probably so fit he rarely broke a sweat. "I was wondering if you'd like a lift to church? Our driver's collecting us in half an hour." She'd called him the previous evening and arranged for him to collect them in time for church.

His blue eyes flickered. "Thanks, but I'll drive myself. I've got to go. Sorry." He hurried off before she could say anything further. She shook her head. What a strange man.

Half an hour later, the minibus pulled into the retreat's circular drive and stopped in front of the main building. Junia and the group of teens had only just assembled after cleaning up after breakfast, so it was good timing. She smiled at Tom, the driver, before shepherding the group into the back of the van. Once they were all in, she climbed in beside him.

"Thanks for coming for us," she said as he put the vehicle into gear and headed back along the road he'd just driven.

"No problem. How was your first night?"

"Good. We did some fire-making, and they all seemed to enjoy it." She nodded her head to the back where Chuck was entertaining the others with a rousing rendition of whatever the latest number one song was.

"Fire-making, ey? I'm sure Chuck was in his element."

She had to shout to make herself heard. "Yep, but I think he learned some stuff as well." Chuckling, she shook her head. Chuck's energy was infectious. She hoped they'd all settle down before they reached the church, especially since they'd never been there before. She didn't want them to make a spectacle of themselves.

Eastbrooke was a small town with a gold rush history, overlooked by mountains on one side and forest on the other. Junia peered out the window at the stunning scenery which was much nicer than the scenery around the inner-city suburb where she'd grown up, where apartment blocks outnumbered trees two to one. What it would have been like to grow up in an area like this where the air was crisp and clean and unpolluted, and cows were more common than cars.

They reached the tiny, white-washed chapel perched on a hill overlooking the small town five minutes later. Tom parked the van and they all piled out before he drove off again, promising to be back in time to drive them back to the retreat. He was staying with friends who didn't attend church.

Standing in the car park with the group, Junia wondered if it had been a mistake bringing them. There didn't appear to be any other young people, and in fact, there weren't many people at all judging by the number of vehicles. But it was too late. Tom had gone.

She drew a deep breath and turned towards the chapel. The first person her gaze landed on was Max. He was standing outside chatting with a plump, dark-haired woman dressed in a light pink, cashmere jacket and white, knee-length skirt. She was perhaps in her late forties, possibly early fifties, and wore a welcome badge on her jacket lapel.

As the group approached, she stepped around Max and beamed widely at Junia. "Good morning, dear. Welcome! I'm delighted you decided to come along."

Junia's brow shot up as she glanced at Max. How did this woman know they were coming to church that morning? *Had he told her?*

He cleared his throat while she took in his stubble and brilliant eyes. "Junia, this is my mother, Jean."

She swung her gaze back to the woman. Yes, there was a family likeness. Jean had the same full lips and dark hair as Max, but that's where the likeness ended. He must take after his father. Not that it mattered. Did the older Mr. Carlton attend church as well? It was strange. From the way he'd behaved so far, she was surprised that Max came from a religious background. But then, this was a small country town and perhaps it was normal for folks to attend church out of tradition, as opposed to conviction or belief.

Introducing herself and the young people to Jean, Junia was pleased her protegees were on their best behaviour. They smiled and greeted Jean politely, including Tasha, although her smile didn't quite meet her eyes. She looked brighter than she had the night before, though, which was promising.

They were about to go inside when a man who resembled Max walked up, hugged Jean, and turned to Junia with a grin. "You must be the new guys up at the retreat. I hope my big brother's treating you well." The man slapped Max on the back and chuckled.

"He taught us to build a fire," Chuck piped up. "Like, a proper one, not with petrol."

The man's eyes widened before his surprised expression turned into a grin. "I'll know where to look if there are any unexplained fires in Eastbrooke, then."

Chuck's face grew red, and when Jean said, "Rob's our Deputy Chief of Police in Eastbrooke," his eyes darted wildly.

"Oh really? How interesting. I imagine it's quiet here, though," Junia said quickly, rescuing Chuck who now looked as though he wanted the ground to open up and swallow him.

Rob smiled, his eyes twinkling. In spite of the physical similarities to Max, his personality was clearly very different. "Most days. But when things happen, they happen. It's never dull."

"Eli's in the force, too," Jean said as two other men approached, both with chestnut hair and broad shoulders. "And Joseph's head of Mountain Rescue."

"Yes," said the man who must be Joseph, "so if Max gets you lost, don't worry."

Max glared at his brother, straightening to his full height. "I never get lost. I'm a wilderness guide."

"That's true," Joseph said good-naturedly. He walked into the church, followed by Rob and Eli, who cast his gaze over the group of teenagers and nodded at Junia as he went inside.

"Shall we go in?" Jean said. "I don't think anyone else will be coming."

Junia blinked. Surely the church didn't consist only of Max's family.

Jean led the way, motioning for the teens to follow her. Junia walked along behind them, Max beside her. "Your family seems lovely," she whispered.

He nodded but didn't respond.

"Does your father come to church, too?" she asked.

"He's dead."

She almost tripped over her feet. She started to apologise for being insensitive, but Max had already strode ahead, making a beeline to the front of the church where his brothers waited.

Glad to see that more than the Carlton family filled the remainder of the pews, Junia directed her group into the back row, shaking her head at Gavin when he sat heavily and sighed with exaggerated boredom.

"Shush, Gavin," Marley tutted before Junia could say anything. "The rest of us voted to come. Deal with it."

Junia hid a smile as she sat next to Tasha, who was looking around the small church with interest.

"It's different to the church building at home," she said. "It's pretty."

Junia nodded. The stained-glass windows and old-fashioned pews made it very different to the stark community building they used at Safe Harbour. "It is," she agreed, trying not to let her pleasure show at hearing Tasha refer to Safe Harbour as 'home' for the first time. It was the first safe home the girl had experienced, and Junia hoped that her use of the word was an indication that she was starting to gain some trust in them.

Tasha peered up at the stained glass, looking suddenly childlike and much younger than her fifteen years. "It's lovely," she said softly. "They've even got angels."

Junia nodded again, not wanting to say anything to interrupt the girl's obvious pleasure.

"Junia?" Tasha asked hesitantly.

"What is it, Tash?"

"Do angels really look out for us?" She spoke quietly, most likely so the others couldn't hear.

Junia nodded. "I believe so. That's what the Bible says."

Tasha looked like she was about to say something else when the organ started playing. Standing to sing the first hymn, Junia worried that Gavin and Chuck, in particular, would get fidgety as it was different from the worship songs they were used to, but they were surprisingly quiet. Marley sang beautifully, while Tasha didn't join in but continued to stare at the depiction of angels on the coloured glass.

After the hymn, Jean introduced the service, reading a passage from Luke and then inviting the pastor, a small, neat man with grey hair, up to the podium to give the sermon. Junia did her best to concentrate but was distracted by keeping an eye on her group, who quickly got bored and started whispering between themselves, and by Max, sitting up ahead, straight backed and still, just slightly taller than his brothers. She felt awful for unwittingly asking about his father and wondered what the story was and if it had anything to do with why he seemed so gruff, unlike the rest of his family. Perhaps, as the eldest, he felt like he had to step into his father's shoes.

The sermon ended and they sang another hymn, which was followed by communion. Junia took the elements with the usual sense of reverence and peace that came over her whenever she participated in the ceremony that remembered the body and blood of Jesus that was broken and poured out at the cross, displaying His sacrificial love. She recalled the very first time she'd ever taken it, not long after she'd been adopted by her foster parents. Not only had she found a family, she'd also found her Heavenly Father, and she remembered that sense of wonder that she was, after all she'd been through, deeply and wonderfully loved. It was a feeling she wanted to convey to all the troubled youth who came through Safe Harbour, many of whom had never known real love at all.

The service ended and Jean invited the group to stay for morning tea. Junia was glad that Tom was already waiting in the car park because she was sure the teens wouldn't cope with small talk and tea, although they might have enjoyed the biscuits. "Our driver's waiting; otherwise, we would have loved to stay," she replied sincerely.

Jean patted her on the arm. "Maybe next week, then. It was nice meeting you, dear." Her smile was genuine and made Junia glad she'd come.

∽

Please babe, I love you.

The heavily tattooed man smirked to himself as he hit send, then growled in frustration as the message remained pending.

His second-in-command looked across the room at him. "What's up? Still not got hold of Tasha?"

The gang leader's lip curled and he shot the other man a glare that kept him quiet. He was not a man to cross, they all knew that...but Tasha running away and refusing to come back had made a total fool of him.

She needed to be taught a lesson.

Of course, he needed to find out where she was first. She'd called him a week ago, as he always knew she would, but in spite of his best attempts to manipulate her, she refused to disclose her location. He'd tried both sweet talking and veiled threats, but although he sensed her weakening, she'd cut the call without warning and hadn't phoned back. He'd texted her every day since, and his blood boiled at the thought that she really might have gotten away. She'd been talking some nonsense about finding God after falling in with a bunch of do-gooders. If he didn't get her back soon, he doubted he ever would.

There were always plenty of girls. A never-ending supply so desperate to be loved they'd believe any nonsense he gave them. It wasn't that Tasha was any different…except that now she was, because she'd left. It had been weeks now, and she should have come back with her tail between her legs, begging his forgiveness.

She was making a fool of him, and he couldn't afford to let that go unpunished.

"She'll be back," he said with more confidence than he felt. *What if she'd gotten rid of her phone?* He'd track her down–there were only so many church projects that dealt with girls like her. But then he would risk being arrested, and he'd promised himself a long time ago that he'd never return to jail. Tasha was underage, and he knew what the penalties were for exploiting a minor. He'd need to play it carefully.

"What if she doesn't come back?" his deputy asked.

He glared at the man. "You questioning me?"

His deputy shrank back but then righted himself with a shrug. "She hasn't come back yet. Aren't you worried she might snitch?"

He balled his hands into fists. It was happening already. His boys were growing cocky, spurred on by Tasha's insubordination and his failure to do anything about it. "She wouldn't dare," he growled.

"But what if she doesn't come back?" his deputy repeated.

Narrowing his eyes, he stared out the window at the grey neighbourhood. *His* neighbourhood. "Then we find her, and we drag her back," he said in a voice that brooked no argument. Tasha would regret crossing him.

He'd make sure of it.

CHAPTER 3

Junia sighed heavily as she made her way to the reception cabin before the evening meal, hoping to find Max there. Their first full day of activities at the retreat had gone well...or would have, if it hadn't been for Tasha. She'd complained loudly through every session, been nasty to Chuck, nearly made Marley cry with her cutting comments, and had been downright rude to every adult who'd spoken to her. Junia had debated sending her back to the dorm on her own, but worried she'd run off. It was unlikely, especially as Tasha would have no idea how to get back to the city, but the sudden mood she was in foreshadowed impulsive and self-sabotaging actions.

It was heartbreaking, because Tasha had seemed so different the day before. Church had left her quiet and reflective, and Junia had hoped that signified some positive change. Two steps forward, one step back was part of Tasha's pattern, and so perhaps Junia should have expected this, but she still felt uneasy, wondering if Tasha was building up to something.

Junia reached the cabin and knocked lightly on the thick wooden door. Despite his aloofness, she felt a fluttering in her stomach as Max's deep voice told her to come in. She stepped inside, and for a moment thought she detected a smile on his face, but it was so fleeting she wondered if she'd imagined it.

"Is everything okay?" he asked with a slight frown.

"I just want to apologise," she began, hovering in front of the desk. "Tasha was so rude today, and she spoiled the day for everyone. I've tried to speak to her, but she doesn't want to listen." She paused, sighing heavily. "The rest of the kids really enjoyed it, though. You're a great teacher."

This time, a small smile did tip his mouth. "Thanks, but don't worry. We've had much worse than Tasha here. Last year a group of rich kids from some posh school came and they were the most badly behaved group we've ever had. She'll settle down."

When Junia didn't answer, he looked at her astutely, lifting his brow slightly. "You don't think so?"

"I'm worried about her." Junia blew out a breath. "She's conflicted, but she won't talk about it, which for her, is dangerous."

Max nodded towards the stool in front of the desk. "Sit down and tell me her story. But first, do you want a hot drink?"

Pleasantly surprised by both his interest in Tasha and his hospitality, Junia accepted his offer as she climbed onto the stool. Her feet didn't reach the ground, so she hooked her boots onto the rungs and started talking as Max fixed the drink. "She's got a sad story. She came to us after running away from foster care and getting involved in a gang. She could have been sent to a government facility for juveniles, but I'm glad she came to us instead."

He shook his head as he set a cup of hot chocolate in front of her, made of real cocoa. The smell made her mouth water.

"No parents?" he asked.

"Her mother died, and her father disappeared when she was young. She hasn't had it easy, and so we try to be as understanding as possible. Her social skills were never going to be great, but her attitude today was something else. She worries me."

Leaning against the wall with his arms crossed, he eyed her carefully. "There's something specific you're worried about, isn't there?"

Junia nodded slowly. Choosing her words carefully so as not to compromise Tasha's safety, she replied. "We think she was involved with the gang leader. Perhaps not sexually–she's underage, although that doesn't always matter to these people–but certainly she developed an emotional dependence. If you've never known a real family, then gangs can seem like a substitute."

Max's eyes softened. He seemed more empathic than she'd initially given him credit for. "I can see why that would happen. So, you think she'll go back?"

Junia shrugged. "It's a possibility, and it's happened with her before, although not while she's been with Safe Harbour. I could be wrong. Maybe she was just having a bad day today, but I get a feeling for these things."

Max nodded thoughtfully and stared out the window before swinging his gaze back to her. "What's she good at? What does she like doing?"

Junia blinked at the change in conversation. "Oh...erm, she always says when she was young, she wanted to be a vet and that she loves animals."

He drummed his long fingers along the windowsill. His

hands were brown and calloused. Hands of an outdoors guy. "I sometimes do a tracking class, identifying animal trails and such. I could do something on it tomorrow, just the basics, and give her a task. Team leader, even. She might feel more engaged." He paused a moment. "Maybe she was out of her depth today."

His sensitivity surprised Junia. Clearly, she'd underestimated him. She smiled. "That's a really great idea, thank you."

He shrugged offhandedly. "I've been doing this for a while. You get a feel for how to manage teenagers, although I certainly couldn't do it all the time. I really admire people who do the work you do."

Junia's cheeks warmed. "I…I can't imagine wanting to do anything else," she said honestly. "My youth worker made such a difference to me that I knew from a young age, it was the job for me." As soon as the words were out of her mouth, she realised she'd revealed much more about herself than she'd meant to.

Max's eyes were kind as his gaze held hers. "You had a similar background?" he asked softly.

Despite her initial uncertainty about him, she instinctively felt safe in his presence. "Nothing as brutal as Tasha's," she said, deflecting her gaze to her hands, "but I was in care after my parents died. I was angry and rebellious and could so easily have gone down a similar path, but like I said," she lifted her gaze, "I had a great case worker, and she placed me with a Christian family who adopted me. Being part of their family completely changed my path. Since then, I knew I wanted to do something similar."

Max nodded with approval.

Warmth flowed through her, but as she sipped her hot chocolate, she hoped that her pleasure in his affirmation wasn't obvious. For some reason, she wanted to impress him, perhaps because she sensed he wasn't easily impressed, but she didn't want him aware of it.

"You weren't a Christian before you were adopted?" he asked.

She shook her head. "No. I don't remember much, but I think I only ever went to church once. My parents never talked about faith, so I don't know what they believed. But they were good people." Well, at least she thought they were. Her memories were tainted by imagination and sometimes she had trouble discerning what was real and what was imagined, but recently, when she'd met up with an aunt she'd found after much research, she learned that her parents had been free spirits and had never stayed in one place long, but that they loved life and loved her. It was a pity they accidentally overdosed on drugs and died.

A shadow crossed Max's face. She guessed he was thinking about his own father. Not wanting him to withdraw again, she changed the subject. "How about you? You seem involved in the church here."

He nodded. "We were all raised with faith, so I've never known anything different. My mother's devout, as well as my brother, Joseph. Rob just goes through the motions, I think, whereas Eli is..." he scratched his head, "resentful."

There was a story there, Junia sensed. "And you?" she asked, holding his gaze.

He hesitated before answering, his expression guarded. "I believe," he said quietly, "although I've always felt closer to God outside in His creation than in church, even as a kid."

"You've always loved the outdoors, then?" she asked, pleased when his face lit up. Obviously, this was an easier topic of conversation for him.

"You bet. Out there, on the mountain, I feel part of everything. Aware both of how small and insignificant I am, and at the same time such an integral part of God's creation. It's where I do most of my praying." He abruptly fell silent, looking faintly embarrassed.

She smiled with encouragement. "I think that's beautiful," she said honestly. "I've never had that much access to the outdoors, not like this, really in the wild. I'm finding it therapeutic, and the skills you teach are interesting and different. You have a real gift for teaching."

His gaze dropped to the counter. "Uh, thanks," he said, for a moment seeming almost vulnerable. Then he looked back up and his voice was brisk. "I'd better get on. So, we have a plan tomorrow, and hopefully it will help Tasha feel more a part of everything."

He was dismissing her. Trying not to look disappointed, she slid off her stool and nodded. "Yes. Fantastic. There isn't a session after dinner tonight, so I guess I'll see you in the morning."

"Yes." He picked up her empty mug, gave a nod, and disappeared through a door.

What had she said to make him cut off their conversation so abruptly? Deflated, she left the cabin, shutting the door behind her. She strolled back to her room, gazing up at the hazy lilac sky over the top of the mountain. A gust of wind blew around her, raising bumps on her arms, and then it just as suddenly died down, leaving the air eerily still. The mountain loomed overhead, somehow distantly comforting, like a silent protector.

A scripture came to mind, seemingly from nowhere.

I lift my eyes to the mountains—where does my help come from? My help comes from the Lord, the Maker of heaven and earth.

Closing her eyes briefly, she felt a subtle sense of God's presence both within and around her, stirring her heart, touching her soul. *"Thank You for this beautiful place, Lord, a reminder of Your immense power and majesty. I stand in awe of Your creation."* Opening her eyes, she continued on, taking in her surroundings. Even the air was different to the city, sharper and clearer, as though it were possible to take a deeper breath. It was both invigorating and yet tiring at the same time. Despite her anxieties about Tasha, at night she was sleeping like a baby.

She prayed Tasha would respond to Max's idea tomorrow, that she'd benefit from his firm, but fair ways. He'd surprised her just then, revealing a whole new side...but then he'd retreated again, closing himself off. As someone who'd been through heartache and grief, she recognised the pain in him, no matter how well he hid it.

There was a story there concerning his father, and as much as Junia tried to tell herself it was none of her business, she found herself thinking about him for the rest of the evening.

CHAPTER 4

The next day, after breakfast, Max sat outside the cabin with a cup of hot chocolate, watching the mountain, enjoying ten minutes of solitude before taking the morning session.

He hadn't slept well, which was unlike him. Although he rarely needed more than a few hours' sleep each night, those hours were deep and he usually woke refreshed. Last night, though, he'd tossed and turned, his dreams unsettled. He couldn't remember much about them other than that they'd featured his father...and Junia.

He didn't want the dreams of his father to return. Nightmares had haunted him for years after his dad's death, and although he'd loved the wilderness since childhood, it had been after his father's death that he'd found himself withdrawing more and more, finding peace only under the open sky, away from the bustle of the town and the familiar faces of its residents. Everyone had loved George Carlton, the Chief of Police for Eastbrooke, a regular churchgoer and generally upstanding guy. Max had loved him too. In fact, growing up, his only answer to the question 'what do you want to be when you're older', was always, 'my Dad.'

His death had affected them all. Max had found solace in the wilderness, Joseph in his faith, Rob by hiding his sadness behind a wall of charm. Eli, who'd still been a child at the time, carried a burning resentment for the world that made Max worry about him. They all knew Eli had entered the police force not so much to be like their father, but out of a desire for revenge. The person who'd planted the bomb that killed George Carlton had never been caught. Eli still obsessively researched the case, hoping to track him down one day. But Max didn't blame the bomber.

He blamed himself.

He sipped his hot chocolate, willing the thoughts away. *Create in me a clean heart, O Lord*, he prayed silently, quoting his favourite line from the Psalms, *and renew a right spirit within me.*

But it wasn't only thoughts of his father that were plaguing him. It was Junia, too. She intrigued him, and her beauty captivated him, but more than that, he felt instinctively drawn to her kindness and resilience. Hearing part of her story the evening before had made him feel protective of her. He hated the thought of her ever feeling lost, grieving and alone. Losing his father had devastated him, but she'd lost both her parents. He couldn't imagine that.

Pushing away his maudlin thoughts, he set his mug down and got to his feet, striding purposefully towards the outdoors teaching area to meet her and her young charges. Animal tracking was usually a popular class, and he hoped he would indeed be able to engage young Tasha. If he were honest, a part of him also wanted to impress Junia.

They were waiting for him. Tasha was off to the side of the others, her arms crossed and a sullen expression on her face. Junia caught his gaze and shrugged, giving him a rueful smile.

He gave a nod before facing the group. "Morning all," he greeted with a firm voice.

Seven pairs of eyes turned towards him.

"Slight change of plan today. We're going to look at identifying animal tracks. Anyone here interested in wildlife?" He didn't look at Tasha as he spoke, but out of the corner of his eye he saw her raise her head.

"Tasha wants to be a vet," Marley offered.

Tasha glared at her as though the other girl had just revealed her darkest secrets.

"Is that right?" Max said. "Okay, Tasha, come and stand with me. You can be team leader for the day."

Her eyes widened and then narrowed, but she didn't refuse. She took a few steps towards him.

"What's your favourite bush or mountain animal?" he asked.

She hesitated, then mumbled, "Tiger quolls."

He raised a brow. A lot of people hadn't even heard of the incredibly rare, possum like creatures that could be found on mountain ranges. She must have studied this stuff, he thought, because she could never have encountered a tiger quoll living in the city. "Well, you're in luck, because they've been spotted on the mountain before," he told her, gratified when her eyes lit up. It was suddenly obvious how young she was now that the permanent scowl had lifted.

"Really? Will we see one?" she asked.

"It's doubtful," he replied honestly. "They're night creatures, extremely rare and very shy, but we can certainly try and find their tracks." He turned to the others. "For those of you who don't know, the tiger quoll is an endangered species and is protected by conservation regulations. They're one of

Australia's largest marsupial carnivores and look similar to a possum, except they're golden with distinctive, large, white spots. They're beautiful animals, but they're night hunters. That's right, isn't it, Tasha?"

She blinked in surprise and then nodded with shy pride. "Yes," she confirmed. "Also, they're marsupials and are sometimes known as 'tiger cats.' They have a really, really strong bite, nearly as strong as the Tasmanian Devil!" She blushed and fell silent, peering up at Max through her fringe.

He sensed her need for approval and smiled encouragingly at her. "I can see I've picked the right person for team leader."

Tasha beamed with pride.

He exchanged a quick glance with Junia, whose eyes shone with joy. He felt a spark of connection between them, and a small flip in his stomach. He broke the gaze quickly. He couldn't be alone with her again like they were last evening. She was beautiful, captivating, a truly good soul...and therefore dangerous to his carefully guarded heart.

He continued with his talk, telling the group about the other animals they might encounter, and describing their prints and scat, which predictably resulted in questions from the boys and murmurings of 'gross' from the girls. Then he took them for a walk at the bottom of the mountain to see what they could identify, letting Tasha lead the way with him while Junia stayed at the rear to ensure no one was struggling. Tasha peppered him with questions all morning, her eyes glowing. Although she was disappointed when they didn't find any tracks of a quoll, she announced it would be her mission for the hike. By the time they returned from their walk, she was happy and laughing with Marley, a complete change from yesterday.

Junia caught up with him as they walked towards the

dining hall as it was time for lunch. The teens had run off in front, no doubt starving. "That was amazing. I've never seen her so enthused about anything. Thank you so much."

He looked away, not wanting her to see just how much her compliments pleased him. "It's my job," he said shortly.

"Yes, of course." She sounded deflated. "Well, thank you, anyway."

He'd been too short with her. Rude, again. He turned to apologise, but she was already hurrying to catch the others. He watched her, the breeze lifting her hair around her shoulders, and felt a pang of longing in his heart he didn't know how to explain.

"SHE'S VERY BEAUTIFUL, that youth worker," Joseph said to him later as they sat in front of the wood burner in his cabin. When he was on the Mountain Rescue night shift, Joseph often visited. Although all the brothers were close, it was Joseph whom Max felt the most affinity with. Like him, Joseph loved the outdoors and connected it with his faith.

Max frowned. What had prompted his brother's sudden observation? *Was Joseph attracted to Junia?* The surge of possessiveness that ran through him took him by surprise. He narrowed his gaze. "Yes, she is," he said warily. "What made you say that?"

Joseph smiled. "I could tell how carefully you were avoiding her at church on Sunday. You like her, don't you?"

Max shifted uncomfortably in his seat. Joseph knew him too well, so there was little point in denying it. "She intrigues me," he admitted. "She's so devoted to the youth she works with, and she seems so genuine...and totally unaware of how beautiful she is. Of course, I've noticed her. I'm only human." He could hear the defensiveness in his tone.

Joseph raised an eyebrow. "But?"

"But what?"

"Well, I'm obviously making you uncomfortable."

"Yes, you are," Max snapped, annoyed at his younger brother's attempts to needle him. "She's a customer at the retreat. Talking about her like this is inappropriate."

Joseph pursed his lips. "I don't objectify women, you know that. It's just...I've never seen you unsettled by a woman before. Maybe it's God's will that she's here right now."

"I don't know what you mean." Max stared into the fire, not wanting to contemplate what it might mean if his brother was right...if God had meant for his and Junia's paths to cross.

"You rarely date. You're always here, at the retreat or up the mountain."

"I like it here. You of all people should appreciate that."

"I do," Joseph assured him. "I just...I worry about you. You're alone too much. I know the guests here keep you busy...but in your heart, you're alone."

Max felt a sudden pang of grief, a stabbing of emotion deep in his chest. His brother was right, because it was a condition that he had deliberately, and carefully, cultivated. He was fine with being a bachelor, and happy to leave it to his brothers to one day give their mother the grandchildren she craved. He was happy with his life...so why were his brother's words stirring the grief in his heart?

"I'm not really in the mood for your psychoanalysis, Joe," he said, although he kept his tone light, hoping that a touch of brotherly humour would distract Joseph from digging too deeply into his feelings. As much as his younger brother loved working in Mountain Rescue, Max often thought his true calling would be as a chaplain or counsellor. Joseph had a knack for seeing inside people that often unnerved someone as self-contained and private as Max.

"I just want you to be happy," Joseph said softly, "and I can't help feeling that this girl might help in that regard."

Max shook his head. "She's been here four days! And you met her once. I think you're running away with this one."

Joseph shrugged. "I just have a feeling. I could be wrong. It's how *you* feel that counts." He left the question in his words unspoken, while Max avoided his gaze and carried on staring into the dancing flames inside the wood burner. He loved fire, the beauty and danger of it.

As if reading his thoughts, Joseph changed the subject. "Are you doing the hike at the end of the week with this group?"

Max nodded. "Yes. There's not a weather warning out, is there?"

"Not yet, but it's the perfect conditions for a bushfire right now. I'll be surprised if a fire ban isn't issued in the next few days. Obviously, you have the fire pits here, but if you're on the hike…"

"I'll be careful. We can do the hike without making fires, if need be. It's not exactly cold right now, even on the mountain. It'd be a shame, though. Kids always love building fires, but there are plenty of other skills we can practice. Putting up the shelters is always fun."

Joseph nodded. "Just make sure your radio's in good working order so you get any warnings. I don't want to have to rescue you if you get stuck."

Max laughed and Joseph grinned back. It was a running joke between them. The laughter cleared the tension that had been raised by talking about Junia, and they sat in companionable silence, sipping their drinks and staring into the fire, both lost in their own thoughts.

CHAPTER 5

*J*unia checked her bag for the second time to ensure she'd packed everything she needed for the hike. It wasn't much since Max insisted they take the bare minimum as they had to carry their own packs. Just a bedroll, a container of high fat snacks, three water bottles, a change of clothes and underwear, and basic toiletries, plus a one-man, pop-up tent. Jay and Sonia had a tent for themselves and the teens had several between them, but Max, so Sonia told her, slept under the stars in his bedroll. Now, that was beyond basic, in her opinion.

As she hoisted her pack onto her back, the prospect of what lay ahead over the next few days sent a fizz of excitement through her.

Not least was the prospect of getting to spend a few more days with Max.

The week had flown by, and she hadn't had the chance to speak with him alone again since that evening in the cabin. Although he was unfailingly polite, she couldn't shake the feeling that he was avoiding her, and after the way she'd opened up to him, the perceived rejection stung. Especially as the more she got to know him, the more admirable she found him. The way he'd gotten Tasha to engage with the group had thoroughly impressed her.

She still worried about Tasha, however. Although she'd become less hostile after Max suggested making her team leader, a role she was treating seriously, something still wasn't right. Too many times Junia had caught her staring off into the distance, and then starting guiltily when she noticed she was being watched. It was just a hunch, but Junia was sure she was contemplating her old life, perhaps even the idea of returning to it. Gang life retained a strong pull on teenagers who found themselves caught up in it, especially those who had little experience of stable family life. Junia had been praying hard all week. She prayed for all of those in her care, of course, but Tasha was most in need of intercession right now. The girl was physically safe, but internally, she was still messed up.

When Junia headed out to meet the others and to do a roll call, the teens all looked eager to get going, including Tasha. Jay and Sonia were going through the list with them, making sure they had everything they needed.

Max looked over at her and gave a nod, and just for an instant he looked almost boyish, his eyes twinkling. She beamed back at him, feeling her cheeks flush, and felt the familiar pang of disappointment when his usual wariness returned. It was almost as though he was scared of her, as if she unsettled him somehow.

"Morning, Junia," Sonia said warmly. "All ready to go?"

"As ready as I'll ever be," she quipped, hoisting her backpack fully over her shoulders, almost stumbling under its weight. How she would ever climb a mountain with this on her back, she had no idea. Pasting a smile on her face, she prayed silently for strength.

Chuck bounced on his heels, obviously eager to get going. Max had appointed him Trainee Fire Marshall, and just as Tasha had responded to her task as team leader, he'd responded with enthusiasm to this vote of confidence. Junia had never seen him so eager to help. Bringing them to the retreat had absolutely been the best idea, even if she'd initially had her doubts.

"Okay team," Max said, the authority in his voice clear. "Let's go."

A FEW HOURS LATER, Junia's muscles felt like she'd run a marathon. She wasn't unfit. She walked everywhere in the city, went to the local swimming pool and a weekly yoga class, but hiking up a mountain with a pack on her back was an entirely different thing. Each step required way more effort than a brisk walk around town.

At least she was bringing up the rear and the teens couldn't see how sweaty and out of breath she was. Max, Jay and Sonia were used to hiking in these mountains, and the teens possessed all the energy of adolescence. As invigorating as the hike was, Junia was relieved when Max announced they'd reached the place where they'd set up camp for the night. Swinging the pack from her shoulders, she collapsed onto a patch of grass for a moment and caught her breath.

Max headed in her direction, his brows furrowed. "Are you okay? You look exhausted."

"Yes, I'm good, honestly," she replied, panting. "It was just much harder than I expected. I enjoyed it, though." She finally caught her breath and looked around. "It's so beautiful here. Even the air seems purer."

He crouched beside her. "It is. It's my absolute favourite place to be. But you must say if it's getting too much. We could have stopped earlier."

"*Now* you tell me." Laughing, she grabbed her water bottle from her bag and took a long, grateful swig, pleased with his change of demeanour.

He chuckled. "Well, you'll be pleased to know we won't be walking nearly so far tomorrow. Just an hour or so in the morning to go a bit higher, and then we'll set up camp and stay there for the next two nights. We'll take the walk back in stages. I want the guys to practice their survival skills, not spend the entire time walking."

"Sounds good to me." She took another slug of water.

Max frowned. "Sip, don't gulp. You'll get cramps, plus our supplies need to last. Although," he winked, "we've brought a bit more than needed, just in case. Most teens aren't great at rationing, especially when it's their first time."

She nodded in agreement as she stretched her leg muscles. "So, what's the plan for the rest of the day?" A few moments resting in her tent would be amazing.

"We'll have a snack and then put the tents up. That's always fun with first timers. Then we'll split into two groups to find firewood and kindling, build the fires and cook dinner, and by then, it'll be time for bed."

She suppressed a yawn. Bedtime couldn't come soon enough.

Putting up the tents was as fun as Max suggested it would be, and then it was time to collect the firewood. Junia and Sonia went with the girls, while Max and Jay went with the boys.

With only two girls, keeping an eye on Tasha was easy.

She'd shown an interest in tracking during the hike, still vocal about wanting to find signs of tiger quolls, but now she'd grown quiet and seemed unenthused. Still, Junia thought, as she yawned loudly, she could just be tired.

With arms filled with kindling, the foursome returned to camp where Max showed everyone how to make a fire pit in the ground, and then Chuck lit the kindling successfully, glowing with pride when Max, Jay and Sonia warmly praised his newfound skills.

Dinner was a quiet affair—it seemed the hike had taken its toll on the teens after all, and they couldn't wait to go to bed.

Once Junia had ensured they were settled in their tents, she headed for the fire and sat on the ground beside it, stretching her legs out, enjoying its warmth. The last rays of the sun were disappearing behind the mountain in a soft hue of orange. Above, the sky had turned from light blue to black, and a few stars popped out overhead. The whole vista was gorgeous and filled her with awe.

∽

TASHA HAD JUST ZIPPED up her sleeping bag when Marley announced she was going to the toilet and wanted her to go with her. Tasha shook her head. "Nah. I've just got all snuggled up."

Marley humphed and unzipped the entrance to the tent, clambered out and then zipped it behind her to keep the cold out. It had been a scorching day, but Max had already warned them that temperatures on the mountain would drop at night. He was right. It was already freezing.

. . .

THE CRUNCH of dry leaves and twigs under Marley's footsteps receded as she headed away from the tent. Tasha should have gone with her. Marley would be scared walking around outside on her own, let alone peeing in the bushes where anything could be lurking, but right now, Tasha needed privacy. Reaching inside her sleeping bag and inside her clothes, she lifted out the mobile phone she kept hidden. The one Junia didn't know about and therefore couldn't confiscate. She held her breath as she turned it on, waiting for the screen to flicker into life and hoping she wouldn't get a signal. If she didn't, it wouldn't be her fault she wasn't answering his messages. He couldn't blame her then.

But he would. She knew he would. It always followed the same pattern. He'd tell her she was his favourite of all the girls in the gang. The clever one, the one he could trust. Then she'd do something wrong, something small, but he'd say she'd been disloyal. She'd let him down and deserved to be punished.

He had a way of making her feel he was right, although most of the time she didn't know what she'd done to anger him so much. But she probably did deserve to be punished, or he wouldn't do it, would he? Not when he told her he loved her and one day when she was older, she'd be his.

Part of her knew this was part of the cycle of abuse. They'd taught her that at Safe Harbour, and she'd recognised straight away that his pattern of behaviour fit everything she'd learned. He was an abuser. He deliberately made her feel worthless and dependent so that she'd remain tied to the gang.

But they were the only real family she'd ever known.

Her heart sank as the message icon flashed on her screen. Thirty-six new messages. Only *he* had this number; he'd given her the phone. It was a 'burner' phone, and the one she'd used to help him sell his merchandise. He always said she was great at it, a 'proper little saleswoman.' Because she looked so innocent, she could smuggle drugs in anywhere.

It had been a very long time since Tasha had felt innocent.

She scrolled through the messages, her mouth growing drier as she read them. His tone changed as she continued to not respond, from loving to stern, to pleading in a way that made her want to call and tell him she was so sorry and would never hurt him again, to outright threats. There were always threats in the end.

I'LL FIND YOU, *Tasha.*

And he would, she knew he would. He could do anything. And then what would happen? It'd be better for everyone if she contacted him, said sorry, and went back. He'd beat her, but it wouldn't be as bad as what he'd do if he tracked her down.

She couldn't be the person Safe Harbour wanted her to be. Who God wanted her to be. They believed in her, especially Junia, and now, Max. But they were wrong. She couldn't be trusted. She wasn't a good girl. *He* knew that. *He* understood.

He was bad, like her.

With her fingers shaking, she started to type a reply, but before she could finish, Marley returned and fumbled with the zip. With her heart hammering, Tasha quickly shoved the phone back into her trousers and hunkered down in her sleeping bag.

"Are you okay?" Marley asked as she crawled over to her own bag. Her headlamp was on and shone in Tasha's face. "You look like you've seen a ghost."

"I'm fine," Tasha said quickly. "I'm just tired." She pulled the sleeping bag tighter.

Marley's eyes narrowed as she shrugged and slithered into her bag before turning the lamp off.

Tasha closed her eyes, willing herself to sleep, and put off facing it all for another night.

But underneath the covers, her hand was tightly clasped around the phone.

CHAPTER 6

Max moved quietly around the campsite, checking that everything was secure. The tents were surprisingly quiet; all of the hiking must have worn the kids out.

In the middle of the site, the fire still glowed in the makeshift fire pit. He headed towards it to put it out but stopped short. Junia sat on the opposite side, staring into the flames, singing what sounded like a hymn. It didn't look like she'd noticed him.

Staying in the shadows, he edged a little closer to hear better, but she looked up. He cleared his throat and approached her. "You have a nice voice."

Her cheeks were red. He guessed not only from the fire. "Oh...oh, thank you," she said, tucking some hair behind her ear.

"Do you mind if I join you? I'll have to put the fire out soon."

She drew her knees up under her chin, wrapping her arms around them. "Of course not."

With the flames flickering near her face, turning her golden hair copper, she looked ethereal. He sat beside her, staring into the fire and enjoying its warmth on his face and forearms.

"The kids enjoyed today." She turned and faced him. "I think this hike's going to be good for them."

He nodded as he poked the fire before placing another log on it. Sparks flew into the air, making a crackling sound. He hadn't planned to keep it going, but how could he pass up the opportunity of sitting in front of a fire with her? As much as he knew he couldn't get involved, she drew him like a moth to a flame. "Tasha seemed subdued tonight," he said, for want of something neutral to say.

Junia sighed heavily, and he sensed her shoulders slumping. "I thought so too. I'll try and talk to her tomorrow."

He nodded again as he studied her face. The light of the fire revealed fine, delicate lines around her eyes he hadn't noticed before. The air around them was still, almost as though the mountain was holding its breath. Out here, in what he considered his territory, some of his usual guardedness dropped away. There was something so natural, so instinctively right, about being here with this woman.

"You do a really good job with them," he said, his mouth curving into an unconscious smile.

She drew a slow breath and dropped her gaze. "Thank you. Sometimes I don't think I do." Her gaze lifted back to his. "I envy you, being able to come up here and escape from it all."

His smile broadened. "I've always loved this mountain. Dad used to bring me and Joseph hiking up here when we were boys. Rob and Eli too, sometimes, but they were more interested in football. And Eli was only little." He swallowed, his smile fading as old loss resurged, leaving a gnawing pain deep in his gut.

Junia was gazing at him, her eyes filled with compassion, making him feel vulnerable. An odd feeling for him.

"You must miss him," she said softly.

He swung his gaze away. "It was a long time ago."

"I still miss my parents, every day. Some losses never stop hurting. I think we simply learn to live with them, don't you?"

He inhaled deeply. "I suppose." He couldn't tell her that it was different for him, because it had never just been grief that kept him up at night. It was guilt. He opened his mouth to say something dismissive, something tough, but instead his thoughts tumbled out unbidden before he could stop them. "The difference is, I'm sure your parents' deaths weren't your fault."

There was a shocked silence before she laid a gentle hand on his arm. As gentle as it was, her touch seemed to burn through the fabric of his shirt. "Do you want to talk about it?"

He should say no. He never spoke about it, so why would he talk about it now, to a woman he barely knew? And yet suddenly, his story felt like a stone inside his chest, something he had to get out if he were to ever breathe again.

"Dad was hunting a white supremacist group," he began, his gaze locked on the fire. "Not that I knew that at the time. Some things about his work he obviously couldn't tell us."

"White supremacists? In Eastbrooke?"

He nodded grimly. "You'd be surprised. Separatist groups love it out here in the wild since there are so many places to hide." He blew out a breath. "A group of white nationals had set up home a few miles out of town. Dad got word they were an active terrorist cell, but there was no proof. They were there for months, and the whole town was talking about it, but we thought they were just some kind of commune. People trying to get back to a simpler way of life." He shrugged. "I was sixteen—I didn't take a lot of notice." He fell silent, remembering that time, fifteen years ago, and remembering his father with a stab of grief that was so sharp as to be tangible, an actual physical pain in his chest.

Junia squeezed his arm, prompting him to continue.

"We hadn't been getting on. I was going through a rebellious stage. I felt like I was expected to join the police force like Dad, but it wasn't for me. Rather than talking to him about it, I started acting out. I often skipped school to go up the mountain." He inhaled deeply as the memories flooded back.

"That morning, I skipped school one too many times and the school actually called my dad. He must have been mortified, being the police chief and all. He went looking for me."

"On the mountain?" Junia asked.

Max shook his head and laughed bitterly. "If only. No, there was this old disused warehouse on the edge of town. Some of the more rebellious kids hung out there sometimes, smoking and stuff. So, Dad checked there first." His chest squeezed like a vice and he forced himself to breathe slowly and not get upset in front of Junia. He never got upset in front of anyone. Ever.

"Stop if it's too painful," she said, but there was no going back. He would finish his story, even hearing the anger and grief in his own voice.

"He didn't find me, or any other kids. Instead, he found two guys from the separatist group. They were making bombs. There was a scuffle. They were armed, and so was my dad. Shots got fired...there were explosives in the room..." He trailed off, unable to finish the sentence.

"The warehouse blew up," Junia said, finishing it for him.

He nodded, swallowing down the lump in his throat. "Yes. All three were killed instantly."

"Max," she said, softly but insistently, "in no way was any of that your fault."

"That's what Mum tried to tell me," he said dully, "but it's not true. If I hadn't skipped school, Dad wouldn't have been there, and it wouldn't have happened."

"It's not your fault," Junia repeated. "The fault lies with the thugs who were there with the explosives, not you. Thousands of kids play hooky. Doing so didn't make you responsible for the tragedy."

"I know that logically," he admitted, "but somehow that doesn't help, because the fact remains that if I hadn't skipped school, then Dad would still be alive, Mum wouldn't be on her own, and Eli wouldn't be so resentful and angry at the world."

"You have no idea what would have happened. Those men posed a threat to the whole town."

"That's what the pastor told me. Mum sent me to him after Dad died and I was racked with guilt. He said that God moved in mysterious ways, and for all I knew, what happened that day could have stopped the whole of Eastbrooke from being blown up. But it didn't help. Then I felt angry at God, and even worse about myself...because I'd rather the town blew up if I could have my dad back." He stopped abruptly as tears welled in his eyes.

Junia was silent for a long moment, and Max felt the sharp sting of rejection. *Did she, too, think he was a terrible person?*

"Max," she said firmly, her voice cutting through his tormented thoughts. "Can you look at me, please?"

He lifted his gaze warily only to see that although her

voice was steady, her eyes shone with tears. "It was not your fault," she said emphatically, "and of course you felt like that. You were grieving. Have you never read the story of Job in the Bible? God understands your grief."

"I've tried to forgive myself," he said quietly, "but it doesn't change the truth of what happened. Over the years I've tried to block it out and get on with life. I don't talk about it, usually."

"Then I'm honoured you've been able to share with me." Her eyes were soft and filled with kindness. But more than just kindness—they were filled with understanding.

He breathed out a long, low sigh, as the stone in his chest softened and dissolved, just a little. "Thank you for listening." Their gazes held for a long moment as the reflection of the flames danced in her eyes.

A spark from the fire landed on the back of his hand. He jumped, and the moment was broken. "I should put the fire out."

She nodded and pushed to her feet. "Goodnight, Max."

He smiled, feeling a rush of emotion towards her that he didn't know how to name. "Goodnight, Junia."

She walked to her one-man tent, knelt and unzipped it before climbing in.

He put the fire out, double-checking that no sparks remained that could reignite during the night, and then climbed into his bedroll. He preferred sleeping under the stars rather than being confined in a tent. Lying on his back, he stared at the sky.

Junia's words about grief and God swirled through his mind, preventing him from falling asleep. After a while, he sat up and reached for his backpack, taking out his mini torch and pocket Bible. He flicked through the pages until he found the book of Job and began to read. The lament of Job reached out to him through the pages.

For my sighing comes like my bread, and my groanings are poured out like water.

Truly the thing that I fear comes upon me, and what I dread befalls me.

I am not at ease, nor am I quiet; I have no rest; but trouble comes.

As he read the story, the outpouring of grief contained in its pages touched his heart. Nothing was held back, and the platitudes and self-righteous arguments given by Job's friends echoed the many well-meaning but ultimately unhelpful things Max had heard over the years. In the midst of it all, Job refused to be comforted, calling instead on God in a grief so potent it became rage, and yet he never lost his faith.

As God liveth, who hath taken away my judgment; and the Almighty, who hath vexed my soul. All the while my breath is in me, and the spirit of God is in my nostrils; my lips shall not speak wickedness, nor my tongue utter deceit. God forbid that I should justify you: till I die I will not remove mine integrity from me. My righteousness I hold fast and will not let it go: my heart shall not reproach me so long as I live. Let mine enemy be as the wicked, and he that riseth up against me as the unrighteous. For what is the hope of the hypocrite, though he hath gained, when God taketh away his soul? Will God hear his cry when trouble cometh upon him?

Such faith in the face of horrendous suffering humbled Max. He'd never blamed God for his father's death. Rather, he blamed himself. Yet now he saw that in doing so, he'd put barriers around his soul that had prevented him from ever truly getting close to God–or anyone else. He carried on reading, feeling a deep stirring within him, when, at the end of the story, the Almighty made His presence known to the grief-stricken man, not, as in other parts of the Word, as the still small voice, or as Jesus Himself, but as the Whirlwind.

Gird up thy loins now like a man: I will demand of thee and declare thou unto me. Wilt thou also disannul my judgment? Wilt thou condemn me, that thou mayest be righteous? Hast thou an arm like God? Or canst thou thunder with a voice like Him? Deck thyself now with majesty and excellency; and array thyself with glory and beauty.

Humbled, Max closed his Bible and lay back, staring up at the mountain and the stars. God's awesome creation, his constant companion. His prayers tumbled from his lips in much the same way as he'd just confided in Junia.

Lord, forgive me my pride and obstinacy. Help me see myself as You see me, and lift this burden of grief and guilt from me. Show me what You would have me do and who You would have me be, for You are the righteous, almighty One. The Great Redeemer. I bow in awe of Your majesty.

It wasn't a whirlwind that answered Max, but a cool breeze coming down from the mountain, stroking his cheek like a caress. Calm settled upon him, and he had a sudden image of his father looking at him with pride. Part of the weight he'd carried for so long lifted from him. He fell asleep feeling more at peace than he had in a long time.

Of course, he had no idea this was the calm before the storm.

CHAPTER 7

Jake, a homeless wanderer who was wild camping a few miles west of Eastbrooke, made a small fire that morning on which he cooked a rabbit he'd caught in the early hours, and boiled himself a tea with his last remaining teabag. Soon he'd have to brave the town and go on a skip dive and visit the church food bank. He was getting low on provisions.

But not today. He looked up at the blue sky, felt the wind on his cheek, and smiled. He liked it out here, where his mind could be as clear as the sky and he didn't have to think about his old life, when things hadn't been so peaceful. There weren't many people here, and that was good, because in his experience, people weren't usually very kind.

He liked birds, though. Birds made him happy. And so, when he spotted a plains-wanderer, one of Australia's rarest birds, he was so distracted that he failed to pay full attention while stamping out his small fire. He walked away, still watching the plains-wanderer, not noticing the tiny embers still glowing faintly on the ground...

Max was already awake and contemplating breakfast when Joseph radioed through to him. He answered with a sense of urgency. If Joseph was radioing this early in the morning, there was a problem.

"Max, can you hear me?" The signal was crackly. Any further up the mountain and they likely wouldn't be able to communicate at all.

"Yes. What's up?"

"There's a bushfire a few miles outside of Eastbrooke. Seems to have started in the night."

Lifting his gaze, Max stared into the distance. Joseph was right. A curl of smoke hovered on the horizon. His insides somersaulted as his thoughts immediately turned to his mother and brothers. "Is it heading for town?"

"Yes, but the whole team of firefighters is on it, and backup's coming. Everyone's hopeful it'll bypass the town. I'm more worried about you guys."

Max blew out a breath and raked his hand across his head. "Okay. Should we cut the hike short? We're only a few hours' walk from the retreat."

Joseph was quiet for a moment before he replied. "No. In all honesty, you're probably safer on the mountain than you are back there."

Max closed his eyes as dread coursed through him. If the fire reached the mountain retreat, he'd lose everything. His livelihood, his home. The thought made his pulse beat erratically. "You think the fire will reach there?"

"I'm hoping not, but things can change in the blink of an eye. You know that."

Max swallowed hard. Joseph spoke the truth. "Okay. What do you need us to do?"

"Stay put," Joseph said firmly. "You should be safe, but don't go any higher unless you're chased by the fire. But I doubt it will come to that. You're probably safest where you are, and Rescue can come for you if need be. Give me a rough location of where you are."

Max gave him rough coordinates before ending the call. He sat and stared into the distance, watching the faint curl of smoke. It seemed far away, but that could so swiftly change. Perhaps it was just his imagination, but it seemed to have gotten closer in the few short minutes he'd been talking to Joseph.

He had to tell the others. He went straight to Jay and Sonia's tent, tapped on the side, and when their heads appeared through the flap, he filled them in on Joseph's news.

Jay's face went ashen, but Sonia was as unflappable and practical as ever. "Let's get everyone up, get some breakfast on the go and we can fill them in if we feel we need to. There's no need to panic. We can stay here for the next two days, and if there's a problem, Joseph will get Mountain Rescue out to us. As long as everyone stays together and stays put, then there's no need to worry."

Max nodded. She was right. If it wasn't for the teenagers under his charge, he wouldn't be anxious.

And, of course, Junia.

He glanced at her tent. There was no sign of movement. He should wake her, give her the news, but doing so felt intrusive and it was pointless to worry her.

He'd relay Joseph's message while they were having breakfast. Downplay it if need be. They could spend the day tracking and foraging without venturing too far from camp. They could have a normal day. Maybe she and her group didn't need to know at all. Why cause them needless anxiety?

He tried to ignore the sinking feeling that things weren't going to go as planned.

∼

IT DOESN'T TAKE MUCH to start a bushfire, really. The right weather conditions and a stray spark is all that's needed.

The embers from Jake's fire had continued to glow that day, kept alive by the gusts of dry wind and the stifling heat. Even so, without the sudden blast of wind down from the north that had lifted the embers swirling into the air, they might have dwindled away to nothing, and the danger might have passed. Instead, they danced into the air and landed on a patch of dry grass and twigs that made the perfect kindling for what could so easily become a huge, roaring wall of flames that would destroy everything in its wake.

The fire sparked, bursting into life amidst the dried wood and leaves. It blazed away merrily enough for a while, until it reached the nearby trees, and the leaves from a hanging branch lit up like fireworks.

Before long, the tree was ablaze. It jumped to other trees, and the fire roared on through the night, driven by the dry winds, and made its way towards Eastbrooke and the mountain that overlooked the town.

Jake woke the next morning, early as usual, but something was wrong. The dawn chorus had taken on an urgent tone, as though the birds were sounding out a warning. He blinked, coming to as the smell of smoke filled his nostrils.

Sitting bolt upright, dread squeezed his chest. Yesterday's fire…the one he hadn't checked was fully out…

Clambering out of the rough shelter he'd made, he stared aghast to the horizon which was alight with more than just dawn. A thick wall of smoke was fast approaching. He laid his head in his hands and moaned. *What had he done?*

He dismantled his shelter and hurried towards Eastbrooke, even though it brought him perilously close to the path of the fire.

He had to warn the townsfolk.

∼

JUNIA STEPPED out of her tent and was raising her face to the bright morning sun when a shriek sounded from Tasha and Marley's tent. She ran over as Marley emerged from the entrance.

"Tasha's gone!" the girl gasped.

Junia blinked, trying to process Marley's words. "Gone? Gone where?" she asked, feeling as though she was speaking through treacle. From the corner of her eye, she saw Max striding in her direction. Jay and Sonia were building a fire, and Chuck, Gavin, and the rest of the boys were piling out of their tent, alerted by Marley's scream.

"I don't know. I just woke up. She's not here. She's gone," Marley repeated, her eyes wide.

Junia took a deep breath, forcing her voice to be calm although her heart threatened to burst through her chest. "Let's not jump to conclusions. She's probably just gone to the toilet."

"She hasn't. Her pack's gone. Why would she take her whole pack to the toilet?"

Icy fear twisted around Junia's heart. This couldn't be happening.

Max reached her side. She spun around to face him. He looked grim, his features drawn tightly across his face.

"We have to find Tasha," she said. "She's not in the tent, and Marley says all her things are gone."

Marley's face was deathly white. "It's my fault," she wailed. "I should have woken up. I knew something was wrong last night."

"It's not your fault," Junia said firmly. "She would have picked her moment when you were fast asleep. There's nothing you could have done to stop her. But what do you mean about last night? Did she say something to indicate where she's gone?"

Marley shook her head, looking miserable. "No, she was just quiet. More than usual."

"Could she have gone back to the retreat?" Max asked. His voice was urgent, and Junia got the impression there was something more, something he wasn't telling her.

"Maybe? Probably not." Junia bit her lip. She knew exactly where Tasha had gone. There was no point in denying it. "She's gone home. Or what she thinks of as home."

"To Safe Harbour?" Max frowned, but then his shoulders fell. "Back to the gang, you mean?"

"How would she get there?" Marley asked. "We're on a mountain."

"She would have told them where she was and where to meet her. Probably the retreat since no one's there."

Max inhaled sharply.

"What is it?" Junia swung her gaze to him. "There's something you're not telling me."

He held her gaze steadily. "Marley," he said in a calm voice while still looking at Junia, "go over to the fire with the boys and get warm. Sonia's making breakfast."

Marley opened her mouth to protest, but one stern look from Max and she left.

Once she was gone, Junia stared at him. "What else is wrong?"

"Don't panic," he said, still in that same, exaggeratedly calm voice. "I've just had a call from my brother Joseph. There's a bushfire outside of Eastbrooke. It's a few miles away and the firefighters are hopeful they'll get it under control, but he did say it was important we stay put."

Junia's insides went cold as she absorbed his words. "The fire...it's heading towards the retreat?"

"Hopefully not...but Joseph said we were safer here."

Bile rose in her throat. "I have to go after Tasha!"

"No. It's dangerous. I'll call Joseph back. He'll find her, that's his job."

But Junia wasn't listening. She was already fleeing the camp, moving faster than she'd even known she could, back in the direction they'd hiked yesterday. She had to get to Tasha.

"Junia!" Max hollered after her. "You have to stay here! It's too dangerous!"

She ignored him and carried on. Within seconds, she heard him thundering after her, still calling her name.

She pushed harder.

∼

TASHA STOPPED and stared in the direction of the retreat. She'd reached the narrow road that ran a short way up the mountain. That meant she wasn't far from it, which was a relief because she'd been walking for hours and was exhausted. Leaning forward, she rested her hands on her thighs as she fought to get her head together.

As soon as he'd answered her call, she knew she'd made the biggest mistake of her life. "Tasha," he'd said, his voice smooth and menacing. "You've been making me wait a long time." The threat was implicit, but having made contact, the old habits had overtaken her and she'd immediately succumbed to his authority.

When he asked where she was, she told him. When he told her to gather her things and he'd come and pick her up at a spot near the retreat, she obeyed without question, although it saddened her to leave them all behind, especially Marley and Junia. But there was no going back now, now that he knew where they all were. If she failed to show up, the whole camp would be in danger.

Her phone, clutched tightly in her hand, vibrated, startling her. Gulping, she answered without speaking. Awaiting his command.

"There's a fire. We passed it on the way," he said. Angrily, as though somehow a bushfire was a deliberate plot on her part.

She had a sudden, wild hope that he might have thought better of it and gone back to the city. Then she could run somewhere he'd never find her. She'd smash the phone and erase his name and number from her mind. But even as she thought it, she knew it wouldn't happen. There was no way he would let her escape again or drive all this way only to return empty handed. That would make him look like a fool in front of his men, and that was something he'd never tolerate.

"Where are you?" he demanded.

"Not far." Her voice came out small. "I've just reached the road. An hour away, maybe."

"Keep walking and we'll drive towards you. The smoke's getting closer. I don't know if we'll be able to go back through it. You're causing me a lot of trouble, Tasha. You know this can't go unpunished, don't you?" His voice was kind, almost remorseful, as though he was distressed by his words.

She nodded dumbly, then remembered he couldn't see her, although she suddenly felt he had eyes everywhere. "Yes," she whispered.

He cut the call. She put the phone in her pocket and trudged on, tears coursing down her cheeks in a silent flow.

She continued on towards her fate. Between him and the bushfire, she'd be lucky to make it out alive.

CHAPTER 8

Max's heart felt it would burst when he finally caught up with Junia. She was surprisingly fast and light on her feet. He was built for strength and endurance, not speed. "Junia," he wheezed, jogging in front of her, "Stop."

She juddered to a halt, her breath coming in jagged, tortured pants. They were halfway to the retreat, but as yet, there was no sign of Tasha. The smoke was visible in the close distance, and wild panic filled Junia's eyes. "We have to find her!" she screamed.

"We're going to," he reassured. "But you won't help her by blindly running into danger. Let me radio Joseph—he can help."

She nodded as she leaned over and clutched her side, her face contorted in pain. Having finally stopped, she no doubt had a stitch.

He pulled his radio out and called Joseph. The signal was weak, but thankfully he got through.

Joseph's voice came urgently over the line. "Where are

you? The fire's gone rogue and is spreading in all directions fast. This could be really bad. We've just picked up the rest of your campers and are getting them to safety, but I got some garbled story about you running after a missing girl…"

Max filled him in quickly, in between the signal intermittently cutting out.

"You can't go to the retreat," Joseph said firmly. "Stay put, or if you have to move, go around the mountain. The fire's spreading fast, Max."

"And Tasha?"

"I'm on it now. I'll get Rob out as well…if there are gang members on the loose, we're going to need more than fire marshalls. Are they armed?"

Max looked at Junia and covered the mouthpiece. "This gang Tasha's with, would they be armed?"

Junia's face had grown ashen. "I'd be surprised if they weren't." Her voice was grim. "They're not nice people."

"Probably," Max spoke into the mouthpiece.

"And are you?" Joseph asked in a too-calm voice that made Max think he was trying to hide his fear.

"Only with a hunting knife," Max replied.

"Get to the other side of the mountain," Joseph said in a tone Max hadn't heard him use before. "Let me and Rob sort out the rest. Don't go too far and stay out in the open so we can find you."

"You have to look for Tasha first," Max urged, afraid that familial love might win out over duty.

"Of course," Joseph snapped, then added in a softer voice, "I'm praying for you. Stay safe, brother."

Max tried to reply just as the signal crackled into nothing. He looked at Junia, warring with himself. There was no way she'd leave Tasha…and truth be told, he couldn't either. But the closer they got to the fire, the more danger they'd be in.

"Joseph's looking for Tasha," he said. "We have to turn back and go around the mountain. He'll find her." He spoke with more confidence than he felt.

Junia shook her head, her body tensed like a wire.

He groaned. She wasn't listening.

But then her eyes widened and she gasped. "Tasha!"

∼

Tasha walked on as he'd told her to. If only she hadn't turned on that phone. More than anything she wanted to run back to the safety of the camp, but that would mean leading him straight to Junia and the others. As much as she was sure the instructor, Max, could defend himself, the others couldn't, and *he* wouldn't care who he hurt, as long he got her back.

When the purr of an engine sounded along the road, her limbs began to shake, even as she craned her neck for a sight of him. Safe Harbour had taught her about trauma bonding, but no matter how much she knew in her head that he was bad news, her heart had different ideas.

When the car pulled up just ahead of her, her heart pounded as she walked towards it, as if drawn by a magnet. Her lips quivered and she prayed he wouldn't hurt her too much.

He wound down the blackened window, revealing him and his deputy.

"Long time no see." The deputy grinned evilly, revealing a gold tooth.

She tried to force a smile, but then *his* arm reached out the window and grabbed hers with a vice-like grip.

"Get in," he hissed, giving her arm a cruel twist when she hesitated. Her heart pounded so hard there was a roaring in her ears and her whole body shook uncontrollably. Something in her instinctively recoiled at the idea of willingly getting into the car. Of enslaving herself again.

"Hurry up!" he yelled. There was something in his voice she'd never heard before. *Fear.* She glanced at the sky, at the thick, billowing swirls of smoke that now filled her nostrils, burning them. *He was scared of the fire.*

She yanked her arm from his grip and fled.

"Tasha! Stop!" he yelled after her.

Her pulse roaring in her ears, she ran the way she'd come, hoping the element of surprise would give her precious minutes. She couldn't outrun a car, but the road narrowed not far ahead and that fancy car wouldn't get through. Or at least, that's what she hoped.

Tears rolled down her cheeks as the car revved behind her. It was hopeless. Her bid for freedom had come too late.

Then her name was called again. But this time, it wasn't him calling. It was Junia. Max and Junia stood ahead, staring at her. Or at least Junia was. Max was staring at the car.

∼

JUNIA SPRINTED TOWARDS TASHA. Max followed, his gaze fixed on the men in the car. Instinct to protect surged through him. Having forgotten all about Joseph's warnings about weapons, he hurtled down the hill as the car veered towards Tasha.

It skidded to a halt, spraying gravel and dust into the air. A door opened and an arm grabbed Tasha. She screamed.

He rushed past Junia, moving quicker than he knew he could. He lunged for Tasha and tried to wrestle her back, feeling like he was in a tug-of-war.

A gun was pointed at him, and for a moment, he froze.

Junia screamed.

The man holding the gun grinned evilly. "There's no need for anyone to get hurt," he said in a voice that was almost pleasant. "The girl belongs to me. Let her go, and you can be on your way."

Tasha sagged in Max's arms, defeated.

Rage surged through him as he glared into the man's eyes. "She belongs to no man," he growled, and pulled Tasha straight out of the guy's grip and thrust her behind him.

A gun shot exploded. Pain ripped through his shoulder and he grunted as the world swam before his eyes. He hit the ground, and the breath was knocked from his body. He braced himself for the next shot, praying it would be for him, not Junia.

It didn't come. The car door slammed and the car took off, spraying gravel into the air.

Max staggered to his feet. His shoulder was on fire.

Tasha had veered off the road and was scampering down an overgrown track. The car was attempting to follow, the engine revving hard. But Max knew the terrain. The car would never make it. She had a good chance of escaping.

If only she wasn't running straight towards the fire.

He tried to follow, but staggered.

Junia appeared at his side, supported him. Her eyes were huge in her tear-streaked face. "Max," she gasped, fear filling her eyes.

"I'm okay," he ground out through gritted teeth before he wobbled.

She caught him again and helped him walk to a rock he could lean against. Her gaze darted in the direction Tasha had fled. "I've got to go after her," she murmured.

"You can't." He struggled to get the words out. "They

won't be able to drive far...so long as she stays away from level ground, she'll escape."

"But what about the fire? She's running straight into it."

Their gazes locked. He had to give her hope. "Joseph will find her." He prayed he was right.

She didn't look soothed, but she crouched beside him and gingerly inspected the wound. There was a lot of blood. He had bandages in his pack...but his pack was at the camp, and Joseph had said not to go that way. He grabbed the bottom of his shirt and ripped part of it off.

"Help me," he grunted, annoyed at his own weakness.

With tender, shaking hands, she quickly patched up his shoulder.

"I'm sorry," he gasped, trying not to show how much pain he was in. "I'm getting blood on your clothes."

"You need a hospital." She glanced at the sky, no doubt hoping to see the rescue helicopter.

"The bullet hasn't lodged. It's just a flesh wound," he said. There might be tendon damage, but he wouldn't tell her that.

She coughed.

A shiver ran down his spine as he looked up. The wall of smoke had grown thicker. It wouldn't be long before they'd see flames. He pulled out his radio, praying for a restored signal. Joseph was their only hope.

The signal was gone.

CHAPTER 9

They were trapped. Max's makeshift bandage was soaked through with blood and his eyes were dark with pain. Although he was trying not to show it, the set of his jaw and the tension in his body as Junia helped him to his feet made it clear he was struggling.

As they stumbled up the mountain to escape the smoke, replaying itself over and over in her mind was the moment he got shot. For a split second after he'd fallen to the ground, she'd thought he was dead. The grief that had roared through her had knocked the breath from her, and the relief that had quickly followed when he moved had been so intense.

She thanked God he'd survived, but they weren't in the clear. Far from it. The only way they'd get through was to not give up hope. She focused her attention on two things—Max, and the mountain peak towering over them, majestic and unconcerned about their plight. The scripture that had come to mind just a few days earlier came back to her and whispered into her troubled soul…

I lift my eyes to the mountains; where does my help come from? It comes from the Lord, Maker of heaven and earth.

"Help us, Lord," she murmured under her breath, fingering the silver cross around her neck with one hand. *"Keep us safe."* Looking up, somehow the mountain looked less imposing now and more like a protector, watching over them as they inched up its side, reaching for safety. She thought of all the times she'd read about mountains in the Bible, and the way these awesome, natural structures featured so prominently at key turning points in the great story of God and His people. Didn't Moses encounter God in a burning bush on Mount Sinai, the same place he received the Hebraic Law? And a thousand years later, Jesus Himself preached His most famous Sermon on the Mount of Olives, the one that turned everything His followers thought they knew on its head. Mountains were considered especially sacred to God by the people of Jesus' day, and the thought gave her some comfort as they trudged on.

It wasn't long before Max began to slow, his shoulders hunching and his gait growing erratic.

"Can we rest for a bit?" she asked, pretending to be more out of breath than she actually was.

He stopped and glanced behind, breathing hard.

"The smoke doesn't seem to be getting any closer," she said. "If the fire was heading straight for us, we'd see flames by now."

"Even so," he said, his chest heaving, "we need to keep going to get to the other side. Bushfires travel fast and change direction fast, especially in this wind. The further from the smoke we can get, the easier it'll be for the rescue team to see us." He panted, drew a long breath. "Let's carry on a while longer, then we can rest."

She nodded, then decided to tackle his condition head on.

"Do you want to lean on me?" she asked in a matter-of-fact voice. "You need to conserve your strength. We don't know how long we'll be here, and we may need your survival skills."

He hesitated. She sensed embarrassment rolling off him. She expected him to rebuff her and was surprised when he nodded and heaved an arm around her shoulders. When he stumbled, she slipped her arm around his waist and took his weight.

His injury was worse than she thought. They should rest, but insisting they did would only annoy and embarrass him further. Without a word, they continued upwards, concentrating on the rough, narrow track that led up the mountain.

They carried on for what felt like hours, neither speaking as the effort sapped what little strength they had left. The terrain was becoming harder to climb and Junia's thighs felt like they were on fire with overexertion. The sky over the mountain top was dimming. The day was drawing in already. It seemed to have gone so fast, and yet at the same time to have lasted forever.

Max stumbled hard and she only just caught him while managing to keep herself upright. If they tumbled down the steep mountain side, they could both die.

"We have to stop," she said firmly. Their plight had gone beyond concerns of saving his pride. "If you pass out, there's no way I can carry you."

He grumbled his reluctant approval. They found a tiny patch of almost flat ground to sit on. Junia's legs felt like jelly as she stopped walking and sank to the ground. Max sat next to her, wincing.

"How's your shoulder?" she asked. His shirt was soaked with so much blood it was almost black. He was losing too much. It didn't look good. There was also the risk of infection, the consequences of which, if they weren't rescued quickly, she didn't even want to contemplate.

"Sore. I can barely feel my arm, which isn't good." He winced again as he shifted to get more comfortable. "It might be worse than I thought. But Eastbrooke Hospital's great. We've got a top-notch surgeon."

This wasn't the time to mention the bushfire raging between them and the hospital. She looked around and sighed. The bush was still thick, making it unlikely they'd be seen. He was right. They needed to go higher and find a clearing, but he could barely walk, and she had limited climbing skills.

"We need to build a fire," he said, cutting through her thoughts. "It'll get cold tonight this high up."

"Wouldn't there be a fire ban by now?"

He laughed, although there was no real humour in it. "I think these are extenuating circumstances, don't you? We'll have to keep turns watching it through the night and keep an eye on the direction of that smoke. I think we're out of immediate danger, though. The wind seems to have eased a little."

With Max guiding her, Junia constructed a makeshift fire pit and gathered kindling and fuel. There were no decent sized logs up here, so keeping even a small fire going through the night would be tough. The thought of spending the night on the mountain, with Max bleeding, no blankets or provisions, and only an intermittent heat source, filled her with terror. She looked desperately at the sky above, swallowing the despair creeping up her throat. *Lord, please watch over us. Let the rescue helicopter find us. Keep Max alive.*

CHAPTER 10

Tasha couldn't carry on anymore. She was completely lost, knowing only that she was on the mountain somewhere, but for hours now she hadn't had any idea as to which direction she was travelling. As long as she was heading away from the smoke, which had been growing thicker and blacker all day, she figured she was choosing the right path.

Although her arms and legs were scratched and bleeding, and her muscles screamed with overuse, she was scared to stop, both because of the smoke and her pursuers, although she must have left them far behind by now. The route she'd taken was rocky and treacherous, and she'd taken it deliberately so the car couldn't follow, but that didn't mean they weren't after her. *He* wasn't likely to give up, because if he did, he'd look a fool for letting her escape. She could only hope that the combination of the bushfire and unfamiliar terrain would have persuaded him not to ditch the car and chase after her on foot.

Her lungs burned as she pushed on. She gasped for air, but the acrid smoke stung the back of her throat. Tears filled her eyes as icy fear twisted in her gut. Would she survive? *And where was Junia?* She was a good woman. She'd only ever tried to help her. The way she and Max had chased after her and tried to rescue her from *him* had touched her deeply. No one had ever cared about her before. They'd placed themselves directly in the path of danger, just for her.

Their care touched her deeply, but guilt also racked her. *What if her pursuers, having given up on her, had turned and gone after Max and Junia instead?* A shiver ran down her spine as she remembered the sound of the gunshot, that loud crack resounding through the air, and Max falling to the ground, clutching his shoulder. How serious was his injury? *Could he die?* As she crumpled to the ground and buried her head in her hands, the events of the day replayed in her mind's eye, each memory bringing with it a fresh wave of guilt. She hadn't even said goodbye to Marley.

And now, she might never see her again.

Emotion clogged her throat. She felt like screaming, but she held it in. What if *he* were close?

She lifted her gaze and looked around, making herself small in case he was nearby. Smoke filled the air below, and the mountain loomed above. She was in big trouble.

Max had taught the group some survival skills, but her mind drew a blank. If only she'd taken more notice. She'd only been interested in how to identify tiger quoll tracks. What use would that be now? She was stuck on a mountain with no way of getting back to civilisation or calling for help. She could die up here.

There'd been plenty of times in her young life when, if anyone had asked her, she would have said that she didn't care whether she lived or died. Her future had seemed bleak. A life of criminality and abuse was all that realistically awaited a girl like her. But then Safe Harbour and Junia came along, and she'd glimpsed something she hadn't known for a long time—hope. Hope that she could have a better future, and that she wasn't a lost cause. She'd gone to Safe Harbour feeling like the worst person in the world, and they'd told her that wasn't true. Everyone was a sinner, and God loved them all, regardless. The idea of being loved simply for who she was, rather than how useful she could be to people, had overwhelmed her. As much as she'd wanted to believe it, a voice in her head–one that sounded a lot like *him*–had told her it wasn't true. For other people, maybe, but not for someone as broken and damaged as her. She belonged with the bad people. They were the only ones who truly understood her. The only ones who could love her.

But that was a lie. Junia had cared enough to come after her, placed herself in danger, just to save her.

And what had she done? She'd repaid her kindness by leading Junia and Max directly to *him*. She pulled her knees tighter to her chest and rested her head on them, as sobs racked her body.

I'm sorry, God, she whispered into her hands. *I'm sorry for everything. Please, please let Junia and Max and Marley and all the others be okay. Don't let Junia and Max suffer because of what I did. Don't let the fire get them.*

Her sobs grew deeper as she prayed, repeating the words over and over again. Did hope exist? Or had she gone too far and now even God wouldn't listen?

As she sobbed, the image of the angel she'd seen in the little church at Eastbrooke came to her. Junia had told her she was never alone. *You just have to let God in, Tasha,* she'd said with a soft smile. How many times had she wished Junia would leave her alone and stop telling her what to do, and yet right now, she'd give anything to see that smile and know her friend was okay.

Junia says You can give us signs, she whispered, still not looking up. *Please let me know Junia's okay. Please, God.*

A rustling sound came from amongst the bushes. She lifted her gaze. A creature sat just a few inches away, staring at her. She sucked in a breath and held it. The animal was the size of a small dog. It had a long tail and a beautiful golden coat with white elongated spots. It had a rodent's face with inquisitive, dark eyes and stared at her with its head tipped to the side as though curious. It didn't seem to be scared at all.

It was a tiger quoll.

It turned and hopped a few steps away, then looked back over its shoulder, almost as if beckoning her to follow.

Still holding her breath, Tasha rose to her feet and followed the animal into the undergrowth.

∼

JUNIA AND MAX huddled in front of the small fire as the sun, a molten ball of burnt orange, slipped behind the mountain, staining the sky a colour that was eerie yet beautiful, and spoke of the fire blazing between them and safety. Against the fierce orange of the sun, the stony peak of the mountain looked harsh and forbidding, more ominous now than protective. Junia shuddered and leaned closer to Max. Ordinarily, their sudden intimacy would seem inappropriate, but with danger staring them in the face as well as the need to keep warm, it felt right to be close.

"How's your shoulder?" she asked, trying to hide just how worried she was.

"Sore," he said, staring into the fire, "but it seems to have stopped bleeding."

"That's something to be thankful for," she replied, trying to sound bright and hopeful. "Maybe Joseph will see us tonight. With our little fire going, we'll be more noticeable, won't we?"

"Maybe," Max replied. He didn't sound convinced. "There are two helicopters, and they'll be tied up with the fire. We have no idea how bad it is down there. Joe will want to look for us, but he might not be able to."

Surely a search party would be looking for them. Isn't that what happened in situations like this? She nodded, trying not to panic. "Okay," she said, choosing her words carefully, "realistically, how long can we survive up here?"

Max grimaced. "If it weren't for the bushfire and my gunshot wound, a few days, possibly more. There's a stream for water and I could forage and hunt small animals...but if we have to keep moving because of the smoke, we'll lose the water and food source and then we're obviously in a lot more trouble."

"How much higher do we need to climb?"

When he held her gaze without saying a word, she knew the answer. Too far.

"And your shoulder. How is it, really?" She sensed he was avoiding telling her the truth.

He continued gazing into the fire for a long time before answering. "It's throbbing a lot," he replied quietly. "Of course, that's to be expected...but I'm worried it's becoming infected."

She closed her eyes momentarily, forcing herself to keep calm and not give in to the panic threatening to engulf her. If

Max's wound was infected, then they needed to be rescued as soon as possible.

"You might have to teach me more survival skills," she said lightly, "in case I end up having to look after both of us. I think I can manage the foraging but hunting, I have no clue about."

"I'll give you a lesson in the morning if Joseph doesn't find us during the night." He sounded exhausted, and the chances were high that he'd be in no fit state to teach her anything in the morning.

"Would you mind taking the first turn to watch the fire?" His voice was starting to slur. "Wake me in a couple of hours."

"Sure. You sleep for a while," she said soothingly. She had no intention of waking him—sleep would hopefully be healing for him. And besides, how could she sleep? What if the helicopter came and they missed it? No, she wouldn't be getting any sleep that night whether Max was awake to watch the fire or not.

He lay on the ground next to her, gingerly placing himself in a position that put no pressure on his wounded shoulder. His head was next to her lap, and as he drifted off, she stroked his damp hair from his brow without making a conscious decision to do so, her natural nurturing instincts coming to the fore.

Lord, watch over Max as he sleeps. Heal him, Lord. Knit his shoulder back together and cleanse his wound. And light the way so that Joseph may reach us.

Stroking his hair, something akin to love surged through her, swiftly followed by hot tears pricking the corners of her eyes. Perhaps it was simply that danger had thrown them together, but there was no denying that she felt incredibly close to him right now, and she couldn't shake the feeling that God had brought them together for a purpose. That gave her hope, too, because surely, He wouldn't bring her and Max together only for them to die in each other's arms on the mountain side. No, she had to believe they would be rescued, and sooner rather than later.

She had to believe that, because otherwise, all hope was lost.

CHAPTER 11

Tasha followed the tiger quoll, stooping so as not to get caught in the small bushy trees as the creature led her deeper into the undergrowth. She was sure it was taking her lower, back towards Eastbrooke, which surely meant nearer the fire, but she figured that no animal would walk directly into danger in that way, so following the quoll seemed as sensible as anything else. At least they were nowhere near the road, so there was little chance of bumping into *him*. Unless he was following her. She glanced over her shoulder but all she saw were bushes. So, she continued to follow, still half dazed by the fact that the creature had allowed itself to be seen, let alone be followed.

It must be a sign, she told herself, and so she carried on, hope flickering inside her even as the undergrowth seemed to go on and on with no sign of ending. She could still smell smoke in the air, but it didn't seem to be getting any thicker, even as the ground seemed to be levelling out.

"Where are you taking me?" she murmured, ducking down low as the creature scrambled through the bushes. She did her best to follow, but there was no way she could squeeze through the gaps the quoll was squeezing itself through. She gave up and straightened, trying not to give in to the sudden despair that filled her. The quoll looked back at her, twitched its nose as though saying goodbye, and disappeared into the bush.

Now she was alone again. Sighing, she sat down for a rest, feeling silly for having followed the small animal. All she'd achieved was to get herself even more lost, and in the middle of the bush like this, no rescue party would ever find her. It was growing dark, and she was tired beyond belief, her limbs exhausted from the day's exertions.

A shadow loomed over her. She gasped in fear, her stomach twisting as she jumped back, her hand up as though warding off a blow.

"Hey, I'm not going to hurt you." A strange-looking man peered down at her.

She breathed a huge sigh of relief. It wasn't *him*, but an older man with long hair and a straggly beard, dressed in mismatched clothes that had seen better days. He had a large pack on his back that was also grubby. He must be some kind of wanderer, and he was probably homeless. Still, his eyes were kind, and oddly for her, she felt instinctively that she could trust him.

"Do you know the way out?" she asked as he hunched down next to her and swung his pack off his back.

He pulled an apple out and offered it to her. She hesitated and then took it gratefully. It had been hours since she'd last eaten.

"That depends on where you're trying to get to," he said thoughtfully.

"Eastbrooke, I suppose."

"That's where I'm headed," the man confided. "I was

trying to warn the towns folk about the fire. I think it was my fault, you see, for not putting my cooking fire out properly. In this weather, the tiniest ember can cause a bushfire that can blaze for days." He sounded desperately sad, and she wasn't sure what to say. He was being a bit hard on himself. Surely it was a mistake anyone could make.

"Did you get lost, then?" she asked.

The man laughed. "Me, get lost? Girlie, I know the bush like the back of my hand. No, the fire came on heavier than I thought and forced me up the mountain, so I've been having to take the long way around. I figure the good folk of Eastbrooke will know all about the fire by now, anyway."

"Do you think they'll be okay?" She thought of the nice people they'd met at church, including Max's family.

The man looked sad again. "I hope so. They usually have good systems in place, towns like that. Living close to the bush, you have to. But you're a city girl, aren't you?"

She nodded. "Melbourne." Then she had a thought. "Hey, have you seen a car with two men in it on the mountain road? A big black one with tinted windows?"

The man shook his head. "I've seen no one until coming across you. My name's Jake, by the way."

"I'm Tasha," she said, holding out her hand. He took it and shook it firmly, his old eyes twinkling.

"Can you show me how to get to Eastbrooke?" she asked.

He pulled at his beard. "I could, if there wasn't a fire in the way. What I'm thinking now is, there should be a clearing just along the way if I've got my bearings right, and it would be a good spot to build a signal and hopefully get seen by any rescue crews. What do you think? Shall we go together?"

She nodded eagerly. It sounded like a great idea. Despite the man's odd appearance, kindness radiated from him, the same sort of kindness that radiated from Junia and Max and the other youth workers. They stood and she followed him, amazed at the way he seemed to blend in with the undergrowth, knowing exactly where to tread, and finding paths she never would have seen. He'd give Max a run for his money when it came to wilderness skills, she thought with a chuckle.

Sure enough, after a little while, they came to a clearing. She sank back down on her haunches, breathing in clearer air. The sky was darkening, but no stars were visible because of the smoke.

"We're not going to get rescued tonight, are we?" she asked. Exhaustion overtook her and she curled up, suddenly cold.

Jake eyed her with concern, then pulled a moth-eaten old blanket out of his pack and draped it over her. "You sleep," he said gently. "I'll keep watch. It will be okay."

The next moment, she wondered if the old man wasn't some kind of sage when the unmistakable whir of a helicopter sounded in the distance and grew louder with every second. Exhaustion forgotten, she leapt to her feet, waving her arms frantically. "Hey, we're over here!"

∼

FLAMES, huge and threatening, engulfed the disused warehouse, while the roar of the fire resounded in his ears. Max looked around. There was no way out. The flames closed in, quick and fast. Trapped by the flames, his father was calling out, "Max! Max!"

"I'm coming!" Max screamed back as he fought his way through the flames to reach his dad, already knowing it was too late.

"Max! Max!" A woman's voice this time. One he knew.

Blinking, he gulped in deep breaths of clear, morning air before fully opening his eyes. A small fire crackled away. Junia sat beside it and peered at him in concern. "You were whimpering and shaking. Is it your shoulder?"

He shook his head. "Bad dream," he said shortly, not wanting to explain its content. He looked around, taking in the landscape as the events of the day before flooded back. His shoulder and arm ached intensely, a gnawing, biting pain that made him grit his teeth. "You didn't wake me," he said. "Have you kept the fire going all night?"

"Yes," she replied proudly. Even having been up all night in yesterday's clothes and covered in soot, she looked beautiful. "It seems you taught me well. I've foraged some berries, too, so we've got breakfast."

"Glad to hear it." He tried to chuckle but winced as searing pain shot through him at the slightest movement. He carefully lifted the crusty bandage and inspected the wound.

"Is it healing?" she asked, craning her neck to see.

"Yes," he said, hoping she couldn't hear the lie in his voice. The wound looked terrible, oozing and raw, and the skin around it was red and tight, with red lines radiating out and snaking down across his chest. It was infected. He might be able to find the right plants to make a paste to hold back its spread, but he needed medical attention soon. He tried to get to his feet to forage for what he needed, but waves of nausea and dizziness hit him as soon as he tried. He lay back down, and cold sweat ran down his brow.

"Max, you don't seem well at all," she said carefully. She was trying to be calm, but he could hear the edge of panic in her voice.

"I'm okay," he reassured.

She bit her lip, clearly fighting with herself as to whether to say more, but to his relief, she turned around and poked the fire.

He stared up at the sky, which was bright blue and clear, with only a few wispy clouds. It should be a beautiful day. But then he painfully swivelled his head around to look back down towards Eastbrooke. Thick, black smoke billowed upwards. It wasn't any closer, but it hadn't retreated, either.

How bad was it down there? Were his brothers and mother safe? Had the town been saved? He avoided thinking about the possibility of the retreat having burned down, taking his livelihood with it. Somehow, it didn't seem that important right now. There were bigger things to worry about.

Like, whether they'd get off this mountain alive. It surprised him that Joseph hadn't found them yet, but his brother wouldn't give up. If only his shoulder wasn't so bad, he wouldn't be so worried, but he knew enough about wounds to know that an untreated infection was dangerous business. He could survive a few days at most, but where would that leave Junia? Unlike him, she hadn't spent a lifetime learning to survive in the bush, and she'd only been taught basic survival skills in their week together. He hadn't prepared her for being stranded in the middle of a bushfire. He'd failed.

Perhaps he should have joined the police force after all.

That made him think of his father and that dream. That horrid dream that tormented him, day and night. He lay down again as his head began to swim and tiredness overwhelmed him. Despair at seeing his father in the flames descended on him once more, and he squeezed his eyes shut against the sudden tears. He must be ill to be this emotional, but he had no strength to prevent his reaction. He felt weak and vulnerable, and he hated that Junia was seeing him like this. All his life he'd been the strong, aloof one, the older brother and protector, but now he felt as fragile as a newborn lamb.

As though sensing his thoughts, Junia turned and crawled over to him, gazing at him with wide eyes that looked like precious gemstones in her pale face. He smiled at her, thinking again how very beautiful she was, then winced as even that action caused pain.

She laid a cool hand on his forehead and gasped. "Max, you're burning up."

"I'm not, I'm cold," he protested, shivering as a chill went through his whole body.

She shook her head. There was no disguising the fear in her expression or her voice now. "The infection's getting worse, isn't it?"

"I think so," he admitted weakly, aware that his words were slightly slurred.

Her voice seemed to come from far away. Somewhere at the edges of his consciousness, he was aware that this was very, very wrong.

"I'm going to get you some water," she murmured. "You need fluids. And I'm going to stoke the fire as high as I can as a signal, okay?"

"Don't waste the kindling," he whispered through struggled breaths.

She smiled, but tears shone in her eyes.

He wanted to lift his hand and wipe them from her cheeks, but any movement now felt like too much effort.

As she got up and went to fetch water from the stream, he blinked to clear his blurred vision to see her better. Even through the fog of his fever, he had a thought of such pure clarity that it took his breath away. *She was meant for him.* God had brought her here, to his mountain, to bring them together. But now it seemed they'd be torn apart, because no matter what he said to her, he knew full well how bad his condition was, and that it was getting worse. Surely the Lord wouldn't have brought them together only for him to die? It seemed cruel, and yet his intuition was right, as crazy as it seemed after such a short time.

She was *the one*.

All his life, he'd carefully avoided becoming close to anyone. Racked with guilt and afraid of feeling such deep loss again, he'd believed he didn't deserve to be happy or have a family of his own. He'd guarded his heart like it was a fortress, locked away from everyone but his mother and brothers, and even with them, except perhaps Joseph, he was often aloof and unable to express his emotions.

What he would give now to see them. To be well, so he could tell them how much he loved them, and how sorry he was that his father had been in the warehouse that day...because of him. Hot tears stung his eyes again. Perhaps this was his punishment. The inner voice of the accuser caused him to bow his head against both the physical and emotional pain.

Then Junia returned, treading carefully with leaves in her hands that she'd used for scooping water. She knelt slowly and gently cupped his head with her hand, raising his mouth to the leaves. As the cold water hit his lips, his stupor lifted a little and he could see that his thoughts were being led down the wrong path. He remembered reading the Book of Job on their first night at camp–how long ago that seemed now! And how it made him realise that sometimes things happened for reasons mere mortals could not and would never be able to fathom. God was not punishing him–and certainly not Junia or Tasha—just because of his youthful mistakes.

If it's my time, it's my time, Lord, but please keep Junia safe...

He finished drinking and laid his head back, exhausted from the effort. He was growing weaker by the minute. He closed his eyes as his vision continued to blur, disorientating him. Junia's cool hand rested on his brow again and he tried to find his voice to say something, to thank her, but he couldn't open his mouth. Instead, a black fog crept around the edges of his consciousness, pulling him under.

CHAPTER 12

*J*unia stared up at the sky through her tears and prayed fervently. She'd stoked the fire, using the last of the kindling, even though Max had wanted her to ration it. She could look further afield if need be, but right now, what was important was being found and getting Max to the hospital. It didn't look as though he had long left.

Now, he lay across her lap, completely oblivious to her, while a thin film of sweat covered his face. He was burning up, and yet at the same time, he was clammy to the touch. His wound was clearly infected, swollen and oozing through what remained of his shirt. She kept talking to him as she stroked his brow, chatting about inane things, simply trying to keep him tethered to her, to this world, before he slipped completely out of consciousness.

She reached for his radio for the twentieth time. There'd be no signal, but she tried anyway. The radio crackled, picked up nothing. She shook her head in frustration as hot tears spilled down her face. She wiped them away roughly.

She had to keep her head, or all was lost. She couldn't afford to panic, but it was hard not to give in to the abject terror that curled in the pit of her stomach every time she looked down at him.

He couldn't die. Not now. The last few days had thrown them together and created a bond that went way beyond mere attraction. Her feelings for him were undeniable, as crazy as it seemed, and yet here they were, in the most terrible of situations, where they may never get the chance to explore what that meant for them both.

It's not fair, she screamed silently, staring at the mountaintop as tears welled in her eyes.

"It's not fair!" she screamed again, this time aloud. Guilt descended on her before she remembered one of her favourite psalms. She prayed it aloud, her voice echoing in the silence of the mountain side.

"Lord, hear my prayer, listen to my cry for mercy. In Your faithfulness and righteousness, come to my relief. Do not bring Your servant to judgment, for no one living is righteous before You. The enemy pursues me, he crushes me to the ground and he makes me dwell in darkness like those long dead. So my spirit grows faint within me; my heart within me is dismayed. I remember the days of long ago; I meditate on all Your works and consider what Your hands have done."

She looked down at Max and stroked his brow. Emotion clogged her throat, but she continued on.

"I stretch my hands out to You; I thirst for You like a parched land. Answer me quickly, Lord, for my spirit fails. Do not hide Your face from me, or I will be like those who go down to the pit. Let the morning bring me word of Your unfailing love, for I have put my trust in You. Show me the way I should go; for to You I entrust my life. Rescue me from my enemies, Lord, for I hide myself in You. Teach me to do Your will, because You are my God. May

Your good spirit lead me on level ground. For Your name's sake, Lord, preserve my life and in Your righteousness bring me out of trouble."

Finishing her prayer, she raised her head. Everything seemed eerily still and silent, as though the mountain itself was holding its breath.

Then a sound in the distance made her heart leap. Hardly daring to hope, she looked up, and there it was, silhouetted against the sky and dropping down towards them.

The rescue helicopter.

Sobbing with relief, she waved her hands frantically, gasping through her tears as it hovered above them, the sound of its choppers roaring. The door opened, and a man she recognised as Joseph waved before winching himself down.

"Is he alive?" he mouthed, fear filling his eyes as he gazed at Max lying prostrate in her arms.

"Yes!" she shouted back. "But he needs a hospital, fast."

"Can you lift him to me?"

Huffing and panting, Junia manoeuvred Max to his brother, who tied him to the winch with him. Max groaned in pain. "I'm sorry, I'm sorry." She felt awful hurting him but deeply relieved at the signs of consciousness.

"I'll be right back," Joseph said before he gave the nod to his partner in the helicopter to winch them up.

Junia's heart burst with joy and relief. They were going to be alright. *Thank You, God, for answering my prayers.*

Ten minutes later, she sat in the helicopter as it headed away from the mountain, with her blood pressure and heart rate being checked by a paramedic. Max lay on a trolley with an antibiotic drip in his arm, which would hopefully hold off the spreading infection until they got him to the hospital.

Joseph passed her a bottle of water and a dry biscuit.

"You're in shock and weak, so they'll want to check you over at the hospital, too, but otherwise you seem fine."

"And Max?" she asked for the tenth time.

His expression stilled. "We'll be there as fast as we can."

She knew from his response that Max wasn't out of danger yet. She looked at him lying on the trolley bed, his skin almost grey, and then laid a hand on her head as she suddenly felt dizzy.

"Eat that; it will help," Joseph ordered.

She took a bite and swallowed, although her mouth was dry and food was the last thing on her mind. "What happened to everyone else?" she asked weakly, wondering if she could bear the answer. "To Tasha?"

"We picked her up in the night. She was in shock and quite faint, so she's still in the hospital, but she's going to be fine."

Junia sagged with relief.

"We picked up the rest of the campers straight away and they're all staying in the church hall at the moment. The fire's being beaten back, and we're expecting rain in the next few days, thank God. Max's retreat sustained a fair amount of damage, but nothing that can't be repaired."

Junia nodded as she tried to take it all in. "And the men who were after Tasha?"

"My brother Rob caught up with them. They're in custody, but they'll have to be released if Tasha decides not to press charges. Rob's talking to people about getting her out of Melbourne to somewhere safer."

Junia nodded. As much as Tasha had been fairly settled at Safe Harbour, it was too close to home for her–and especially if she pressed charges. "I'll talk to her," she murmured.

"Right now, you'll relax," Joseph said, "and try and rest. You've been through quite an ordeal."

And it may not be over. Junia gazed at Max's unmoving form. They still had to get him to the hospital.

Joseph's gaze followed hers and his mouth set in a grim line. He didn't need to say anything for her to know he was worried.

The flight to the hospital couldn't have been very long, but each minute felt like an hour. Junia took Max's hand, trying to will her own strength into him. She'd known him little more than a week, and yet after everything that had happened, it felt like a lifetime. *Don't let me lose him now, God. Not now that we've come this far.*

Finally, they arrived at the hospital. Other paramedics took Max straight to the Emergency Room while Joseph stayed with her in the waiting room until the doctor came. She felt desperately tired and needed to lie down and sleep, although she suspected that worrying about Max would only keep her awake.

"Will he be okay?" she asked Joseph, breaking the weighted silence that lay between them.

He sighed heavily. "I hope so. If only we'd found him sooner..."

"You did all you could," Junia reassured him. "And he wouldn't want you to blame yourself."

"No," Joseph agreed with a sad smile. "He'd be telling me to buck up and get on with it." His eyes searched her face, and then he added, "You care about him, don't you?"

She felt herself go bright red. Was it that obvious? Before she could answer, he continued. "He cares about you, too. I could tell, as soon as you arrived."

"We didn't even know each other!" she protested.

He shrugged. "I know my brother."

The doctor called them both into a small room but addressed Joseph. "Your brother has a nasty infection. I'm hoping we caught it in time, but the next few hours will be crucial. We may have to operate on that shoulder, but he needs to stabilise first."

Joseph and Junia exchanged a worried glance, then Joseph stood to leave, telling her he'd send his mother to pick her up when she was discharged. Junia thanked him, and as he walked away, she thought how much like Max he was.

"They're a lovely bunch of boys, the Carltons," the doctor said, picking up on her train of thought. "If George were only here to see them, he'd be so proud."

CHAPTER 13

Max was vaguely aware of people near him, rushing around his bedside, and of voices he recognised, although he couldn't make out what they were saying. He felt like he was floating, and he drifted in and out of consciousness.

At some point, everything went dark, and he was alone. Even the beeping of the machine he was hooked up to had stopped. In the silence, all of the pain and fever had gone. He opened his eyes.

He was on the mountain...except this time, he was alone.

Strangely, he wasn't scared. The sun was pleasantly warm and a fresh breeze rustled his hair. Birds were singing, and he smiled. Feeling thirsty, he got up and walked to the stream. A man was already there, and it felt like the most natural thing in the world to go over and sit next to him. The man didn't look up, and Max didn't look at him. He had a vague feeling he knew him, and he felt comfortable in his presence.

Using his hands, he drank from the stream and was

amazed at how fresh and pure the water tasted. "This water is really good."

The man next to him nodded. "Of course. It's mountain water. Straight from the source."

Max gasped. He knew that voice.

"Dad?" he asked, his eyes filling with tears as he turned to the man.

"Son," his father said, his voice warm and his eyes shining with love...and pride.

Max shook his head, hardly daring to believe his own eyes. "Dad," he whispered, as grief flowed through him like a river, "I'm so sorry. The warehouse...it was all my fault."

George Carlton shook his head. "No, Max. You were a kid. The fault lies with the bomb makers, not with you. If I hadn't come across them that day, the whole of Eastbrooke was in danger."

"It's still not fair," Max said.

His father smiled, his eyes filled with understanding. "I know, son. I know. But it's time you let all the guilt and anger go. Leave it here. Let the water wash it away. You don't need it anymore."

"I can't stay with you?"

His father shook his head. "Not today. But one day, son. One day we'll see each other again...and we'll never be separated."

A great weight lifted from his heart as he heard the truth in his father's words as clear as a bell. His tears dried on his face as calm came over him. "I need to go back," he whispered.

"Yes, you do. But remember, I love you...and I couldn't be prouder of the man you've become."

Max gazed into his father's eyes, feeling a deep wound within him finally close. His eyes grew heavy, and as he lay back to let sleep claim him again, a smile curved his lips as his eyes closed.

"He's smiling!"

"Mum! He's awake."

Max blinked his eyes open, his vision blurred as he took in the shapes around him. His vision slowly cleared. His mum, Joseph and Eli crowded around the bed. He tried to sit, but as a wave of nausea rolled over him, thought better of it.

"Lie down," his mother urged. "Elijah, go and get a doctor."

Eli went to do his mother's bidding while Max stared around the room, trying to get his bearings. Then his eyes flew wide open. "Junia?"

"She's fine," Joseph reassured him. "Mum's going to take her home tonight. The doctors checked her over and other than mild shock and dehydration, she's fine. I'll get her once the doctor gives the okay."

Max nodded. His head was swimming as the events of the last two days came back to him in a blur of images.

"Where's Rob?" he rasped, his throat dry. "Tasha? Where's Tasha?" He tried to sit again, his heart thumping.

"Okay," Joseph said calmly, placing a steadying hand on his good shoulder. "Let me answer in order."

Max swallowed hard and settled his head back on the pillow, steeling himself for bad news.

Joseph released a breath. "Rob's at the station, liaising with the police in Melbourne. He apprehended the two men who tried to kidnap Tasha and they're in custody. Tasha's here in the hospital, and she's safe and under observation. I don't know any more details, but right now, everyone's safe."

"And what about the fire?"

His brother winced. "Eastbrooke was missed, thank God, but..." his voice trailed off, and Max knew instantly what he was referring to.

"My retreat," he said grimly.

Joseph gave a slow nod.

"How bad is it?"

"It can be repaired, but it'll need a few months' work at least."

The news was bad, but it could have been worse. A lot worse.

Eli returned with the doctor, who was delighted to see him awake. He proceeded to check Max's wound and vitals. "Looking better. You're one lucky boy. The shoulder will probably need surgery as there's a lot of tendon damage. We'll do some more tests first though." He made some notes and gave a nod. "I'll be back soon."

Max exhaled slowly. So much for it just being a flesh wound. But he was incredibly fortunate. He still had his arm–and his life.

Eli and Joseph left, leaving him alone with his mother, who took his good hand and squeezed it. "I was so scared when they couldn't find you," she murmured. "I stayed up all night, praying."

For some reason, her words reminded him of his dream–or whatever it had been–and he smiled, that same calmness washing over him again. "Mum," he said softly, wondering how she'd react, "I saw Dad."

She frowned. "That's not possible."

"When I was drifting in and out of consciousness," he tried to explain. "I had a vision, or a dream, or something...I saw him by the river." Tears filled his eyes. "He told me he was proud of me...and that it wasn't my fault."

"It was never your fault," his mum said firmly. "We all

tried to tell you that. You've been carrying that burden all these years?"

He nodded. "I never realised just how much my guilt and grief were hardening my heart. Shutting me off from others...and even from God, to some extent. These last few days have changed everything."

She gave a lopsided grin. "Would that lovely young woman have anything to do with that change?"

"I think so," he admitted. "But how do I tell her? I've only just met her, and she'll be going back to Melbourne."

"You both know how to drive. You can visit and get to know each other better. Just tell her what's on your heart, Max. Don't close it again."

They embraced, carefully because of his shoulder, and even through the pain and stiffness, for the first time since his father died, he felt free.

CHAPTER 14

Tasha stared at her phone, scrolling through the old text messages from the man who'd once meant so much to her, and who she now, finally, knew was an abuser. Could she dare hope that this could all be over now?

Rob promised that if she gave a statement, she'd be protected, and they'd find her a safe place to stay, well away from Melbourne. "The church has links with an organisation that houses survivors like yourself," he'd told her kindly.

She'd felt a flutter of hope at the thought of being part of a proper family, just like Junia had. She'd miss everyone at Safe Harbour, but if she was going to fully break free, emotionally as well as spiritually, she needed a fresh start.

"But what if I don't want to give a statement?" she'd asked, fear overtaking her. If she gave one, he'd know. She'd be a snitch.

"We'll still look after you just the same, Tasha. Our help doesn't come with conditions." Rob had seemed surprised that she would assume otherwise, and she didn't know how to tell him that in her world, nothing was freely given.

Grace is. She heard Junia's voice in her head. Perhaps this was grace. She'd thought she was going to die until she'd seen the tiger quoll and then Jake. The thought of the eccentric old man made her smile. He'd gotten out of the hospital as fast as he could, claiming he needed to be in the open air, but he'd dropped by her room to say goodbye first.

As she scrolled through the messages, they didn't have the same power over her anymore. She was still scared of him–that was rational–but the emotional ties, for now at least, had withered away. Watching him shoot Max had been the last straw, and she had no doubt he wouldn't have cared if her and her friends died. That told her all she needed to know.

By the time Rob returned, she'd made up her mind. She handed him the phone. "All the text messages are on there. You can have it," she said, swallowing hard as she deliberately went against all of the conditioning that gang life had taught her. Her hand shook as he took it from her.

"Tasha, thank you. This is incredibly brave. I have good news, too. It turns out he had a whole stack of outstanding warrants. He's been extradited to Melbourne. Even without your statement, he's going to prison."

Gasping, she buried her head in her hands and sobbed.

Rob laid a fatherly hand on her shoulder.

"Is everything okay?" a familiar voice asked.

She looked up. Junia stood in the doorway. She was wearing a hospital gown and looked exhausted. Tasha sobbed with joy and held her arms out. "Junia! I'm so glad you're okay! How's Max? Is he going to be alright?"

"I hope so." Junia's eyes shimmered with tears which she wiped with the back of her hand. "I haven't had an update yet." She stepped closer and slipped her arms around Tasha. "How are you, Tash?"

"I'm so, so sorry," she sobbed. "I put everyone in so much danger, and Max got hurt. I was so stupid. Can you ever forgive me?"

Junia stroked her hair. "Of course, I can. I'm so, so glad you're okay." Pulling back, she perched on the edge of Tasha's bed and searched her gaze.

There were things that needed to be said. Explained. Tasha swallowed hard. "I'm giving a statement," she said quietly.

Junia's brow lifted. "Really? Oh Tasha, I'm so proud of you. But listen, it's okay if it feels like too much. You'll be taken care of, either way."

"I know, Rob told me." She fell silent for a moment and stared down at her hands on the blanket. Everything still felt surreal. "I saw a tiger quoll," she said. "It made me see where I've been going wrong. How I've been running back to the bad because it's what I know, but actually the good has been in front of me all along." She lifted her gaze. "I want to get baptised, Junia."

"Wow." Junia's mouth gaped. "You got all that from a tiger quoll?"

Tasha burst out laughing, as did Junia. They hugged again, tears rolling down both their cheeks. This time when they pulled apart, another Carlton brother stood in the door. Joseph. He was grinning, and Tasha felt her heart lift further as she knew it could only be good news.

"Junia, Max is awake. He wants to see you."

∽

As Junia followed Joseph to Max's room, her breath caught in her throat and she silently thanked God that he was awake and alive. So many blessings in one day, after so much despair up on the mountain, made her feel as though she was living in a dream. Except it was real, and everything was just as it was meant to be.

She hesitated behind Joseph and took a deep breath before entering Max's room. Their mother Jean sat by the bedside but stood to make room for her.

He was pale and looked strangely vulnerable lying in the bed with a drip in one arm and the other shoulder heavily bandaged. But he was still the Max she'd gotten to know, and when their gazes met, all she wanted to do was throw herself into his arms. She didn't, but as she sat in the chair beside the bed, taking his hand felt like the most natural thing in the world to do.

"I thought we'd never get off the mountain," she said honestly, giving voice to the reality of the situation they'd just escaped.

"I know," he said, his voice barely above a whisper. "Thank you for caring for me."

"You're welcome." Junia smiled, and they stared deeply into each other's eyes. There was so much to say, but somehow it felt impossible to voice her thoughts, let alone her feelings. They'd known each other for less than two weeks.

The thought of leaving there and never seeing him again, and the whole experience becoming simply a great testimony to tell at church, something that had once happened, didn't feel right. Somehow, this shared experience had changed everything. She'd never be the same person she'd been before she went up that mountain...and she could never forget Max.

But how do I tell him? He'd think she was crazy. Besides, now certainly wasn't the time. He needed to recover. That was the priority. Instead, she told him about her conversation with Tasha.

"I've told Tasha she can stay with me until they find her a place," Jean said. "I've got plenty of room. So can you and the rest of the group, Junia. Although it'll have to be sofas and blankets." She laughed gently.

"Thank you," Junia said, overwhelmed by her kindness. These were good people.

"Don't let her feed you cake," Max warned. "She doesn't know when to stop."

They laughed together, but his eyelids were drooping, and his speech growing slower.

"You need to rest," she said softly. "I should go. The doctor will be coming round to discharge me soon."

He nodded, then lifted his gaze over her shoulder at his mother, and from the corner of her eye, Junia saw her give a subtle nod.

"I'll be in the waiting room, dear," she said to Junia, and then left with Joseph following.

Slightly puzzled, Junia turned back to Max.

He swallowed. "This is going to sound crazy, I know," he began, his voice wobbling as he took her hand.

Hope surged within her. "Go on," she whispered.

"I think–no, I know–that I'm developing feelings for you. If I was avoiding you last week, it's because I was drawn to you, but it scared me. Ever since my dad died, I've not let myself get close to people. But after this, I can't let you leave without telling you."

She couldn't stop herself from smiling as joy bubbled inside her. "I feel the same. I don't know how this will work, but I'm willing to give it a try."

"I should ask you out on a date," he said, his eyelids fluttering.

"You should," Junia agreed, chuckling.

His eyes closed and his breathing deepened. She looked at

their joined hands and smiled. From the moment they met, despite his crustiness, she'd known there was something special about him, and now, her heart swelled with feelings she'd thought she might never experience.

As she stood to leave, he murmured, just loud enough for her to hear, "You can tell my mother–I'm going to marry you."

"Are you sure you're not still delirious?" She laughed, but there was no answer. He was fast asleep.

EPILOGUE – SIX MONTHS LATER

Max turned to his brother Joseph and smiled as he passed him the rings. Two, thin bands of gold, engraved with a line from the Song of Songs. *'I am my beloved's and my beloved is mine'* in the tiniest, most delicate writing. Perfect, just like this moment. Just like her.

Junia stood in front of him in white lace, her hair softly curling on her shoulders, waiting for him to slip the ring on her finger. The ring that would signify they were husband and wife.

As he placed the gold band on her slim finger, he smiled into her eyes, taking another moment to appreciate just how beautiful this woman was. His woman...and now his wife. His brothers–and Junia herself–might have thought he was crazy when he came round in the hospital and announced they would be married, but even in his compromised state, he'd known he was more serious than he'd ever been about anything. He could have lost her up on that mountain, and he wasn't going to let her slip through his fingers once God had saved his life.

"With this ring," he said loudly, his voice resounding around the small church, "I thee wed."

They'd dated for a few months, Junia driving up to Eastbrooke at weekends, while he'd waited for a good time to formally propose, not wanting to rush her. When she'd tearfully announced one day that she was being made redundant from Safe Harbour due to funding issues, he'd wondered if the time would ever be right. Then Sonia suggested giving her a job at the retreat–once it was open again, of course, as it was still being repaired from the fire at that point–and Junia had jumped at the chance. She loved Eastbrooke, loved the retreat...and loved him. On hearing those words, he'd produced the ring he'd bought in hope months before, and she'd thrown her arms around him with a tearful yes.

Now, here they were, on their wedding day. He held out his own hand for her to slip on his ring, a ripple of joy flowing through him as she pushed it on to his finger.

She looked up at him, her eyes shining with love. "With this ring," she echoed, "I thee wed."

It was done. As the pastor pronounced them man and wife, Max pulled her into his arms and lowered his mouth to meet hers. Her lips were warm and she gave herself freely to the passion of his kiss, much to the delight of their guests. He didn't want the moment to end, but this was only the beginning.

He'd anticipated a small wedding, but as it turned out, half of Eastbrooke were there, as well as all of Junia's former colleagues and some of the kids from Safe Harbour, and her adopted family. Tasha had even flown down with her new foster parents, looking happier than he'd ever seen her.

As they walked down the aisle, arm in arm, he reflected on how incredibly blessed he was to have so many people in his life who loved him.

Thank You, Lord, he prayed, gratitude bubbling within him. *Thank You for opening my heart and bringing Junia to me.* He couldn't wait to see what the future held. After their honeymoon in New Zealand, they'd come back to a refurbished centre and lead their first retreat together. And hopefully, he thought with a smile, they'd think about starting a family. He knew his mother was eagerly awaiting grandchildren.

Junia squeezed his hand as they reached the door where they posed for a photo before he kissed her again.

"I love you," she whispered. "I'm so happy."

"So am I," he said seriously, gazing into her eyes. "And now we have the rest of our lives together."

As they walked outside to take the wedding car to the reception venue, he glanced up at the mountain in the distance and remembered how they'd met.

She followed his gaze and smiled. "We should be grateful to God for that mountain since it brought us together. Even if it did feel like a brush with death at the time, I wouldn't change a thing."

"Me either." He kissed the top of her head, breathing in her sweet, floral scent, enfolding her in his arms. "I'll always be there for you, Junia."

"I know. And this is where I feel the safest. Right here in your arms."

Before they got into the car, his mother rushed over with Rob behind her. She wrapped Junia in a hug. "I thank God for bringing you into my son's life," she said, smiling through tears. "You've both made a mother very happy."

Rob rolled his eyes and grinned at Max.

Jean shook her head and chuckled. "It could be you next, Rob. You need to settle down someday."

Rob's eyes widened in horror. "I don't think so, Mum."

"Why not?" Max teased his brother.

"Why not, indeed?" Junia asked before Rob could respond. "After all, who knows what God has in store for any of us?"

I lift my eyes up to the mountains – where does my help come from?
My help comes from the Lord, the Maker of heaven and of earth.
He will not let your foot slip. He who watches over you will not slumber.
Indeed, He who watches over Israel will neither slumber nor sleep.
The Lord watches you. The Lord is the shade at your right hand.
The sun will not harm you by day, nor the moon by night.
The Lord will keep you from all harm and He will watch over your life.
The Lord will watch over your coming and going, both now and forevermore.

UNDER HIS WATCH

PROLOGUE

*R*ob circled the block near Emma's house, a warning voice whispering in his head. *Something is wrong.* A sense of urgency tugged at him, the inner voice growing louder…

She's in danger.

Years of being on the police force had taught him to trust his instincts. He hit the gas and sped towards her house, rehearsing what reason he'd give for turning up on her doorstep unannounced. After everything she'd been through, the last thing he wanted was to scare her even more. But if nothing was wrong and he came up with a lame excuse, like inviting her for coffee again, what would she think? That he was pushing her?

Not that he didn't want to see her again, but the next time, he'd properly ask her on a date. That was, after she'd had the chance to know him better and see for herself that he wasn't the flirtatious guy who dated a different girl every weekend. He only had himself to blame for her opinion of him. It was a carefully cultivated image, designed to stop people from getting too close.

Yet, with Emma, things were different. He wanted her to see the real him, even if that thought scared him beyond all comprehension.

Please, Lord, he prayed spontaneously as he slowed for a corner, *please let her be okay*. But, as though in reply, the sense of urgency came again. He drove even faster. He should have sent an officer to check on her earlier. Insisted she stay at his mother's, where she wouldn't be alone. She was a witness to a murder, and that placed her in danger. Although she thought the killer hadn't seen her clearly enough to identify her, she could easily be wrong. The more he thought about it, the more he was convinced she was in acute danger.

As he turned onto her street, his worst fears were realised. A black sedan with frosted windows was parked outside her house. Two men, with balaclavas on and weapons drawn, jumped out of the vehicle and ran up her front path. They didn't bother to knock. One of them shot the front door open before they both ran in.

Rob's heart pounded as his adrenalin spiked. His first instinct was to leap out of the car and tackle the men himself, but his years of training took over. It would be a foolish move. Although he was armed, he was outnumbered against two obviously dangerous criminals, and if shots were fired, Emma could be hurt—or worse. His stomach lurched as he screeched to a halt behind the sedan and radioed his partner Jerry.

"Two masked, armed men entering Emma Humphries' house. Forced entry. Send immediate back-up." He paused, then barked, "I'm going in." He wouldn't wait for back-up. She'd be dead before they arrived. He pulled his police issue gun out of his dashboard compartment and jumped out of the car, heart in mouth.

He prayed he wasn't too late.

CHAPTER 1

Two weeks earlier

Rob tried his best to look interested as Marion described her day to him. Not that she was uninteresting. Not at all. In fact, her job at the dog grooming salon probably came with a lot of entertaining anecdotes, but his mind was on other things. He and his partner Jerry had taken a call from Police Headquarters in Melbourne earlier that day warning them of possible drug gangs moving in on the Eastbrooke area, and Rob was eager to start investigating. His last three cases as one of Eastbrooke's most respected law enforcement officers had involved a missing cat, a stolen bicycle, and an ongoing feud between neighbours.

Eastbrooke was a small, quiet town, and while it was a wonderful place to live, nothing much happened on a daily basis. The last major drama, over a year ago now, had involved an attempted kidnapping and a police chase in the middle of a bushfire. The same bushfire that had endangered his brother Max's life. He just couldn't seem to find a happy medium.

Helping to take down a drug ring could be just what his career needed, and this time there was no chance of it getting personal. After the bushfire, Rob had found himself obsessively checking on his mother and three brothers, suddenly aware of their mortality after nearly losing his older brother. His vigilance had only served to annoy everyone, particularly Max, who as the oldest had always been the protector and had no wish to see their sibling roles suddenly reversed.

Rob became aware of Marion looking at him expectantly, clearly wanting a response to something she'd just said, which he'd completely missed. He flashed her his best smile and hid his discomfort. His heart simply wasn't in this date, but he was too much of a gentleman to say so.

The smile seemed to placate her, as she blushed and smiled and carried on talking. He did his best to focus, but something was wrong. He enjoyed the company of women, but he was twenty-nine years old and hadn't had a steady relationship since his girlfriend in college. They'd broken up when she realised he wasn't about to propose any time soon, and as Christians, their relationship had nowhere else to go. It had been an amicable split, and he'd secretly been somewhat relieved, although his mother Jean had been disappointed. For years she'd despaired of having any of her four boys happily settled, although now, since Max had married and was expecting his first child, she'd stopped hinting at Rob. This date, though, had been her idea. His mum was friends with Marion's mother–she seemed to know everyone in Eastbrooke–and had passed the word on that Marion had her eye on Rob.

"Why don't you take her for a nice meal?" his mother had suggested. "I haven't seen you date anyone in months."

"That's because you told me to stop dating all the eligible young women in town if I only intended on leading them up the garden path and not to an altar, or words to that effect."

She'd shaken her head with such a look of patient perseverance that he'd agreed to take Marion out. He knew he was handsome, and as an up-and-coming law enforcement officer, was considered a good catch. And he wasn't in any way disrespectful to women. He prided himself on being the perfect gentleman and had never slept around, but at some point, most of the pretty girls in Eastbrooke had been on a date with him, until he'd sworn off after a lecture from his mum. But now it seemed she was encouraging him again.

He told himself that he simply hadn't found *the one*, but to be honest, he wasn't really looking. His job kept him busy, and he was chasing promotion. He loved his family and saw as much of them as he could. He didn't have time for anything serious. Or, at least, that's what he told himself. If there were other, more deep-seated reasons for his reluctance to settle down, well, he wasn't the introspective type.

"Are we having dessert?" Marion asked.

"Sure." He smiled generously. "Order whatever you'd like."

"Oh, but I'm watching my weight," she pouted.

He fought not to roll his eyes. "Okay, shall we get the bill?"

She looked disappointed. "I thought we could share. This cheesecake looks great."

"Sure," he said again, giving his usual, easy-going smile. He glanced at the clock. Twenty more minutes and he could take her home, then call Jerry to talk about the information they'd received that day.

His work phone buzzed in his pocket. "Sorry. I need to take this."

She gave a nod.

He retrieved it quickly from his pocket. Jerry's name flashed on the screen. Pressing the green button, he glanced at Marion before saying, "Hey partner. What's doing?"

"Are you busy?" Jerry's gruff tones came over the line.

"Sort of. What's up?"

"We need you down at Jacob's Creek. We've got a body."

Rob's brows hiked. Swivelling around, he kept his voice low. "A drowning?" The creek was small and not very deep. It seemed unlikely.

"Nope. The dude's been shot."

Rob whistled under his breath. "I'll be there as soon as I can." He cut the call and smiled apologetically at Marion. "I'm so sorry, but I have to go. Work emergency. I'll drop you home."

She looked both disappointed and curious. Before she could question him, he turned and signalled for the bill.

He drove her home, his mind on Jerry's news. *A shooting? In Eastbrooke? Did it have anything to do with the drug smuggling ring?* Although such a thing seemed unthinkable in their sleepy, out of the way, picturesque town, it wouldn't be the first time over the years. Eastbrooke was nestled beneath a mountain range and plenty of passes led to the coast. It was a smuggler's dream.

"Is it serious? The call out, I mean?" Marion asked as they pulled up outside her apartment.

"I can't say, but yes, it's definitely urgent." He tapped his fingers on the steering wheel as she opened the door, his head already on the shooting. *Why was she taking so long to get out?*

She looked at him expectantly. "So, I'll see you again?"

He went to agree, but then his natural honesty came to

the fore. "I couldn't really say right now. It looks like I'm going to be pretty busy."

"Well, goodbye then." She pushed the door and climbed out.

He gave a half-smile. "Bye, Marion."

"It's Marla." Her voice was as cold as ice. She slammed the door and stormed off.

Rob winced as he pulled away from the kerb. This date had been a bad idea from the beginning. Now he'd offended a perfectly nice woman who deserved a more attentive companion, and his mother would be disappointed. Hopefully when Max and Junia had the baby she'd forget about his non-existent love life.

He high-tailed it to the creek. Romance, he knew little about, but crime—that was a totally different story. It was right up his alley.

When he arrived, Jerry hurried to the car, his face grim. "What took you so long?"

Rob grimaced. "A date my mother set up."

Jerry shook his head and let out a small chuckle.

"Forensics got here quick." Rob jumped out of the vehicle and nodded towards the tent set up by the side of the creek.

"Yeah. Quicker than you."

"Come on, give me a break." Rob let out an exasperated breath, although he knew his partner was only toying with him.

"Sorry. You know I don't mean it. Come on." Jerry led him to the side of the creek where the body had been dragged out and was now being examined by the forensics expert.

"What do we know?" Rob asked.

"Shot to the back of the head at close range."

"This wasn't a crime of passion then," he said, raising his

brows. "That's an execution. Do you think this could be related to the drugs line that Melbourne warned us about?"

"Let's not jump to conclusions," Jerry replied. It was a familiar pattern between them, and one of the reasons they worked well together. Rob went on instinct and tended to think creatively, while Jerry was more cautious. He was a solid police officer, but it was Rob whom everyone knew was on the fast track for promotion. He'd been told numerous times that he reminded everyone of his father, George Carlton, who'd been Police Chief in Eastbrooke until his premature death when Rob was thirteen.

"Looks likely though, doesn't it?" Rob continued. "Was he killed here, or did the creek carry him down?" They were at the creek now, and he addressed his last question to the forensics expert, an older woman with a steel grey bob.

"Killed here," she confirmed. "He's been dead at least twelve hours, I'd say, so some time in the early hours."

"Let's get Search and Rescue on the lookout for a weapon," Jerry said.

Rob nodded, although he doubted they'd find one. "I'll call Joseph and get him and his team onto it. Is Johnson coming?" Al Johnson was the current Police Chief in Eastbrooke, nearing retirement and fast losing enthusiasm for the job.

"I called him," Jerry replied. "He was on a weekend break with his wife, but he's on his way back now."

Rob frowned. "I don't suppose he was happy about that."

"You suppose right."

The pair exchanged a wry smile and then Rob got on the radio. Joseph was his younger brother who headed Mountain Rescue, whereas Eli, the youngest, was also on the police force. At twenty-four, he was their newest recruit, eager and bright. When he'd announced his intention to sign up, Rob had been worried about future rivalry, but Eli was intent on moving to the city once he'd served his time here.

Rob studied the bloated body. Who was he? How had he ended up here? "Nothing to identify him?"

Jerry shook his head as his phone rang. He took the call, and after a few moments of nodding and the odd word here and there, he faced Rob. "That was the chief."

"I figured that much. What did he want?"

"Seems you might be right. He spoke to Melbourne. An informant told them a gang member called José Moreno had been kidnapped by a rival gang. The same one they believe is moving in on the mountains. There's been a feud brewing for a while, it seems."

Rob's adrenalin kicked up a notch. Why had he ever complained about Eastbrooke being boring?

"Why kill him all the way out here?" Jerry scratched his head of thick, brown hair.

"To send a message." Rob instinctively knew he was right. "It's a way of saying, this is our territory now."

Jerry shook his head. "I hope you're wrong. This can't be happening in Eastbrooke. Nothing like this has happened here since your father's day."

"Yeah," Rob said, his voice like flint, "and it killed him."

Jerry shuddered. "Sorry, mate. That was insensitive."

"Not at all. But let's pray this gets cleared up quickly."

Jerry nodded.

Rob's gaze swung to the mountain towering above like a silent sentinel, and then to the body. A tremor ran though him. No. This wasn't going to get cleared up quickly. Don't ask how he knew. He just knew.

CHAPTER 2

Emma glanced at the clock and was surprised that it was nearly time to go home. The day had flown. But then, she adored her job as a first-grade teacher at Eastbrooke Primary.

After qualifying as a teacher, she'd re-joined her parents at their missionary camp and taught in the small school in the compound. She'd loved it, but the poverty and harsh conditions broke her heart. It had been a life-changing experience, and she'd expected it would be the sort of work she'd always do, having grown up with missionary parents. However, while home on a trip to see her grandparents, an advertisement for a first-grade teacher at Eastbrooke Primary caught her eye. She felt God calling her to answer it. Her parents urged her to follow that call, and so here she was. Living and working in the small and peaceful town of Eastbrooke was a huge change from Ethiopia, and she sometimes wondered how long it would be before she grew restless. It wasn't the type of place where much happened.

Which was why, she supposed, the news article that

appeared yesterday about the body of an unknown man found in Jacob's Creek had caused quite a stir and had been the talk of the town ever since. The consensus was that it must have been an accident, perhaps an unlucky camper who didn't know the mountains well, although there was a rumour it had been a murder.

Emma had been in Eastbrooke for three months, and had found it a welcoming place, having made good friends with her colleagues and the women from the local church, especially Jean Carlton, an older woman with a nurturing manner that reminded Emma of her own mother. Jean was a well-loved figure in the local community, ran the women's group at Eastbrooke Baptist Church, and had taken Emma under her wing and helped her feel at home. Jean was a widow with four grown sons, and she treated Emma like the daughter she never had.

"Miss," Josie, a cute blue-eyed five-year-old with golden braids, looked up from her drawing. "Robbie's stolen the red crayon."

"I had it first." Robbie pouted.

Josie promptly picked up the green crayon and scribbled all over Robbie's picture, to which Robbie let out a huge yell.

Emma was about to intervene when the bell sounded. Relieved, she reprimanded them both gently, helped the children pack up, and then saw them out.

She was doing a last-minute tidy of the classroom when her colleague Mary came in and asked, "Will you be at church next Sunday?"

"Of course." Emma smiled.

"A few of us are going for a walk afterwards if you'd like to come. We're thinking of making it a regular thing."

"Oh. I'm going to Jean Carlton's for lunch this Sunday,

but I'll definitely come the week after. I love a good walk, and a regular walking club sounds like a great idea."

"Great, I'll sign you up," Mary said on her way out, leaving Emma smiling after her. Mary was always trying to sign her up to something. Last week it had been the crochet club, which Emma had tried, only to discover she was terrible at it.

She locked up and left, saying goodbye to the caretaker on the way out. It was a bright, sunny day and she decided to walk the kilometre home–practically the entire length of Eastbrooke–rather than waiting for the bus, which was unreliable at the best of times.

She was halfway down High Street when Rob Carlton approached from the opposite direction. She knew who he was because she was friends with his mum, and she'd met him at church. She'd heard the rumours about him being a sort of playboy, and had to admit he cut a dashing figure in his police uniform. She felt her cheeks warm when he smiled at her. She wasn't immune to his good looks, but he wasn't her type. Not that she had a type—a life devoted to missionary work had never left time for romance, but her type definitely wasn't a man like him. Not that he wasn't a good man. The town held him in high regard and he was evidently a good police officer. On the few occasions she'd spoken to him, he'd been unfailingly polite, but he also had a reputation as the town's most eligible bachelor. His easy confidence suggested he was aware of his charms. She'd always thought of herself as something of a plain jane, and certainly not the glamorous type someone like him would choose to be with.

"Hello. Emma, isn't it?" he asked politely as they reached each other.

"Yes, from the school," she said, lowering her gaze. She'd

only ever spoken briefly to him when they'd been in a crowd at church, and never alone.

"Eastbrooke Primary's a great school. All of us Carlton boys went there, as did my mum and dad."

"Wow. That's really lovely to have roots like that." She lifted her gaze, suddenly wistful. As a result of her parents' travelling, she'd gone to five different schools and been home schooled throughout her adolescence. She wouldn't have changed the experience for the world, but even so, the sense of belonging Rob described painted a touching picture.

"You've come from Africa, haven't you?" he asked.

His interest momentarily flattered her, but then she reminded herself that he was the type of guy who could make *anyone* feel he was interested in them, not in a deliberate sense, but just because of his natural charm and easy manner.

She gave a nod. "Yes. Ethiopia. I worked at a missionary school my parents set up. I'm Melbourne born and bred, though. My grandparents still live there."

"I'd love to do more travelling. I've been to New Zealand, but that's about it. You must have loads of stories."

"A few," she agreed, smiling.

"You'll have to tell me about them sometime." A charming grin hitched up the side of his face, sending an involuntarily tingle up her spine. Before she could reply, he was on his way.

She huffed with annoyance as she stared after him. How dare he have that effect on her. Chiding herself, she hoisted her bag onto her shoulder, and lifting her chin, continued on her way. She had more important things to think about than Rob Carlton. What to have for dinner, for one.

Her turn of the century, two-bedroom cottage was on a lovely, leafy lane, surrounded by other similar cottages.

Colourful annuals filled her front garden—not that she was a gardener. Far from it, but her nan had given her some tips when she first moved in, and now, the whole garden looked really pretty. Smiling, she headed to the front door and went inside, quickly changing into sweatpants and a tank top.

She contemplated making a casserole for dinner before deciding against it, and instead, put a ready-made meal for one in the oven. She had a lot of lesson planning to do and didn't have the patience for cooking. She'd bought a stack of ready-meals last week for evenings like this. As she put it in the oven, she recalled the pitying look on the shopkeeper's face as he'd rung them through the till. "A young lady like you shouldn't be on her own," he'd said kindly. "I'm sure you'll meet someone soon."

"I'm not actually looking for anyone," she'd mumbled, thrusting her shopping into her recyclable bag and hurrying off, mortified. She was only twenty-six. Not quite a spinster yet. Even so, the last two times they'd spoken on the phone, her mother had asked if she'd met any nice men in Eastbrooke.

"Mum!" she'd protested. "I'm not planning on staying here forever."

"Well, you were led there for a reason," her mother said, "and I do worry that mine and your father's lifestyle has meant you've missed out."

"I've had a wonderful life," Emma had said sincerely. "Stop worrying. Things will happen in God's time. Isn't that what you always tell me?"

As she tucked into her meal for one half an hour later, she thought that even so, a date might be nice. Unbidden, the face of Rob Carlton came to mind. She quickly pushed the image away. She didn't know him well, but he definitely wasn't her type.

After finishing her lesson plans and having a hot bath, she climbed into bed and opened her Bible. She'd been prayerfully reading through the Psalms, and her eyes alighted on Psalm 61. She slowly and mindfully read it aloud.

"Hear my cry, O God, listen to my prayer. From the ends of the earth, I call to You, I call as my heart grows faint, lead me to the rock which is higher than I. For You have been my refuge, a strong tower against the foe. I long to dwell in Your tent forever and take refuge in the shelter of Your wings. For You, God, have heard my vows, You have given me the heritage of those who fear Your name."

She paused, allowing the beautiful words to sink into her heart and soul before praying silently, in thanks, and for her parents and her students. She also added a prayer for the family of the man whose body had been found in the creek.

As she drifted off to sleep, her thoughts once again shifted to Rob, but this time in his capacity as a protector of the town. She trembled as she remembered the rumours about the body, which meant Rob might be hunting a murderer.

"Keep him safe, Lord," she murmured sleepily, before she fell into a deep, undisturbed sleep.

CHAPTER 3

Luis stifled a shudder under Eric's glare, his boss's eyes hard, like shards of ice. Luis had seen the consequences of that look once too often. Any sign of weakness would be a further sign of failure, and his boss didn't tolerate failure. He paid well, but the costs of letting him down were higher. Much higher.

"I told you," Eric said slowly, as though speaking to a disobedient three-year-old, "to send a message to the gang in Melbourne, and take care of both José and Rick. Instead, you let Rick get away, and leave José's body where it could be found."

Luis bit his tongue while considering how best to reply. It was pointless saying that Eric's instructions had been less than clear. He had a brilliant criminal mind, but he expected everyone else to read it and keep up with his unscrupulous schemes without the need to spell them out. He was impossible to please, and in Luis' line of work, that did not bode well for a long life.

"By *send a message*, I assumed you wanted the body

found," Luis said in a matter-of-fact tone. Pleading wouldn't get him anywhere with Eric.

"No, Luis. I meant, send evidence of his death to our rivals in Melbourne. Oh, I don't know, a body part or two. *Not leave his body floating in a creek, alerting the small-town hicks of Eastbrooke to our presence here in the mountains.* And how did Rick get away?" He angled his head slowly, his gaze boring into Luis'.

Luis swallowed. It was his fault. He'd assumed he could handle both executions by himself. It had never occurred to him that Rick might put up a fight, cutting him in the process. Luis knew better than to tell Eric he'd sustained a knife wound to his side that he'd stitched up himself.

"I did injure him," Luis said, effectively dodging the question. "He's probably dead somewhere up in the mountains by now."

Eric's eyes blazed. He leaned forward, his voice low. It was more like a snake hissing than a soothing murmur. "But you don't know that for sure, do you? You've left us vulnerable, Luis."

Luis hung his head, hoping that contrition would be enough. He was Eric's right-hand man, and Eric kept his team small–especially as he had a penchant for eliminating non-performers.

"Tell me what I need to do," he said, his gaze fixed to the floor, his heart beating in his throat. Eric's gaze was on him. He could feel it. He'd be lucky to get out of this alive.

Finally, Eric's chair creaked.

Luis lifted his gaze slowly, holding his breath.

"Get people looking for the body. If there is one," Eric ordered in a tone that suggested if there wasn't, there'd be unpleasant consequences for Luis.

"Done," Luis said with as much confidence as he could muster.

Eric drummed his fingers on the arm of the chair. "What do we know about the police in Eastbrooke? Are they just small-town hicks, or do we need to worry about how far they'll investigate José's death? And how likely are we to turn one of them as an informant?"

"Not very," Luis replied, answering his boss's last question. "These small-town cops aren't as jaded as those in the city."

Eric narrowed his eyes. "There's something you're not telling me."

"No," Luis said hurriedly. Probably too hurriedly. He swallowed hard. "It's just that…"

"What?" Eric snapped again.

"The chief here's getting old and has taken his eye off the ball. He couldn't catch us if he tried, but it might be wise to keep an eye on the officer below him."

Eric cocked a brow. "What's this officer's name?"

"Robert Carlton. His father, George Carlton, was the old chief, well respected in the town. I wasn't able to dig up any dirt on him; he seems to be clean."

"Carlton," Eric mused, scratching his chin. "Why have I heard that name before?"

"George Carlton was blown up in an explosion fifteen years ago that was believed to have been linked to a white supremacist cell. The White Legion. There's a rumour they've started up again." Luis studied Eric's face closely. His boss had youthful links to white supremacists, but his expression betrayed no recognition. From what Luis had gleaned, his boss had never been overly involved; he was more focused on criminality, power, and profit than serving any ideology that didn't benefit him.

Eric tapped the arm of the chair again. "No. I'm thinking more recent. The son, Rob. Why does his name sound significant?"

"He was the cop who caught that gang leader up here last year." The removal of that leader had allowed Eric and his men to encroach on his weaker successor's turf. José and Rick had been part of that gang. Eric was now one step closer to achieving his goal of dominating the drug trade in Australia–and not just drugs. The mountain passes offered opportunities for other, even more lucrative cargo.

But Eric didn't seem impressed. He shrugged. "Sounds like he just got lucky. Rob Carlton won't be a threat. And if he is…well, you know what to do."

CHAPTER 4

Rob beeped his horn outside his mother's house. Moments later, the front door opened and she came out, dressed in a neat floral dress and cardigan, her plump face full of smiles as she hurried down the path towards the car. He was driving her to church, and today, he was looking forward to going. It had been a busy week at work and he craved the quiet of Eastbrooke Baptist Church, which always gave him a sense of peace even if he didn't always understand what the minister was talking about–mainly because he had a tendency to zone out and think about other things.

He had faith, although he was aware it had come easily to him since he'd grown up in the church. He'd never really questioned it or wrestled with it or felt a need to look deeper. He believed because he was brought up to believe, and as far as he was concerned, that was good enough. He did his best to be a good man and live by solid principles, which was surely the important thing. His mother and younger brother, Joseph, were devout enough for the rest of them, although his oldest brother, Max, had recommitted to his faith after meeting his wife the year before. Eli, the youngest, seemed more rebellious and was seen at church increasingly rarely these days, greatly concerning both his mother and Joseph.

His mum reached the car and slid into the passenger seat before enveloping him in a big hug. "Morning, son."

"No Eli?" Rob lifted his brow. At twenty-four, Eli was the only Carlton brother still living at home.

"No," she said with a sigh. "He's gone fishing with his friend, Scott." Her face showed clearly how she felt about her youngest son skipping church to do his own thing yet again.

"You can't make him come, Mum," Rob said softly but firmly. "You'll only make him more hostile. This is something he has to figure out for himself."

She huffed out an exasperated sigh as she stared out the window. "I know. I just worry about him. He's always been the most sensitive of you all, and I worry his grief over your father has turned into a big ball of resentment that he just won't address. He was so young when it happened… I think it affected him more than I realised at the time."

Rob patted his mother's hand before starting the engine. "He knows we're all here for him, Mum, and honestly, I think you worry too much. He's doing great at work."

"Chasing murderers." Her tone left no question about how she felt about that.

Rob suppressed a smile. His mother often wished her sons had chosen regular, safe occupations. Instead, she had two police officers, a Mountain Search and Rescue expert, and a wilderness guide. No wonder she was always worried.

"Well, Eastbrooke doesn't get very many of them," he said. "This week has been most unusual, but we'll get to the bottom of it." He didn't tell her about the possible links with organised crime in Melbourne. That was the last thing she needed to know.

They were halfway to the church before she mentioned his ill-fated date with Marion. Whoops. Marla.

"So, I take it you haven't spoken to Marla since your date?"

"She's a lovely girl," he said diplomatically, "but I'm really not looking for anyone, Mum. And especially right now, with a case like this taking up my time. If I get to the bottom of it, it could be my chance to get promoted. It's always been my dream to follow in Dad's footsteps. You know that."

Her face softened as she touched his wrist. "I know, and he would have been so proud of you. Of all of you. I just want to see you settled and happy. Life can't be all about work. Your father was one of the most hard-working men I knew, but it didn't stop him being a family man."

She was right. His dad had been the best. If he could be half the policeman and family man he'd been, Rob would be happy. But he didn't want his mother matchmaking. He'd hoped that with Max about to give her the first Carlton grandchild, she'd ease up on him, but it didn't seem she had.

"There's a wonderful young woman I think you'd get along with…" she continued.

He groaned audibly. "Mum, no more!"

"You already know her," she continued, regardless of his protestations. "Emma, that lovely new teacher from the primary school."

"I saw her the other day," he said quietly. He kept his gaze glued to the road, sensing his mother's gaze on him.

"You like her!"

"She seems very nice, yes," he said neutrally. "Shall we have the radio on?"

As he drove and his mother mercifully started singing

along to the local gospel station, he thought about Emma Humphries. Or rather, tried not to think about her. His mother was right. He did like her, although he couldn't put his finger on what it was about her that he felt drawn to. She was attractive, but hers was a quiet beauty that she made little effort to adorn. She was always neat and well-presented, but unlike most young women her age, she seemed to have little interest in her appearance and always looked demure. Perhaps it went with the teacher image, or the fact that she'd spent most of her life on mission in Ethiopia with her parents, a fact he knew through his mother. With those kinds of priorities, he supposed hair and make-up took a backseat.

Nevertheless, there was a quiet dignity about her and a self-sufficiency that he found intriguing and made him want to get to know her. Except, he felt an uncharacteristic pang of shyness whenever he bumped into her, perhaps precisely because she stood out so much. No doubt his mother would continue trying to set them up, and although he didn't dislike the idea of dating her, it made him nervous. He'd always thought of himself as a confident person, yet felt somehow inferior compared to Emma. She needed someone better than him. A better Christian, for a start.

"Oh look, there she is," his mother announced gaily as they pulled up outside the small church.

Emma stood at the entrance, chatting to the meet- and-greeter. Dressed in a simple shift dress and flat pumps with her hair pulled back in a loose bun, she looked effortlessly pretty.

He climbed out of the car and walked with his mum towards the church. And Emma.

When she lifted her head and caught sight of them, her

eyes widened as her gaze briefly met his. She quickly directed it to his mother and gave her a smile.

The pair embraced warmly.

"Emma's coming for lunch with us after church, Rob," his mother said with a grin.

His head snapped up and he stared wide eyed at her before he pasted on a smile and turned to Emma. "How lovely."

She returned his smile with an equally fake one.

Ushering his mother inside, he left Emma to continue her chat.

Eastbrooke Baptist Church was an old, stone building that dated back to some of the early settlers, and the simple altars and pews stood in contrast to the impressive stonework and pretty stained-glass windows depicting frolicking angels. There was a sense of peace in the old building that soothed Rob as soon as he entered, and he followed his mother into a pew near the front, where Joseph, Max and Junia were already seated. Junia was five months pregnant, and her belly swelled against her loose cotton trousers.

Rob grinned as he kissed her cheek. "How's my little nephew doing?"

Junia laughed. "Rob, you know we've opted not to know the sex."

"The Carltons run to boys," he told her. "Look at us."

"I'd love a granddaughter," his mother said wistfully, "although, of course, the child will be loved regardless of what gender it happens to be."

"She's already bought a stack of pink onesies," Rob whispered. Junia laughed, and then the organist began to play. They stood to sing a traditional hymn, *How Great Thou Art*, before a young woman with an acoustic guitar got up to do a more modern version of *In Christ Alone*. Rob sang along, and for once found himself reflecting on the words which were, he realised, quite beautiful.

In Christ alone, my strength is found, He is my light, my strength, my song. This cornerstone, this solid ground, firm through the fiercest drought and storm...

As he absorbed the music, he felt a sudden pang of gratitude for all that he had. His family, his church...he'd always had the privilege of feeling grounded and protected. Although losing his father so young had of course been devastating, he'd always known he was loved.

His thoughts flashed to the body in the creek, who'd now been formally identified as José Ingala, a drug dealer from Melbourne. What had gone wrong in the man's life that he'd ended up like this? Although he wasn't someone likely to garner much public sympathy, he was still someone's son. Someone's brother. Perhaps even someone's husband. Regardless of what he'd done and whatever had caused him to be killed, Rob vowed he'd do whatever was needed to bring his killer to justice. After all, that was why he'd chosen to be a policeman.

His dad had talked a lot about justice to his young sons, and about how man's justice would always be fallible. Many would say that José had gotten the justice his life had deserved, but Rob knew what his mother would say about that... *God weeps for every lost soul.* A shiver went up his spine. He glanced up at the sunlight pouring through the stained-glass window and grew mesmerised, so much so that he barely realised when the singing was over and Max nudged him to sit.

The minister read out the week's notices and then began his sermon. He was a small, elderly man with a commanding presence, and his voice carried across the small church, capturing the attention of his congregation.

Rather than allow his thoughts to drift as he usually did, Rob listened as the minister began by reading a passage from the letter of Paul to the church in Ephesus, known as Ephesians.

"*As for you, you were dead in your transgressions and sins, in which you used to live when you followed the ways of this world and of the ruler of the kingdom of the air, the spirit who is now at work in those who are disobedient. All of us also lived among them at one time, gratifying the cravings of our flesh and following its desires and thoughts. Like the rest, we were by nature deserving of wrath.*

"*But because of His great love for us, God, who is rich in mercy, made us alive with Christ even when we were dead in transgressions—it is by grace you have been saved. And God raised us up with Christ and seated us with Him in the heavenly realms in Christ Jesus, in order that in the coming ages He might show the incomparable riches of His grace, expressed in His kindness to us in Christ Jesus. For it is by grace you have been saved, through faith—and this is not from yourselves, it is the gift of God—not by works, so that no one can boast. For we are God's handiwork, created in Christ Jesus to do good works, which God prepared in advance for us to do.*"

Although Rob had heard this passage many times before, he'd never really stopped to ponder its meaning.

When the minister began to preach, talking about what it meant to be saved by grace alone, Rob leaned forward, taking in every word, although it felt uncomfortably like each one was directed straight at him.

"Paul is telling us," the minister said, his gaze momentarily landing on Rob, "that no matter how good our works, or how righteous we think we are, none of this saves us. We're saved only by the grace of God. Christ alone is our salvation. We can't work our way to heaven."

Rob sat very still. How had he missed this? He'd always assumed that because he was from a good, church-going family and he tried to live a good life and do good works, he'd earned his place in heaven. He was one of the 'good guys'. He'd always assumed that was enough, and he didn't have to worry about forgiveness or salvation in the way that someone like José, for example, would. Yet the minister was saying that was wrong, that Rob, as much as anyone, needed the grace of God. But if that was true, didn't it mean all his arduous work had been for nothing? Once again, the minister spoke as though answering his very thoughts.

"Of course, this doesn't mean that works are not vital to God's kingdom. We're commanded to live as Christ told us, and James says 'faith without works is dead.' But we can't get to faith, or grace, by works. Rather, it's God's grace that inspires us to do good works, for His glory. For any good works we do for our own glory are surely the works of a hypocrite. For Jesus Himself tells us in the Gospel of Matthew, *'Be careful not to do your acts of righteousness before men, to be seen by them. If you do, you will have no reward from your Father in Heaven.'* Yet how many of us take pride in our own righteousness?"

The minister's strong words had Rob reeling. He sat back in his pew, hardly able to grasp what he was hearing. Everything he'd taken for granted, all his categories about who the good guys and bad guys were, was being completely upended. How on earth had he managed to come to church all his life and never understood this? He glanced over at his mother and brothers to see if they too looked shocked, but they were nodding along happily, clearly familiar with the message.

"We must remember," the minister concluded, his voice

softer, "that we are *all* sinners. By God's grace alone we are saved. And that this…this is *good news*. Let us pray."

As the minister prayed aloud, Rob bowed his head and prayed silently, his heart filled with remorse. *Lord, I'm so sorry. I'm not sure how I missed this, and I'm not sure I understand it all, but I want to. I want to know more about You, more about Your grace. More about Jesus. I don't want to be self-righteous or proud. Help me to know You better, Lord.*

The service ended with another song, and then everyone moved out of the church, shaking hands, and chatting, but he felt disorientated.

Joseph studied him, frowning. "You okay, brother?"

"I think so," Rob replied uncertainly. "That sermon really got to me."

Joseph clapped him on the back. "I've got to go but call me during the week. We'll talk about it."

"Thank you."

As Joseph left, his mother approached with Emma in tow. "Emma can come in your car with us, can't she, Rob?" she asked, her eyes twinkling.

Blinking, he replied, "Of course."

CHAPTER 5

*E*mma felt strange and awkward sitting in the back of Rob's car as he drove his mother and her to Jean's house for lunch after church. He was quiet, his usual easy smile replaced by a reflective, faraway look which she assumed was because of the body discovered in the creek. The local press had been reporting on it all week, obviously excited at something sensational to print.

The whole of Eastbrooke was talking about the tragedy, to the point that some of her pupils had raised the topic in class, having heard the adults around them discussing it. She'd done her best to reassure the little ones that the police would catch the bad guys, and not to worry. Luckily, smaller children were resilient and easily distracted, especially when she'd allowed them to get the modelling clay out in an effort to do just that.

Today though, the idea that anything bad could happen in Eastbrooke seemed surreal. The sun was out, the service that morning had soothed her soul, and Jean chatted away happily as they headed to her house. She lived in a detached, white brick home with a huge bay window and large front and back gardens. It was the same house Jean had raised her four boys in with her husband.

"Joseph sends his apologies," Jean said, turning her head slightly, "but he had to dash off to work straight after church. I hoped Eli would be here, but he's gone fishing. So, it's just us, Max and Junia."

"Oh, lovely," Emma said, pasting on a smile. That left her and Rob as the other 'couple.' She hoped Jean wasn't playing Cupid. Her friend was eager to see all of her sons settled, so it wouldn't surprise her. Emma glanced at Rob as they walked towards the door, but he seemed miles away.

Max and Junia arrived just as she was taking a seat at the table while Jean laid out a simple cold buffet. She'd never spoken much to them—they lived a short way out of town on a resort-style retreat they ran, facilitating wilderness programs for city kids, and Max in particular wasn't very talkative. But she got on with Junia, who seemed both outgoing and kind.

"How are you feeling?" Emma asked sympathetically when Junia winced while easing herself into the seat opposite.

"I'm really good, actually, but just this last week I keep getting a trapped nerve. I think it's the way the baby's laying, although he or she doesn't stay in the same position for long."

Emma glanced at Junia's swelling belly, wondering at the miracle of life and how it must feel to be blessed with a child in your womb.

"Do you want children, Emma?" Jean asked, her eyes gleaming.

Emma blinked and tucked a strand of loose hair behind

her ear. "Oh, I suppose. I haven't given it much thought as yet, but in the future, yes. I guess so."

"Ignore her," Max said gruffly. "She's obsessed with marriage and babies. Junia and I would have a whole football team if she had her way."

"Oh goodness, no." Junia laughed. "Two or three, maybe." She rubbed her stomach affectionately.

Jean took the seat at the head of the table, leaving Rob to sit next to Emma. He smiled as he sat, seemingly having snapped out of his reflective mood, and despite herself, Emma felt her cheeks warm. His blue eyes were piercing against his tanned skin and dark hair, and she felt acutely aware of his nearness.

"How's the case going, Rob?" Max asked, spearing a tomato.

Rob groaned. "You know I can't talk about it. But to be honest, it isn't. As the paper has reported, the victim's from out of town and we haven't found any local leads, so it'll probably be passed onto the city police."

Max narrowed his gaze. "You're not happy about that."

Rob shrugged before taking a sip of Coke. "Just protective of my jurisdiction, I suppose. It's a cop thing."

"Your father was the same," Jean said. "You're so much like him." She squeezed his wrist and smiled.

Rob pulled in a deep breath, and if Emma wasn't mistaken, a knowing look passed between the brothers.

She quickly tucked into what was a very tasty lunch. She hadn't been hungry that morning and had skipped breakfast, so she felt famished now. She listened as the Carlton family chatted away, swapping stories past and present. She felt at ease with them, not like an outsider at all. It made her a little homesick for her own parents who were a close couple and devoted to her, their only daughter.

"You grew up in Africa, didn't you, Emma?" Junia asked.

Emma nodded. "Ethiopia. My parents still run missionary projects there. It's a tough place to live, but it has a stark beauty despite all the hardships."

"Seeing all the poverty must be difficult."

"Yes. It sure makes you grateful for what you have. Nothing gets taken for granted, and everything, where possible, is shared. I've heard some people say that such places test their faith, but it only strengthened mine."

Rob looked at her with admiration.

She abruptly went quiet and nibbled her sourdough roll.

Oblivious, Junia continued. "It's very different, of course," she said, "but I grew up in a rough neighbourhood in Melbourne. Nobody had a lot. Of course, many people in that kind of situation turn to crime or alcohol, but on the other hand, our community church was strong. I think people often come together in the face of adversity, and that adversity can make them stronger."

Max nodded. "Definitely. We see it with the kids up at the retreat. Although some of them can be…trying."

Rob threw his head back and laughed. "I don't envy you, brother. I'd rather deal with a town full of criminals than a bunch of teenagers."

Junia, a youth worker, rolled her eyes and chuckled.

"You should try five-year-olds," Emma quipped. "They're little tyrants sometimes."

They all laughed as she regaled them with a couple of funny stories, and before she knew it, lunch was over and it was time to go.

"Can you drop Emma off, Rob?" Jean asked.

"Oh, it's no trouble to walk," Emma said, flustered.

"No, not at all. I pass near your street anyway," he said.

She drew a slow breath and accepted the offer graciously since it would be rude to say no.

After thanking Jean for a lovely lunch, and saying goodbye to Max and Junia, she walked to the car with Rob and got in the passenger side. As he slipped in beside her, she tugged a piece of hair and wrapped it around her finger. Other than bumping into him in the street, she'd never been alone with him before and suddenly felt at a loss for anything to say.

He, too, seemed suddenly awkward, then as he pulled away from the kerb, he asked abruptly, "What did you think of the service this morning?"

Her forehead creased as she faced him. She hadn't expected that question. "Oh...I really enjoyed it. It's a lovely church."

"I'd not heard that message before."

"Really?" His admission surprised her. After all, grace as a free gift was a cornerstone of the Christian faith. While she supposed that was second nature for her, having grown up with devout parents, the Carltons had been going to church all their lives, too. It seemed he wanted to talk, so she waited for him to continue.

"It really got to me." He drew a slow breath and braced his hands on the wheel. "All that stuff about works and self-righteousness. I've always believed that I'm a good guy, as opposed to a bad guy, but it hit me this morning that I've always assumed I'm in God's good books because of the work I do. Hearing that works don't mean a thing shook me."

"I can definitely understand that." She gave an empathetic smile. "I mean, I come from a missionary family. I grew up thinking we were good." She spread her arms wide and chuckled. *"Look at us, saving the world.* It was a while before it sunk in that only God saves. There was nothing wrong in what we were doing, but at the end of the day, we were still sinners in need of God's grace. There's real freedom in understanding that."

Rob frowned. "You understand it?"

"Yes," she said lightly, not wanting to belittle him. "Imagine if we did have to earn God's favour through works. The quest for perfection would be exhausting. I think many people and institutions fall into that trap."

Rob nodded thoughtfully. "You're right," he said after a few moments. "I think I've been trying to prove something my whole life."

For a long moment, she studied him. He was much deeper than she'd originally thought. "I imagine your job can be high pressure," she said softly.

He tapped his fingers on the steering wheel and looked at her. "Yep. But I love it."

As they pulled up outside her house, an odd twinge of disappointment that the journey was over so quickly flowed through her. She'd seen a side to him she doubted few outside his family ever saw, and she would have liked to continue their chat.

"Thanks for listening," he said gently as she unstrapped her seatbelt. "You're really easy to talk to."

"Not at all. I enjoyed spending time with you," she said sincerely.

"Perhaps we should go for a coffee some time. Maybe next weekend?"

A small breath escaped her lips. She wanted to say yes, but something stopped her. Although she was sure he was simply being friendly and not at all inappropriate, the gossip she'd heard about him dating every pretty girl in town ran though her mind. She didn't want to be just another girl on that list, especially when it would spread around Eastbrooke like wildfire.

"I'm afraid I'm busy next weekend," she said primly. "I have a whole month's worth of lesson planning to do."

Disappointment flashed in his eyes, but he shrugged and looked as easygoing as ever. Perhaps she'd imagined the disappointment.

"No worries. I'll see you around," he said casually as she reached for the door handle.

She smiled. "Sure. Thanks for the ride."

As he drove off, she stood on the grass and watched until his car turned a corner and disappeared from sight. Mixed feelings surged through her. Why had she turned him down? It was only coffee, not a date. And since when did she care what people thought? As much as she felt sure that her response was the right one, part of her wondered what might have happened if she'd said yes.

CHAPTER 6

*R*ob arrived at work the next morning completely out of sorts. He'd slept badly, kept awake by ruminating over the minister's words and the abject humiliation of being turned down by Emma. He'd only invited her for coffee, and he'd definitely only been offering the hand of friendship, but her refusal smarted.

A woman had never turned him down for a date. Never. Not, of course, that it would have been a date.

It wasn't just his pride that was stinging over the rejection. He'd seen the look on her face, however fleeting, almost of disappointment, when he'd invited her. He couldn't stop wondering what it meant and could only conclude that she'd thought he was being inappropriate. Perhaps Marion, no, Marla... *why couldn't he get her name right?* had said something. Small town gossip was rife, and for once he felt resentful of his reputation as a charmer. For some reason he wasn't prepared to look at too deeply, he wanted Emma to think more highly of him.

Coupled with the revelation the minister's words had

given him, he had the distinct sense that his entire world view, not least of himself, had just been upended. He was eager to get started on a new week at the station. As a cop, he knew where he was and what he was doing.

After entering the building, a stone structure construction as old as the town, he made a beeline for the kitchen to grab a coffee, but as he passed through the open plan work area, Jerry looked up and asked, "Hey Rob, did Johnson call you about this morning?"

Pausing, Rob shook his head. "No. What about this morning?"

"Joseph found a guy hiding on the mountain. He was picked up and brought into custody a few hours ago. Same gang tattoos as our friend José. He had some minor injuries, so he was taken to the hospital. Eli's on guard."

Rob shook the fog from his head. He needed to focus. "Have we contacted Melbourne?"

Jerry grinned. "I thought you might want to question him yourself first. If something's going on in those passes, it's our jurisdiction as much as the heavies. And you've got a knack for getting answers."

Feeling much more himself, Rob nodded eagerly. "I'll grab a coffee and we'll go and question him. Do we know his name?"

"Not yet. He's refusing to say, but we know José ran with a guy named Rick, and our man matches his description."

"Has the boss got him pegged as the killer?"

Jerry shrugged. "I think Johnson considers the whole thing a nuisance. He wants a nice, easy couple of years before his retirement. But Joseph said the guy seemed almost relieved when he was picked up. He was scared...but not of being brought in."

"Then he was a target as well," Rob said, taking a deep

breath. "And he most likely knows who killed José. Getting him to tell us will be the hard part. Forget the coffee. Let's go."

As they strode into the hospital fifteen minutes later, Rob was pumped. He wanted to nail this case. It was his chance to prove he was the right choice for Police Chief when Johnson retired…and to follow in his father's footsteps. God's grace might not need to be earned, but promotions sure did.

His brother Eli stood outside the room where the suspect was being kept. He'd been on the night shift and looked both tired and relieved to see Rob and Jerry.

"How's our guy?" Jerry asked.

"Not saying much, but polite enough with the hospital staff. Refusing to say a word to me, of course."

"He'll talk to Rob," Jerry said confidently.

Rob hoped his partner was right.

The man, whom they assumed was Rick, lay back on the pillows with his arm in a sling. Heavyset with a shaved head, all visible parts of his body, including his head, were covered in gang markings. He narrowed his eyes as the pair entered the room and stood at the end of his bed. "I'm not telling you anything," he spat.

"We haven't even said hello yet," Jerry said, pulling up a chair beside the bed.

Rob sat on the other side with his arms folded. "Hey, Rick."

The guy flinched then glared at him, not acknowledging his name. His reaction said it all, though. They had the right guy–now they needed him to talk.

"You're a long way from your usual territory," Rob said amiably, almost with disinterest. He was examining his fingernails and could have been talking about the weather, a tactic that seemed to rile a suspect, playing to their ego.

Someone like Rick wanted other men to know he was important and someone to be reckoned with. Sensing the guy glaring at him, Rob yawned, stretched his hands behind his head, and looked around the room.

"You don't know what you're talking about," Rick snarled.

"No?" Rob quirked a brow.

"No. You're just a small-town hick. You think you can do better than those flash city cops? They've never managed to catch us."

Rob gave an easy smile and Rick clamped his mouth shut. He'd said too much, and he knew it.

"Someone caught José, though," Jerry chimed in.

Rick folded his arms across his chest, or at least tried to, given his wounds. "I don't know what you're talking about."

"That's what you just said about us," Rob said. "We're going to be here a while if you don't know, and I don't know, and Jerry here doesn't know. Jerry, want to go and grab some coffees? Looks like we need to get comfortable. Let the officer outside know he can go home."

"Sure." Jerry stood and left the room.

Rob started whistling under his breath, still leaning back in his chair.

Rick glared at him. "You guys think this is funny?"

"Think what's funny, Rick?" Rob leaned forward, still smiling, but his tone had changed. "The fact that you're in hospital, obviously a wanted man, or the fact that the same person who killed your friend and put you in here is up to no good in my area? Actually, I think neither of those things are funny. Like you said, I'm a small-town cop. I like an easy life. I don't like bodies washing up in my jurisdiction, upsetting everybody." He paused. Rick continued glaring at him, his dark eyes wild.

"The way I see it," Rob continued, "you have two choices.

You don't tell me what you know, and I turn you over to Melbourne, who no doubt have warrants out for your arrest, or you do tell me what you know, and then I turn you over to Melbourne."

Rick frowned. "That makes no sense. Why would I talk if there's nothing in it for me?"

"Because you might just be our star witness. And star witnesses can make bargains. You might even stay out of jail, get a new name, start again."

"I'm no snitch." He turned his head away.

Rob shrugged and sat back again, folding his arms. "Okay, then I can't help you. Take your chances with Melbourne– and whoever's after you."

Rick closed his eyes, wincing with a pain that Rob guessed was caused by more than just his arm. When he opened them again, they were dark with fear. Rick was scared of whoever had shot him and killed José.

But scared or not, he was no greener behind the ears than Rob. He narrowed his eyes and sneered. "You forgot the third option."

"Which is?"

"I walk out of here. I don't see no arrest warrant."

"That's right," Rob said amiably, "because we're not arresting you…yet. We're just asking you a few friendly questions. And if you're the fine upstanding citizen I'm sure you want to be, you'll cooperate."

"I want a lawyer." Rick's mouth took on an unpleasant twist.

"Why would you want a lawyer, Rick? Like I said, we're just asking you a few questions. You don't need a lawyer for that."

"I don't know anyone called Rick."

Rob raised a brow. "Let's cut the pretence, okay? You're

not being recorded. I know who you are, and I don't care what you got up to in Melbourne. I do care about José's body washing up in Jacob's Creek, and the implications of that for my town. This is a lovely place. A good place. We don't have organised crime around here.'

Rick snorted. "Tell that to your father."

Rob stiffened, a chill going down his spine. "What," he said, enunciating each word carefully, "do you know about my father?"

Rick lay back on the pillows and turned his head away. "Nothing. I'm tired, I need to rest. I'll tell the nurses you're harassing me."

"The nurses will do whatever Rob tells them," Jerry quipped, stepping back into the room carrying two steaming cups of coffee. "Officer Carlton is Eastbrooke's most eligible bachelor. Isn't that right, Officer Carlton?" Jerry winked as he handed him his coffee.

Rob took the polystyrene cup without the smile and joke Jerry was expecting. Emma flashed into his mind, but he pushed away her image. *Not now.* He wanted to know why Rick had mentioned his father, because there was a reason, and instinct told him it was related to this case.

"You mentioned my father," he said coldly. "Let's cut the bull, Rick. This is off the record, okay? For now, anyway. Why would you know anything about Police Chief Carlton unless you were either a cop or a criminal? *Who shot José?*"

"He's definitely not a cop," Jerry said when Rick didn't answer. "A cop wouldn't have left his mate to die."

The barb hit home. Rick sat up, wincing, but glaring at Jerry so hard that his eyes bulged. "You weren't there!"

Rob smiled slowly. "But you were, clearly. Tell us what happened."

Rick sighed, defeated as he realised his mistake. He lay

back on the pillows again, his face grey. "I'm not naming any names."

Neither Rob nor Jerry responded.

Rick sighed. "Let's just say I heard some stuff, okay? That's all I'm saying."

"Okay, that's good." Rob nodded encouragingly. They were lucky to get that much.

"So, maybe I heard that this José guy was sent here to check out the mountain pass, okay? That he heard it was a good place for, ah, certain exchanges of goods."

"Right." Jerry nodded. "Goods."

Rick shifted in the bed. "Except, maybe someone else wants it too. Someone trying to start something bigger. Take over the whole trade. Because things in Melbourne have been…messy."

Rob's eyes narrowed. His arrest of a prominent gang leader last year had disrupted Melbourne's drug trade, which of course was a good thing…if only there weren't so many others ready to step straight into the gap. "Okay, that makes sense. So, the civil war in Melbourne has spilled all the way to Eastbrooke because of the mountain passes?"

Rick shrugged. "This is all hearsay, okay? It's not quite that simple. This guy–the word is he's not even from here. Not even an Aussie. He's got ties to some big people."

Jerry's eyebrows shot up. "The mafia?"

Rick rolled his eyes. "You've been watching too much TV. No, worse."

Rob frowned. Who could possibly be worse than the mafia? Then he had a sinking feeling. Rick had mentioned his father. "Neo-Nazi groups," he whispered.

Rick nodded. "Yeah. And I don't just mean some city gang. That group your father disrupted…their roots went deep."

Grief and long buried fury squeezed Rob's heart. The real leaders of the group that had killed his father had never been found. If this guy had ties to them…Rob shook his head. He couldn't afford to dredge up old grievances right now.

"That's it," Rick said. "That's all I know. Before you tell me it's off record or try and start bribing me, I don't know the guy's name, okay? I just know that whoever he is, he's worrying a lot of people who aren't easily worried." He closed his eyes, signalling he was done.

Jerry opened his mouth to say more, but Rob shook his head. They wouldn't get any more out of Rick today. He stood to leave, looking down at the man on the bed. "Rick…"

"The name ain't Rick…" he mumbled, his voice slurred.

The pain killers were kicking in. "Okay, whoever you are…" Rob said, "think about my offer. We can help you. Otherwise, what options do you have? We can't keep protection on your door without a good reason. You can't go back to Melbourne. You can't stay on the loose here. What are you going to do, take your chances on the mountains again? People die up there."

"I don't need your help. Leave me alone or I'll ring my buzzer. That matron doesn't look like she'll fall for your charms too easy."

"You'd be surprised," Jerry muttered under his breath as he walked out.

Rob followed, then paused at the door and glanced back at Rick. On his arm, amidst all the gang tattoos, was an intricately inked cross. Impulsively, he asked, "Are you religious, Rick?"

Rick opened one eye. "I was raised Catholic," he said suspiciously. "Why?"

"No reason," Rob said as a strange wave of pity flowed through him. "But maybe it would be a good time to pray."

Rick laughed bitterly. "God don't listen to the prayers of people like me." He had both eyes open again, and for a second he looked oddly vulnerable.

Rob caught his gaze and said quietly, "I believe He does. Try it." Then he left and hurried after Jerry, once again feeling unsettled. It was turning out to be a strange couple of days.

A SHORT WHILE LATER, back at the station, Rob looked up as Jerry stormed in, his face dark. "Johnson!" he harrumphed as he flopped into his chair.

"What's happened?'" Rob asked, frowning.

"He pulled the guy who replaced Eli off Rick's door. Said we don't know who he is, and he's not an official suspect or witness, so we can't afford round-the-clock protection."

Rob groaned and rolled his eyes. "Did you tell him he gave us a lot of information? I've just sent it down to Melbourne."

"Yeah. He said it was just hearsay. He wants it gone so he can retire quietly. And leave us to deal with the future consequences."

Rob let out a heavy sigh and leaned back in his chair. "Hopefully, Melbourne will get up here to question him before he decides to discharge himself."

"Too late. That's what I'm mad about. The hospital just called. He's already gone. We're back to square one."

"Not necessarily," Rob said, trying to remain upbeat. "Let's see what we can find out about this neo-Nazi guy."

"Melbourne won't share information with us. This will be taken out of our hands now."

"No," Rob said firmly. "It might come to that, but I'm not giving up yet. The whole town is terrified. No one will go near the creek. I'm not having criminals moving in on Eastbrooke."

Jerry angled his head. "You're an odd guy. You're too talented for a small-town force, but you really love the place, don't you? Is that why you stay? Is it because of your dad?"

Rob blinked. "Have you been taking classes in psychoanalysis or something?"

Jerry laughed and the tension dissolved, but he was right. This was starting to feel personal.

That meant it would for his brother, too.

"Jerry," he said quietly, leaning forward, "we're not telling Eli about this. He's off this case. Stick him on traffic, or something."

Jerry whistled. "He won't be happy about that. He's another one who's wasted on Eastbrooke."

"Even so," Rob insisted.

Jerry nodded, and Rob knew he understood. Of the four brothers, Eli still carried the most bitterness around their father's death. Any indication that this was even loosely related would send him off on a search for revenge. Rob wasn't about to risk his brother getting hurt.

The rest of the afternoon went by in a blur. There was no sign of Rick, although they drove around to look for him anyway, and they put Joseph on alert. The Melbourne special forces were angry he'd slipped through their fingers, and, as predicted, refused to share any information regarding what Rick had told them, other than to say there was an 'ongoing investigation.'

Rob had a horrible feeling that if they didn't get this resolved quickly, it would blow up out of proportion, potentially endangering the citizens of Eastbrooke. Jerry was right; he loved the place, and like his father before him, he felt fiercely protective of it.

As he drove home that evening, he passed by Emma's house and found himself slowing down, hoping for a glimpse of her. He sped up again, telling himself not to be so silly. She'd made it clear she wasn't interested, and besides that, she wasn't his type.

Even so, she remained on his mind all evening, and when he laid down in bed and tried to clear his head for sleep, images of her, laughing with him over lunch on Sunday, were there again, jumbled with images of José's body in the creek, snippets of the minister's sermon in church, and the tattoo on Rick's arm. After a while, he sat up, frustrated. Usually, he was asleep as soon as his head hit the pillow.

Instead, he did something he hadn't done before sleep in a long time. Putting his hands together, he prayed. He prayed for Rick, who was wandering somewhere out there, in pain and in danger, and for Eastbrooke to be protected and safe from harm. He prayed for God to keep Eli away from bitterness, and for Max and Junia's baby. Then, finally, he prayed for Emma, although he didn't quite know what to pray for. *Keep her safe, Lord. Let her be happy in life and find someone to cherish her...even if that can't be me.* His own silent words surprised him, but they were from the heart. He lay back down on the pillow, feeling oddly more at peace although nothing was resolved.

CHAPTER 7

*E*mma began to wish she'd accepted Max's offer to pick her up as she made her way up the track that led to the retreat. Or at least, she was fairly sure this was the shortcut Junia had described. The directions had sounded a lot clearer on the phone than the terrain appeared in real life, and she had a definite feeling that at some point she'd walked straight past the turning she should have taken. The track was starting to incline steeply, but she thought the retreat was at the bottom of the mountain, not up it.

She'd been distracted, thinking about Rob, and hadn't paid enough attention to where she was going. It annoyed her that he'd been haunting her thoughts for the last two days, and the more she tried not to think about him, the more her mind insisted on conjuring him up. His invitation to have coffee had taken her by surprise, but after her knee-jerk refusal, she had mixed feelings. Perhaps she'd been too presumptuous in assuming his invitation was for a date, not just coffee. He may have simply intended to be friendly; after all, she was relatively new to town and was friendly with his mother and sister-in-law.

But something made her wary of him. Plus, she wasn't looking for a relationship. Friendship, maybe, but even that could be dangerous with someone like him.

She'd only had one serious boyfriend—another trainee teacher she'd met while doing her degree. He'd wanted to get married; she wasn't ready to commit, so he broke it off. The experience had left her a little jaded, and when she returned to Ethiopia, she'd been far too busy to think about relationships, anyway.

The path grew steeper and she began to puff. She peeled off her jacket and tossed it over her shoulder. She was just about to retrace her steps when she came across a turn. Perhaps this was it.

She hadn't gone more than five minutes down the path when she hit a wall of bushes. Her first guess had been correct. She'd missed the turn way back down the track. With a sigh, she turned to head back the way she'd come when she heard voices nearby, a little further into the undergrowth. Male voices, and they sounded, not quite angry, but definitely threatening.

Holding her breath, she peered through the undergrowth, trying not to make a sound. The light was poor, but she made out two men.

One of them had a gun.

She froze.

A heavyset man with a bald head and tattoos was being forced to his knees by the other man holding the gun which was pointed at the back of the tattooed man's head. Once on his knees, he seemed resigned to his fate, staring straight ahead. His lips were moving and he looked up, to the sky. She got the impression he was praying.

She wanted to say something, shout out, do something to help, but her limbs were frozen and when she opened her mouth, nothing came out. The shot, when it came, was so loud in the quiet of the bush that she jumped, startled, before she could stop herself, rustling the leaves around her.

The man holding the gun looked up, and even through the leaves, his gaze met hers as he looked straight into her eyes. "Hey!" he shouted, and started towards her.

She fled, her limbs no longer frozen, moving faster than she knew she could. She screamed as another shot rang out behind her.

He was shooting at her.

Her breaths came fast as she sprinted to get away.

Back on the track, she fled in the direction she'd come, screaming at the top of her voice, hoping that being on the open road would deter her pursuer. Not that anyone would be out here on the mountain. Another shot rang out, and this time she was sure the bullet whizzed past her, just inches from her head.

Lord, she screamed silently, *please lead me to safety. I need to tell someone what I saw.* She prayed for the man on his knees, even though she knew there was little chance of him still being alive.

Footsteps pounded down the road behind her, gaining on her. Her side cramped with pain as she pushed harder. Her eyes burned with tears. Her flight was futile. Despite her prayers, she would be caught. Shot dead.

Then, there it was. The turn she'd missed. It was small, like Junia had told her. She veered off the track and took it, praying the man hadn't seen where she'd gone. The space opened up and lights shone in front of her. "Max!" she screamed at the top of her voice. "Call the police!"

. . .

As she neared the building, she glanced over her shoulder. Relief filled her. She wasn't being followed. She keeled over as cramps tore through her body, holding onto her calves and trying to catch her breath.

In front of her, a door opened. It was Max with a shotgun in hand. He raced to her side. "Emma?"

"He had a gun," she babbled, her words tripping over themselves. "The man was on his knees and he was praying and then he was shot. The gunman saw me and shot at me and …" She fell against Max, sobbing. He helped her to the house.

Junia stood on the front porch, her arms out. "Come inside," she said soothingly, "and tell us what happened. Max, is anyone out there?"

"Not that I saw. Where did this happen, Emma?"

"Up the track a bit. Off to the side."

Junia helped her inside and settled her into a chair by the fire. She was grateful for its warmth because she was suddenly freezing all over. Dimly aware that she was in shock, she felt oddly disassociated from herself, as though the real Emma was watching this shaking, crying woman from somewhere far away.

"I'll call Rob," Max said.

The blood drained from Emma's face. "He could get shot. I shouldn't have put you all in danger by coming here. The guy could have seen where I went." Her hand flew to her mouth as she thought about Junia and the baby.

Junia took her hand, her voice low and calm. "Whatever happened out there," she said softly, "you've done the right thing by coming here. You're safe now. Max has a gun, and we're going to call the police and get this sorted, okay?

You're safe," she repeated, but although Emma nodded, her teeth chattered.

Junia squeezed her hand. "Let's pray," she said, bowing her head.

Emma followed suit, although her thoughts felt too scattered to pray.

"HEAVENLY FATHER," Junia began, *"let Your peace settle on Emma. You are our rock, our refuge and our shield. Be with her now, guard her as Your most precious daughter. In Jesus' name, I pray. Amen."*

"Amen," Emma echoed, and she felt, if not exactly at peace, then at least a little calmer. She exhaled slowly. "Thank you."

Max had left the room to call Rob. He returned with a mug, which he handed to her. It smelled potent. She frowned.

"It's brandy," he said. "I know you don't usually drink, and neither do we, but it's good for shock."

She nodded slowly and sipped the small amount of brown liquid. It burned her throat but felt pleasantly warm as it settled in her belly.

Junia patted her hand.

"I preferred the prayer," Emma quipped, starting to feel a little more like herself again, "but thank you. I feel warmer now." Hesitantly, she recounted what had happened.

Junia's face paled and Max pursed his lips angrily, shaking his head. "Whoever this guy is, the police will catch him. Neither Rob nor Eli will stop until this is over. I know my brothers."

"Would you recognise him if you saw him again?" Junia asked.

Emma nodded. "Maybe." But she shuddered at the

thought of ever seeing him again. Suddenly, Eastbrooke didn't seem such a tranquil haven after all.

A knock sounded on the door, the sudden noise making her nearly jump out of her skin.

Max went to answer it. "It'll be Rob."

But he took his shotgun, nevertheless.

CHAPTER 8

*R*age, and an urge to protect, surged through Rob as Emma recounted her story to him and Jerry. When she described the man, and then described seeing him pray, he closed his eyes briefly, remembering his last words to Rick, who, of course, the unfortunate man had to be.

His rage turned into a steely determination to find those responsible, but the urge to protect only grew as Emma finished her tale and then seemed to deflate into herself, exhausted. She'd been through a huge ordeal, but this instinctive feeling to watch over her and keep her safe was entirely personal.

Right now, though, he had a job to do. As Jerry took her statement, Rob contacted his officers and Mountain Rescue to search for the scene of the crime. And the body.

Joseph answered the Mountain Rescue line and listened in silence as Rob recounted what had happened and gave him a rough location based on what Emma had told him.

When Rob finished, his younger brother took a deep breath. "This is all getting quite alarming, isn't it?"

"It's certainly more than we're used to dealing with," Rob agreed, "but we'll catch whoever's behind this. The city police have been reluctant to share their information, but I think at this point they'll have to. But I doubt we'll be on this case much longer. This is bigger than we can handle."

Rob couldn't help feeling a twinge of hurt pride as he uttered those words. This was his jurisdiction, and the thought of officers from out of town taking over the investigation annoyed him, even though he knew this was bigger than anything a small-town force could cope with. Now that Emma was involved, it had also become personal. The thought of how close she'd come to getting shot filled him with a terror he wasn't yet ready to analyse.

"Are Junia and Max okay?" Joseph asked.

"Yes, just alarmed. Junia's been great with Emma. Max is frothing at the mouth to go and search the mountain himself, but thankfully he's a bit more sensible these days now he's about to become a father."

"Right, I'll fire the helicopter up and keep you posted. God be with you." Joseph rang off and Rob returned to the lounge. Emma's face was white, her eyes huge against her pale skin, and with her knees drawn up to her chest and her arms hugging them, she looked unbearably fragile.

He had the urge to sweep her into his arms and take her far away from here. Somewhere that was safe.

She looked up and smiled weakly.

He hadn't seen her since she'd politely turned down his offer of coffee, but that didn't seem to matter now.

"Do you want to stay here tonight?" Junia asked her. "It's probably a good idea to have some company. You've had a terrible ordeal."

Emma winced. "Thank you so much, and I'd love to

spend time with you and Max, but…it's so near to…to what happened."

Junia nodded with understanding and looked up at Rob. "Perhaps you could take her to your mother's place?"

"Good idea. I'll call her now."

Emma straightened, twisting her hands together. "I don't want to be any bother. I'm fine, honestly. I probably just need a good sleep."

Rob shook his head. "I'd rather you had some company tonight. Junia's right. You've gone through an ordeal. And Mum will insist. Trust me, if she finds out I took you home and left you alone instead of taking you there, she'll make my life a misery for at least a decade."

Behind him, Max chuckled.

Emma laughed weakly but looked relieved. "I probably could use the company," she admitted.

"That's what I thought. Come on."

He and Jerry drove her to his mother's house and when they arrived, Rob filled both her and Eli in on what had happened.

Horrified, his mum immediately fussed over Emma as Rob had known she would.

Then Jerry got a call.

The body had been found.

As Rob headed out the door with Jerry, Eli called him back. His younger brother's eyes blazed with anger.

Rob suppressed a sigh. He knew what was coming, but did Eli really have to pick right now? "I've got to go," he said.

Eli ignored him. "Why have you bumped me off this case?" he demanded angrily. "I know it came from you and not Johnson."

"We needed someone on traffic. Especially with the road leading to Jacob's Creek closed."

Eli glared at him. "I'm better than standing around waving road directions at people."

"Even I started on traffic, Eli," Rob pointed out.

"I'm not a newbie, Rob."

"You're twenty-four."

"And I've been a police officer since I was twenty. As have you. You're pushing me out. This has something to do with Dad, doesn't it?"

Rob sighed heavily. He couldn't lie to him, not about this.

"Not directly, no. You know I'd tell you if it did. But it's a possibility that whoever's behind all this had ties to the gang Dad was hunting."

The look of sheer rage that came over Eli's face and the mumbled cursing under his breath convinced Rob he'd been right to keep him away. "You're hot headed, Eli, and I understand, but I can't have you making this personal."

Eli narrowed his eyes. "I'm going to get whoever killed Dad one day, I swear."

Rob stared at him in sympathy. If only there was something he could do to soothe the hurt in his baby brother's soul. "Go and look after Mum and Emma," he said softly before leaving him and jogging after Jerry.

THE BODY WAS where Emma had described. Face down, with a bullet wound to the back of the head. As expected, there was no sign of a weapon or the perpetrator. It was another execution.

Even before the body was rolled over, Rob knew it was Rick. The man was bald and had a cross tattoo on his arm.

A wave of sadness washed over him, but then he recalled Emma saying she'd seen the man pray. Rob hoped the gangster had found some sense of repentance and peace before his premature death.

∼

Eric's face was a mask, his grey eyes hard as flint, his expression unreadable–unless, like Luis, you'd seen that look before and knew what it meant.

It didn't bode well.

"So, let me get this straight," Eric said slowly, his accent subtly coming through, "you were seen. And you left the body. Again."

Luis sucked in a breath. If he got out of this room alive, he'd be a lucky man.

"We were in the middle of nowhere, surrounded by bush. There was no way I could have known some woman would come blundering in."

Eric blinked, impossibly slowly, his eyes fixed on Luis' like a snake's. As usual when he was talking to Eric, Luis had to do his best not to show any fear. He was certain Eric could smell it.

Like all predators.

Luis was no innocent. He'd been a criminal since the tender age of fifteen, when his father had told him it was about time he was inducted into the 'family business.' His father had been gunned down by a rival gang five years later and Luis had taken over–and taken such retribution on the gang in question that it was spoken of throughout Australia's criminal network to this day, twenty years later.

He knew no other life than drug dealing, arms smuggling and thuggery. Few people intimidated him…apart from Eric. It wasn't only the rumours Luis had heard about how his latest boss dealt with his enemies. After all, there were plenty of those going around about Luis himself. It was more that Eric exuded a coldness that Luis hadn't seen before. The man didn't have a flicker of humanity in him. Worse than that was the borderline insanity and the pleasure he displayed in controlling and hurting those around him, the only emotion he showed other than the icy rage that currently radiated from him. Luis wondered what the real reason was for Eric leaving the white supremacists. If perhaps he'd been kicked out. After all, even they had their limits.

Luis doubted Eric had any.

Two things Luis did know about his boss. He detested failure, but he hated insubordination even more.

"You should have made sure you were further from civilisation. This whole operation's now in danger of being aborted…and I've put a lot of time and money into it. Two bodies? We're in danger of having the Feds on top of us, and that would be unbelievably bad, Luis. Especially for you."

Luis nodded, his pulse throbbing in his jaw. "I understand. What can I do?"

Eric stared at him until Luis dropped his gaze. The minutes ticked by while he waited for Eric to speak. When he did, his tone was almost nonchalant, which unnerved Luis even more. "Would she be able to recognise you?"

Luis looked up. "The girl?" He shrugged. "Maybe not. It was getting dark, and when I caught her eye, she ran. She didn't look back when I gave chase."

"When you gave chase and somehow managed to lose her, you mean? Even though you were armed and she wasn't?"

Luis swallowed. "She was zig-zagging, and then she ran towards a building…I saw the lights come on." He was practically stammering, and he hated himself for his weakness.

Intense anger flashed in Eric's eyes. "You carried out an

execution...within walking distance of *someone's home?* Were you trying to get caught, Luis?"

Luis closed his eyes. Why had he mentioned the building? "I didn't know it was there. It was set back from the road. Hidden. I thought the spot was deserted."

"Because you clearly didn't scope out a wide enough area."

Luis nodded. He was a hair's breadth away from begging for his life, but that would only antagonise Eric even more. He could do nothing but wait and accept his fate. "You're right," he said, the words sticking in his throat. "I failed."

"You know," Eric mused, "I really am incredibly disappointed. You came well recommended, Luis. I expected better. Instead, you've been something of a disaster from start to finish."

Luis didn't reply. He was wondering how Eric would kill him−or have him killed. He would have prayed for it to be quick, but he'd given up praying long ago.

"Would you recognise her?" Eric asked abruptly.

Luis blinked. "Who? The girl?"

Eric rolled his eyes. "Obviously, the girl."

"I...I think so. Maybe. Yes," Luis added, as anger seethed in Eric's eyes again.

Eric pinned him with his steely gaze. "Find her, and finish her."

Luis' eyes widened.

"What?" Eric snapped. He wasn't a fan of being questioned.

"Another murder...won't it arouse even more suspicion? The drop off happens in four days..."

"Let me worry about that," Eric said. "You won't be there, Luis. Consider yourself demoted. Permanently, if you mess this one up."

Luis knew exactly what that meant.

"Make it look like a break in. Give them something else to worry about for a few days. Understand? I want it done tomorrow."

Luis gulped. *Tomorrow?* He had no idea who the young woman was. He wasn't about to argue, so he nodded. As he turned to leave, Eric called him back. He smiled, but there was no mirth in it.

"Yes, boss?" Luis asked as coolly as he could manage.

"If you mess this up, you're a dead man."

As Luis left the room, he had the sinking feeling that whether he messed up or not, his days were numbered.

CHAPTER 9

The next morning, Rob stopped by his mum's house en route to the station. The team from Melbourne was heading to Eastbrooke, and while he wasn't looking forward to them taking over, after a long night filled with nightmares of Emma being shot in his arms, his pride was stinging less. The most important thing was that these killings stopped, and that she was safe. If that meant handing the case over to the city cops, well, so be it.

Arriving at his mum's place, he greeted her with a kiss, feeling a twinge of disappointment when she told him that Emma had already left, although he tried not to show it. "Oh...how was she this morning?"

"Quiet. She left a little while ago to get changed for school. She wouldn't hear of having the day off. Said there wouldn't be enough time for them to get a replacement teacher. Very conscientious young woman."

"Yes," Rob murmured, reaching for an apple from the fruit bowl, and lifting his gaze when he felt hers on him. "What?"

"You like her," she said quietly.

He rolled his eyes and went to protest, but his mother raised a hand, a serious look on her face. "I'm not matchmaking, Rob, I just have eyes. I saw the way you were with her last night, and Sunday at lunch."

"I was nothing but polite."

His mother nodded. "That's what I mean. You're not your usual, charming, smiley self around her. You're almost… awkward. I've never seen you like that around a girl."

HE SIGHED HEAVILY. There was no point lying to his own mother. She knew him better than he knew himself. Emma had gotten under his skin, and was curling herself around his heart, and the more he tried to deny it, the more he felt it. "It doesn't matter, anyway." He shrugged. "She turned me down."

"You asked her on a date?" His mother's eyes widened.

"Not really…just coffee. It was completely spontaneous. We were talking in the car…she's really easy to talk to, and you know I don't often confide in anyone. I was just being friendly."

"And what did she say?"

"That she was busy," he said glumly.

"Oh…" She looked at him with puppy-dog eyes.

"She may as well have said she was washing her hair." His shoulders drooped.

His mother slipped her arm around his shoulders. "Perhaps it was a little premature. I don't think she's a casual date kind of girl, at least that's the impression I get."

"But what if I'm not casual about her?" he blurted, then felt his cheeks warm. "I'm just tired," he said, blowing out a beath and rubbing his eyes.

"You don't have to be ashamed of having feelings, Rob," his mother said softly. "It's about time, don't you think?"

He dropped his gaze to his hands, feeling uncomfortable, like a little boy under his mother's scrutiny. "I don't know what you mean."

"I think you do," she said, sitting next to him at the table. "I've watched you over the years. You get on with everyone, and yet you get close to no one, except your brothers and me. You hide it well, but in some ways you're as aloof as Max."

"I'm not!" He was nothing like Max. He'd practically lived alone on the mountain before marrying Junia.

"You're scared of love," his mother said matter-of-factly. "And I know why. It's because of your father."

Her words tightened a cord around his heart. He pushed his apple away, no longer hungry. "It's a bit early for psychotherapy, Mum," he joked weakly, but she wasn't letting it go.

"You can't let what happened to your father stop you from living your life, Rob. Not now you've found someone you could potentially share it with."

"I barely know her," he protested. "And you've been on your own since Dad died," he pointed out. His mother was still an attractive woman, yet she'd never considered remarrying.

"That's not because I'm scared." Her face softened and her eyes took on a faraway look. "It's because I'm content with having had your father for as long as I did. He was my soulmate. I wouldn't want to marry anyone else. And I'm not lonely. Or bitter."

He searched her face. Her eyes were clear. She spoke the truth—her words were from the heart.

"I remember how much the two of you loved each other." Grief tugged at his heart as he recalled his childhood. They'd been such a happy family, and he put that down to the special relationship his parents shared. "And us," he continued, his voice thick. "We had the perfect family...I don't suppose I appreciated that."

"You were just a child," she said gently.

"When Dad died, he left such a hole in our lives." He blinked back tears as that raw place inside him surfaced. "Don't you ever think...if it wasn't for the fact that you had us kids...it would have been better to not go through that?"

A small breath escaped his mother's mouth as she lifted a hand and gently brushed the back of it against his cheek. "Oh, my darling," she said softly. "Do you really not know the answer to that? I wouldn't change a second that I had with your father, not a single moment. Yes, it hurt to lose him... and it hurt even more to see you boys having to deal with the loss, but I still thank God every day that he was a part of our lives. And besides," she added with a smile, "I'll see him again, in eternity."

"You really believe that?" He'd grown up with the notion of an afterlife, but it had never been more than an abstract concept, while the certainty in his mother's voice was tangible.

"With all my heart," she confirmed, smiling. Moments ticked by before she stood and put the kettle on.

"None of it matters anyway," he said lightly. "Like I said, Emma turned me down. She's not interested. I really doubt I'm her type."

"Nonsense," his mother said briskly, retrieving two mugs from the shelf. "I see the way she glances at you when she thinks no one's looking."

"Really?" Emma might actually like him? A grin spread across his face, and for a moment he felt like a schoolboy, but then he shook his head. "You're just imagining it, Mum."

"No, I'm right. I'm telling you," she insisted.

"Then why would she say no to coffee?" He didn't understand.

His mother sighed. "For someone so handsome and clever, you really don't know much about women, do you?" She raised an amused brow. "Emma isn't a frivolous girl, Rob, whereas *you* are a charmer."

"It's just the way I am." He shrugged, grinning. "But I'm never disrespectful. I'd never treat a woman badly."

"I know that, and I'm not saying for one moment that Emma would think anything else…"

"But?"

"But…you go for coffees all the time. You date."

"The last two, *you* set me up with," he pointed out.

"All I'm saying," she continued, ignoring his comment, "is that Emma is the sort of girl you need to make an effort for. You have to woo her, not expect her to just fall at your feet. You've been too used to that. Everyone likes you, Rob. No one could refuse you anything as a child with that smile of yours, least of all me and your father." She smiled indulgently as she handed him a mug of coffee.

He mulled over her words as he sipped the steaming drink. Maybe she was right. Maybe he did need to make more of an effort. Make Emma feel special. There was only one problem with that.

They were in the middle of a murder investigation. He sighed. "At the moment she's a witness to a murder in what is still currently my case. She's under my protection. I can't think of her in any other way."

"Maybe not right now, but just remember what I said…I would rather have had the time with your father and lost him than never have had him at all. Trust God, Rob. Let Him lead you in this."

He nodded. He wanted to tell her about his feelings at church on Sunday, and how he'd been praying ever since, but there wasn't time now. He swigged back his coffee, got up and kissed her on the cheek. "I'd better go."

"Stay safe, son. I'll be praying for you."

CHAPTER 10

*E*mma walked to the staff room to grab her cardigan. She was on her lunch break, and while she usually brought sandwiches, that morning she'd turned down Jean's offer to make her something for lunch. After a night tossing and turning, reliving that horrid event, she hadn't felt hungry, nor anticipated ever feeling so again.

Now, though, her stomach rumbled. She needed something to eat after all. There was a café at the end of the road, and apart from grabbing something, getting away for half an hour or so might do her good. Clear her head. Settle her nerves. She'd thought that going to work as usual was the best thing to do, but all morning she'd been jittery, startling at every noise, and she knew her class had noticed that something was wrong.

The image of the man on his knees, followed by the sudden loud crack of the gunshot, so loud it seemed to pierce the very air, replayed over and over in her mind. Growing up in Ethiopia, a place beset by poverty and unrest, she was hardly sheltered when it came to the harsh realities of life, but she'd never witnessed a murder and had never been pursued by someone shooting at her. No matter how much she tried to soothe her mind by praying continually, her nerves were on edge and her thoughts scattered. Why hadn't she listened to Jean and given herself a few days off? She was too conscientious. She knew that. But she was doing the children a disservice if she couldn't read a story without images of the armed man flashing through her mind.

She'd somehow finish the day and take tomorrow off.

Slipping on her cardigan, she buttoned it, feeling cold in spite of the warmth of the day. She left the school by the side gate that turned onto High Street and walked towards the little café that she often thought looked inviting but had never yet visited. The woman behind the counter, who had long dark hair and a timid smile, took her order and then waved her to a small corner table, where Emma sat and watched people passing by, going about their day, feeling oddly detached from normality.

How could Rob stand being a police officer, dealing with this kind of thing constantly? Perhaps that was the reason for the barrier behind his casual friendliness, a wariness that prevented him from getting close to people. Smiles on the surface, but hardened underneath. His way of coping.

Thinking about Rob warmed her, and a smile played on her lips despite herself. She believed his concern for her the night before had been genuine. A small crack in his armour.

Maybe she should have accepted his offer of coffee after all.

She ate her sandwich and sipped her juice in silence. After finishing, she still felt shaken but less jittery and detached, and more able to get on with the afternoon. She carried her plate to the counter, thanked the dark-haired woman, and left the café to walk back to the school, feeling more prepared for her afternoon class.

As she walked, however, her spine tingled. Was someone watching her? Her heart thudded as she stopped and turned, her head jerking around sharply.

She scanned the area. No one suspicious. A few cars parked further down the road; an old man walking by on the opposite side of the street with his equally old dog; a young mother pushing a baby in a pram a few metres behind her. She drew a slow breath, turned around and picked up her pace. Although she'd seen no one suspicious, the sense of being watched didn't leave her.

~

LUIS WAITED until the woman turned down a side street, then started the car and drove down the road at a deliberately casual pace. When she'd turned and looked back, her eyes had seemed to look right through him just as they had the night before, seconds after he shot Rick. Luckily, she hadn't noticed him hunched behind the steering wheel.

As he passed where she'd turned, he craned his head. It was an alley way that led directly to the primary school. She must work there. All he had to do now was wait for the end of the work day and discretely follow her home. Then, when it was dark, he'd strike, ensuring it looked like a robbery gone wrong. Without a witness, there was no danger of being caught. And no matter how hard the local authorities searched the surrounding mountains, they were unlikely to find his and Eric's bunker which was hidden so well that even aerial patrols wouldn't find it. Eric's plan to use the most hidden and dangerous of the mountain passes for his new business interests was ingenious, and Luis knew that if it wasn't for his own recent mistakes, the police would have no idea they were even in the area. He was lucky that Eric had let him live, but he suspected it wouldn't be for long. In fact, he had an extraordinarily strong suspicion that once he cleaned up this mess with the woman, he'd be a dead man himself.

He'd do the same if he were in Eric's situation. He could run, but where to? Eric would hunt him, regardless of where he went. He'd entertained the idea of taking Eric out before Eric took him, but quickly discarded it. Eric was too powerful, and the rest of his henchman were always nearby, watching. The best Luis could hope for was that he got things right from now on and that Eric would change his mind. That meant getting rid of the girl.

He sped up and headed out of town before pulling over on a deserted road. Taking his phone from his pocket, he took a deep breath as he scrolled through to Eric's name and then called him.

Eric picked up halfway through the first ring. "Have you found her?" His voice was gruff and demanding.

"Yes. She works at the school. I'll follow her home and strike when it's dark."

"Take Elliot with you," Eric said in a tone that sounded almost bored. "And don't mess this one up, Luis. For your own sake." The line went dead.

Luis clenched his fist. He couldn't mess this up. He had to do away with the girl.

If he wanted to live, he had no option.

⁓

EMMA WALKED HOME that afternoon with the same unnerved feeling that someone was watching her. She refused to give into it and look behind her, but she walked home at double her usual pace. Once she got inside the house, she locked the door behind her, then checked the back door. She briefly considered calling Rob but decided against it. She had nothing to tell him other than she thought she'd been followed with absolutely no evidence to support it. *I need to get a grip. It's just my imagination running wild.*

After a shower and a light meal, she felt a little better. Messages from Junia and Jean flashed on her phone. She messaged back rather than calling. Although glad of their support, she couldn't face talking about the previous evening. There was also a brief message from Rob. *Hope you're okay. Call if you need anything.* She stared at it for a moment, then simply replied *thanks*. She set her phone down and took her files out, hoping that doing next week's lesson plans would take her mind off everything.

It was getting dark when she finally put her paperwork down and went into the kitchen to make a hot chocolate before having an early night. While stirring her drink, the back porch light snapped on. Because it was sensory activated, she jumped and let out a little scream. With her heart thumping, she peered through the window into her small back garden.

Nothing was there. *It's probably just an animal crossing through. A possum, perhaps.* The light went out after a few seconds and she returned to her hot chocolate.

Moments later, her front door was shot open and she screamed.

CHAPTER 11

Rob blinked his tiredness away as he started to drive home. He'd worked a twelve-hour shift and it was growing dark. He longed for a hot shower and bed. It had been a frustrating day. Scouring the mountains, even with Joseph's help, had revealed nothing. Searching for the gunman was like looking for a needle in a haystack, it seemed.

He'd also spent most of the morning on the phone to the officer heading to Eastbrooke with a small team to take over the case. While he knew it was for the best, it still rankled his pride. This was *his* case, and *his* town. In the end, he'd gone into the station's restroom and prayed for humility, which had left him feeling marginally better. Deep down he knew this situation was beyond a small-town force, and the important thing was wrapping the case up, capturing the person behind it all, and ensuring the people of Eastbrooke were safe.

Making sure Emma was safe.

. . .

He'd thought about her all day, despite trying not to. He kept seeing her sitting before Max's fire, her face pale, her hands shaking, and feeling the rage again at the man who'd shot at her. It was probably best he wouldn't be in charge much longer; it was becoming way too personal.

He hadn't expected the call he'd received that morning, however, for it hadn't been an officer from the Melbourne force. Instead, the case was being turned over to the Feds. Whoever they thought might be in charge of this operation, it was someone big.

Driving home, he passed the end of Emma's street. He should go and check on her. Her response to his earlier message was brief and told him nothing; he wanted to know that she was truly okay. But turning up to her house late at night unannounced could be considered unprofessional. However, as he drove on, a nagging feeling from somewhere deep inside told him he *needed* to check on her. He turned back and circled the block near her house, feeling that something was terribly wrong. A sense of urgency tugged at him, the inner voice louder now...*she's in danger.*

Years of being on the police force had taught him to trust his instincts. He hit the gas and sped towards her house.

Please Lord, he prayed spontaneously, *let her be okay.* As though in reply, the sense of urgency came again, and he drove faster. He should have sent an officer to check on her earlier. Insisted she stay at his mother's where she wouldn't be alone. She was a witness to a murder, and that placed her in danger. Although she thought the killer hadn't seen her clearly enough to identify her, she could easily be wrong. The more he thought about it, the more convinced he was that she was in acute danger.

As he turned the corner into her street, his worst fears were realised. The street lights revealed a black sedan with frosted windows parked outside her house. Two men, with balaclavas on and weapons drawn, jumped out and ran up her front path. They didn't bother to knock. One of them shot the front door open before they ran in.

Rob's heart pounded as his adrenalin spiked. His first instinct was to leap out of the car and tackle the men himself, but his years of training took over. It would be a foolish move. Although he was armed, he was outnumbered against two obviously dangerous criminals, and if shots were fired inside, Emma could be hurt—or worse. His stomach lurched as he screeched to a halt behind the sedan and radioed Jerry.

"Two masked, armed men entering Emma Humphries' house. Forced entry. Send immediate back-up." He paused, then barked, "I'm going in." He wouldn't wait for back-up. She'd be dead before they arrived. He pulled his police issue gun out of the dashboard compartment and jumped out of the car, heart in mouth.

He prayed he wasn't too late.

When a woman's scream came from inside the house, he could barely draw breath.

He raced through the front door, his gun drawn and held close, ready to fire if necessary. The sound of Emma's voice pleading, almost crying, came from the back of the house. He hurried down the hallway.

A man stood in the kitchen doorway, blocking his view. "Shoot her," he said in a calm voice.

Rob raised his gun, took careful aim, and shot the man in the back of the thigh. The man cursed and crumpled to the ground, clutching his leg. Rob leapt forward and snatched the weapon he'd dropped. He aimed his own gun at the other man standing in the kitchen with his weapon pointed at Emma.

She was backed up against the kitchen counter, tears

streaming down her face, lips quivering. Her gaze flicked to Rob's, pleading with him to save her.

"Put the gun down," he ordered. His voice was emotionless, although his heart pounded.

The thug sneered and jabbed his gun closer to Emma.

She cringed, let out a small gasp.

Where was Jerry? Rob fought to keep calm and not let his anger, or fear, show. Emotion would only escalate the situation.

The man cursed in a language Rob didn't recognise.

"Put the gun down," he repeated. "No one else needs to get hurt."

There was a horrible, long moment that could have only lasted a few seconds, yet seemed to go on forever, where the man continued to point his gun at Emma, and Rob at him They were in a stalemate that couldn't possibly end without someone being hurt badly. Or killed.

Lord, Rob prayed silently, his heart pounding, *please help us.*

Police sirens suddenly wailed outside, breaking the silence. *Jerry.* Relief filled him.

The thug jerked. Rob took a step forward and cocked his gun. "Drop it," he ordered again.

The thug turned and fled out the back door just as Jerry and Eli flew into the house through the front. Everything happened at once. Eli sprinted out the back door, chasing the still armed man; Jerry cuffed the injured man on the floor, read him his rights and rang for an ambulance. Rob moved towards Emma, who collapsed in his arms, sobbing.

HE PUT his arms around her, the only thing holding her up as she trembled with shock. "Shhh," he murmured into her hair, his voice low and soothing. "You're safe now."

From now on he'd do everything in his power to protect her.

Even if it meant not letting her out of his sight.

CHAPTER 12

An hour later, despite his resolve not to leave her, Rob left Emma with his mother and Max to go to the hospital with Jerry to question the man who'd been shot. He knew they'd look after her, but it was difficult tearing himself away. He was furious with himself. She should have been in protective custody, or at the very least, not been left alone. She'd witnessed a murder, and these guys weren't amateurs–despite the mess they'd made over the past few days.

He said as much to Jerry as they drove to the hospital. "This is the second time in two weeks we've questioned an injured suspect. They're supposed to be organised criminals."

Jerry nodded. "They're panicking, and probably have been since the first body was found."

"Emma said the guy I shot was the same man she saw shoot Rick. I've taken her statement, but she's in shock. It might not stand up in court, but I believe her. The guy's trying to cover his tracks. Or, more likely, has been ordered to. Hence the panic and sloppiness. Which means we might be able to get some information out of him."

Jerry glanced sideways as he drove. "Is that why we're in a rush to question him tonight, instead of leaving it until the Feds arrive tomorrow?"

Rob shrugged. "The more information we can give them, the happier they'll be."

Jerry narrowed his eyes.

"What?" Rob demanded.

"Ordinarily, I'd say this was just about your pride. Wanting to show the Feds you can do your job without their interference, but right now, I'm wondering if it's more about a certain young lady."

Rob glared at him. "What's that supposed to mean?"

"Come on." Jerry smirked. "It doesn't require a genius to see how taken you are with her."

Rob groaned and slumped in his seat. "Not you as well. You sound like my mother."

"Your mother's a very perceptive woman," Jerry said.

Rob ignored the comment while Jerry snickered beside him as they headed to the hospital.

THE MAN, who'd given his name only as Luis, was handcuffed to the bed and looked mutinous. His eyes were like daggers as Rob walked into the room. "You're the one who shot me," he growled.

"That's right," Rob said, his voice like flint. He didn't have time for the games he'd played with Rick. This guy wasn't just a potential witness. He was in custody, a murder suspect. Rob had no doubt he'd gone to Emma's house with the sole intention of killing her, and his blood boiled in his veins. He wasn't a violent man, and violence went again all the morals that had been instilled in him during his Christian upbringing, but he had to jam his fisted hands in his pockets as he looked at Luis.

"Why were you at Miss Humphries' house?"

The man glared at him and didn't answer. There was a steely toughness to him that made Rob groan. He'd be harder to crack than Rick. Perhaps Jerry had been right about leaving this to the organised crime experts. He wanted, more than anything, to get back to Emma to ensure she was okay. *What if someone else was sent to finish her off?*

His phone rang. It was Johnson. Giving Jerry a nod, Rob stepped into the hallway to answer it.

"Chief?"

"Are you at the hospital?"

"Yes," Rob replied. "I'm about to question the man we apprehended at Emma Humphries' place."

"I wouldn't bother." Johnson sighed. "The Feds are on their way."

"Tonight? I thought they were coming in the morning."

"As soon as they heard the name Luis, they got excited. Leave the questioning to them but stay until they arrive. I don't want another suspect going missing and getting killed. Relieve the junior officer, and you and Jerry guard the suspect. Don't let him out of your sight."

Rob swallowed his annoyance at being ordered around. Johnson was the boss, after all, but Rob was used to being left in charge. It seemed he really did need to work on his pride. "Yes, Chief," he said as agreeably as possible. He ended the call and motioned for Jerry to join him outside the room. In a low voice, Rob quickly filled him in.

"Great," Jerry grumbled, "we're on watch duty again."

It was three hours before the two plain clothed Federal police officers arrived. One was tall and blond, perhaps in his forties, the other heavyset and dark, reminding Rob more of a Hollywood gangster than a Serious Crimes detective.

"Detective Myers," the blond man introduced himself, "and this is Detective Weaver. Are you Officer Robert Carlton?"

Rob nodded and extended his hand, which Myers shook.

"Let's grab a coffee," Myers suggested. "Weaver can wait with your partner."

Detective Weaver looked none too pleased, but Rob appreciated Myers' attempt to treat him as a professional equal. He led the way to the cafeteria, which was all but empty at this time of night, and they sat by the window with their coffees. Rob raised a brow at Myers. "So, I'm guessing this isn't simply about getting to know each other."

Myers grinned and Rob decided he liked him.

He lowered his voice, his expression serious. "The suspect you have in custody is Luis Regan. He's been evading us for years. Drug dealing, arms smuggling, and five suspected murders that we know he either committed or ordered, but we've never been able to pin on him. I wanted to say thank you for bringing him in."

Rob shrugged off-handedly. As much as he wanted to bask in the praise, he'd simply been in the right place at the right time, for which he thanked God, recalling the whisper that had urged him to check on Emma. "To be honest, he got sloppy, breaking into Miss Humphries' house like that. And I got lucky…I happened to be driving past."

Myers nodded. "See, this is what's worrying us…and why we've been called in. Melbourne tipped us off. They think Luis's working with someone we've had our eyes on for even longer…and not just us, Interpol."

Rob's eyebrows hiked. "This is where the neo-Nazi ties come in?"

CHAPTER 12 | 211

Myers nodded grimly. "You've heard of the White League?"

The muscles in Rob's jaw tensed. "The group my father was tracking...they were a splinter cell, if I'm correct."

Myers' gaze held steady, as if studying him. "Yes. The guy we believe Luis is working for was a major player with the group, although he left a long time ago...not long before your father's death, I believe."

Disappointment flowed through Rob. For a moment he thought they might be tracking the man responsible for killing his father. "Why did he leave?"

"He preferred crime to ideology," Myers said wryly. "His name, if we've got the right guy, is Eric Hausbaden, and he's a nasty piece of work. From South Africa originally. He makes Luis look like a pussycat."

Rob whistled through his teeth. "So, Luis is your way of getting to Eric?" No wonder Myers wanted to thank him for bringing him in.

"Hopefully. Someone like Luis won't turn informant easily, but we think he'll be in Eric's bad books after this week. He'll be fearing for his life. If we offer him witness protection, he might just take it."

"What if he doesn't?"

Myers shrugged. "Then we threaten him with a long prison sentence. But we'll need Miss Humphries to identify him."

Rob bristled at the thought of causing Emma further distress, but she was the only one who could confirm it was Luis who killed Rick.

Myers' next words sent an icy chill through his body, confirming Rob's earlier fears. "She needs to be in protective custody, or at least be guarded. She's your only witness. If

Eric sent Luis to dispose of her, he has even more reason to want her gone now."

Rob swallowed hard and fought to keep his voice even. "I've already thought of that. I'll guard her." He was suddenly glad he'd been demoted on this case, as now he could take on the role of Emma's protector until this was over. He wouldn't let anything happen to her. Not on his watch.

They returned to the ward and Rob left Myers and Weaver to question Luis, who went grey as they walked into his room.

"Do you think he'll talk?" Jerry asked as he and Rob strolled to the car.

"Probably not." Rob sighed. "Not straight away, anyway. Emma will need to identify him…and she needs to be in protective custody."

"In a safe house?" Jerry asked.

"With me."

Jerry blinked and looked at him curiously.

"I'll keep her safe," Rob said, his voice firm.

"I know," his partner said quietly. "I was thinking more about you. I've known you a long time, my friend. You're falling hard."

Rob let out a slow breath. Jerry spoke the truth. He could no longer deny his feelings for Emma. She was capturing his heart, and there was nothing he could do about it.

BACK AT HIS mother's house, Rob joined Emma in the lounge room. She was curled up on an old brown sofa with a crocheted blanket over her. She lifted her head as he walked in. Her eyes were guarded. She seemed tense, as well she might, considering what she'd been through.

"The homicide case has been taken over by the Federal

police," he said, perching on the edge of the matching armchair. He leaned forward, held her gaze.

"I'm in danger, aren't I?" she asked, her voice faltering. "They came to kill me."

He hated the fear in her eyes. It tore at him, and all he wanted to do was wrap her in his arms and keep her safe. "Yes. And you might still be in danger. It's not safe for you to be alone."

She straightened, pulling the blanket around her. "So, what do I do?" Her voice was steadier, and he felt a pang of pride at her show of resilience.

"You'll stay with me until it's over."

Her eyes widened. "With you?"

He groaned inwardly. What a fool. He should have been more sensitive. She was a Christian, and having been raised with Christian principles himself, he understood her reluctance to be alone with him.

"Emma," he said quietly, holding her gaze, "I'm not sure there's any other way. We can't allow you to stay on your own. I understand why you might not want to stay with me on your own, but I can assure you that I'm not in any way trying to take advantage of you. This is purely about keeping you safe, it's part of my job. If it wasn't so dangerous, we'd stay here with my mother, but I can't put her in danger, too. I can get a female constable to stay with us, if that makes you feel better."

Her expression softened. "I wouldn't want to put your mother in danger. It's an odd situation, and I…I do trust you, Rob, but I think I'd like a female constable to stay as well."

He bit his lip to stop a grin splitting his face. Despite everything, he heard the truth in her words. Her trust gave him a burst of joy amidst the horror of the day.

"I'm glad." He smiled. Clearing his throat, he stood and

said more formally, "I'll drive you back to your house first so you can pick up some things. Pack enough for a few days."

"Do you think it'll be that long?"

"At the moment, I know as much as you do." While she went to the bathroom, he quickly made a call to Jerry, asking him to arrange a female constable to meet him at his house, and then he went into the kitchen and told his mother and Max the plan. As expected, his mother suggested she come with him to look after Emma.

He shook his head firmly. "No, Mum. It's dangerous. Absolutely not."

Max nodded in agreement as he fetched his coat. "I'd better go. Junia's at a friend's place and I need to pick her up. Stay safe, brother." He slapped Rob on the back, which was about as affectionate as Max ever got with anyone except their mother and Junia.

Emma came into the kitchen, her cardigan buttoned up and her handbag over her shoulder. Her eyes were puffy, but she held her chin out defiantly. "Okay, bodyguard. Let's go."

CHAPTER 13

Emma drew a steadying breath as she approached the damaged front door of her house. It was past midnight, and the house was shrouded in darkness. A shudder raced up her spine as she recalled the moment the door had been shot open and the men ran inside. It felt like the house had been violated, and she wondered if she could ever live here again.

Rob turned his flashlight on so she could see where she was going. A temporary lock had been placed on the door. He took the key from her and opened it, switching on the lights.

The kitchen was cordoned off with crime scene tape and there was blood on the hall carpet. She averted her eyes, feeling nauseous at the whole scene, trying to block the flood of memories. It had only been hours earlier, yet time seemed to have warped. It felt as though it had simultaneously occurred weeks ago and just minutes before.

"I'll wait down here while you get your things," Rob said politely.

She went up the stairs, her legs feeling like lead. In her bedroom, she found her hold-all at the back of her wardrobe and quickly threw in some jeans, T-shirts, underwear and pyjamas, then went into the bathroom to fetch some toiletries. She caught a glimpse of herself in the mirror above the sink and startled at how pale she looked. She splashed some water on her face, and after brushing her hair, felt marginally better.

As she walked back down the stairs, her gaze landed on Rob and her breath hitched. He looked so handsome in his uniform, standing sentinel-like, protecting her. She was glad of his protection, although the idea of staying with him was strange. She felt safe in his presence, and she appreciated that he understood her discomfort. Without knowing why, she did trust him, but it wasn't just because he was a police officer and his job was to look after the witness.

"Ready?" Concern filled his eyes as he searched her face. "It must have been difficult, coming here." His voice was soft. Caring.

She nodded, averting her gaze from the kitchen as she headed for the front door. "It feels like the place has been violated," she said quietly.

"I'll make sure it gets cleaned up before you return," he said. "It won't take away what happened, but at least it'll be back to normal."

"Thank you," she said softly, stepping out onto the path. It was well past midnight and she suddenly felt exhausted. The air was cool on her face, and she wrapped her cardigan tighter. As they drove to his house in silence, she struggled to keep her eyes open.

He lived in a small house on the outskirts of town. The front lawn was neat and the front door looked to be freshly painted. Inside, it was tidy and minimalist, with the only personal touch being a large photograph of him and his brothers when they were children, with a young, pretty Jean and a handsome man Emma guessed was his father.

"Is that your dad?" she asked.

"Yes," he replied with a quick smile. "You can tell, can't you?"

"You all look like him, that's for sure."

He showed her upstairs to a small guest bedroom. There was nothing in it other than a bed and a small dresser.

"I'm sorry it's not much," he apologised, looking embarrassed. "I'm not used to having people stay over, unless it's one of my brothers."

"It's fine," she assured him. Right now, she could probably sleep on a wooden bench.

He hesitated in the doorway, his gaze darting. "Can I get you a hot drink, or anything?"

"I just need to sleep, but thank you. For everything."

"You're welcome. The female constable will be here soon. Goodnight, Emma."

"Goodnight, Rob," she said, but he'd already left. She shut the door quietly and changed into her pyjamas. After taking the pocket Bible from her handbag, she climbed into bed. Although her eyes were heavy and her body desperate for sleep, she needed the comfort of the Word after such a harrowing night. Once again, she turned to Psalm 61, and this time the words seemed more poignant than ever.

Hear my cry, O God, listen to my prayer. From the ends of the earth, I call to You, I call as my heart grows faint, lead me to the rock which is higher than I. For You have been my refuge, a strong tower against the foe. I long to dwell in Your tent forever, and take refuge in the shelter of Your wings. For You, God, have heard my vows, You have given me the heritage of those who fear Your name.

She placed the Bible down by the side of the bed and

closed her eyes, reflecting on the words she'd just read, allowing them to sink in and penetrate her soul.

"You are my refuge, Lord," she whispered, "my rock and my strong tower. I thank You that I'm safe and well. Thank You for Rob and Jerry, that they came to my aid when I needed them, and for Jean and Max and Eli. Thank you for sending friends and protectors. Please keep the people of Eastbrooke safe from the dark forces gathering around. Place a hedge around the town, Lord. Help the police apprehend the villains before anyone else gets hurt. Keep us all in the shadow of Your wings, for You are the Almighty God, our Lord and Saviour."

Her thoughts drifted to the moment the two men burst into her house, and she shuddered as she recalled the fear she felt when the gun was pointed at her. Yet, for all of their evil acts, those men were children of God—they just didn't know Him. "Help me, Lord," she prayed fervently, "to forgive those who tried to hurt me, for vengeance is Yours and Yours alone, and You are a just and merciful God. I pray that they may see the error of their ways and find their way to You, in humility and repentance. In Jesus' name I pray, Amen."

Finally, she turned off the lamp on the dresser and allowed much needed oblivion to claim her.

EMMA PUSHED her way through the undergrowth; branches scratched her face. The moon shone overhead. It felt like she'd been lost for hours. Surely that was Max and Junia's house up ahead, yet she seemed to be going around in circles. Panic mounted inside her; she could barely breathe. She kept trying to pray, but she was unable to speak.

"Hello, Emma," a voice sounded behind her.

It must be Rob, come to show her the way. She spun around, relieved.

A man stood there, pointing a gun at her, his eyes glinting with evil.

She turned and fled, but it felt like she was moving through treacle. He was gaining on her… She tried to scream, but all that came out was a pitiful whimper.

"Emma," he called behind her, "Emma…"

"Emma! Emma, wake up."

She sat bolt upright, her mouth open, ready to scream, her heart thundering in her chest.

It was Rob, and she was in his house. She was safe. Her panting slowed, and she breathed out a shaky sigh of relief, then buried her head in her hands. "I'm sorry," she murmured. "I was dreaming…I was lost near the retreat, and that man was there…pointing a gun at me."

Rob sat carefully on the edge of the bed. "It's okay," he said soothingly. "You're safe, it was just a dream."

"I'm sorry," she said again, embarrassed that once again he'd witnessed her at her most vulnerable.

"There's no need to apologise. It's only natural that you'd have nightmares after everything you've been through. You've been incredibly brave."

"I don't feel brave. I feel terrified."

"It's going to be okay." He gave a comforting smile. "I won't let anything happen to you."

She nodded, feeling a little better as the memories of her dream drifted away.

His gaze settled on the Bible next to her bed. "Do you read it every night?"

She nodded again. "Yes, and then I pray. Don't you?"

He winced. "Not as much as I should, although I've been praying more this week."

"Because of everything that's happened?"

"Kind of, but not really." His gaze dropped to his hands, and he looked so vulnerable that a surge of protectiveness for him flowed through her. "It was the sermon last week; it really got to me." He lifted his gaze and met hers. "You know, when the minister was talking about being saved by grace, as opposed to works."

She smiled. "It's the essence of the gospel, and why Christianity really is such good news."

"Well, the thing is, it didn't feel like good news. It made me uncomfortable. I've been exactly the person the minister spoke about, taking pride in how righteous and good I am. Knowing that because of what I do, everyone sees me as a good guy."

"You *are* a good guy."

"Maybe," he said, "but it's a source of pride for me. A big part of my identity. To the point that I've made it the centre point of who I am, instead of God. And it makes me judgmental of others. Like, if I'm the good guy, then others must be the bad guys. So, *I'm* okay with God. I'm in, they're out. But this week, after hearing that sermon, that whole way of thinking has been upended."

Emma studied him. It wasn't easy baring your soul. Admitting you're wrong. She got the feeling he'd never talked to anyone like this before. He seemed genuinely open, vulnerable.

"That's not a bad thing," she finally said, softly. "Because it's so radical, the gospel can and does make people uncomfortable. No one can earn their way to heaven. But that's not a cop out…it means we have to admit we're sinners and accept the gift of Jesus' saving grace. That's the only way we can be saved. We must always try to live the way He wants us to, but we should never be proud of our works for their own sake."

"Which is what I've always done," he said contritely.

"Don't beat yourself up. We're all sinners, remember? Just pray humbly and honestly, and God will help you figure this out."

Rob smiled, and there was such an open expression on his face that she felt a sudden connection between them, one that went beyond mere attraction. As though they'd known each other forever. "You make it all sound so simple," he said. "I wish I could be more like you."

Her cheeks flamed. His admiration was heartwarming, but she was a sinner too, and far from perfect.

His gaze dropped again. "Now I'm sorry," he murmured. "You've just had a nightmare, and here I am pouring out my soul to you."

"It's okay. I'm glad you feel you can talk to me. Embrace the journey, because it certainly sounds as though you're on one."

"Yeah, I guess I am." He gave a small chuckle.

They sat in companionable silence for a few moments, and then he pushed to his feet. "Will you be able to go back to sleep? Because if not, we can watch some terrible early morning TV if you need the company. Whatever you need."

She laughed. "That's very sweet, but I think I'll try and grab some more sleep before I resort to the shopping channel. Thank you, honestly. You, and your whole family, have been amazing."

"You're pretty amazing yourself." Their gazes connected, and for a moment, time stood still before he turned and left the room, closing the door softly behind him.

Her mind spun and her heart pounded, and there was a tingle in the pit of her stomach. Maybe her emotions were exposed because of the events of the day, but if she were honest, she was falling for Eastbrooke's most eligible bachelor, and it seemed he was falling for her.

She eased her head onto the pillow. Too much was happening for her to figure out what that meant, or what it might signify–if anything–for her future. Rob was looking after her as part of his job, she knew that, but she'd seen a different side to him tonight, and it drew her closer to him. God was working on him, softening him, and that made her glad.

She pulled the blanket tighter. It was too much to think about right now. She started to murmur the Lord's prayer under her breath, but she was asleep before she reached the third line.

This time, there were no nightmares.

CHAPTER 14

Rob glanced at Emma as they walked into the station. Her face was pinched and dark circles hung under her eyes, no doubt from her broken sleep the night before.

"Are you sure you're ready for this?" he asked.

She gave a nod but didn't speak.

"If at any time it gets too much," he told her, "just say the word and I'll get you out of there."

"Thank you," she murmured, giving him a grateful smile. She'd been quiet all morning, turning down his offer of breakfast and nibbling on a cheese sandwich for lunch. They'd sat and watched sitcoms together and she'd seemed more relaxed, but when the phone rang, she flinched.

When he told her that Myers wanted her to pick the shooter out in a line-up, however, she'd nodded defiantly.

"You don't have to do it," he said. "You're not under any obligation."

"I want to," she replied in a tone that brooked no argument, and he'd again been impressed by her quiet strength.

Having her around the house had been both pleasant and unsettling. He tried hard not to think what it would be like having her around on a more permanent basis. While the female constable had been there, it was almost as if she wasn't, like she knew she was simply there out of protocol.

He held the door open for Emma and then led her to the viewing room. Detective Myers was there. He stood and held his hand out. "Good afternoon, Miss Humphries. Thanks for agreeing to do this."

"You're welcome," she said quietly, but her gaze flicked to Rob as though for reassurance.

"That interior window," Myers said, nodding at the far wall, "is a mirror on the other side. In a moment, seven men will line up. All you need do is take a good look at them, and if you see the man who attacked you yesterday, tell me the number. They can't see you."

"But he'll know it's me," she pointed out.

"It's to keep him from intimidating you. To make you as comfortable as possible."

She took a deep breath and stepped towards the window. "I'm ready."

Behind the glass, seven men trooped in and stood in an orderly line, facing what to them was a mirror. The sixth man stared into the mirror as though he could see through it, a clear look of menace in his eyes. *Luis.* Rob swallowed down his rage at seeing him again, remembering the way the man had so coldly given the order to shoot Emma. He wouldn't let himself think about what could have happened if he hadn't followed that small voice within and swung by her house.

"Number six," she said immediately.

"You're absolutely sure?" Myers asked.

"One hundred per cent." She faced Rob, her eyes pleading. "Can we go now?"

He nodded. "Yes, let's go." He spoke to Myers. "Keep me updated?"

"Of course."

Back in the car, Emma rested her head against the seat and exhaled a long breath. "I'm glad that's over."

"Well done. It must have been difficult so soon after yesterday. And you identified the right guy. It's not always as obvious as you think–shock can do funny things to memories."

She faced him and gave a small smile. "The limp confirmed it. I thought he'd be more injured, though."

"Just a flesh wound, but a painful one," Rob said. "We shoot to wound, not to kill."

"Does it ever scare you?" she asked as he started the engine and pulled out of the car park.

"Shooting people?"

"Not so much the actual act, but…having all that power over someone's life."

He pondered the question. He'd never thought of it that way. "I don't suppose I've ever really thought of it as power, just a responsibility. We're here to protect the public, not gun down criminals unless we have to. Although cop shows make it look more glamorous, I suppose."

She smiled again. "You're a good guy," she said decisively.

His heart warmed at her appraisal, although their conversation the night before came to mind. "You think so?"

She nodded and laid her head against the seat and closed her eyes. "You're a hero," she murmured.

He didn't reply, but a ripple of pride flowed through him, despite trying to keep it in check since the pastor's sermon had moved him so much. For some reason, though, Emma's opinion felt more important to him than most, and somehow, it felt right.

Back at his house, she went up for a nap while he pottered around doing some chores. It felt odd not being at work. Almost like a holiday, but he was ever watchful. He couldn't afford to drop his guard.

She came back down in the early evening and they ordered a takeaway and watched a film about the American Civil War. They'd invited Constable Jenkins to join them, but she said she was happy to do her own thing. As the credits rolled, he caught himself looking at Emma and studying her profile. She had an elegance about her that was wholly natural and that she seemed completely unaware of. He averted his gaze as she turned to him, embarrassed that she'd caught him staring.

"Is everything okay?" she asked.

"Yes," he said quickly. "I meant to tell you that Myers phoned while you were asleep. After you identified Luis, they offered him a plea deal, and he gave them details of the operation. There's a deal happening in the early hours of the morning."

"Wow, that all happened quickly."

He nodded. Myers was good, although admitting it irked him. "Luis would have been pretty desperate, facing both a long prison stretch, and the boss man unhappy with him. Men like Eric Hausbaden have a long reach. Luis wouldn't be safe anywhere without protection; in jail or otherwise."

Emma shook her head, her eyes wide. "This is a whole new world to me; I'm just an average schoolteacher."

"Hardly average." Rob chuckled lightly, then said, "You grew up in Ethiopia. I'm sure things are hard there."

She nodded thoughtfully. "It's not an easy life. There's so much suffering, but people have such strong faith. Probably stronger than in the developed world where things are easier."

Rob glanced down at his hands. "I admire that about you," he said quietly. "Your faith, I mean." He lifted his gaze to hers. "You remind me of my mother. No matter what life throws at her, even losing Dad, she never wavers in her faith or her values. I wish I were more like her."

Emma's brows lifted. "You seem a highly principled person, just like her."

"Well, in that respect, maybe. But faith doesn't come as easily to me as it does to her. Like I told you last night, there's so much I've realised I don't know, even though I grew up in church."

She smiled at him with her gorgeous, soulful eyes. "Faith isn't an intellectual exercise," she said softly. "It doesn't come from the mind, as much as our minds are a blessing. It comes from the heart."

He felt a sudden and uncharacteristic urge to pour his out to her, just like he had the night before. It wasn't like him to want to open up, but her calm acceptance of him made it seem the most natural thing in the world to do.

"I think maybe that's where my problem is." He took a deep breath. "I've always guarded my heart. Ever since Dad died, I've kept a part of myself locked away. It's only now that I understand how that has affected my relationship with God as well. It's always been about keeping the commandments and being 'good' and taking pride in that. But now I get it, it's about a relationship with Him."

Her eyes sparkled. "That's exactly what it is. And it's the best relationship you'll ever have."

He smiled wryly. "It's not like I have much to compare it to."

"Really?" She raised a disbelieving eyebrow.

His cheeks warmed. "I know I've got a reputation as a charmer," he admitted sheepishly, "and I've been on a few dates—Eastbrooke's a small town—but that's as far as it goes. I don't sleep around, and I've always been wary of relationships. I tell myself it's because of my job, but I know it's also about keeping my heart safe. I think I use the charmer image as a bit of a front."

Her gaze narrowed. "So, when you asked me out for coffee…"

"I meant nothing disrespectful. I genuinely wanted to get to know you." There was a pause, perhaps one of the most uncomfortable of his life as he stopped himself from leaning forward and kissing her. "I'm sorry," he said, "I shouldn't be telling you all this."

She shook her head. "Not at all, I'm honoured you have." She looked thoughtful, and then asked, "Can I pray for you?"

He blinked. "Pray for me?" It should be him praying for her… He cleared his throat and agreed. What else could he do?

She bowed her head and clasped her hands together. He did the same. When she spoke, her voice was low and soothing, but also throbbing with emotion, and Rob felt a whisper of something long buried move through him.

"*Lord, watch over Rob and keep him safe. He's Your precious child, and You're always there for him, whether he knows it or not. Open his heart that he may come to You fully, Lord, in humility and with awareness of Your deep and abiding love for him. Give him the assurance that he doesn't need to earn Your grace, and that You love him because He's Your child, not because of anything he achieves or does. Free him from fear, so that his heart may be open to love. In Jesus' precious name. Amen.*"

"Amen," he echoed. He kept his head bowed as a sudden stillness came over him and a peace he'd never felt before flowed through him, soothing his frazzled nerves. He felt the sense of a presence around him, a sense of being held and cherished, and it brought tears to his eyes. He blinked them back, and when he looked up, Emma was smiling at him.

"That was wonderful, thank you." He got up and cleared the plates and rubbish away, needing to ground himself in the ordinary.

When he returned, Emma was standing up, stretching. "I don't know why I'm so tired," she complained, "but I think I need an early night. Will you wake me if you hear anything from Myers?"

"Of course," he said. "Goodnight, Emma."

"Goodnight, Rob," she said as she headed up the stairs.

CHAPTER 15

The smell of cooking bacon wafted through the house the next morning. It was early, but Rob was clearly up and making breakfast. It had taken Emma a long time to drift off as she'd replayed the line-up over and over again, the man's dark, unwavering gaze trying to intimidate her, threaten her, as she'd flashed back to him standing in her kitchen doorway, ordering the other man to shoot her. It had taken more bravery than she'd known she possessed to turn to the detective and say 'that one; number six.'

She hadn't been worried about nightmares as she'd tossed and turned, though, as interspersed with the memories of Luis' face had been her talk with Rob, and the tangible presence that had settled in the space between them as she'd prayed for him. She felt closer to him, and grateful to God for putting him in her path. Even if they were never destined to be any more than friends, although she had to admit to herself, finally, that she wanted more than that, she was glad she'd been able to inspire his commitment to faith in some small way. And she could hardly fail to be grateful to him for protecting her. A shudder ran up her spine. Without him, she may well not be here.

As she approached the kitchen, the smell was now suspiciously like bacon burning, and as she entered, Rob was grumbling under his breath and throwing pieces of charred meat into the bin.

He looked up with a sheepish expression on his face. "I was hoping to surprise you with breakfast, but…well, you can see it's not going according to plan."

She laughed at his expression. "I could smell it before I could see it. Do you want me to try? I enjoy cooking."

He rubbed the back of his neck. "That was the last of the bacon…it was my third attempt. I'm not usually such a terrible cook."

"Okay." She laughed again. "Do you have eggs, milk and flour?"

"I think so."

"Right. Move over, we're having pancakes."

He grinned apologetically and moved out of the way as she headed to the counter, then he opened the cupboards and passed her the ingredients she asked for.

"Do you have lemon and sugar?"

"Yes, one moment. I'm getting spoiled…this reminds me of being a kid." He flashed a boyish smile that made him look incredibly vulnerable and her heart melted. She looked away, suddenly shy at the feelings welling in her. She combined the ingredients and started to mix the pancake batter, making enough for both them and Constable Jenkins who was taking a shower.

Ten minutes later, she and Rob sat together around the table, Constable Jenkins opting to have hers on the porch in the sun, tucking into what Rob announced were the best pancakes he'd ever tasted. "Don't tell my mother that," he said with a laugh.

"I won't," Emma promised.

As nice as it was to sit together and share such a normal, domestic moment, tension filled the room. They were up early because they were anxious for the phone call that would tell them what had happened in the early hours of the morning. Whether the sting had gone as the detectives had hoped, and Eric and all the others involved in the arms smuggling ring were safely in custody. Then, perhaps, although she'd never be able to forget the traumatic experience, life could hopefully go back to normal.

Rob seemed to pick up on her thoughts. He swallowed the last of his pancake and met her gaze. "It's horrible, isn't it? This waiting."

"It certainly seems to make a minute seem like an hour," Emma said, sighing. "But this must be harder for you. I imagine you're used to being in the middle of the action."

"Yes." He nodded. "And I did feel like that when I was first taken off the case. But honestly? I'm glad I'm here with you."

He held her gaze, and her insides grew warm as she stared into his eyes, acutely aware of the deepening connection between them. When he opened his mouth to speak, her chest tightened with anticipation, but whatever he was about to say would be left unsaid because his phone rang loudly, making her jump.

He snatched it up. "Hello?" He turned it onto speakerphone and set it in the middle of the table so she could hear. "It's Myers," he mouthed. "Get Constable Jenkins."

Emma hurried to the front of the house to get her. She didn't want either of them to miss what Detective Myers had to say.

"I have mixed news, I'm afraid," Detective Myers began in

a clipped tone. He sounded exhausted, and Emma guessed he'd had a long night.

"Go on," Rob said warily.

"We intercepted the meeting and apprehended most of Eric's men, and those on the other end of the deal…I'll give you those details when Miss Humphries is not in earshot."

"Of course. You said Eric's men…but not Eric?" Rob's eyebrow quirked.

"He wasn't present. I imagine because he suspected Luis informed. No doubt he'll be long gone, although we have a manhunt after him since we can finally pin something on him."

The detective sounded angry, and Emma felt sympathy for him. To have their target so nearly in their grasp and then have him slip away, no doubt to cause more havoc in the world, must be incredibly frustrating. She glanced at Rob. He, too, looked grim, echoing Myers' mood.

"What happens with Luis now? I presume you still have to uphold his plea deal?" Rob asked.

"Well, yes. He gave us the information, and other than Hausbaden himself, we do have the other perpetrators in custody. But this is the problem…Luis had to come with us, to show us the exact location…there was something of a skirmish, and in the chaos…he got away."

Emma's heart stopped. She glanced at Rob. He was staring at the phone, and his face paled.

"Is…is Emma in danger?" he asked quietly.

There was a pause before Myers replied. "I hope not. To harm Emma now would be counterintuitive, but so was running away after we offered him a deal. Of course, he might have assumed it wouldn't hold since we didn't get Eric."

What Myers said made sense. There was no reason for

Luis to come after her now, but Rob was still staring at the phone, worry etched in his features.

"There's a 'but' in your voice, Myers, I can hear it," he said.

Myers sighed. "Take Miss Humphries off the call please, Carlton."

"No," Emma said quickly.

Rob's brows drew together as he lifted his gaze.

"I mean, assuming it isn't classified information, if it concerns my welfare, I have a right to know what you're going to say," she said.

He gave a nod. "She's right," Rob said to Myers.

Myers sighed audibly through the phone. "This is just a gut feeling, but Luis is unstable, he won't be thinking straight. He tested positive for crystal meth at the hospital, and he was clearly in withdrawal yesterday. It might make him more likely to act rashly and aggressively. It would make little sense for him to come after Emma again, but…I'd like to keep her in protective custody while we try and locate him. He's probably left town, but he might not have. We have a team trying to locate him."

Icy tendrils of fear squeezed Emma's chest as her gaze darted around. She inhaled sharply, barely registering the last part of the call as Rob finished the conversation with Myers.

He leaned across the table, his eyes searching her face. "Emma, are you okay?"

She nodded, willing herself to be brave. "Yes," she said, though her mouth was dry. "I'm fine. Myers worried me a bit, but like he said, there's no real reason for Luis to come for me now, is there?"

Rob nodded reassuringly. "I'm sure Myers is simply

taking precautions," he told her, but Emma didn't miss the flicker of anxiety in his eyes.

The phone rang again. Jean's name flashed on the screen. Rob pressed the answer button. Jean's cheerful voice echoed through the small kitchen. "Hello, love. I was just passing by so I thought I'd stop by and check on Emma's place. Do a little clean-up for her."

Emma smiled at Jean's kindness. "Thank you," she replied. "That's really lovely, but honestly, you shouldn't have."

"Oh, it's no bother, dear," Jean trilled. "I'm just phoning because it seems you have left your back door open."

The hairs on Emma's arm stood up as she lifted her gaze to Rob's, whose dawning horror reflected her own.

"It wasn't left open," Emma whispered.

"Mum!" Rob shouted urgently. "Get out of there!"

There was a sudden noise, followed by a scream.

"Mum!" Rob yelled.

The line went dead.

CHAPTER 16

Rob inhaled deeply as he approached the front door of Emma's house, with her slightly behind him. This had to be the craziest plan he'd ever heard of in his life, and he still couldn't quite believe that he'd been crazy enough to agree to it.

The minute the phone had gone dead, he'd grabbed his gun and sprinted to the front door, yelling at Emma to stay with Constable Jenkins and ordering her to call Myers back, then he'd spun around as the phone rang again.

"It's your mum," Emma said, her face deathly white as he answered it.

Rob had been praying that something had just startled his mother and that nothing dreadful had happened to her, but as Luis' deep voice came through the speaker, terror and rage rolled through him. "Where's my mother?" he growled, his hands shaking.

"You can have your mummy back," Luis said in a mocking tone, although Rob hadn't missed the edge of desperation to it, "when you bring me that little snitch of a teacher. I'll do a trade."

Rob fought to keep his voice calm. Antagonising the man would only make the situation ten times worse. "You don't need to do this, Luis. Just hand yourself in. I spoke to Myers just now. The deal's still on the table. You'll blow it if you get yourself into more trouble."

There was a pause, and Rob prayed that Luis would see the sense in what he was saying, even as he knew that desperate men were rarely able to think straight. But Luis was also in the grips of drug withdrawal, and thus even more on the edge.

"I don't believe you," he spat.

"It's true," Rob said quietly, trying to sound convincing. Generally, he had good negotiation skills, but this was way beyond anything he'd ever faced. *His mother's life was in danger.*

"You're a liar," Luis growled. "Bring the teacher if you want your mother back in one piece." The phone went dead again. Rob roared with frustration. He ran out the door, only to turn and see Emma and the female constable following.

"You can't come," he told Emma.

"But it's me he wants," she said simply. "If you turn up on your own, won't you make him even angrier? Let's at least get in the car, and you can phone Detective Myers on the way and tell him what's going on."

Her common-sense approach snapped him back into cop mode, and he nodded as the three of them got into the car. He still wasn't happy with the plan of entering the house with Emma, offer to do the trade for his mother, and lure Luis outside somehow, where Myers' men could close in and take him into custody without using violence.

The whole thing was a terrible idea and he believed it

would be better if he went alone rather than putting Emma in danger as well, but she'd agreed with Myers and said she was going whether Rob liked it or not. He had no choice.

When they arrived, he gave her his spare, unloaded gun and showed her how to hold it. Fear filled her eyes, but she bravely swallowed it down. Before he got out, he instructed her to stay put, but she didn't listen and got out of the car and followed him.

Although he couldn't see them, he knew that Myers and an armed team were surveilling the house. If he had the time to look, he'd spot the cars and possibly a hidden sniper or two. He had to hand it to Myers, the man had assembled his team and got them into position within minutes of Rob's frantic phone call.

He cautiously approached Emma's front door trying not to think what he might find inside.

Please God, he prayed fervently, *keep both my mother and Emma safe. I don't care about myself, but please, give them Your protection, I beg of You.* He'd never felt so in need of the Lord's intervention as he did now.

"Luis?" he yelled through the door. "It's Officer Carlton. I have Emma Humphries with me. You need to bring Jean Carlton out."

Movement sounded inside, then Luis called through the door, "I'm not stupid." He all but growled, sounding even more unhinged. "Bring her in here."

"I'm not going to do that, Luis, at least not until I see that my mother's safe," Rob called back, fighting to keep calm and not just kick the door down and rescue his mum. Thankfully, his years of training were serving him well, helping him to maintain calm. Eli was at the station under the watchful eyes of Jerry and Johnson. His hot-headed younger brother wouldn't be able to keep his cool in this situation.

"I'm not coming out," Luis yelled back.

Rob swallowed his frustration. He'd expected this. "Okay, Luis, I'm coming in, but Miss Humphries is going to wait out here for now, okay? I need to see that my mum is safe and well."

There was a pause while Luis clearly thought through his options. "Come into the hallway," he yelled eventually, "but with your hands up. And I want to hear the snitch."

"I'm here," Emma yelled.

"Stay out of the doorway, and don't follow me," Rob told her, nudging the door. It pushed open. He stepped inside and held his hands up. His gun was in his holster. He was quick, but would he be quick enough if he needed to use it? Luis stood at the other end of the hall, his own gun to Jean's head.

Rob's insides roiled with fear. She seemed unhurt, however, and although clearly shaken, she seemed less terrified than Rob would have expected. "Are you all right?" he asked, trying not to betray emotion in front of her captor.

"As much I can be," she replied. "I've been telling Luis that he doesn't need to do this. This isn't the way. God will forgive him."

Rob stared at her. This was hardly the time for evangelism, yet she seemed completely sincere. He glanced at Luis. The man looked pale and clammy, and his eyes were unfocused. Blood seeped through his clothes from where the wound in his leg must have re-opened. He was clearly in a bad way, and this would only make him more volatile and unpredictable.

"Higher," Luis snapped.

Rob complied and raised his hands higher. "Let her go, Luis," he said quietly, "and we can talk about this. None of this needs to happen. I promise you—the deal's still on. Let my mother go and there won't be any further charges."

"Of course not," his mother agreed soothingly. "I've been telling Luis that he needs to get back to the hospital. He doesn't look well at all."

Luis blinked, looking disorientated. Rob wondered if it was from his withdrawal or his mother's calmness, which was surprising him, too. Really, his mother was an amazing woman.

"This is a trick," Luis snarled.

"It isn't," Rob promised. "Miss Humphries is outside, but you don't need her, Luis."

"Not good enough," he said, shaking his head, his gun still pointing dangerously at Jean. "I want her to retract her witness statement. She made a mistake. It wasn't me she saw."

"Okay," Rob said agreeably, although the request was pointless since he'd already confessed.

"You're lying," Luis snarled. He looked almost feral. He was very close to the edge. If Rob showed any anger, or fear, matters would escalate quickly, but keeping his emotions in check when the man had his mother at his mercy felt like more than he could bear. His gaze flicked to his mother's, and although she was obviously scared, there was a serenity in her gaze that immediately humbled him.

Rob prayed silently. *Lord, give me strength.*

A sense of certainty rushed into him, the feeling that somehow all would be okay. He looked Luis dead in the eye. "Luis," he said quietly but firmly, "you know this won't end well for you if you continue. Let my mother go and we can talk, you and me. I'll throw my gun on the floor. I can get the deal back on the table for you, as long as nobody gets hurt."

Luis' eyes flashed wildly, and for a moment Rob felt sympathy for him, in spite of the situation. He thought of

Rick, and wondered what happened to men like these to make them who they were, so far from God's plan for them.

"How do I know I can trust you?" Luis' eyes narrowed, but there was a ring of hope in his voice.

"Because right now I'm your best, in fact, your only, chance of getting out of this."

"I could run, and take her with me," Luis threatened.

Rob didn't reply, and after a few moments, Luis sagged with defeat. "I'm surrounded, aren't I?"

Again, Rob didn't answer. For a long, terrible moment, they all stood still, Rob and his mother holding their breaths, waiting for Luis' next move. Then he let her go and pushed her forward. "Go," he said.

Slowly, carefully, she walked past Rob and towards the front door, pausing only to murmur, "God keep you safe," as she passed him.

Rob's arms ached from still being in the air. He turned to Luis. "Okay, I'll throw down my gun, and you put yours back in your belt, and we'll sit down and talk, okay? We'll negotiate with Myers." He was taking a risk, but he'd rather he was Luis' hostage than his mother or Emma.

Slowly, Luis nodded and started lowering his gun while Rob carefully reached for his.

Afterwards, Rob never knew what spooked the man, whether he saw movement through the open door, or it was simply his paranoia from the drug withdrawal, but suddenly he whipped his gun back up and pointed it straight at Rob with the clear intention of shooting him in the head. Rob reached for the gun in his holster, even while knowing he might not be fast enough.

A shot rang out behind him from one of the snipers. Luis crumpled to the floor, clutching what had been his uninjured thigh. As officers rushed in behind him, Rob ran out the door to where his mother and Emma stood on the front lawn, holding each other and sobbing with relief. He threw his arms around them both, clutching them to him.

"It's over," he said, praising God in his heart. "It's all over."

At some point, he was never sure when, his mother stepped away and it was just him and Emma hugging. He looked down at her, and their gazes met, and something passed between them that he could no longer deny.

"Finally," his mother said, a grin on her face as she looked from one to the other.

EPILOGUE - SIX MONTHS LATER

Emma checked her hair in the mirror and grabbed her purse as a car horn beeped outside. It would be Rob. She hadn't seen him all week, and anticipation fizzed in her stomach like it did every time she saw him. His smile still made her weak at the knees, and sometimes she had to remind herself that she was dating Eastbrooke's most handsome and former eligible bachelor. And not only was he also a town hero after the events of six months ago, but he also seemed to utterly adore her. For someone who professed to once having been too scared to get past more than a few dates with a girl, he'd surprised the whole town with his commitment to her, and the way that he so clearly cherished her.

Even so, in the past few weeks she'd begun to wonder if their relationship was stalling. They'd established a familiar routine of date night on Friday, going to Max and Junia's on Saturday, and lunch at Jean's after church on Sunday. Sometimes he'd pop round for dinner in the evening if he finished at the station early enough. It was a routine that had taken a few months to build. After that awful afternoon when Luis had taken Jean hostage, it had been obvious to everyone they had feelings for one another, and so their relationship had begun, slowly at first, dating only once a week. After such a traumatic time, she'd needed the space and time to go slowly, and he'd respected that.

His commitment to his faith had grown, too. Just as he'd let down the barriers he'd erected against committing to a relationship, the barriers around his heart had slipped away as well. Over the course of the last few months, she'd found it inspiring to watch his faith and trust in the Lord grow stronger with each day.

So, she was definitely very happy…but a part of her couldn't help wondering…what next? He'd told her he loved her, and she believed him, but there'd been no real talk of future plans as they enjoyed taking things day by day. Did he see a future with her? Maybe even marriage one day? She was scared to raise the subject in case she ignited his old fears around commitment.

Help me not to be impatient, Lord, she prayed, *and trust that things will happen in Your time, and as You decree.*

Feeling better for having handed it over to God, she left the house and went to the car, smiling as Rob jumped out to open the door for her.

"You look beautiful," he said, his eyes admiring.

"Thank you." She felt her cheeks blush a little. She'd had her hair done that afternoon and was wearing a new, pale-green wrap dress that matched her colouring perfectly. She felt pretty, and with the admiration in Rob's eyes, she felt beautiful.

"Where are we going?" she asked. She was sure they must have exhausted every spot in Eastbrooke over the past few months.

"I thought we'd go back to the restaurant where we had our first proper date," he said as he strapped in and drove off. He seemed both distracted and fidgety, nothing obvious, but not quite his usual easy going self.

"Did you have a tough day at the station?" she asked sympathetically. Johnson had finally retired two months ago and Rob had been made Chief at just thirty, a huge honour, and the ambition he'd held since childhood was finally realised. She was incredibly proud of him.

"Same old, really. Things are pretty quiet."

"Oh." Maybe she was imagining things, but by the time they reached the restaurant, he seemed even more on edge, even nearly spilling the water as he poured her a glass.

"Are you sure everything's okay?"

"I'm just tired," he said with an apologetic smile, but he seemed more nervous than tired.

Finally, after dinner, she discovered what was causing his nerves. After the waitress took their plates, he fixed Emma with a steadfast gaze while nibbling his bottom lip, and took her hand over the table. "There's something I need to ask you," he said, his voice low.

She held her breath, hardly daring to hope. "Yes?"

He slid out of his chair and onto one knee in front of her.

She was crying happy tears even before he had the chance to open the small box he'd pulled from his pocket. He opened it to reveal a beautiful sapphire and diamond engagement ring.

"Emma Humphries," he said, gazing into her eyes, "I love you so much. You're the only woman I've ever loved and I want to spend the rest of my life with you. I know this is soon, but Emma…will you marry me?"

She threw her arms around his neck while the other

diners in the restaurant burst into applause. "Yes," she gasped through happy tears. "Of course, I will!"

A little later, as Rob drove her home, he asked if it was okay to drop by his mother's house.

Emma raised a brow and chuckled. "She knows, doesn't she?"

He grinned sheepishly. "Yes. And she'll be chomping at the bit to know what you said. Err, I think Max, Junia and Joseph will be there too. Mum might have made a cake."

Emma laughed, shaking her head. "No wonder you didn't suggest dessert. But what if I'd said no?"

"Well, I guess they would have all been there to commiserate with me."

As they walked into his mother's house, everyone piled into the hallway smiling. Emma held out her hand to show them the ring amidst cheers and whoops of congratulations.

Junia hugged her, looking as excited as Emma felt. "I can't wait to have a sister-in-law. And Polly can't wait to have an aunt." Polly had been born a few months before, and was the cutest little thing.

Emma felt even more overjoyed, if that was possible. God was good, and she'd never felt more thankful.

They shifted into the kitchen. The gigantic cake Jean had made adorned the table. "You've really outdone yourself," Emma said with a laugh. "There's enough here to feed the five thousand."

Jean's generosity never failed to warm Emma's heart. The woman seemed to have an abundance of love and there was not an ounce of bitterness in her heart. After Luis had been sent to prison, albeit for a reduced time given the information he'd passed on that had allowed the smuggling ring to be apprehended, Jean had requested to write to him, and now she did so regularly. Luis was reading the Bible and visiting the prison chaplain, something Emma doubted would have happened without Jean's unconditional forgiveness. She was thrilled to gain this woman as a mother-in-law, not to mention three brothers-in-law, a sister-in-law and a niece!

Max gave her a warm hug, and then announced that he was going to phone Eli to give him the good news. Eli was away in Melbourne taking a counter-terrorism training course. The events earlier in the year had convinced him he wanted to be more than a cop in a small town, and so he was following his dreams. Jean was worried he was on a revenge quest, but only time would tell. "It's in God's hands," she said.

Joseph was the next one to congratulate them, pulling Rob and Emma together in a hug. "I'm so pleased for you both," he said.

"Aren't you dating yet?" Rob teased. "You're the next in line, you know."

Max clapped Joseph on the back. "That's right, little brother," he said with a wide grin. "I wonder what God has in store for you?"

Joseph shrugged. "We'll see," he said simply.

Emma smiled, a wave of peace settling over her. They *would* see, in time, what God had in store for all of them, and while she may not know exactly what the future held, there was one thing she knew for certain.

God did.

> *Hear my cry, O God;*
> *listen to my prayer.*
> *From the ends of the earth I call to You,*
> *I call as my heart grows faint;*
> *lead me to the rock that is higher than I.*
> *For You have been my refuge,*

a strong tower against the foe.
I long to dwell in Your tent forever
and take refuge in the shelter of Your wings.
For You, God, have heard my vows;
You have given me the heritage of those who fear Your name.
Then I will ever sing in praise of Your name
and fulfill my vows day after day.

WITHIN HIS SIGHT

PROLOGUE

Holly, Makayla and Joseph wove their way carefully down the mountain slope. With only a torch and moonlight to guide their path, they couldn't hurry, although Holly felt the urge to do so. The further she got from that place, the better.

Halfway down, the sound of twigs snapping came from behind. They stopped. Listened. *Someone was following*.

Heart pounding, Holly turned around slowly, although she already knew who it was. It was too late to escape. Karl stood there, gun raised and pointed at them. With the moonlit shadows dancing behind him, he looked the epitome of evil, not the holier than thou leader of the Pure Light commune she'd been staying at undercover for the past several weeks.

Joseph stepped forward, spreading his arms as though trying to shield her and Makayla.

Karl jerked the gun so that it pointed directly at Joseph. "One more move, Carlton," he sneered, his eyes glittering dangerously, "and I'll shoot."

Crackling came from the radio in Joseph's hand. *Was someone trying to get through?* Holly thought she could hear a voice.

Please, Lord, please let someone hear us and know we need help.

"Put the gun down," Joseph ordered loudly but calmly. But was it loud enough for someone on the other end to hear? The radio crackled again.

Karl's gaze momentarily shifted to it. "Get rid of it." He nodded towards the bushes, his voice quiet but menacing.

When Joseph hesitated, Karl jerked the gun aggressively towards Holly.

Joseph tossed the radio, and any hope Holly had of getting out of there alive sunk in her chest like a stone.

Karl was going to kill them. And up here on the mountain, who would ever know? Their bodies might not be found for days. Or months. Or years.

Joseph raised his hands. When he spoke, his voice was even, but Holly was close enough to see the pulse throbbing in his neck. "Let the girls go," he said. "They're no use to you. You and I can sort things out between us—man to man."

Holly shook her head even as admiration for his bravery rushed through her. After everything she'd been through, she couldn't bear to lose Joseph now.

"Do you think I'm stupid, Carlton?" Karl sneered. "They'll go straight to the police—to your brother, no doubt. It must be so hard for you to know that you're powerless to protect your little friend. Not quite the hero now, are you?"

Holly sensed Joseph flinch, but he didn't outwardly react to Karl's words. Beside her, Makayla sobbed, the sound cutting pitifully across the otherwise silent mountainous terrain.

Karl's gaze pivoted to her, although his gun was trained firmly on Holly. "I'll deal with you later," he threatened.

Makayla cringed, her entire posture seeming to collapse under his words.

Then Karl turned his attention back to Holly, and the hatred in his eyes was so palpable, she gasped.

"As for you," he spat, "there's only one way to deal with traitors."

"Don't touch her," Joseph ordered through gritted teeth. "Or I swear I'll hunt you down until the end of your days."

Karl tipped his head back and laughed raucously, the evil sound reverberating around the mountain making Holly shudder from head to foot. She closed her eyes, grasping for a comforting phrase from the Bible to calm her panicked thoughts, but suddenly, comfort seemed far away as Karl's laughter continued to echo.

"Oh, don't worry, Carlton," Karl continued to taunt. "You'll be with her. I hope you really love this mountain, because I'm going to make sure you're buried here forever."

A long, ominous silence followed. Karl continued to point his gun steadily at Holly, sneering silently at Joseph as though challenging him to do something.

But there was nothing he could do.

There was no escape.

CHAPTER 1

&

Three weeks earlier

"We'll have to walk the last mile or so." Sally turned to Holly, her eyes gleaming. "The Jeep can't get that far up the mountain. You'll be alright with your luggage, won't you?"

"Of course," Holly murmured. She had no choice but to be alright. Although Sally had told her to travel light, her rucksack was filled to the brim. *You won't need much up at the commune,* Sally had said. *We live simply there.* Still, Holly had gone out and bought too many new clothes since nothing in her wardrobe was particularly suitable for life on a mountain commune that had only one generator, no television, and zero gadgets.

Her smartphone with its small solar battery was tucked in her cami under her loose shirt where she hoped it wouldn't be seen. She'd been too worried about being searched to put it in her pack. Phones were banned at the commune, and if the leaders discovered why she needed hers, then she'd be banned, too. A shiver of excitement at being this close to a big story ran through her, but close on its heels came a chill. The group seemed benign, but if the rumours were true, she was placing herself in danger for the sake of her career. She hoped it was worth the risk.

She loved her career as a journalist, and with her parents having moved abroad and her fiancé having left her for someone else—a supposed friend—nearly a year ago, her career provided her only purpose right now. The thought of a big story, one that would propel her to the national papers, kept her awake at night with excitement.

She only hoped she was right about this one, or she was in for a boring few weeks.

Pure Light was a small but rapidly growing New Religious Movement that called themselves radical Christians and quoted the Bible, but it was nothing like the Anglicanism she'd grown up with, and she was still trying to figure out exactly what Pure Light's rather vague theology was, other than believing in a back to basics and close to nature lifestyle, away from the temptations of the modern world. They'd been described by one magazine which had covered them as Australia's version of the Amish, albeit without the use of wagons. But there was nothing primitive about Sally's Jeep.

Then there were the rumours, which every story about the group had mentioned, but which the members vehemently denied and there seemed to be no concrete evidence for that. Pure Light was, under the surface, a white supremacist group, with links to suspected domestic terrorists. Holly's editor at The Post, William Long, knowing that her hunches usually worked out, had agreed for her to get close to the group, but he hadn't been too impressed about paying her wages while she disappeared up a mountain, near the little town of Eastbrooke. *What if it turns out to be nothing, and they're just a bunch of hippies?* he'd grumbled, but Holly wouldn't let it go. After attending Pure Light's small church in the city twice a week and being thoroughly love bombed by everyone there, especially Sally, she was convinced that the rumours were true and something more sinister was going on, although she couldn't really explain why. Everyone was just a little too nice, a little too sincere, and there was an emphasis on spiritual purity that simply seemed, well, off. She was certain she was right.

If she were wrong, William wouldn't give her another chance at a big story like this for a long time. If ever.

"Right," Sally said, cutting through Holly's thoughts, "this is as far as we can go. I'll park up by these trees and we'll get going. We need to hurry to get there before dark."

Holly climbed out of the Jeep, hoisted her rucksack on her shoulders, and followed Sally through the suddenly dense thicket of trees. The path was steep, and before long, her thigh muscles burned. As the sun sank over the mountain and daylight disappeared fast, a sense of foreboding came over her.

However, when they emerged from the thicket, she gasped. The view was amazing. The sky, blood orange, bled bright against the grey and green of the mountain. Her gaze dropped to the valley below where the small town of Eastbrooke twinkled in the semi-dark. They were higher up the mountain than she'd thought.

"Beautiful, isn't it?" Sally said, her eyes gleaming again. There was something odd about the almost rapturous expression on her face.

Holly hugged her arms around herself, suddenly wondering if she'd bitten off more than she could chew.

"It's so unspoiled up here, so pure," Sally said. That word again.

"It is stunning," Holly agreed. "What's the town like?"

"We won't be going down there," Sally said, so sharply that Holly blinked. "We built this place so we had somewhere that was clean and close to God, not polluted like most places these days. You won't need to leave the commune. Everything you need is there. Come on." She turned on her heel and continued at a brisk pace.

With her rucksack weighing heavily on her back, Holly struggled to keep up. She lost her footing several times as she scampered over loose rocks. She wasn't taking enough care. But how could she? Sally's abrupt change of mood had disorientated her. Somehow, when Sally talked about pollution, Holly felt certain she wasn't talking out of concern for the environment. A shiver ran through her and she rubbed her arms.

Sally glanced over her shoulder. The sharpness had disappeared, replaced with her usual, almost motherly, concern. "We're nearly there, you'll see it in a minute," she said. "It'll be bedtime when we arrive—we sleep and wake with the sun—but I'll make sure you get something to eat. And I'll introduce you to our Head Pastor, Karl. He's looking forward to meeting you."

"And I'm looking forward to meeting him," Holly responded with genuine enthusiasm. She'd unearthed very little about Karl Hawthorne, the leader of Pure Light, but what rumours there were about the group tended to circulate around him. Yet, all her investigative skills had turned up nothing about his background or upbringing. Nothing.

Which meant his name wasn't Karl Hawthorne. Of course, it was hardly unusual for cult leaders to adopt a new name, but one as ordinary and unassuming as 'Karl

Hawthorne?' No, she was sure that could only mean he was deliberately hiding his identity. If there was a story, it rotated around this mysterious man.

The compound came into sight, and it was as basic as Holly had expected. There was a long, open-ended hall she guessed was used for meetings or dining, probably both, and a series of small timber cabins. There was also a chicken coop and a goat. Surrounded by the backdrop of the woods and the mountain, with the now pink sunset casting its rosy glow over everything, it looked wholesome enough.

Sally led her to a small cabin and drew out a large chain of keys from her extra deep pocket. "Here you go. Since you're new, I've given you one of the smaller rooms. Most of us share in bunks of up to six, apart from married couples, of course."

"How many members are here?" Holly asked.

"About sixty; it's one of our smaller places. We have larger communes that cater to families." Sally opened the door and waved Holly in, turning on the solitary light bulb that hung naked from the ceiling of the tiny cabin. "You'll be sharing with Makayla who arrives tomorrow. She's a city girl, too. I'm sure you'll get on."

"Right," Holly said as she took in her surroundings with dismay. The cabin was a far cry from her well-equipped, modern apartment back home. The room contained one bunk bed with thin mattresses covered with rough looking blankets, a dresser and one chair. And it smelled musty.

"The toilet's through there." Sally pointed to an internal door. "The shower block is down the slope behind the dinner hall. Ladies shower in the morning after breakfast, men in the evening. We don't have much electricity, so it's important to stick to times."

"Gotcha." Holly tossed her rucksack onto the bottom

bunk and let out a weary sigh. It had been a long day, but lugging the heavy pack up that mountain had all but done her in. Plus, she was starving. Hopefully Sally hadn't forgotten her offer of food, because the cabin was bare.

"Come and meet Karl, and then I'll get you something to eat."

Relieved, Holly followed her across the compound which was eerily quiet. Where was everybody? Surely they weren't all in bed already, although Sally did say they woke and went to sleep with the sun. It wasn't quite six p.m. How would she ever grow accustomed to this? She wasn't a night owl, but six p.m.? That was ridiculously early to be in bed.

Sally led her to a larger cabin which was slightly set back from the others. Not only was it larger, but it also had a small wooden porch. Clearly, the leader of the group wasn't expected to live as simply as his followers. Sally knocked on the door almost timidly, and Holly noticed how the woman put her head down, her whole posture changing from that of someone in charge to someone submissive. It was such an immediate and obvious change that Holly frowned. Was Sally scared of Karl? She'd never spoken of him with anything but reverence, but this change was significant.

"Come in," a rich, deep voice called.

Holly followed her inside. Karl's cabin was far nicer, and warmer, than her basic one. A fire crackled in an open fireplace; there was a comfy looking sofa, and a double bed with a plump quilt, probably down. A large rug covered the floor, and a small kitchenette lined one wall. Her gaze was drawn to a large picture of a very blond-haired and blue-eyed Jesus hanging on the wall, but her attention quickly turned to Karl himself.

Tall and well-built with a healthy tan, dark hair and dazzlingly white teeth, his presence could only be described as commanding. There was a natural arrogance to him, and as he held out his hand, Holly wouldn't have been surprised if he expected her to kiss it, as one did with royalty. She shook it, trying not to wince at the strength of his grip.

"Welcome," he said. His gaze was so piercing that she was tempted to look away.

"Nice to meet you," she replied, trying to smile but feeling suddenly claustrophobic in the cabin with him towering over her and Sally hovering at her side. "I'm Holly."

"Oh, I know who you are," he said, staring at her so intensely she wondered if he knew her true identity. Not Holly Smith, retail assistant, but Holly Davidson, aspiring investigative reporter. Her mouth went dry. Surely her cover wasn't blown already.

"I hope you'll enjoy your time here, Holly," he went on. "Most people do. It's a retreat from this fallen and broken world, a taste of what is to come—God's kingdom on earth. Most people never want to go back. If you decide you want to be part of our family, we'll baptise you into Pure Light. Your life will never be the same again."

His words were warm, and he was smiling, but a chill ran through her, nevertheless. Her smile felt frozen on her face. "Thank you so much for having me," she gabbled. "I can't wait to, err, get to know you all and learn more."

"Good." He gave a nod and turned his attention to Sally, effectively dismissing her.

"I'll be giving a sermon in the morning, before breakfast. Make sure the hall is ready."

"Of course, Pastor," Sally replied so reverently Holly expected her to curtsey.

"That will be all." He turned, walked to the fire and rubbed his hands. It seemed they were both dismissed.

Holly felt dazed as she followed Sally outside.

"He's wonderful, isn't he?" Sally gushed, her eyes gleaming again as she led Holly to the large hall.

Holly nodded, hoping Sally couldn't read her thoughts. She didn't find Karl wonderful at all. In fact, she found him intimidating. Scary, even.

After handing her a pre-made egg and lettuce sandwich, Sally accompanied her back to her cabin and handed her a key. "Sleep well, Holly."

She smiled. "Thank you. I'm sure I will."

Left alone, she devoured the sandwich and quickly changed into her pyjamas before crawling into her bunk, her head whirling and her body shivering. Although the blankets felt rough to the touch, they were heavy, and hopefully warm. She curled her body under the blankets and wrapped them tightly around her. Finally, she stopped shivering.

Reaching for her phone, she turned it on, and under the cover of the blankets so no light would be emitted, she texted William to let him know she'd arrived safely. She then turned it back off and slipped it inside the pillowcase.

A few moments later, an owl hooted near the window and made her jump. She was a city girl, used to traffic noise, not owls hooting. As she pulled the blankets tighter, she wondered what other creatures might be up here on the mountain. Foxes? Snakes? Dingoes? Spiders? *Why had she come?*

Sleep eluded her. Sometime later, as she lay on her back, staring at the ceiling, she thought through the events of the day. So far there was nothing to raise any serious flags, but it was too soon to tell. They wouldn't want to scare newcomers away. Yet, as she reflected on what both Karl and Sally had said, she again sensed a more sinister meaning behind their words. All Sally's talk about cleanliness and purity might not mean anything. Those weren't bad things, but her hostility towards the town below had seemed out of place for someone Holly had only ever heard preach about love and light back home.

As for Karl...his words about the kingdom of God were the sort of thing one could expect to hear from a preacher, yet Holly felt certain he had his own interpretation, one that wasn't in line with the Bible.

If only she could remember exactly what it said.

She'd been raised a Christian, and as a child, she'd attended church every Sunday, but as a young adult at college and then during her apprenticeship, her attendance had fallen away. She believed in God, but she didn't feel she truly understood her faith and often wished she'd paid more attention at church. Especially now.

She'd gone a few times with Chad, her ex-fiancé, but those memories were bitter ones now, and besides, she'd been attending more to please him more than anything else.

Although she'd stopped overtly practicing in many ways, she'd never *not* believed and had always tried to live by the Christian values her parents had taught her. It had been important to save herself, in the intimate sense, until marriage, and when at twenty-one she'd met Chad, she'd been pleased when he felt the same.

Once they were engaged, that all changed. He'd begun pressuring her for more, and it had become a bone of contention between them until one day she discovered he was being unfaithful. She handed his engagement ring back and took time off work, heartbroken and humiliated. She'd wasted three years of her life. Then her parents moved, and William, her boss, made it clear that she either got back to The Post or she'd be fired, and so for the past three years, she'd thrown herself into her work. She hadn't thought about God, or perhaps had deliberately chosen not to, even though her mother had encouraged her to attend church again. But she hadn't. It simply reminded her too much of Chad.

Now, though, she felt the beginnings of an old longing. For the first time in many years, she clasped her hands together and closed her eyes. As she said the Lord's prayer quietly, a familiar peace settled over her.

It was enough to allow her to drift off to sleep until she was woken by the sound of birdsong over the mountain and Sally ringing the bell for morning worship.

CHAPTER 2

Joseph sat forward in the pew and listened intently to the minister. Pastor Peter's sermons always touched him, but this morning it felt as though the older man was speaking directly to him. When his gaze fixed momentarily on Joseph's, Joseph had the uncanny feeling that the man knew exactly what effect his words had on him.

"God's calling on our lives is not always one we initially welcome," he said sombrely, the deep timbre of his voice resounding through the small chapel. "Often our Lord calls us from our safe, predictable lives into a wholly new adventure, and we may not, at first, want to respond. We may protest, as Moses did, that we're not good enough for the task He's calling us to do. Like Gideon, we may think we're not strong enough, and like him, say to God, *But I am the least in my father's house.*" The pastor paused and chuckled. "God had other ideas for Gideon, just as He may have for you."

The words reverberated inside Joseph's head and heart.

The least in my father's house... He tried to avoid the uncomfortable feelings the phrase triggered for him, touching as it did on old insecurities that logically he knew weren't true.

But since when did the human heart ever run on logic?

He shifted uncomfortably in the pew. He didn't believe in coincidences. If the sermon sounded as though it was meant for his ears, then it was, even if the pastor himself couldn't have known when he prepared it. Of course, there were others in the congregation for whom it would also resonate, but Joseph was under no illusions that God was speaking very clearly to him, and it had been happening for some time.

For the past year, he'd felt restless with his life. As the pastor had said, it was safe and predictable. Perhaps not always physically safe since he headed up Eastbrooke's Mountain Rescue team, but his life on a whole was steady, lacking emotional ups and downs. Boring, almost. After his one and only girlfriend, Terry, ended their relationship three years ago, he'd concentrated on his work and his family. Three brothers and a widowed mother meant he never felt alone. The Carltons were a close family, perhaps even more so since the brutal loss of their father and husband seventeen years earlier.

At first, he'd assumed the restlessness was due to his still being single at twenty-seven while both his older brothers were now married. The eldest, Max, had one child and another on the way, and Rob had recently returned from his honeymoon with Emma, one of the local primary school teachers. They'd all been single for so long that the changes were bound to ripple through the family.

Deep down, however, he knew that wasn't the real reason for his restlessness. He felt only happiness for his brothers, and he loved being an uncle. Neither was he looking for a relationship. His relationship had failed because Terry had accused him of putting his faith before anything else. And she was right. God came first, and trying to have a relationship with someone who didn't fully share his commitment had been a mistake. No, he was content enough to leave that aspect of his future in God's hands.

It was only now, listening to the pastor's words, that he understood truly what the feeling was.

He was being called.

He'd often thought about training to be a minister but had pushed the thoughts away. Like Moses and Gideon, his reaction had been, *Me, Lord?* He was a Carlton. The Carlton brothers were known for their toughness and strength. They were protectors and alpha males. Ministry simply didn't fit that image. Their father had been the Police Chief of Eastbrooke, and now at just thirty, Rob had taken over that role. Max lived at the bottom of the mountain where he and his wife Junia ran a wilderness retreat for teens. The youngest, Eli, was a police officer and was currently in the city training with the counter-terrorism unit, while Joseph headed up the Mountain Rescue team. It was a running joke in Eastbrooke that whatever danger you found yourself in, a Carlton brother would be there to save you. Just like their father had been.

Joseph had always loved his job, but now, it was starting to feel old. As if he should be doing something else.

But ministry?

As the pastor wound up his sermon, Joseph felt that once again he was speaking directly to him. "It is perhaps natural for us to resist God's call the first time we hear it. Maybe even the first ten times, or a hundred times. But if we're serious about being disciples of Christ, sooner or later, we must lay down our resistance. For as Jesus was recorded as saying in the Gospel of John, *'You did not choose Me, but I chose you and appointed you so that you might go and bear fruit—fruit that will last—and so that whatever you ask in My name, the Father will give you.'* We must ask ourselves, then, what have we been chosen to do? What fruit is ours to bear?"

As the sermon concluded and Pastor Peter finished with prayer, Joseph's head whirled. As everyone stood to leave, the pastor announced that he was happy to pray with anyone his sermon had touched, anyone who wanted to explore God's calling on their life.

Joseph hesitated and was about to step forward when his brother Rob came up behind him and slapped him good-naturedly on the back.

"Hey, bro! Are you coming to Mum's for lunch? There's something I need to talk to you about."

In spite of his brother's usual jovial tone, Joseph recognised the glint of concern in his eyes and nodded. Talking to the pastor would have to wait.

Sunday lunch at the Carltons happened most weeks, but it was rare that the whole family was there together given their irregular work shifts. Today, it would be just Joseph, Rob and Emma, and of course, Jean, the boys' mum. Max and Junia were visiting friends, and Eli no longer lived in Eastbrooke.

Joseph missed his little brother. As the youngest, they were close, even though in many ways they were like chalk and cheese. Joseph was quiet and reflective whereas Eli could be a hothead, acting before he thought; Joseph was devout,

CHAPTER 2 | 271

and Eli was most emphatically not. In fact, he was the only one of the Carltons who didn't attend church. Joseph and his mum had both tried to counsel him, but Eli had no interest in discussing faith issues, and since he was an adult now, they had to leave him to make his own choices, although they prayed for him continually.

Joseph sat opposite Rob at the large, wooden table and dug into his mother's homemade bread. "This is amazing, Mum," he said appreciatively.

Beside him, her face lit up in a broad smile while she patted his hand. "Thank you, Joseph. You're too kind."

"I'm not, Mum. Your bread's the best. Don't you agree?" He lifted a brow at Rob and Emma who both nodded, their mouths too full of the crusty bread to say anything.

"So, what did you want to talk about?" Joseph asked Rob once he'd finished his mouthful.

Rob glanced at Emma.

She angled her head and looked at her husband pointedly. "Is this about the commune?"

He shrugged and gave an apologetic look.

She blew out a breath. "I wish you'd stop trying to protect me from every bit of news, Rob." When the pair met, it had been because she was a witness in the case that had made his career, and Rob was fiercely protective of her after everything they'd gone through together. Perhaps a bit too protective by the look on her face.

"The commune?" Joseph asked, his brows drawing together as he glanced between the pair. "I've been keeping an eye on the construction. They haven't done anything to break planning permission."

Leaning back, Rob rolled his eyes and blew out a breath. "I'm not bothered about that. It's what they *are* that bothers me."

"Aren't they just back-to-basic types?" Joseph frowned. As someone who loved the mountain and had grown up going on wilderness camps with his brothers, he could understand the appeal of giving up modern life to live closer to nature.

"Well, that's what I thought, but now they've moved in, it seems they're actually a cult called Pure Light. Heard of them?" Rob asked.

Joseph shook his head, bemused. The word 'cult' made him think of weird temples and bright robes. "Are they New Agers?"

Rob shook his head grimly. "Christians, or so they say. Rumour is they're anything but. I need to speak to Eli and see if he's heard anything about them."

Joseph frowned again. This might be more serious than he thought. "What's the rumour?"

"That they're white supremacists." A muscle flicked angrily in Rob's jaw.

Joseph felt his mother stiffen. It had been a neo-Nazi group that had planted the bomb that killed their father. A shiver went through him. "Really? White supremacists, up on the mountain?"

"There may be links, that's all I know." Rob shrugged and leaned forward. "It doesn't mean they're dangerous. They could simply be separatists and be keeping themselves to themselves, but it's something we need to be aware of." He paused, toying with his glass of water. "I was wondering if you could keep an eye on them?"

"Of course." Joseph nodded. "I was planning on going up there anyway to introduce myself and to let them know we're there in case anything happens. It's easy to get lost on the mountain. I'll keep my eyes and ears peeled."

"Thanks." Rob gave a grateful nod and then turned his

attention to the chicken Caesar salad their mum had just placed on the table.

As she and Emma started chatting about recipes, Joseph stared out the window. It was a sunny day, and yet a chill went through him. That group on the mountain was bad news, he just knew it.

CHAPTER 3

Holly pulled her blankets tighter and tried to shut out the annoying ringing of a bell. She was drifting off again when someone banged on the door. She groaned and opened one eye. It was still dark. Where was she? And what was the banging? And then she remembered... she was at the commune, and Sally had told her everyone rose at dawn. Groaning again, she dragged herself out of bed and yawned. Why had she thought this was a good idea?

Flicking on the measly light, she quickly changed out of her pyjamas and slipped on a sleeveless vest and a long skirt. Women weren't to be seen in their night attire, so Sally had also told her. But where was her cardigan?

Another bang, louder than before, sounded on the door. "Holly, time to rise." It was Sally, and her tone was officious.

Holly reached for the door and opened it, trying her best to summon a bright smile while she rubbed her arms briskly.

Sally's gaze travelled over her attire. "I hope you have something more modest to put on."

Holly blinked. Her vest was neither low-cut nor especially tight. "Yes. I was about to put on a cardigan," she replied defensively.

"See that you do," Sally snapped. "We prefer women not to have bare arms here. There are a lot of single men—and married ones, too. Come to the hall when you're finished. Karl's giving a message before breakfast." Her tone was more cheerful as she said those last words, as if Karl speaking was the best thing that could happen at this time of day.

Holly nodded, trying not to show the offence she felt at Sally's comment. Thank goodness she'd bought new clothes for the trip. Wanting to fit in with the way she'd seen the other women from Pure Light dress, she'd bought plenty of long skirts and blouses. She hadn't anticipated her attire being policed in this manner, though.

After finding her cardigan, she brushed her teeth in the sink and plaited her long hair before leaving the cabin, satisfied she looked suitably wholesome.

The crisp, morning air embraced her as she stepped outside. Shivering, she pulled her wool cardigan tighter. The scent of pine needles and smoke hung in the air, and a thick layer of mist covered the valley below. The early morning twitter of birds rang through the trees. She smiled. Now she was up, it was actually quite lovely and peaceful. A pity she needed to go inside and listen to a message. But that's what she was here for.

Reaching the open-ended hall, she looked longingly around for coffee but was sadly disappointed. The only refreshment on offer was water. She took a glass and hovered at the entrance, discretely eying those already inside. There was a uniformity in appearance that was unsettling. The men were all clean shaven with closely cropped hair and casual clothes, khakis and T-shirts, mainly. They were hardly stereotypical neo-Nazis. The women, like herself and Sally, wore long sleeves and skirts, and were make-up free. Those with husbands hovered at their sides demurely with their eyes cast down. A few wore head scarfs, knotted neatly under their chins. There was nothing particularly sinister looking about any of them. They were simply very traditional, but Holly couldn't stifle a creeping uneasiness. Especially when they all gazed expectantly at the stage, waiting for their pastor.

Pastor, she thought wryly, *or guru?*

She perched on a bench seat towards the rear. Moments later, Karl appeared, striding purposefully onto the stage. He wore a white shirt and beige cargo pants that set off his dark hair, and his presence was immediately commanding, just as it had been the night before. He was obviously charismatic and a natural leader. Qualities that could be used for tremendous good—or tremendous evil.

He welcomed the newcomers, which included pointing them out, and Holly was soon surrounded by the other women greeting and hugging her. They all seemed genuinely pleased to meet her and have her with them, and it was hard not to be touched by their hospitality and genuine joy in welcoming a stranger. This was more like the church she remembered.

By the time Karl started his message, she felt relaxed and genuinely interested in what he would say. Perhaps she'd gotten this group all wrong.

Even so, the reporter in her listened carefully to his words, waiting for anything that might betray more nefarious motives. If only she had a way of taking notes rather than relying on her memory when she was barely awake. There was nothing, however, that seemed to be a major cause for concern. His voice was almost hypnotic, and his congregation listened intently. He was passionate about his subject, telling the story of the Israelites journeying to the promised land, trusting God for their nourishment. Holly couldn't help but feel inspired.

Only towards the end did he say something that set off her internal alarm bells—a dissonant beat in what had otherwise seemed like a genuine sermon.

"The Israelites came out of Egypt," he boomed, "just as we at Pure Light have been called out of the world. Called away from the corruption of the Egyptians. We have to ask ourselves, who are the Egyptians today? God's chosen people were one people, one race, and God wanted them to stay that way. There were divine penalties for those who did not keep the blood pure."

Holly's skin crawled and she had to try hard to keep nodding and smiling along with the others, who didn't seem alarmed at all by what he'd just said.

This wasn't the Christianity she remembered from going to church with her parents. What happened to the story of Ruth, who joined the Hebrews? Or the Good Samaritan? Or the commission of Christ Himself to take His message to all the corners of the world? This was a perversion, and Holly felt sick.

On her very first day, she had gained proof that her hunch was true, but her first reaction wasn't one of excitement at getting her story.

Instead, her stomach clenched in alarm.

MAKAYLA, the girl Holly was to share her cabin with, arrived early that evening while Holly was freshening up for dinner. She'd spent all day in the women's study group run by Sally, which seemed to be obligatory, and she felt drained. There'd been no more mention of race, but rather a lecture on the correct roles for women, which seemed to consist of having as many babies as possible and being quiet. Everything was more intense than the weekly meetings she'd infiltrated back home, and although she was here undercover, after several hours, the shaming messages Sally was doling out had started to upset her. She'd kept quiet in the group but had battled to keep her anxiety at bay. It had been a relief when the sessions were finally over.

There'd been no lunch, either. "We fast through midday," Sally had told her. "Breakfast and supper only. You'll get used to it."

The alarm bells were coming thick and fast. Keeping members tired and hungry, policing their dress and thoughts…Holly knew enough to know that this was typical cult behaviour, but she hadn't been prepared for how it would make her feel. She wanted nothing more than to abandon the story, go home and cover a local fashion show or something similarly innocuous.

I can't give up, she told herself firmly. *This could make or break my career.*

She'd laid her phone on the windowsill in the sun to charge and nearly jumped out of her skin when female voices sounded outside the door. One belonged to Sally, the other would be her new roommate. She quickly stashed the phone back inside her pillowcase, her heart thumping as the door opened. She plastered what she hoped was a welcoming smile on her face, although it felt more like a grimace.

"I hope I haven't interrupted your personal prayer time," Sally said, raising an eyebrow.

Holly bit her lip. The free time before supper was supposed to be spent in prayer. "Not at all," she said, raising her chin.

Sally's gaze narrowed before she ushered the young woman inside. "Holly, this is Makayla. I'm sure you two will get on well together." Her voice was matter-of-fact, not friendly at all.

The young woman couldn't be much more than twenty, although it was hard to tell. She was very pretty, with dark wavy hair and huge green eyes. The grin she gave Holly was infectious. "Nice to meet you, Sister," she said, greeting her the way Pure Light members did.

"You too, Sister." Holly gave a warm smile, but all the while wondered how she'd ever be able to use her phone while cooped up with this girl in such a small cabin.

"Well, I'll leave you two to get to know each other," Sally said. "Maybe you can pray together." She left, closing the door behind her.

"So, where have you come from?" Makayla asked, her gaze travelling around the cabin.

Holly gave the practiced version of her backstory. "From the city. I was searching and found Pure Light. How about you?"

"Oh, Sally and Karl are my cousins," the girl said.

Holly blinked. *This girl is Sally and Karl's cousin?*

"I didn't see much of them growing up," Makayla continued, "but I went to live with them when I was sixteen after my parents died."

"I'm so sorry," Holly said sincerely, but then she processed what Makayla had said. "Hang on, Karl and Sally are related?"

"They're brother and sister. Didn't you know?" Makayla's brows furrowed.

Holly shook her head. *Why hadn't Sally mentioned that?* It explained her hero worship of him, though. She must have grown up listening to him and his radical ideologies. The thought made Holly shudder. She felt sorry for the other woman even though she was growing increasingly wary of her.

"You've been a member of Pure Light for a while, then?" Holly probed. There was a vibrancy about Makayla that didn't seem to fit with the submissive nature of the other women she'd met here.

"Not at first." Makayla leaned against the bunk bed and crossed her arms. "I was away at theatre school and then university—I studied choreography. So, I've only recently started to take much notice, but I love the simplicity of Pure Light. There was a lot of crazy stuff going on at university—drugs, promiscuity, you know the score. In my final year, I just kept thinking more and more about the contrast between all that and the way Pure Light live. None of my uni friends ever really seemed happy, so," she shrugged, "I thought I may as well give it a try. And Karl's great. He's so passionate about everything."

She'd lurched from one extreme to the other. Holly looked at the girl with compassion. There was a sweetness to her that made Holly feel protective. Makayla reminded her of herself, before Chad had broken her heart and she'd thrown herself into her career.

"But don't worry," Makayla chattered on, "I won't be getting special treatment. If anything, Sally is doubly hard on me. Maybe that's why she didn't tell you that Karl's her brother, so you don't put her on a pedestal."

"Maybe," Holly murmured.

"Anyway," Makayla said, pulling her Bible from her backpack, "shall we pray? Sally's given you a Pure Light prayer guide, right?"

"Right," Holly said dully, picking her copy up from the

bed where she'd thrown it, and following Makayla's lead, she knelt down.

This was going to be a long, few weeks.

~

Walking away from the cabin, Sally clenched her fists. Karl had been right—she'd invited Holly here too soon. She wasn't ready to fully surrender to the tenets of Pure Light. Her rebellion was subtle, but it was there, nonetheless.

Karl was rarely wrong. He was a modern-day prophet, inspired by the Lord, not a wishy-washy version most people worshipped these days, those who ignored their true heritage as a people set apart, and who still mixed with the fallen, degenerative races who were beyond redemption. Sally knew better than anyone just how special a man her brother was, and she would follow him to the ends of the earth.

She wouldn't allow anyone to get in the way of Pure Light's mission. Not even her cousin Makayla, who was too flighty by half. Karl had agreed to bring her into the group because she was a family member, and Sally deferred to him as she always did, even though she personally wished that Makayla had stayed at university. Who knew what corrupted influences she'd fallen prey to while there?

Karl had placed Makayla and Holly together so Sally could keep a close eye on the pair and keep them firmly under her wing, but now she felt uneasy, worried they might corrupt each other further. She didn't know what Holly had been doing when she opened the door, but she'd looked startled, as though caught in the act of something forbidden. She certainly hadn't been praying as she'd been instructed, that was for sure.

That was insubordination, and neither she nor Karl tolerated insubordination. The time was coming when Pure Light would be instrumental in the world to come, and women like Holly would need to adhere or be thrown out.

They had a vision for the future, and no one would stand against it.

Karl would make sure of that.

CHAPTER 4

*B*alanced precariously on a ledge, with sweat trickling down his brow, Joseph looked with disdain at the sheep inching its way further up the crumbling rock face.

He'd been on his routine walk when the sound of a bleating sheep higher up the rocky mountainside caught his attention. Concerned the sheep might be in trouble, he'd scrambled after it. He should have called his partner, John, for backup, but at first glance it had seemed an easy enough task. If only the sheep had stayed put. Instead, it seemed more frightened of him than of a potentially deadly fall, and it kept going further up the rocky outcrop. Now Joseph's jacket and radio were on the ground below while he was halfway up the same crumbling ledge the silly sheep had wandered onto.

"You know I have better things to be doing," he called out loud. Lately, he seemed to be rescuing more sheep than people, and his job was becoming less than fulfilling. Not that he didn't care about the animals, but he'd never imagined when he signed up to lead the Mountain Rescue team just how much of his time would be taken up rescuing sheep.

He shook his head at the animal, which was trembling as he inched closer to it, and a wave of compassion swept through him. It was little more than a lamb, and it was God's creature, after all.

He'd just gotten within touching distance when it panicked and jumped, exactly the opposite of what he wanted it to do. The outcrop was perilous, jutting over a sheer face that dropped straight to the valley below. Fall the wrong way, and you'd plunge to your death. He grabbed for the animal but lost his footing and slipped.

His heart pounded, and for one terrifying moment, as the drop beneath loomed in his vision, he thought he was a goner. Then his hands and feet found solid ground and he clung on for dear life. Breathing heavily, he scrambled back across the ledge to safety, flopping onto the ground and sucking in a deep breath before releasing it slowly. That was way too close for comfort, and exactly why he should have called for backup. He drummed safety first into all the new trainees, yet here *he* was, taking silly risks. He huffed out another breath. He could have died, but thank God, he hadn't.

And now, the sheep stood a few feet away, eyeing him curiously. It was fine.

"You probably could have jumped down by yourself the whole time, couldn't you?" Joseph accused.

The sheep walked off and then paused to pull up some scrubby grass as if nothing had happened.

As Joseph stood, he felt both foolish and intensely grateful that he was still alive. He touched the small silver cross he wore under his clothes. "Thank you, Lord, for looking after me." The story he'd loved as a kid of the shepherd risking all to go after the one lost sheep came to mind, and he smiled wryly.

He recalled his conversation with Rob several days earlier. Maybe the people at the commune were lost sheep, too.

He needed to go there and introduce himself, and, as Rob had requested, get a feel for what was happening at the commune. He glanced at his watch. There was enough time to drop in on his way back to base. It was only a slight detour round to the other side of the mountain, which was flatter and a lot easier to navigate, making it an ideal place to set up a camp.

He got there fifteen minutes later. Not much had changed since his last visit, which was before the group had officially moved in. The structures, though basic, were sturdy and well built, and they were obviously planning on staying a while. There was already a buzz about the group down in Eastbrooke, but he doubted that buzz had reached them up here. As far as he knew, none of the commune members had set foot in town, even to restock.

As he approached what looked to be the main cabin, about twenty people milled around, all seemingly busy with various tasks. Men carried firewood and women, laundry. There appeared to be no children, which he thought odd. Weren't places like these breeding grounds?

A woman's voice, sharp and suspicious, came from behind him. "Excuse me, can I help you?"

He turned. A tall woman with sharp features and an unmistakably hostile expression stood before him. She was dressed in a long-sleeved dress that reached to her ankles. She appeared to be a similar age to him. Behind her stood two other women, one younger with unruly dark hair who looked fresh-faced and not much more than college age, and another who caught his eye immediately.

This woman's gaze was intelligent, and a sudden, unexpected warmth rushed through him. She was also beautiful. Not just physically; there was something intangible about her that called to him in a way he didn't understand. A flash of surprise in her amber eyes suggested she felt it too, and although Joseph had never seen her before, he felt as though he knew her on some deep level.

Tearing his gaze away, he smiled politely at the taller woman. He was about to explain who he was when the women's gazes shifted to something—or someone—over his shoulder. Joseph glanced around. A man, tall and dark haired and carrying an air of steely arrogance emerged from the main cabin. Warning shivers immediately spiralled down Joseph's spine. The man narrowed his eyes and approached him with a slightly menacing air, but Joseph held his gaze and lifted his chin. He was a Carlton, after all.

"You're trespassing," the man said with an undisguised snarl.

Joseph extended his hand, but the man simply stared at it without taking it. Stifling his annoyance at the man's rudeness, Joseph said, "Actually, I'm here to make sure all is well. I'm Joseph Carlton, head of the Mountain Rescue team in Eastbrooke. I wanted to give you our base location and our contact details in case you have any queries or emergencies." He rubbed his jaw, the prickle of his day-old stubble rough on his hand. "You've chosen a good spot here, but the mountains can be more treacherous than they look. It's not advisable to go walking around without knowing your way about."

"We'll be fine," the man said pompously. "We're under the protection of God."

"That's great," Joseph responded. "But even so, I think God expects us to take practical care of ourselves, and you've got quite a few people here. So, if you want to…"

The man stepped closer, his eyes dark and threatening. "Are you suggesting I can't look after my people?"

Joseph shook his head and shrugged. "Not at all. I'm simply doing my job."

"Well, thank you, but we have all the information we need. And we have no radios or phones, and only the electricity we need. We don't want communication with the outside world. If that's all?" The man angled his head and lifted a brow, effectively dismissing him.

"Yep, that's all. And please, if you're not willing to accept the help of professionals, make sure that none of your group goes wandering around out here." As Joseph turned to leave, the three women caught his attention again. The youngest was wringing her hands and looked anxious. The taller one had her arms folded and was glaring at him, clearly in agreement with the man. But the other woman, the one with the dark caramel hair and amber eyes, stood watching him with an expression he couldn't place, and immediate concern for her rushed through him. Although she was dressed in the same manner as the others, there was something about her that didn't fit. She didn't belong here.

Nodding politely at the trio, he walked off, but he sensed hostile eyes boring into his back the whole way, almost as though there was a target painted on him. When he got far enough away, he released a huge breath.

He had no idea if Rob's information about neo-Nazis was correct, but it was clear something was very wrong at that place, and the man had made his skin crawl, prickling it with warning. It wasn't the usual feeling of status rivalry that Joseph had sometimes picked up from other men, who saw his strong build and handsome features and reacted out of some kind of male need to prove themselves; this was something else entirely. This man was dangerous.

But to whom? To the people of Eastbrooke? That seemed far-fetched. But what about the people at the commune? He'd called them 'his people' in a tone that spoke more of ownership than affection.

If right, that meant the woman with the amber eyes was in danger. Joseph didn't understand the strange pull he felt towards her, but just like the pastor's sermon the previous Sunday, he knew when the Lord was trying to tell him something.

If only he knew what it was.

CHAPTER 5

Well, I can add 'hostile to outsiders' to my cult warning signs list, Holly thought as Karl glared after the man who had just introduced himself. Joseph. It was a nice name.

But it was his surname that Karl seemed more interested in. He looked at Sally and spat out the word "Carlton," as though the very shape of it left a nasty taste in his mouth.

"We knew they'd check on us," Sally said quietly.

Karl grimaced. "Yes, but we didn't expect one of them to literally be patrolling the mountain. This should have been checked out properly." His mouth took on an unpleasant twist, and his gaze darted around as though he was looking for someone to blame.

Sally visibly stiffened, although when she spoke, her voice was soothing. "He won't be a problem. We're not doing anything wrong by being here."

Karl nodded, looking somewhat mollified. "No, we're not. We're doing the Lord's work." His gaze swept over Makayla and Holly, finally settling on Holly. "And how are you finding us?"

"I love it here," she said quietly, trying to strike a balance between sounding enthusiastic about the commune and being suitably subdued, as women here seemed to be expected to present themselves.

"Good. Sally tells me you haven't been keeping to our prayer schedule?"

Holly blinked and glanced at Sally, who returned her gaze coolly, one eyebrow slightly cocked as though challenging her to complain.

"No," Holly protested, flustered. "It was just the first day… I wasn't used to my day being scheduled so much. But I'm used to it now."

"We pray together," Makayla interjected, defending Holly. "We're helping each other."

Karl gave a pleased nod. "Excellent." His gaze swung back to Holly, and it was so penetrating that a shiver ran through her. "See it doesn't happen again," he said.

"It won't," Holly promised, her mouth dry. *Was he threatening her?* It sounded that way. But with what? As he turned and sauntered away, she realised her hands were trembling.

Karl frightened her.

"Come on," Sally said briskly. "You're both on kitchen duty for the rest of the day."

"I need to go to the toilet," Holly said. It wasn't a lie; she felt sick.

"Five minutes," Sally snapped. "We'll meet you in the hall." She walked off with Makayla following, although she glanced back over her shoulder and gave Holly a look filled with sympathy.

Back at the cabin, her heart beating double time with fear of being caught, Holly turned on her phone. While she sat in the bathroom waiting for the nausea to pass, she googled Joseph Carlton's name.

At first, all that came up were the details for Mountain Rescue, which she scrolled quickly through, pausing briefly to look at Joseph's photo and remembering the strange sensation she'd felt when their gazes met. It was almost as though she knew him. There'd been a connection there that made no immediate sense to her, a pull towards him that was almost magnetic.

There was no denying he was attractive, but men and dating couldn't be further from her mind, especially here. Yet, she'd noticed Joseph Carlton in a way that made her cheeks tingle like a schoolgirl with a crush. Thankfully, neither Sally nor Karl had seemed to notice.

As she continued to speed scroll, a newspaper article from a year ago jumped out at her. It didn't mention Joseph, but it did mention the Carlton family from Eastbrooke and their late father. He'd been the Police Chief for the small town and its surrounding areas and he'd been killed in an explosion set by a terrorist group seventeen years earlier.

A white supremacist terrorist group.

Now, according to the article, his son Rob had been made Police Chief after helping to foil a smuggling ring in the mountains, whose leader had past ties to white supremacists.

No wonder Karl seemed to hate the family, which meant there had to be links. A new wave of fear trembled through her. Pure Light being a secret supremacist group was one thing, but could they have ties to international terrorism? Drug and firearms smuggling? Her stomach lurched.

This was way above her paygrade. If she had any sense, she'd get herself out of here and go home. She hadn't signed up for this level of danger.

The temptation, however, was too strong. The voice of

raw ambition reminded her that if she could get this story, then her career was made. This was important. Being the one to fully expose Pure Light would make *her* important.

No longer just the lonely woman who'd been cheated on and dumped by her fiancé, she would finally be someone.

Hearing footsteps outside, she quickly hid her phone in her cardigan, stood and flushed the chain.

"Holly? Are you okay?" It was Makayla.

Holly emerged from the bathroom, smiling weakly. "I just felt a little sick. I'm not used to working all day with no lunch."

Makayla nodded with understanding. "It's hard at first, isn't it? When we get used to it, though, we'll feel so much better; cleaner and lighter. Karl says that's how we make ourselves more receptive to messages from God. All the saints used to fast, didn't they?"

Holly nodded, recalling stories from Sunday school, including those featuring false teachers and prophets. She decided not to mention them to Makayla. She'd already drawn too much of Karl's attention to herself.

"I came after you because I wanted to say," Makayla chattered on, "don't worry too much about Karl telling you off like that. It's for our own good, and he's a great guy, really."

"I know," Holly said neutrally, although inside, she cringed. She liked Makayla, and it hurt to hear her starting to worship her cousin in the same way Sally did. Makayla seemed younger than her years and was obviously impressionable, and Holly couldn't help feeling upset at the way her older cousins—who should be looking out for her—were so clearly brainwashing her into their ideology.

"Let's go before Sally reports us," Makayla said, her eyes wide.

Holly had already noticed how anxious the young woman

was around Sally. In her own way, Sally was as intimidating as Karl.

But if Holly wanted this story, then it was precisely Sally and Karl she needed to grow close to. From now on, she'd be the perfect Pure Light member, hanging off their every word.

She followed Makayla back to the kitchen, her phone still hidden inside her cardigan, burning through the fabric with its secret knowledge.

CHAPTER 6

"Little bro! How are you?"

Joseph was pleased to hear from Eli. It had been a while. His brother was busy in Melbourne training with the counter-terrorism unit and Joseph was often busy at the Rescue Lodge on the mountain, so coordinating times when they could talk was often challenging. Even so, they tried to catch up with each other at least every few weeks.

When Eli spoke, however, he sounded grim. "I've been missing you all, but this isn't a social call."

"Oh? What's up?" Joseph was immediately on alert. Eli was grown up and could look after himself, but as far as his older brothers were concerned, he would always be the baby of the family.

"I was talking to Rob about Pure Light—the guys that have moved onto yours and Max's mountain."

In spite of the serious subject, Joseph couldn't suppress a smile. Eli had been referring to the mountain as his and Max's ever since they were teenagers, since the two of them had spent most of their time hiking and camping on it.

"Yes, I was up there yesterday," Joseph said. "Rob asked me to have a look around, and I wanted to introduce myself anyway and let them know how to contact Mountain Rescue. They weren't very friendly."

That was an understatement. The open hostility from the sharp-faced woman and their dark-haired leader bordered on enmity. The face of the brunette flashed into his mind and he felt his cheeks grow warm as he recalled the way he'd felt suddenly pulled to her.

His little brother didn't need to know about that.

"Did you meet their leader, Karl Hawthorne?"

"Dark-haired guy, very tall? Yes. He made it quite clear they wouldn't be needing my help and I wasn't to go back. Rob told me there are suspicions they're a white supremacist cult. I don't know about that, but their setup certainly seems cult-like, not that I know much about these things."

"More than a suspicion, now," Eli said gravely. "I've been researching Karl Hawthorne for a while. It's not his real name, of course. His real name is Karl Hausbaden."

Joseph frowned as a memory nagged at him. "I should know the name, shouldn't I?"

"He has an uncle from South Africa called Eric Hausbaden. He's the guy who got away last year. You remember that huge smuggling ring that Rob stumbled across?"

Joseph whistled out a slow exhale. Of course, he remembered. How could he forget? This was serious. "They can't be attempting to use the mountain passes again after last year. Surely they wouldn't be that crazy."

"I don't think Eric has much to do with Pure Light. I've been digging around on this for months, and although he was involved with white supremacy when he was younger, he left it behind and went full pelt into organised crime. We suspect he may occasionally bankroll some of their activities, but he's not an active member. No, the link is his brother, Karl's father, Johannes. He's the leader. It's been suspected for years, but only recently proved, thanks to some dedicated undercover agents."

Joseph's head spun. This was so far out of his field of experience he wasn't sure if he was keeping up. "So, this Johannes is the real leader of Pure Light?"

"No," Eli explained patiently. "Karl's the 'religious' one. Pure Light is his baby. Johannes is the leader of The White League."

Joseph felt sick as he realised exactly where he'd heard that name before. "Didn't they have something to do with Dad's death?"

"Yes. The group Dad intercepted was a splinter cell of the League. We thought they'd disbanded years ago, but it turns out they've consolidated and grown. They have links to all the other big supremacist groups, here and in the States. Seems they're bankrolling Ryan Spencer—you've seen him on the news, right?"

"He's an alt-right pundit, isn't he? Wasn't there a fuss about whether we were going to let him into the country a few months back?"

"Yes," Eli said shortly, "but he got in in the end. He's got definite links to Karl."

"Hang on," Joseph said, confused as he remembered an image of the man yelling into a reporter's mic and practically frothing at the mouth about something or other. "Isn't Ryan Spencer a prominent atheist?"

"He was. Now he's a member of Pure Light, and he's setting up the first American group."

Joseph let out a groan and ran a hand wearily across his forehead. This was all more than he could take in. Avalanches and wildfires were a breeze compared to this; he was glad he'd never followed Rob and his father into the police force as Eli had.

"So, the reason I'm phoning," Eli said, "is to ask you to keep an eye on the group, see if anyone turns up matching Spencer's description. Obviously, Rob's aware, but he doesn't spend all his time on the mountain like you do."

Joseph shook his head. Eastbrooke had always been such a quiet town, but the last few years, one thing after another had happened, and they all seemed to be linked, somehow, to this White League.

Including his father's death.

He shuddered as he realised what this might mean for Eli. They all were aware that the reason the youngest Carlton had joined the counter-terrorism unit in Melbourne was because of his unresolved anger over their father's murder. Eli had been just a child when it happened, and the wound went deep, but unlike the rest of the family, he had no real faith to speak of to help him through it.

Not for the first time, Joseph felt his heart bleed for his younger brother. "Eli," he said gently, "please don't let hunting this Johannes guy become a crusade for you. The work you do is amazing, but don't do it from a place of revenge."

"Too late for that, bro," Eli said lightly, as though they were discussing nothing more pressing than the weather. "I'm determined to be the one who brings him in. Besides, it will make my career."

At what cost? Although an icy tremor sliced through him, Joseph said no more. If he continued to push, Eli would clam up.

It seemed he already had. "I've gotta go," his younger brother said abruptly. "Speak soon." And then he was gone.

. . .

THOUGHTS OF ELI stayed with Joseph all evening, remaining there even when he got into bed and picked up his Bible for his nightly devotions. It would be far from the first time he'd prayed for his little brother, and he was sure it wouldn't be the last.

He snuggled down into his comfy double bed, glad to be in his own apartment rather than bunking in the lodge yet again. He went to open his Bible at the Psalm he'd been praying through, but instead, it fell open somewhere in the New Testament as though it had a mind of its own.

Joseph looked at the passage in front of him. It was the Gospel of Luke, chapter fifteen. A shiver ran down his spine as he read.

Now the tax collectors and sinners were all gathering around to hear Jesus. But the Pharisees and the teachers of the law muttered, "This man welcomes sinners and eats with them."

Then Jesus told them this parable: "Suppose one of you has a hundred sheep and loses one of them. Doesn't he leave the ninety-nine in the open country and go after the lost sheep until he finds it? And when he finds it, he joyfully puts it on his shoulders and goes home. Then he calls his friends and neighbours together and says, 'Rejoice with me; I have found my lost sheep.' I tell you that in the same way there will be more rejoicing in heaven over one sinner who repents than over ninety-nine righteous persons who do not need to repent.

The passage seemed so appropriate for Eli. He was the lost sheep of the family in many ways, the only one currently outside the fold. But God loved him, just like the parable said, and He would never stop seeking Eli to bring him back into the fold. It provided great comfort to Joseph.

He pressed his hands together. "Lord," he murmured softly, "I know You're the good Shepherd who cares for His flock. Please help Eli overcome his anger and pain and all the hurt that's blocking him from receiving Your abundant love. Let his eyes be opened so that he may truly see You and all that You are. Help him to come back into the fold and realise how much You love him."

As Joseph prayed, his thoughts turned again to the alluring woman at the Pure Light camp, and this time a wave of compassion for her, and all the members of the cult, including the leaders, swept through him. They were lost sheep, all of them, led astray by hatred and fear masquerading as truth. He had to pray for them as well.

"Jesus," he beseeched, his voice low and sincere, "watch over Your lost sheep at Pure Light and help them see the error of their ways. Reveal to them the truth of who You are, so that they might reject the doctrine they've been brainwashed with. May they come to know Your amazing love, and may they humble themselves before You and be freed by Your love. In Jesus' precious name. Amen."

Joseph closed his eyes and basked in the peace he always felt when he communed with the Lord in prayer. Time seemed to stand still in those moments when he was aware of nothing but the connection between him and his Saviour.

Then a thought entered his mind, as though it had been spoken directly into his consciousness.

Joseph, I need you to minister to My lost sheep. Heed My call, Joseph.

He opened his eyes and stared into the dark as tears of humility rolled down his cheeks. "Yes, Lord," he whispered. "I hear you."

CHAPTER 7

Once out of sight of the camp, Holly paused and released the breath she felt she'd been holding for days. The tension from being constantly watched had affected her more than she realised. She rolled her shoulders and rotated her neck, gulping the mountain air in as deeply as she could.

She wouldn't have long before she was missed, and she was taking a risk venturing this far from the camp, but she'd go crazy if she didn't get away for a short while. With a rare afternoon off from the constant work, sermons and Bible studies, she was determined to make the most of it. It also gave her a much-needed chance to make some notes on her phone and send a text to William. He must be worrying about her by now, or more likely, worrying about how the story was coming along.

The story. Some days she felt that she was starting to forget why she was even at the commune. It had only been a week, yet the relentless schedule and the way the days all blurred into one, made it feel as if she'd been there for years and her normal life had faded to a dream. It was easy to see how people became indoctrinated; she was so used to listening to the warped views of Pure Light that they no longer seemed unusual to her. Already she instinctively cast her eyes down when a man came near without having to remind herself to do so. She'd memorised the prayers, and she'd even been asked to lead a Bible study group. Sally was pleased with her and had stopped treating her with suspicion, and Holly knew that her objective to appear as a fully committed member had so far been achieved.

But she was in danger of losing herself.

As she walked, she typed shorthand notes into her phone, recalling Karl's recent sermons. The Pure Light ideology was indeed white supremacist; the theology of the cult centred around the idea that the ancient Hebrews were the ancestors of the 'white race', and all other races were 'fallen.' Cursed by God, even. Only true Christians who kept themselves 'pure' and separated themselves from the world would inherit the Kingdom of God. It was the most disturbing rhetoric Holly had ever heard, and she didn't need to be an expert in the background of her faith to know that the nonsense Pure Light spouted was both un-Christian and unscientific. It was ludicrous, and it amazed her that so many people were willing to believe it. Especially Makayla, who seemed to have a genuinely good heart and who Holly couldn't imagine wanting to harm a fly.

So, her hunch had been right. The only problem was, it wasn't much of a story. It might make a good feature piece in the Post, even a national magazine, but she wanted a front page in the tabloids, or at least a centre story. Although the members of Pure Light were abhorrent racists and were separating themselves and living up a mountain, they weren't causing any outright harm or breaking any laws. To get her big break, she needed more. If this commune wasn't the only one, there had to be a bigger structure and it raised questions about just who was bankrolling the groups. She needed more.

Lost in thought and rapidly typing her notes, she gasped as the ground gave way and she half fell, half skidded down a steep drop before landing heavily on a ledge. Her ankle twisted painfully beneath her, but she barely registered it. Instead, she stared at the sheer drop, and the town that was a tiny speck below. Her heart thudded as nausea churned her stomach. Two inches more and she would have slipped off the edge and fallen to her death. How had she been so careless? Gulping, and with her pulse thrumming in her ears, she reached behind and inched further from the edge, slowly feeling her way back to safer ground. She should have heeded Joseph Carlton's advice that day he'd visited the camp. Why hadn't she believed him when he'd warned them the mountain could be treacherous? At least she hadn't fallen.

After a few moments to catch her breath, she began retracing her steps, paying much more attention to where she was walking. Her phone was still in her hand, her fingers wrapped so tightly around it that her knuckles had gone white. At least she hadn't dropped it. She picked up her pace. Sally would notice if she didn't get back soon, and who knew what the consequences would be.

Walking quickly, her heart still thumping from the fall and panic rising at the thought of Sally's wrath, it wasn't long before she realised she had no idea where she was. Absorbed in her notes, she'd clearly wandered off the main path and now had no clue as to how to retrace her steps to get back onto it.

She was lost.

Her chest heaved and she began to hyperventilate. She tried to take some deep breaths to calm herself as she gazed around. It all looked the same. She couldn't afford to panic; that would make it worse. Not knowing what else to do, she did what she used to do as a child when she felt scared; she prayed. Looking up at the blue sky above, she murmured the Lord's Prayer, letting the familiar words wash over her.

> *Our Father, which art in heaven,*
> *Hallowed be Thy Name.*
> *Thy Kingdom come.*
> *Thy will be done on earth,*
> *As it is in heaven.*
> *Give us this day our daily bread.*
> *And forgive us our trespasses,*
> *As we forgive them that trespass against us.*
> *And lead us not into temptation,*
> *But deliver us from evil.*
> *For Thine is the kingdom,*
> *The power, and the glory,*
> *For ever and ever.*
> *Amen.*

When she finished, something moved in the trees in front of her. It was a young sheep, cocking its head and staring at her with interest.

"Hi there," she said.

The sheep lost interest and started eating the dry grass at its feet, but from behind the animal, a figure emerged from the patchy trees, and her knees practically buckled in relief.

It was Joseph Carlton.

"Hey," he said, his brows drawn in concern. "Are you okay?"

Holly nodded, although tears pricked her eyes. Even through her fear, she felt that magnetic pull towards him again. Instinctively she felt safe with him, as though she could trust him.

Even so, she had to stick to her story.

"Yes," she said, her mouth suddenly dry. "I had an hour for exercise and I got lost. And I nearly fell," she added, remembering the drop and feeling the fear again.

He stepped towards her, his expression soft and compassion in his eyes. "You're shaking." The stress and anxiety of the previous weeks welled up in her.

"I'm sorry," she said, wiping her eyes and feeling foolish.

"Don't apologise," he said gently. "You've had a scare. The Mountain Rescue lodge isn't far. Let's go and get you a hot drink."

"I'll be late back," she said, panic sounding in her voice. "I'm already late."

"Late for what?" He angled his head, his brow creasing.

"Oh…just chores and stuff," she said, not wanting to alert him to everything that was going on at Pure Light. Sally had drummed it into them that the rest of the world wouldn't understand.

She felt sick as she realised just how much Pure Light was getting inside her head.

"I can take you back on the motorbike," he said softly. "It'll be a lot quicker. I want to make sure you're okay; it's my job."

She nodded, blinking away tears while fuming at herself for her weakness, and started to follow him through the trees. She was aware of a dull ache in her ankle now, but it was just a twist. She didn't want to think what could have happened if she'd broken it out here. Or worse…

The Mountain Rescue lodge wasn't far, just on the other

side of the thicket of trees. It was rustic and homey, and a very welcome sight with smoke coming from the chimney and curling into the air, drifting away slowly in the slight breeze, leaving a trail against the sky.

Joseph stood aside and allowed her to enter ahead of him. She passed through the small reception area into a room with an old, comfy couch and a small fire. She sat gratefully, sinking into the cushions. Off to the side, another man clattered around in a tiny kitchen.

"That's John," Joseph told her.

The man, tall and sturdy with a pleasant face, turned and waved. He brought her a hot chocolate and then went out to the reception area, closing the door behind him.

Holly couldn't help but think of what Sally and Karl would have to say if they knew she was in a room on her own with a male.

Especially this one.

The day he'd visited the commune, Karl had spoken Joseph's name with such venom. What would his reaction be to Joseph dropping her back? At least it would confirm she was telling the truth about getting lost, and what choice did she have? She had no idea how to get back to the commune.

She drank her hot chocolate, grateful for its warmth, although she wished it was coffee. Some of her shakiness subsided.

Joseph watched her with a guarded expression. "So," he said after a while, "how are you getting on up there?"

"Oh, it's great," she said, not sounding very convincing even to her own ears.

He didn't look like he bought it, either. "You guys are Christians, right?"

She nodded.

His gaze narrowed. "It seems strange that a Christian group would live so isolated up a mountain."

Had he heard the same rumours about Pure Light that she had? She guessed so, since his brother was the Police Chief.

"Oh, we just believe we should model the Kingdom of God here on earth," she said lightly. "So, we keep away from the sins and temptations of the world."

"I suppose that makes sense," he said diplomatically. "Didn't medieval monks do things like that? Hermits and the like?"

She nodded, glad that she remembered a little of Sunday school. "Yes, it's just like that," she said, although she felt a strong urge to tell him more. To confide in him.

"What about your leader, though?" he asked, pressing a little more, his brow lifting. "He seemed quite hostile to outsiders. Or was it just me?"

"We have to keep the group pure," Holly said automatically, then flinched at the sound of Sally's words coming from her mouth. "Erm, I mean, free from bad influences."

His gaze met hers and held. "Do you think I'm a bad influence?"

As she gazed into his deep brown eyes, she felt that sudden awareness she'd felt on their first meeting, a connection between them, and her heart pounded so loudly she thought he must be able to hear it. "No," she said, her voice coming out in a whisper.

Their gazes held for a long moment before he tore his away, although it seemed an effort to do so.

He stood abruptly. "Let's get you back before it grows dark." He led her outside and fetched helmets for them both. He climbed onto the motorbike and then reached around and helped her onto the back.

"Hold tight to my waist," he instructed as he strapped his

own helmet under his chin. "The ground's uneven and we don't want you bumped off."

She did as he instructed, trying not to notice the firmness of his torso and the breadth of his shoulders as she clung on. This close to him, it was hard to think of anything other than his nearness and the way her arms fitted around his waist.

Her anxiety was forgotten until they reached the commune. Sally stood outside the cabin Holly shared with Makayla, glaring with open animosity as the motorbike approached. "Where've you been?" she snapped as Joseph stopped the bike. Her eyes seemed to bore into Holly's soul.

Joseph answered for her, his voice calm but firm. "I found Holly here wandering near the rescue lodge, very clearly lost. It seems she rambled too far during her exercise. She was in a little bit of shock, so I gave her a hot drink before I brought her back on the bike. She'll need a hot meal and a good sleep."

"Thank you for the advice," Sally said sarcastically, still glaring at Holly.

Joseph shot her a sympathetic look before he turned to leave. "You have our location and number if there are any problems," he addressed Sally. "And Holly, stay close to camp in future."

"I will. Thank you, Mr. Carlton," she said quietly, her eyes cast downwards. She tried not to watch as he rode away, although his leaving left her with an acute sense of loss. Would she ever see him again?

As she lifted her gaze to Sally's furious face, she somehow doubted it.

CHAPTER 8

"Makayla, go inside," Sally ordered, her words whiplike. She kept her gaze pinned on Holly as Makayla scuttled inside, although not before shooting her cousin an apologetic look.

"You brought an outsider into our camp," she hissed at Holly, anger boiling inside her. All the work that had gone into this place, and now it had been invaded twice by someone who'd never understand their purpose. Someone, in fact, who could jeopardise everything they were working for.

The stupid woman blinked at her in surprise. She clearly had no understanding of what she'd done. "I was lost," she said. "He simply brought me back. That's his job."

Sally's hand twitched with the urge to strike the impudent woman across the face. But she would do better than that. She would take her to Karl.

Her hand snaked out and grabbed her wrist. She ignored her yelp of pain as she pulled her between the buildings towards his cabin.

"I'm sorry, Sally," the woman gabbled as she hurried to keep up. "I didn't mean to cause any harm."

Sally ignored her, keeping a vice-like grip on her arm. When they reached Karl's cabin, she knocked lightly on the door.

He opened it and measured her with a cool, appraising look. Perhaps she'd made a mistake coming to him since he expected her to keep the women in line.

"What?" he asked.

"She brought an intruder into the camp." Sally pulled Holly forward.

He turned furious eyes to the woman who was visibly quivering. Sally smirked with spite.

"I got lost on the mountain. Mr. Carlton brought me back. If he hadn't found me..." Her words trailed off and Sally shook her head. Did she think that her wellbeing was more important than the integrity of Pure Light? She clearly hadn't been learning as fast as Sally had thought.

"Go," Karl said, his eyes flicking over her dismissively.

Sally was used to that, but it stung, nevertheless. She nodded and let go of Holly's wrist, noting with satisfaction when she immediately started to rub it as though in pain.

"I'll deal with this...infraction," he said, pulling Holly inside his cabin and shutting the door in Sally's face.

∽

HOLLY SQUIRMED under Karl's gaze, feeling claustrophobic inside his cabin. She'd not been alone with him and all her nerves were on edge, screaming at her to get out of there. Her wrist ached painfully where Sally had manhandled her, and she was certain it would bruise. Would Karl hurt her as well? Fear made her rigid as she stared at the ground in front of her, trying to appear as submissive as possible, even though all her instincts screamed at her to run.

"Do you understand what you've done?" His voice was soft, but there was no kindness in it; it reminded her more of the hiss of a snake.

"I shouldn't have brought an outsider into the camp," she said demurely. "And I'm truly sorry. I didn't mean to. I got lost, and fell, and ..."

"Do you think I care?" he shouted.

She jumped, her pulse throbbing in her jaw as she clenched it tight. *This is it. I'm getting out of here.* The thought brought nothing but relief. Her desire for career success seemed in that moment like nothing but foolish vanity and a temptation that had led her straight into danger.

But then, a voice whispered, *all of this would have been for nothing.* And did she really want to fail at her work just as she'd failed in love?

"No, of course not," she said, hoping she sounded convincing. Her fear was certainly real. "I shouldn't have let him bring me back. I see that now. Please, allow me to repent."

He seemed mollified by that, at least, and his voice was less harsh when he spoke again. "Repentance is good," he said approvingly. "And repent you shall. You'll be on extra chores, longer prayers in the evening, and you will fast for three days."

Her heart sank. She was already exhausted and hungry.

"I will also be watching you closely," he added. "Now, go to bed. I'll inform Sally of your new duties."

Holly nodded and left without lifting her gaze. Only when she was outside did she breathe a sigh of relief. She'd fully expected that Karl would hurt her in some way.

Although, working her to the bone and not feeding her for three days was nothing short of abuse.

She made her way to her cabin, feeling faint at the thought and wondering how she would get through the ordeal. She had a visual image of Joseph Carlton's handsome face and kind eyes and wished he was there, even though she knew that was impossible.

Only once she was in bed and Makayla was asleep did she allow her thoughts to take free reign. Today had frightened her deeply, but at least she had definite evidence that both Karl and Sally were abusive, and that Pure Light was a cult. Not only did the leaders brainwash their members, they mistreated them, too.

For the first time, she felt that her very life was in danger. Even so, she knew without a shadow of a doubt that as soon as she got the chance, she had to see Joseph Carlton again, and not just because she felt compelled to.

If she were to stay here, then she needed someone other than William, whom she didn't trust to have her best interests at heart, to know what was going on.

And to know her true identity in case something happened to her.

CHAPTER 9

Joseph was resting on the couch in the lodge. He was on night shift and was finally drifting off just a few hours before dawn. At first when he heard the slight knock at the door, he thought he was dreaming, but then it came again.

He opened it and stared at the woman standing there. "Holly?"

She smiled sheepishly. "Sorry to bother you…there's something I need to talk to you about. I checked the website and figured it was your shift."

"It's two a.m. How did you get here?" He opened the door wider to let her in. As the light fell on her face, her cheeks looked hollow, as though she hadn't eaten for days.

"I remembered the way. It's a fairly straight run to here if you don't leave the path, isn't it? I used the torch on my phone. The one I'm not supposed to have." She grinned, looking almost manic.

"Holly," he said softly, "are you okay? Are you in trouble of some kind?" She must be, to turn up here like this. Yes, it was a fairly straightforward route from the compound to the lodge, but it was steep and at least a thirty-minute trek, and she'd done it in the middle of the night?

She nibbled her lip. "You could say that," she said quietly. Her hair fell over her face and she looked away, her arms folding around her body. "I shouldn't have come," she murmured.

"Don't be silly. You're safe here. Come and sit down. Can I get you something to eat or drink?"

The way her eyes lit up, he figured she must be starving. "Yes, please. Anything will do."

"Beef sandwich and hot chocolate?"

She nodded and sat on the couch while he went to the kitchenette, trying to hide his alarm. Something was very, very wrong, but he didn't want to push in case she clammed up. He was flattered that she felt able to come to him, but his overriding emotion was the fierce urge to protect her from whatever was bothering her. He thought of Karl and bristled. If he had hurt her…

Taking a deep breath to calm himself, he carried her sandwich and drink to her and then sat in the chair opposite. She gulped the sandwich down fast enough to give herself indigestion.

"Don't they feed you up there?" he asked lightly, as though it was a joke.

"We fast a lot," she said, not meeting his gaze.

He waited for her to finish before he asked gently, "So, what's going on?"

She took a deep breath as though to prepare herself, and then it all tumbled out as he listened in shock.

"I'm not really a Pure Light member. I'm a reporter, investigating the group. I knew that going undercover and joining them was the only way I would find anything out."

She leaned forward. "You can't say anything; I'm on the verge of a really big story that could make my career. But I wanted someone to know…just in case." She swallowed hard.

"Just in case? Are you in danger, Holly?" On the one hand, he admired her intrepid spirit, but on the other, he thought she must be crazy to willingly live with those people. It certainly didn't seem to be doing her any good.

"No," she said quickly, but her gaze darted away and he wasn't sure that he believed her. "But I'm not sure what will happen if they discover who I am. They watch the move of every member, and I'm not allowed to exercise alone after the other day…hence why I'm here at this time of night. I can't stay long; we rise at dawn."

He shook his head. The conditions surrounded horrendous. "What is it you're investigating them for?"

She looked at him, her gaze unflinching. "White supremacy," she said grimly. "Your brother is Chief of Police; he must know."

"There are rumours." Joseph nodded. "But you can't arrest people just for having abhorrent ideas."

"That's the thing," she said. She seemed brighter now that she'd eaten, and a little colour had returned to her cheeks. He tried not to think about how pretty she was. "I've seen and heard enough to know that the rumours are true," she continued. "They believe that the 'white race' are God's chosen people and the only ones who will inherit His Kingdom, but other than that, there isn't much to report. Yet I know there's more. It feels like they're building up to something. Something is being prepared for…and it isn't just the afterlife."

He felt sick. "Holly," he said urgently, "you have to get out of there. You have no idea how dangerous they could turn out to be, or what they could do if they find out who you are. How can a newspaper story be worth all that?"

She lifted her chin. "It's my career. I've never wanted to do anything else. Can't you understand that?"

He considered her words and could relate to the crossroad he was facing about his own life. He was still resisting what he knew to be his calling, while this young woman was plunging into danger for the sake of what she felt to be hers. He thought, too, about Eli and his comment about how catching Johannes Hausbaden would make his career, even though they all knew that wasn't the whole story. What was Holly's story that she'd put her life on the line for a moment of glory?

"I can," he agreed, not elaborating on his thoughts, "but surely there'll be other opportunities. Ones that aren't so dangerous."

"I know what I'm doing," she said firmly, and he heard the annoyance in her voice. Just like Eli, she would back off if pushed.

"Okay," he said again, softening his voice. "It's your choice, after all. But can I pray for you at least?"

She blinked. "You're a Christian?"

"Yes," he said proudly. Now wasn't the time to mention that he was thinking of becoming a minister, but her question reminded him that he had an appointment with the pastor tomorrow. It would be the first time that he'd properly discussed what he now knew for sure was God calling him to ministry.

She looked oddly pleased. "That's great. After all this time at the camp, I'm in danger of forgetting what real Christianity looks like. Although, I've been praying more than I have in years."

"You believe, too?" he asked, and wondered why that

filled him with joy that was more than simply finding a fellow person of faith.

"Yes," she said, but her gaze dropped to her hands. "I grew up going to church. I wish I'd paid more attention though, because although I believe in God and try to live in a godly way, I don't know much about it all, really." She lifted her gaze and held his.

There was more to the story, some hurt she hadn't disclosed, but now wasn't the time, not when she was already in the middle of what he suspected was a more traumatic situation than she was letting on.

"You know enough to know that what Pure Light is teaching is wrong," he pointed out.

"Yes, and I thank God and my parents for that. I never used to understand how people could become brainwashed by these things, but after living among them, I'm starting to get it. It's almost like spiritual abuse."

Joseph shuddered. "That's exactly what it is." He inhaled slowly and looked into her eyes. "Holly, can I pray for you?"

She sniffed, as if his offer touched her deeply. "Yes, please."

He gave a small smile and then bowed his head. "Heavenly Father, thank You for Your unconditional love which is beyond measure. Father, I pray for everyone at the commune, but I pray especially for Holly. Watch over her, Lord, and may she be aware of Your constant presence with her. Keep her safe from harm, Lord, and let this endeavour be used for Your good purposes. Fill her with Your peace, Lord. In Jesus' precious name, I pray. Amen."

"Amen," she echoed softly.

As he opened his eyes, he saw that hers were moist.

"Thanks." She smiled, and taking a tissue from her pocket, dabbed her eyes. "You know, there's something powerful in your voice when you pray. You should be a minister or something." She chuckled lightly.

Joseph blinked. He wasn't a great believer in signs from God, but if he were, this would be one.

"I liked that part about God using what I'm doing for good," she went on. "It isn't just about me and my career, is it? This is affecting peoples' lives…and their spirits."

Had he said the wrong thing? The last thing he wanted was to encourage her to stay in such a dangerous situation. He'd feel a lot better if she went home and forgot all about Pure Light and getting her story.

Or would he? If she left, he'd never see her again.

Frowning at his thoughts, he stood abruptly. "We'd better get you back before you're missed."

"You can't take me back," she said hurriedly. "If they see you…"

"What would happen?" He raised a brow.

She shrugged and released a slow breath. "I'd never hear the end of it."

"I'll walk with you up to where the road runs out. It's straight up from there. I'll lend you a torch."

"It's okay. I can use the light on my phone."

She was quiet on the walk back, and he sensed her anxiety rising the closer they got to the commune. When they reached the spot where he had to leave her, he turned and faced her. Her hair shone silver in the moonlight, and she looked almost ethereal.

"You don't have to go back," he said softly.

"I do," she whispered. "I don't know why, but I do."

"Take my personal number, at least," he insisted. "And I'll give you my brother Rob's, too. If you need anything, or if you sense that you're in any danger, call us. In fact," he said as an idea occurred to him, "do you think you could try and text me every couple of days to let me know you're okay? If I don't hear from you, I'll put out a Rescue Alert."

He worried that was too much and she'd back off at his protectiveness, but she looked relieved as he gave her the numbers and she typed them into her phone.

"Thank you, and yes, I will. I feel safer knowing someone's looking out for me. You're a good man." She squeezed his hand before she left.

Rooted to the spot, he stared after her, even as she vanished from his sight, his hand still tingling from her touch.

CHAPTER 10

The next day, Pastor Peter waved Joseph into the sitting room and directed him to the couch. "Good to see you, Joseph. What did you want to talk about? It's not often I get a ministry request from any of you Carltons."

"I suspect it's usually my mother who comes to see you." Joseph smiled as he chuckled lightly. Easing onto the couch, he took a deep breath. Now he was here, his hands had grown clammy. Thanks to his long night worrying about Holly and pondering her visit, he was also exhausted. But he couldn't put this off any longer.

The calling needed to be answered.

He cleared his throat as the pastor waited patiently for him to speak. The older man's eyes were kind and helped to settle him.

"You gave a sermon recently about answering God's calling on our lives," Joseph began, then hesitated.

The pastor nodded encouragingly. "It spoke to you?"

"Yes, although it wasn't a new feeling. Ever since, though, it hasn't left me. Then the other night, after speaking with

Eli, I was praying and I got a strong sense that God was telling me to minister to the lost." He felt almost embarrassed now that he was stating it out loud. *Could God really speak to him like that?*

The pastor didn't seem surprised at all, however, and instead nodded thoughtfully.

"For a long time," Joseph continued, twisting his hands in his lap, "I've felt a call to ministry, but never this strongly. I've always tried to tell myself it couldn't be real, that it wasn't for me...but I can't ignore it anymore."

"And the idea that you're being called in this way, how does that make you feel?" the pastor asked, studying Joseph intently.

Joseph bit his lip. "Honestly? Frightened and unworthy."

To his surprise, the pastor looked pleased. "If you didn't feel that way, I'd be questioning if you were ready, or if you were truly discerning your call," he said. "Like I mentioned in that sermon, those whom God calls are never 'up to the job.' We're called, not on our own merits, but because God can work through us. Humility is vital."

"I suppose I never thought of it like that." Joseph drew a deep breath and added hesitantly, "So, if it's real, what do I do?"

"Well, I can't say I'm surprised. I've thought for a long time now that God may have His hand on you in this way. I'd be more than happy to sponsor you to go to Bible College, if that's what you decide. But that's a few months away. For now, I'd suggest we meet regularly and pray together, so we can confirm that this is indeed what you're being called to."

Joseph exhaled in relief. This had been easier than he'd expected.

But straight after the relief followed doubt. "You don't

think I've got it wrong? I mean...ministry? I'm Mountain Rescue. My brother and father are, or were, police chiefs."

"And that means you can't be in ministry?" The pastor raised a brow.

Something else from his sermon came back to Joseph. Gideon had protested that he was 'the least in my father's house.' Childhood anxieties flooded through him. He'd always felt like the weak one, the sensitive one. The one who always had something to prove next to his ultra-macho brothers and the heroic memory of their father.

"You look deep in thought." The pastor leaned forward.

Joseph met his gaze, feeling suddenly raw and vulnerable. It wasn't a feeling he enjoyed. "I'm a Carlton," he said, as if that explained it.

The pastor, however, seemed to understand. "You think you'll be letting the family name down."

Joseph nodded.

Inhaling deeply, the pastor folded his arms and settled back in his chair. "Do you really think that being called to the ministry is an easy path? I can assure you it isn't. There might be less physical danger, but it's not a role for the faint-hearted."

"Yes, I suppose I know that," Joseph said. "But that's another thing...I don't know if I'm good enough. I understand the importance of humility, but what if I'm simply not up to it?"

"Don't you think that's for God to decide?"

The pastor's words pierced him, cutting through his self-doubt and lack of self-esteem. Of course, it was true. All through scripture the Lord called the last and the least, not the strongest or the proudest.

"I don't need to be better," he said with wonder in his voice. "I just need to surrender."

"Exactly," the pastor said with a smile.

They prayed together, asking for God's guidance in discerning Joseph's next steps, then they chatted for a while over a pot of tea, with Pastor Peter sharing stories about his own early days as a minister, and how he, too, had questioned it all at first. Joseph left feeling both nervous about his future prospects, and relieved that he'd finally taken the plunge.

Now he could resume worrying about Holly.

Her appearance last night had concerned him. He was certain she wasn't being fed properly, and he'd noticed bruising around her wrist. She was obviously in danger but too stubborn to give up her mission. He admired her tenacity, even as it frustrated him.

Rob had a rare weekday off work, so after leaving Pastor Peter's place, Joseph decided to call on his older brother on his way home. He lived not far away, in a small worker's cottage that he and Emma had bought just before they got married.

When Joseph arrived, his brother was doing some odd jobs around the house. "Don't you ever relax?" he chided.

Rob laughed. "You can't talk; you spend every spare minute on that mountain. How are things up there? Any news on our resident cultists?"

"That's actually what I came to talk to you about," Joseph told him.

Rob's smile slipped. He set his drill down and led Joseph through to the kitchen where they both sat at the table. "Go on," he said.

Joseph told him about Holly, while Rob listened intently.

"She's in danger," Joseph concluded. "But I can hardly go launching a rescue mission if she doesn't admit it. Can you do anything?"

"No," Rob said, the frustration evident in his voice. "As abhorrent as they sound, they're not breaking the law. Police Chief or not, I can't go issuing warrants with no evidence, or unless she's explicitly stated that she's being abused, in which case it would be a safeguarding concern."

Joseph shook his head. "No. She spoke about their beliefs, which are sinister, and they're clearly operating as a supremacist cult, but that's not illegal, is it?"

"Not yet," Rob said. "If they were to get involved in actual neo-Nazi activity, they'd become an illegal group, but so far, we don't have any evidence of that. Keep the lines of communication open with Holly. If anything does happen, within the cult or to her, we'll go straight in. It's good that she's got you looking out for her."

Joseph didn't answer.

Rob peered at him and then raised an eyebrow. "What does she look like, this Holly?" The way he asked made Joseph defensive.

"Why's that relevant?" he asked.

"It isn't." Rob shrugged, grinning. "But your reaction to the question is. You like her, don't you?"

"I barely know her," Joseph protested, but he felt his cheeks go warm. His brother knew him too well.

"I barely knew Emma when I first realised how I felt about her. I fought it and tried to tell myself it was silly, that it wasn't real...but deep down, I knew better."

"That's different," Joseph mumbled.

"Is it? How, exactly?"

Joseph couldn't answer.

Thankfully, he was spared from his brother delving into the topic any further by the time. Rob checked his watch and stood up. "Talking of Emma, I've got to pick her up from the school as her car's in the garage. Do you want to wait? You can stay for an early dinner."

Joseph shook his head. "I'd love to, but I need to get some sleep or I'll be dead on my feet."

"Okay." Rob slapped him on his back. "Take care, then."

Joseph gave a nod and they stepped outside together. As he headed back to his house, he thought about his brother's words. *Was his attraction to Holly that obvious?*

CHAPTER 11

Three days after she'd gone to see Joseph in the middle of the night, Holly was feeling a little brighter. She was no longer fasting and some of her strength had returned, along with her resolve. She'd been praying every night—but not the prayers that Sally expected her to say, which were all about preserving the sanctity of Pure Light and creating their version of God's Kingdom on earth. Instead, she'd started talking to God again, just like she had as a kid, and in spite of the danger she knew she could be in if she were caught, she felt an intuitive sense of protection.

Knowing that Joseph was thinking of her made her feel less alone, too. She'd texted him every time she had the chance to let him know she was doing okay, and every time she snuck into the toilet cubicle to turn her phone on, her heart fluttered when she saw a message from him. Not that he was ever anything but cordial and professional, but even so, she sensed that she'd found a friend.

Occasionally, she wondered if he could have been more than that, had they met under different circumstances, but she pushed those thoughts away as quickly as they came. She was hardly in a position to meet anyone right now, and besides, she'd sworn off men after Chad. Especially church-going ones.

But Joseph was nothing like Chad. Although she barely knew him, something inside her sensed that he was trustworthy.

There was no point thinking about it, though. As soon as she had her story she'd be out of here, hopefully to move onto bigger and better things.

"Holly?" Sally looked up and pursed her lips as Holly entered the kitchen.

Holly's head jerked up. It was her turn, again, to peel potatoes for dinner. It was a good few hours' work, and the rusty potato peeler kept cutting her fingers. "Am I late?" she asked, looking suitably subservient. It wasn't entirely an act; Sally was incredibly domineering, and Holly often felt her confidence wilting around the woman.

"No, you just look miles away," Sally said suspiciously. "I've noticed you seem lost in thought these past few days. Is there anything you want to tell me?"

Holly shook her head, hoping she didn't look as guilty as she felt. She took her place at the wooden counter, picked up the peeler and made a start on the potatoes, next to a young girl peeling carrots, who couldn't be much more than sixteen. Holly had never heard her speak.

Sally wasn't peeling anything, of course. She was supervising.

"I think I'm just tired, I'm sorry," Holly said contritely.

Sally stepped closer, almost leaning over the counter.

Expecting a tirade, Holly flinched.

When Sally spoke, though, her voice was surprisingly soft, as though inviting Holly to confide in her. "Has one of the young men caught your eye? You can tell me if they have."

Nearly dropping a potato, Holly shook her head. "No, no, of course not."

Sally tutted. "I'm glad you're modest. Of course, we don't tolerate wantonness here, but you are at an age where you should be partnered. If there's someone you're interested in, tell me. You're one of us now, and Karl is very fair. He always tries to make sure the marriages are welcomed by both parties. A godly marriage is for life, after all."

Holly blinked, trying not to react with revulsion as she understood what Sally was saying.

They were trying to arrange a marriage for her.

It made sense, given that Pure Light believed it was a woman's place in life to be a good wife and to produce many offspring to continue the 'Chosen Race,' but she still felt shocked. She nodded, hoping the nausea she suddenly felt didn't show on her face. Hunching over the potatoes, she peeled faster to disguise the fact that her hands were shaking.

Thankfully, Sally turned her attention to the girl next to her, snapping at her to hurry up with the carrots.

"It will be all hands on deck this weekend," Sally said to no one in particular, but her eyes had lit with excitement. "We have a very special Brother coming to visit us. Phase two of our mission begins!"

Holly forgot about the arranged marriage issue as her curiosity piqued. A *'special' visitor?* This sounded newsworthy. She wanted to ask who it was and why he was coming, but that would only rouse Sally's suspicions, so she kept quiet.

Two hours later, her hands were red, raw and chapped

from all the peeling, and she made her way back to the cabin to freshen up before afternoon Bible study.

Makayla was in the cabin, praying on her knees.

Holly tiptoed quietly past her. The younger girl worried her. As time passed, the more attached she grew to her, but she was also witnessing the sweet young woman becoming more and more brainwashed. It was so hard to watch, knowing that when she left, Makayla would still be here, in the clutches of her cousins.

Karl had been taking a particular interest in Makayla recently, often having her in his cabin for private instruction, and until now, Holly had simply assumed it was because the two were related and he was grooming her to become a leader like Sally. After learning about the arranged marriages, however, she couldn't help wondering if Karl had other plans for her.

Surely not, since they're cousins, she reminded herself, but somehow, that didn't put her mind at rest.

Finishing her prayers, Makayla rose to her feet. She, too, looked tired and thin, but unlike Holly, there was a feverish glint in her eyes.

Holly shuddered. That glint reminded her of Sally's.

"How are you, Holly? I was with Karl all morning, so I didn't get to have breakfast with you. Exciting things are about to happen."

Holly's brow hiked. Did Makayla know more about the visitor than she did? Had Karl told her about him? "Yes," Holly said, trying to sound suitably enthusiastic. "Sally told us all in the kitchen."

"Oh, did she? I thought they'd wait for Karl to announce it to everyone," Makayla said innocently. She was so free of guile that it made Holly feel fiercely protective and want to get her away from her predatory cousins as fast as she could.

But how? Although they were developing a bond from living in such close quarters, Holly felt sure that Makayla's bond with Karl and Sally was now a lot stronger than it had been when the girl first arrived. If Makayla found out what she was really doing at Pure Light, Holly was sure she'd have no hesitation telling them. She'd see it as the morally right thing to do.

"Well, we have to get ready for his visit," Holly said casually.

Makayla nodded fervently. "Ryan Spencer is practically a celebrity in America, isn't he? I can't believe he's coming all this way to preach to us."

Holly frowned. The only person in the public eye that she knew with that name was a controversial far-right speaker. He was certainly alleged to have neo-Nazi links, but he was also a prominent atheist, as many of them often were.

"Apparently it was Karl who personally ministered to him and baptised him into Pure Light, and he was a total non-believer," Makayla chattered on, confirming that Ryan Spencer was indeed the same person.

Holly's head spun, and the threat of Karl and arranged marriages was forgotten again as her journalistic instincts came to the fore.

She was on the verge of something big, she could sense it.

That wasn't all she sensed. As Makayla left for Bible study, telling Holly to hurry up before she was late, Holly sat heavily on the bed and pressed a hand to her forehead, overwhelmed with the shocks of the morning.

It wasn't just the story that was big. The danger level was ramping up. Part of her desperately wanted to take Joseph's advice and leave, and that part was becoming almost as strong as the hard-nosed journalist persona she'd spent so long trying to cultivate. But there were other reasons to stay.

The world needed to know what was going on up here, and the more she'd been praying, the more she felt there was a purpose to her being here that went way beyond her own selfish ambition. Then, of course, there was Makayla. Holly didn't want to believe that the girl was now entirely under Karl's spell, but it wouldn't be long before she was.

Retrieving her phone from inside her pillowcase, she turned it on. Her fingers flew over the keys as fast as her heart was beating at the thought of getting caught.

She had to tell Joseph. More than that, she had to see him and discuss all this in person. She couldn't think straight here.

There've been developments, she texted. *Can you meet me at midnight? The place where you dropped me off before?*

His answer came back almost immediately.

I'll be there.

Her heart pounded with equal mixtures of fear and anticipation at seeing him again. She turned her phone off and hid it before hurrying from the cabin. She'd just make it in time for Bible study.

∽

IT WAS NEARING midnight and the commune was deathly quiet. Lights out had been hours ago; early nights and early mornings were part of the schedule. Sally, however, couldn't sleep. The impending visit by Brother Spencer required a lot of organisation on her part, and the list of things she needed to oversee was running around on a loop in her mind, preventing her from getting any rest.

Everything had to be perfect for this visit. She couldn't let Karl down.

He didn't tolerate failure.

At least Holly was back on track. Satisfaction lifted Sally's lips. The punishment seemed to have worked, reining in the rebellious spirit she'd sensed within her. It was definitely time to arrange a partnership for her. A husband would keep her in line.

Sally would never marry. Endometriosis had resulted in an operation in her early twenties that had left her unable to conceive. It had been a huge blow, because there was no greater duty for a Sister than to bring racially pure babies into the world. She knew that in some of the Elders' eyes she was defective, but she made up for it with her unswerving and faithful devotion to their vision, and it had paid off. She was the only woman in Pure Light with anything resembling a leadership role, and Karl treated her like a cherished Sister, which was all she wanted. She needed no one else.

She turned restlessly on her hard bunk. Sleep was hopeless. Maybe a walk in the fresh air would help. Sitting up, she pulled a shawl over her pyjamas. She wouldn't go far since women were forbidden to walk around on their own after dark, but as the female leader, she could make an exception for herself, although she was also conscious of setting an example.

Stepping out into the night felt almost rebellious, although no one else was around. The camp was silent, broken only by the occasional hoot of an owl. Stars twinkled overhead, so clear from this high on the mountain that she could almost reach out and touch them.

A flash of light from over near the trees at the edge of the compound caught her eye. Peering in the direction it came from, she frowned. It looked like a small torch.

Pulling her shawl tightly around her shoulders, she headed in the direction of the quickly vanishing light. Was someone creeping around beyond the trees? Spying on them? Joseph Carlton, maybe? She wouldn't put it past the man. Karl thought he was trouble, and given the family background, she sensed her brother was right. The Carltons were nothing but a small-town family, yet they seemed to have a history of getting in the way. Her Uncle Eric was still cursing Rob Carlton for foiling his plans last year.

But God worked in mysterious ways, and if that hadn't happened, they wouldn't have been able to start the commune here. It was the perfect place...or would be, if the Carltons weren't patrolling the mountain and surrounding areas.

As she crept through the trees, the light appeared again. She crouched down and peered through the branches. A figure was moving down the mountain, away from the commune. She inched forward, peering through the shadows. *Who was it?* Whoever it was wore a long skirt, and a long plait trailed down her back. Sally's eyes shot open. *It was a Pure Light woman!*

An owl hooted and the woman turned her head, just enough for Sally to catch a glimpse of a profile, lit up by the faint light from the torch. She couldn't be certain, but she was almost sure it was Holly. She clenched her fists. How dare she! Although Sally wasn't surprised. She'd suspected Holly's subservience was too good to be true.

But where was she going? Keeping to the shadows and moving as silently as she could, Sally followed.

Whatever Holly was up to, she would be roundly punished for it. It was time she got what was coming to her.

CHAPTER 12

*J*oseph was there, waiting for her. He flashed a light which Holly hurried towards, glad to no longer be on her own.

"Thanks for coming," she said almost breathlessly when she reached him. "I didn't mean to drag you out on your night off."

"It's fine. I was going to pop into the lodge to check on John, anyway." His forehead creased as his worried gaze swept over her. "So, what's wrong? Your text sounded urgent."

She told him about the impending visit from Ryan Spencer, and, although she hadn't intended to, she also mentioned the arranged marriages and her worries over Makayla.

"I may have gotten completely the wrong idea about what Sally and Karl have planned for her," she said with a frown, "but whatever it is, it isn't good. She's their family, after all; they could be grooming her for some kind of position in the cult. Although apart from Sally, so far, I haven't met any of the women who do anything other than cook, clean and go to study group. We don't even really speak to each other. We call each other 'Sister' but there's no real sisterhood."

"But you feel close to Makayla," Joseph pointed out.

"I wish I didn't." She sighed heavily. "It would make it so much easier. I almost feel I'm betraying her. She's such a sweet girl, and they have their claws right into her. It worries me what will happen to her after I leave. When she first arrived, I don't think she bought into it all, not the racial stuff anyway. But now she hangs off every word Karl says."

JOSEPH NODDED GRIMLY. "He's a typical charismatic leader. Rules through equal parts charm and fear."

Holly shuddered. There was nothing about Karl that she found remotely charming. Subconsciously, she started rubbing at her wrist where Sally had twisted it, only realising what she was doing when Joseph's gaze followed the movement. Concern filled his eyes. She wanted to tell him just how bad things had been, but she was sure that if she did, he'd feel duty bound to report it.

"I just thought I should tell you about Ryan Spencer's visit. Things seem to be ramping up and I get the feeling that something huge is being planned, but I don't know what, exactly. I'm not in the inner circle."

"You sound disappointed in yourself."

She took a deep breath. "Perhaps I am. This was supposed to be the big undercover mission, but instead, I've gotten myself into this impossible situation. But I can't give up now."

She wasn't sure who she was trying to convince—Joseph or herself.

"I can't tell you what to do," he said in a low voice, "but it sounds as though you should get yourself out of there. It's no reflection on your skills as a journalist, Holly. This is dangerous stuff."

His concern brought tears to her eyes. She swiped them away. "I can handle it," she said in a defiant tone.

He didn't reply, and she suddenly felt foolish. Why had she even messaged him to meet her? She could have simply texted him about Spencer's visit. The truth was, she was hungry for human company outside of the cult. Joseph had become a touchstone for her, a link with the outside world.

Then, of course, there was her growing attraction to him, which she was in no state to process right now, but which she couldn't deny, either. She lifted her gaze to his handsome face. If only they could have met under different circumstances. Feeling a rush of emotion, she stepped towards him, then flinched at his next words.

"I have to tell my brothers about this, Holly. It's important. Eli's been tracking this guy, Spencer. Him coming here could be really significant. You need to be out of there before there's any kind of showdown."

With a jolt, she realised that Joseph might not be motivated by concern for her at all. He had a stake in this, because of his police officer brothers and his position as steward of the mountain range. An insidious little voice whispered inside her head, *He probably doesn't care about you at all. He's just like Chad.*

Suddenly, she couldn't think straight. All the hunger, fatigue and fear of the last few weeks caught up with her at once. Maybe she'd been wrong, and she couldn't trust Joseph Carlton at all.

Maybe she couldn't trust anyone.

"I should never have told you," she snapped.

His eyes widened, and his jaw dropped.

"This isn't the time for the police to move in at all. It's just a speaker coming," she continued.

"One with potential terrorist links." He folded his arms and stared at her, piercing her with his gaze. "Are you really prepared to take that risk for a story?"

That stung. Turning, she began to walk away, back to the commune. Where else did she have to go? She was alone.

"Holly!" he called, coming after her.

She whirled around to face him, anger bubbling inside her out of seemingly nowhere. "Leave me alone! You've just been pretending to befriend me this whole time, just so you could report back to your brothers."

He breathed in deeply, shaking his head. "That's not true, Holly," he said firmly, but gently.

She was so angry she stormed off. She didn't need him, or anyone. She would get her story, and then she'd be out of there.

He didn't follow, but although she didn't turn back, she could feel his gaze on her back.

By the time she tiptoed into the camp, her anger had abated somewhat. Perhaps he was right. Perhaps it *was* time to get out. To admit that she'd bitten off more than she could chew.

She stopped in her tracks. So lost in thought, she hadn't seen Sally standing in front of her cabin until she almost walked into her. Sally wore a triumphant grin as she waved Holly's phone in her hand.

Holly groaned. How had she forgotten to take it? The battery had been low so she'd found a small torch in the kitchen and taken that instead, but she still should have taken her phone.

She turned to run, but it was too late. Sally's other hand lashed out like a whip, grabbing her arm. Holly tried to grapple with her to get free, but Sally was a lot stronger than she looked.

Holly screamed, hoping that somehow Joseph would hear her. Instead, lights flickered on in all the cabins around the camp while Sally dragged her towards Karl's.

He stepped out onto his porch, and once his gaze landed on the two women, he hurried down to them. "What's going on?" His voice boomed like thunder while his eyes darkened dangerously.

Holly froze. She looked around desperately, but everyone stared at her and Sally. They'd be after her in a heartbeat if Karl uttered the word, she was sure of it.

There was nowhere to run.

Sally handed Holly's phone to Karl. "Holly isn't who she says she is," she hissed. "She's a journalist, undercover, looking for a story. She's also been meeting up with Joseph Carlton. She's been spying on us."

He took the phone, but his gaze was on Holly. "Is this true?"

Holly couldn't speak. Her mouth was dry and her lips wouldn't move. There was no defending herself. How could she? It was true. Her gaze flickered towards her cabin. Makayla stood out front, staring at the spectacle. Did she already know about the phone? After all, Sally would have searched the cabin to find it.

Which meant that either Sally had seen her leave, or Makayla had. She gazed at the younger girl, wishing she could read her thoughts.

She screamed when Karl grabbed her and pulled her along towards the storage building.

"Get off me!" She struggled with all her might, but if Sally was strong, Karl was ten times more so, and she had no hope of fighting her way out of his grip.

"Someone, help me!" She screamed louder, but none of the onlookers moved.

When they reached the solid timber structure, Sally unlocked the door before Karl thrust Holly inside so roughly that she fell onto the hard dirt ground. Clambering to her feet, she rushed for the door, but it was locked firmly. She threw herself against it. "Please, let me go," she sobbed, now truly terrified.

Karl's voice came from outside, and she thought she could hear pleasure in her suffering. "You'll stay there until our work is done," he said loudly, no doubt as much for the benefit of the rest of the camp as for her. "You will not stand in the way of the Lord's mission...and for this, you are condemned."

His footsteps retreated, and she was left in the dark. Although screaming was pointless, she hurled herself against the door again and again, but the thick wood and the large metal bolt weren't going to give. Exhausted and petrified, she sunk in a heap on the ground, sobbing as terror overtook her.

Her eyes slowly adjusted to the faint gloom from moonlight coming through a barred skylight in the roof. She took in her surroundings. Boxes of supplies were stacked against each wall. At least she'd have food to eat.

But as the writing on the side of the crates grew clearer, a fresh wave of terror filled her.

They weren't boxes of food.

They were explosives.

CHAPTER 13

As the minutes, then hours, ticked by, Holly huddled in the corner of the storage building, curled in a ball, shivering, trembling, and thinking she'd been left to die. No one was coming. As the night wore on it grew even darker until the moon came out from behind clouds and shone directly through the skylight, revealing a perfect circle of light in the middle of the earth floor. Without knowing why, she crawled towards it and sat under the moonlight, gazing at its serene beauty.

Lord, if You really are there, please help me. It was a desperate prayer, her doubt born out of fear that she would be left there to die, and her parents would never know what had happened to her. Silent tears slipped down her cheeks; she had no energy to wipe them away.

Her gaze shifted to the boxes of explosives. She didn't want to think about what they could signify. There was a dusty shelf above the boxes, and for some reason, she was drawn to it. Tucked into the corner of a shelf was a small book.

For a single moment, the moonlight seemed to shine directly on it.

It was a Bible.

She reached for it, and then sat, cross-legged, within the circle of light. The spine was cracked, and it fell open instantly in her lap. Her gaze dropped to the open page, and the words stared up at her, highlighted by the moonlight.

Psalm 51.

Slowly, haltingly, she read aloud.

Have mercy on me, O God, according to Your unfailing love, according to Your great compassion, blot out my transgressions... Create in me a pure heart, O God, and renew a steadfast spirit within me. Do not cast me from Your presence or take Your Holy Spirit from me. Restore to me the joy of Your salvation and grant me a willing spirit, to sustain me. The sacrifices of God are a broken spirit. A broken and contrite heart, O God, You will not despise.

The words pierced right to her very soul, as though they'd been written directly for her. She saw, with a clarity that seemed to illuminate every dark corner of her psyche, just how she'd allowed the hurt Chad had caused to turn her away from God's presence, and instead chase fame and fortune in a bid to prove herself worthy.

"Forgive my transgressions, Lord," she sobbed, echoing the words of the Psalmist. She felt scrubbed raw and entirely unworthy of God's presence after the way she'd turned from Him to pursue the lure of the world. To make a name for herself. She looked at the Book again, and the true meaning of the words flooded over her like a balm to her scarred heart. Yes, she had transgressed, but the Word told her that the Lord did not despise her, but instead, He loved her unfailingly and with great compassion. She didn't need to be 'worthy' in the eyes of the world, or God

Himself, for all were sinners. She needed only to offer contrition and her broken heart to Him, and she would be forgiven.

She read the words of the Psalm again, slowly, like a prayer, because that's what it was, punctuating them with her own heartfelt cries to the Saviour she had forgotten.

Have mercy on me, O God. Create in me a pure heart and renew a steadfast spirit within me. I am Yours. Forgive me for ever doubting that. Don't cast me from Your presence, but restore me to the joy of Your salvation. My broken heart is Yours, Lord. Do with me as You will.

The moon seemed to shine brighter, almost blinding her with its pure light. She became transfixed as the Spirit swept through her, drying the tears on her cheeks and filling her with a gentle joy that transcended the fear of her situation. A smile grew on her lips as her heart soared with gratitude.

"Thank You, Lord," she whispered. The light around and above softened. She exhaled slowly as the bubbling joy subsided, leaving in its place a gentle sense of calm. She would be okay. Even if she did die here, everything would ultimately be okay.

The door rattled, and a key turned in the lock before the bolt slid back. Her heart pounded as she stood and pushed as far back into a corner as she dared. The door opened and her heart pulsed even harder. It had to be Karl or Sally coming to intimidate her again.

But it was neither of them. It was Makayla. Holly breathed a sigh of relief.

The girl stood there, her dark hair wild around her pale face, her eyes huge with fear…but also with determination. "Quickly," she whispered. "Everyone's asleep. I stole the key, but you have to go now. It will be dawn soon."

Holly ran to her and pulled her into a tight embrace.

"Thank you so much," she said as she let her go. She held her at arm's length and peered into her eyes. "But why?"

Makayla shook her head, her face pinched with terror. Something had happened.

"It was my plan to let you out if they didn't," she said. "Journalist or not, you don't deserve this." She drew a deep breath. "I've been having my own doubts these past few days, ever since they started telling me more, but I've had to act as though I went along with everything. If I'd known who you were, I would have told you."

"It's not your fault," Holly reassured. "They've been brainwashing you for months. They've gotten to me too, made me question my own thoughts. But something else has happened, I can see it in your eyes."

Makayla hesitated.

Holly stepped aside so she could see the boxes behind her. "These are explosives," she said grimly.

Makayla nodded without surprise. "I didn't know they were here," she whispered, "but last night, I found out a bomb attack is being planned. The whole camp is clearing out after Ryan's Spencer's talk, and the attack will go ahead. All the men are in on it."

Holly's eyes widened. "Where are they going to bomb?"

"A refugee shelter in the city, and a smaller attack in Eastbrooke."

Holly's hand flew to her mouth. *Joseph.* She had to warn him. "Please come with me, Makayla. You need to get out of here, too."

When Makayla hesitated, Holly grabbed her hands and pleaded with her. "Karl and Sally will know that someone let me out, and if you seemed reluctant about their plans, it won't be hard for them to work out it was you. You're in danger, Makayla."

Her pretty face paled, but she still shook her head. "They're my family."

"I know," Holly said softly. "But do you trust them?"

Makayla blinked back tears. Finally, she replied haltingly, "I've never really known them. I have no idea what they're truly capable of."

"Then please come with me," Holly begged.

Makayla sniffed and nodded slowly. "Okay." Her voice was timid, as if she were still torn. Holly could understand that. It had to be hard learning what your family members were capable of, but still not wanting to betray them.

"Good girl," Holly said, smiling. She took Makayla's hand and together they crept through the camp. Holly's heart thumped so hard inside her chest that she felt sure the sound of it would give them away.

CHAPTER 14

On the cot at the lodge, Joseph tossed and turned as images of trekking up the mountain towards the commune disturbed his sleep. In his dreams, he'd been hiking for hours and not getting any closer. The moon, low and huge, emitted a sinister, yellowish light that made the landscape look ghoulish.

He stopped to pray, but to his horror, he couldn't remember any words. He sank to his knees in despair and sobbed.

He was never going to get off the mountain.

Somewhere in the distance, a woman was sobbing, too, and the sound wrenched at his heart. It was Holly. He tried to call out to her, but his voice wouldn't work. He tried to get to his feet to find her, but his body felt like it was trapped in treacle. The wind rustled as though it was laughing at him, mocking his feeble attempts to get up and go to her.

Then everything changed.

He was in his mother's kitchen, alone. The room was sparkling clean and filled with soft white light that made him feel clean. He suddenly couldn't remember what he'd been scared of a moment before.

"Joseph," came a voice from behind him.

He turned. A man stood there.

George Carlton.

His father.

"Dad!" Joseph's voice choked on a happy sob as he took in his father's appearance, remembering every happy moment of his childhood. Then he shook his head sadly. "I've let you down."

"You could never let me down," his father said, love sounding in his voice and shining from his eyes. "I'm so proud of you, son."

"But I'm not like my brothers," Joseph said. "I try to be, I really do, but I'm not a hero like them. Like you."

"There are different types of heroes in this world," his father said. "You have a different calling. Embrace it. If you need my blessing, you have it. You always have."

Joseph's eyes filled with tears of joy. As he stepped forward and embraced his father, strength flowed into him.

"You have to go now," his father whispered.

Joseph felt like a child again. "Can't I stay with you?"

"You have to wake up. Holly's in danger."

Joseph sat bolt upright. Blinking, he looked around, puzzled, as the interior of the lodge became clear and the edges of his dream faded. But he remembered his father's words...

Holly's in danger.

He jumped to his feet. He had to go to her. The dream was too vivid not to be true.

He pulled out his radio to call the police station and talk to Rob, but then hesitated as he thought through what to say. Could he really call the police over a dream, and request them to go up the mountain in the middle of the night? No. He put the radio down and went into the other room where John was yawning while sitting at the desk reading the newspaper.

"Everything okay, bud?" he asked. "It sounded like you were having a bad dream at one point; I was going to come in and wake you."

"I'm not sure. I might take a walk up the mountain towards the commune," Joseph said.

"At this time of night?"

"I've got a bad feeling. I want to check it out."

John looked skeptical but shrugged. "Okay, whatever. Take your radio, just in case."

Joseph nodded and left. He was halfway to the commune when he wondered if he should have brought the rifle that was kept in the locked cabinet in the lodge. It had only ever been used for putting sheep with broken legs out of their misery, but he had a feeling that tonight it might be needed for something more.

He hesitated. Should he go back for it? By the time he decided he would, it was too late. Someone, or something, was hurtling towards him.

Heart pounding, he peered into the distance. It looked like two women, and he was sure one of them was Holly.

~

AN OWL HOOTED SOMEWHERE OVERHEAD, waking Sally from her slumber. She yawned and stretched like a cat before rolling over to get comfortable and go back to sleep, smiling to herself as she remembered the events of the day.

She was glad Holly had been exposed. She'd taken great pleasure in revealing the contents of her phone to Karl. Holly was the snake in the garden, sent to plot their downfall, but Sally had caught her, and now her ability to bring harm to Pure Light had been neutralised, just in time for their plans to go ahead.

The time for the great battle had come and Sally couldn't wait to be a part of it. She welcomed every chance to show her brother that she was worthy of his love.

That awful Holly could have destroyed everything.

The more she thought about it, the angrier Sally grew. Sleep eluded her as she stewed on her resentment. Holly had pulled the wool over her eyes completely, making her look a fool. She wouldn't tolerate it. She was worried she'd gotten to Makayla, who'd been quieter than usual when she was let into their plans. She should have been proud and honoured that she'd been brought into the inner circle. What poison had Holly been dripping into her ear?

It was pointless staying in bed. She'd go and question Holly herself, taunt her a little, just to let her know her place.

But when she went to get the key from the box under her bed, it wasn't there. Curses slipped from her lips. This couldn't be happening!

In a panic, she sprinted across the camp to the storage cabin. The door was wide open. The stupid woman had escaped. *But how?*

Drawing a slow breath, Sally inspected the door. There were no signs of forced exit. Someone had taken the key and let her out. *But who would do such a thing and show such insubordination?*

Makayla. It had to be Makayla. Sally's stomach twisted. Surely her meek little cousin wouldn't dare, especially after discovering Holly's true identity. She'd looked heartbroken at the revelation.

Sally hurried to the girls' cabin, already knowing what

she would find. She was right. The cabin was empty, which could only mean that Makayla had let Holly out and they'd gone off together.

She needed to tell Karl.

She sprinted across the camp, but as she hammered at his door, she cringed while anticipating his reaction.

The door opened and he glowered at her. "What do you want, Sally? It's three a.m."

Shock and rage filled his eyes as she stammered out the news.

"We have to go after them and drag them back before they do any damage." He disappeared inside and then returned with a gun.

Sally's gaze locked onto it. "Do we really need that?"

Karl's slap to her face took her by surprise and almost knocked her off her feet. She clutched her cheek, staring at him with hot, humiliated tears filling her eyes.

"Don't you dare question me!" he hissed. "It was you who brought that woman here in the first place!"

Sally bowed her head and followed him obediently.

CHAPTER 15

Holly ran straight into Joseph's open arms. As he wrapped them around her and held her tight, she was certain everything would be okay. The sense of safety she felt in his arms was both alien and yet oddly familiar.

He finally released her and stepped back, placing his hands on her upper arms as he stared into her eyes.

"What are you doing here?" she gasped.

"I stayed at the lodge in case anything happened. I woke with a feeling you were in danger…it was the Holy Spirit that made me aware, I'm sure of it. What's happened?"

Holly stared at him as she absorbed his words. Clearly, she wasn't the only one the Holy Spirit had showed up for that night, and she felt the fledgling bond between them deepen further…but there was no time to talk about that now.

"Sally caught me coming back in, and Karl locked me in the storage cabin." She swallowed hard. "There are explosives in there. A lot of them." She turned towards

Makayla, and the girl stepped forward into the moonlight, nodding her head with a grim expression on her face.

"I let Holly out," she said. "Karl—our pastor, and Sally, are my cousins. They've been mentoring me, but I didn't realise what they were up to until tonight. Ryan Spencer is coming, and they're planning a terrorist attack in the city and in Eastbrooke."

Joseph's eyes shot open. He reached for his radio. "I have to call Rob," he said, glancing at Holly.

She nodded. "Of course. I'm sorry I got angry with you before. I've been so silly."

"Don't apologise. I'm just glad you're safe. Come on, I'll take you both to the lodge while I call Rob and get him and his team up here."

The trio started weaving their way down the slope. With only a torch and moonlight to guide their path, they couldn't hurry, although Holly felt the urge to do so. The further she got from that place, the better.

Halfway down, the sound of twigs snapping came from behind. They stopped. Listened. *Someone was following.*

Heart pounding, Holly turned around slowly, although she already knew who it was. It was too late to escape. Karl stood there, gun raised and pointed at them. With the moonlit shadows dancing behind him, he looked the epitome of evil, not the holier than thou leader of a so-called Christian community.

Joseph stepped forward, spreading his arms as though trying to shield her and Makayla.

Karl jerked the gun so that it pointed directly at Joseph. "One more move, Carlton," he sneered, his eyes glittering dangerously, "and I'll shoot."

Crackling came from the radio in Joseph's hand. *Was*

someone trying to get through? Holly thought she could hear a voice.

Please, Lord, please let someone hear us and know we need help.

"Put the gun down," Joseph ordered loudly but calmly. But was it loud enough for someone on the other end to hear? The radio crackled again.

Karl's gaze momentarily shifted to it. "Get rid of it." He nodded towards the bushes, his voice quiet but menacing.

When Joseph hesitated, Karl jerked the gun aggressively towards Holly.

Joseph tossed the radio, and any hope Holly had of getting out of there alive sunk in her chest like a stone.

Karl was going to kill them. And up here, on the mountain, who would ever know? Their bodies might not be found for days. Or months. Or years.

Joseph raised his hands. When he spoke, his voice was even, but Holly was close enough to see the pulse throbbing in his neck. "Let the girls go," he said. "They're no use to you. You and I can sort things out between us—man to man."

Holly shook her head even as admiration for his bravery rushed through her. After everything she'd been through, she couldn't bear to lose Joseph now.

"Do you think I'm stupid, Carlton?" Karl sneered. "They'll go straight to the police—to your brother, no doubt. It must be so hard for you to know that you're powerless to protect your little friend. Not quite the hero now, are you?"

Holly sensed Joseph flinch, but he didn't outwardly react to Karl's words. Beside her, Makayla sobbed, the sound cutting pitifully through the otherwise silent mountain.

Karl's gaze pivoted to her, although his gun was trained firmly on Holly. "I'll deal with you later," he threatened.

Makayla cringed, her entire posture seeming to collapse under his words.

Then Karl turned his attention back to Holly, and the hatred in his eyes was so palpable, she gasped.

"As for you," he spat, "there's only one way to deal with traitors."

"Don't touch her," Joseph ordered through gritted teeth. "Or I swear I'll hunt you down until the end of your days."

Karl tipped his head back and laughed raucously, the sound reverberating around the mountain with pure evil that made Holly shudder from head to foot. She closed her eyes, grasping for a comforting phrase from the Bible to calm her panicked thoughts, but suddenly, comfort seemed far away as Karl's laughter continued to echo.

"Oh, don't worry, Carlton," he continued to taunt. "You'll be with her. I hope you really love this mountain, because I'm going to make sure you're buried here forever."

A long, ominous silence followed. Karl continued to point his gun steadily at Holly, sneering silently at Joseph as though challenging him to do something.

But there was nothing he could do.

There was no escape.

Stepping towards them, Karl swung his gun in a slow arc, encompassing the trio. With a menacing leer, he motioned with his other hand towards the mountain. "Carlton, you're going to lead us back up to the camp," he said in a tone that was almost conversational.

"I don't think so," Joseph said through gritted teeth.

Karl's leer widened, his expression in the eerie light made Holly think of a shark. "You don't really have a choice, do you? You'll go first, followed by Holly, with my gun in her back. Try anything and I'll kill her before you can blink." He glanced at his sister. "Walk behind with Makayla." His lip curled with contempt as he spoke his cousin's name, and

Holly shuddered to think what 'punishment' would be in store for the girl.

Joseph glanced at Holly briefly before he began to walk, but his gaze remained firmly on Karl as he passed the man who was now showing his true colours.

"You'll pay for this, Hausbaden," he told him quietly.

Karl flinched at the use of his real name, but just then, a shot rang out and Holly screamed. *No! Not Joseph*...Fear, stark and vivid, swept through her. But he was still standing, as was Karl.

Karl swung his gun around as he looked in the direction of the gunshot.

Another man approached slowly with his rifle pointed. Holly recognised John, Joseph's partner from the Rescue Lodge. She was about to breathe a sigh of relief when Karl made a sudden grab for Makayla and pushed his gun into the side of her head.

Everyone froze. John stopped a few metres from them. His eyes flickered nervously as he kept his rifle trained on Karl, his gaze darting towards Joseph as though waiting to be told what to do.

Joseph took a step sideways, closer to Holly, but stopped when Karl snarled at him.

"Stay put, Carlton, unless you want blood on your hands."

"You can't hurt Makayla!" Holly gasped. Tears streamed down the other girl's face as she stood trapped in Karl's arms. "She's your family."

"The true lord requires sacrifice," Karl said calmly.

Makayla whimpered.

Holly felt sick as she understood just how warped Karl's ideas really were. There was nothing of the true God in his twisted ideology.

"Hausbaden," Joseph said firmly, an undercurrent of

anger and fear in his tone. "Let her go. You don't want to do this. It's over."

"You don't get to tell me when it's over," Karl responded with hate blazing from his eyes.

Holly's gaze turned to Sally, who had barely moved throughout the whole interaction, standing as still as a statue as she watched events unfold. Holly searched her face for a trace of compassion and empathy.

"Sally," she begged. "You can't let him hurt Makayla. She's your cousin. You took her in."

Sally smiled almost serenely. "Makayla is a traitor."

With those words, Holly's hopes of any help from her faded. Karl was so far inside his sister's head that Holly suspected nothing would break her loyalty.

Karl inched backwards, dragging Makayla with him. Sally followed. There was nothing any of them could do.

"We'll meet again, Carlton," Karl hissed at Joseph. "I'll make sure of it. But right now, if you try to come after me, I'll shoot her without a second thought. And I know you won't let me do that," he continued, taunting, "because you all have to be heroes, don't you? But not this time."

Karl and Sally, with Makayla between them, had nearly disappeared into the trees when a loud roar filled the skies and a blue light swept over them.

"It's Rob," John murmured just loud enough for Holly and Joseph to hear. "He radioed through to me at the lodge because he knew I'd get here quicker."

So, Rob had heard the radio. Euphoria filled Holly. *Thank You, Lord.* The helicopter continued to lower until it hovered just above them, the sound of the rotors deafening as dust was whipped up and swirled around.

A voice, sounding a lot like Joseph's, shouted through

some kind of megaphone. "This is the police. Drop your weapons and raise your hands."

Karl shoved the gun harder into Makayla's head. She squealed loudly. Then, a red dot appeared on both Sally and Karl's foreheads.

"I repeat, drop your weapons," Rob said again. "Or I'll give the order to shoot."

Now that her own life was in danger, Sally's demeanour finally cracked. Sobbing, she pleaded with her brother. "Karl, let Makayla go."

Although Holly hoped the woman had gathered some empathy for her young cousin, she doubted it. She was starting to believe that Sally was as evil as her brother.

In a sudden movement, Karl tossed the gun and pushed Makayla into the path of John's rifle before turning and making a run for it towards the trees.

Springing into action, Joseph raced past Holly. Within moments he caught up with Karl and wrestled him to the ground as the helicopter lowered further and Rob and another police officer jumped out.

Feeling weak, Holly sank to her knees on the ground as nausea overtook her. Her head was spinning and everything around her seemed to blur. For a moment she thought she would faint, but then strong arms were around her, lifting her to her feet, and her strength came back. Joseph gazed down at her with eyes filled with emotions so far unspoken.

"Is it over?" she asked, her voice shaking. She looked around. Karl was being led, hands cuffed behind his back, into the helicopter. He looked smaller somehow, his entire body language expressing defeat.

"For now," Joseph said softly. "And for you, yes. He can't hurt you now."

She couldn't believe it. IT was finally over. "Where's Makayla?"

"I'm here," the girl said, her voice as shaky as Holly's. She stood with John, visibly trembling but looking ever so relieved.

Holly laid her head on Joseph's chest for a moment and then stepped back, wiping her eyes as she realised she was crying.

"Come on," he said softly. "I'm going to take you and Makayla to Max's. He lives at the retreat at the bottom of the mountain. We'll be safe there until Rob gets back."

Overwhelmed with gratitude, Holly nodded. Then she frowned as she looked around.

"Where's Sally?"

CHAPTER 16

Holly and Makayla sat in front of Max and Junia's log fire, hot chocolates in hand. Makayla was silent, staring into the flames, while Holly spoke to Junia in low tones. Joseph felt simultaneously relieved that they were safe, and furious with Karl for threatening their lives. However, Sally was still at large. John was out searching for her with a police officer, while Rob had taken Karl back to the station to read him his rights. Joseph wondered if it would be Eli who would come to pick him up to take him to Melbourne. The counter-terrorist division would have a lot of questions for him. Joseph suspected Karl would tell them nothing, but if anyone could crack him, it would be his brother.

Returning to the room after taking a phone call, Max motioned to Joseph. Joseph set his cup on the side and crossed the room.

"There's no sign of Sally," Max said quietly. "They'll look again tomorrow."

"I'll join them."

Max shook his head. "No, brother, you'll take a few days off. You've been through a lot."

"Not as much as the girls have." Joseph glanced back at the women around the fire, although he only had eyes for Holly.

Max followed his gaze. "She means a lot to you, doesn't she?"

"I barely know her."

"Like I barely knew Junia when you said the same thing to me," Max reminded him. "And you were right, remember?"

Joseph looked down, unable to put words to the tumult of emotions swirling through him. Seeing Karl with a gun pointed at her, he'd known in that moment that if he lost her, he could hardly bear it. He'd felt certain then that she was his soulmate. Now, he wondered if that was a crazy thought.

But then, the whole night had been crazy.

"How did you know to go back?" Max asked curiously.

For a moment, Joseph wondered how much to tell his oldest brother. He finally settled on the truth. "I had a dream about Dad. He warned me, I think. Or God did. The details are slipping away now."

Max looked at him with empathy, as though he understood the journey Joseph had been on. "I had a dream like that about Dad once," he said in a quiet voice. "It changed my life. It wasn't just about Holly, though, was it?"

Joseph shook his head. "No," he admitted. He swallowed hard and drew in a breath. "I've been thinking about going to Bible College. To be a minister." He held his breath, waiting for Max's reaction. Would his most rugged of brothers scoff or try to talk him out of it?

He needn't have worried. Max smiled and looked genuinely delighted. "Finally," he said.

"Huh?" This wasn't the reaction he'd been expecting.

"Joseph," Max said patiently, "we've all been waiting years for you to figure this out. I had you pegged for ministry when we were teens. You were always the best listener, and the one for whom faith came so naturally. Mum will be over the moon—she's always longed for at least one of us to go into ministry."

Joseph could hardly believe his ears. "You're not disappointed?"

"Disappointed? Why would I be?" Max looked genuinely baffled.

"I'm a Carlton," Joseph said, as though that explained everything. "You know how people see us...rugged, hero types. Especially since we took down that gang and Rob made Police Chief. I'm expected to rescue people, and the occasional sheep. Not souls."

"And you've done a great job at Mountain Rescue," Max said, "but that doesn't mean you have to do it forever. I don't understand why you think we wouldn't be supportive."

Joseph took a deep breath before blurting out his feelings. "I suppose I've always felt like I have to live up to Dad."

Max nodded. "I think we've all felt like that."

"But all of you do," Joseph continued. "Whereas I thought that if I entered the ministry, I'd be letting his legacy down somehow. I've always felt like..."

"Like what?" Max angled his head.

Joseph sighed. This wasn't easy. "Do you remember that sermon a few weeks ago about calling, and Pastor quoting Gideon when he said he was 'the least in my father's house?' Joseph blinked, lowered his gaze. "I guess that's how I feel sometimes."

"Little brother, get that ridiculous idea out of your head.

You are the very best of us. Do you know, I used to feel jealous that I thought you were Dad's favourite?"

Joseph looked up, and despite himself, a grin grew on his face. "Really? I always thought it was you or Eli."

"And Eli thinks it was Rob." Max chortled. "Sibling rivalry, hey? The truth is, he loved us all equally, exactly as we are, as does Mum. Don't ever apologise for being who God has called you to be." His voice had grown serious.

Joseph nodded and thanked God silently for the wisdom of older brothers.

"So," Max continued, "now you've got that crazy notion out of your head, are you going to do it? Bible College, I mean?"

Joseph nodded. "Yes. Peter is going to sponsor me."

Max clapped him on the back. "I'm proud of you. Now, what are you going to do about Holly?"

"Shush!" Joseph hissed as Holly caught the sound of her name and looked up. Their gazes met. With the flames dancing across her face and hair, turning her eyes to gold, she looked gorgeous. It was all he could do to keep his eyes off her.

He pondered Max's words and wondered what the answer would turn out to be.

What was he going to do about Holly?

CHAPTER 17

As Holly made her way to the baptistry font, her face glowing, Joseph sat in the front pew beside his mum, his gaze fixed on this woman who had captivated his heart.

This was a big day for Holly, and he was honoured to be witnessing it. Although her parents had her christened as a child, she'd made the decision to be baptised as an adult to not only be obedient to the Word, but as a way of rededicating herself now that she had a renewed commitment to her faith. She'd told him about her encounter with the Holy Spirit that night she'd been locked in the cabin, and he'd been filled with awe at the way God worked in peoples' lives at times.

The fact that her encounter must have happened at around the same time as his dream hadn't been lost on him, either. He'd taken it as yet another sign to follow his calling to ministry.

Sometimes he couldn't help wondering if it was *another* sort of sign as well. One that indicated a deeper bond between him and her. In the weeks that had passed since the incident on the mountain, she'd stayed in Eastbrooke with his mother while the media frenzy died down. Quickly growing bored with inactivity, she'd started helping out at the local paper.

They were becoming firm friends, their shared trauma making them closer, but sooner or later she would return to Melbourne. After all, her career was there...and just as she had wanted, she was set for bigger things.

She'd written her story for the Post, detailing her infiltration of Pure Light and the life-threatening events that had ensued, and just as she had dreamed, it had been a national hit. A major tabloid had rerun the story and it had been featured in international news, too. Offers of interviews and radio shows were pouring in thick and fast. She didn't seem as enthused about it all as Joseph would have expected, given her earlier insistence on getting a good story at all costs, but no doubt her recent experiences had derailed her. He was sure that once she recovered fully from the shock and trauma, she'd return to her career—and the city—even if she was content to lie low for the time being.

It couldn't last forever, but he was holding off revealing how he really felt about her, telling himself that it was too soon and that she wouldn't want to be held back by a small-town pastor.

After plucking up the courage to tell his brothers and receiving their unwavering support, he'd discovered that there were no longer any internal barriers to prevent him studying for ministry. Pastor Peter had sponsored him, and just this week, he'd received his acceptance into Melbourne Bible College. He would start in a few months, staying in the city for study every two weeks. He was excited, if not a little nervous, knowing that he was finally following the path God was placing in front of him.

The only thing missing was someone to share it with.

As the pastor immersed Holly in the water and lifted her back up, Joseph's heart swelled with pride and happiness for her. For a moment, she caught his gaze and a surge of electricity flowed through him. But it was more than simple attraction; what he felt for this woman was as spiritual as it was physical.

But he couldn't tell her. She'd been through so much in this tiny mountain town that he was surprised she hadn't gotten out as fast as she possibly could. With all the new career opportunities that awaited her, it could only be a matter of time. And although he would be in Melbourne every two weeks, Bible College would give him no time for social calls.

No, he had to accept that because of their changing circumstances, it wouldn't work. It was too complicated.

Even if an inner voice kept telling him otherwise.

Trying to distract himself from his train of thoughts, he glanced around the small church. It was more packed than usual, filled not just with regular churchgoers but all the Eastbrooke residents that had been following Holly's story. Given that she might well have saved the town from being bombed, she'd become something of a local hero. As for Joseph, he was currently the Carlton brother in the spotlight for heroic deeds, and as the guy who had brought Karl Hausbaden in. Even counter-terrorism agents had been calling to thank him. He had all the heroic acclaim he had ever wanted...and wasn't surprised to find that, in fact, he didn't really want it. He had accepted that his path lay elsewhere.

In the church. He smiled at the thought that one day he

would be standing where Pastor Peter was right now, baptising new members of the Lord's flock.

After the service, they went back to his mother's place where she had prepared a small luncheon buffet to celebrate Holly's baptism. Max and Junia were there with Polly, his niece, and Rob and Emma, but as usual, Eli was missing, although his little brother had promised to come and visit soon. Right now, he was intent on tracking down Ryan Spencer and Johannes Hausbaden.

Makayla was also in Melbourne. She was in a safe house, going through a deradicalisation program while also helping the counter-terrorism department with their enquiries. She kept in touch with Holly as much as was safe, and she seemed to be doing well, although no doubt she was still reeling from the terrible betrayal by her family and of discovering their true intentions.

Karl Hausbaden was awaiting trial, both for plans to commit terrorist acts and for assaulting and kidnapping Holly. There was no doubt he would get a long sentence, particularly as he had refused to give any information about either his father or the White League, denying any links even though they were now quite obvious. There was no sign of the older Hausbaden, and Ryan Spencer was still in America, peddling thinly disguised Nazism on national television. They didn't have anything on him that would stick, something that Eli was still furious about.

Joseph was just eternally grateful that Holly was safe.

Sally was still at large and there had been no sightings of her. Joseph hoped that she would stay well away from her family from now on, and perhaps find repentance and rebuild her life. Then he remembered the woman's unwavering devotion to her brother and suspected not.

Still, at least she was gone and couldn't hurt Holly

anymore. A surge of protectiveness washed over him as he once again recalled the details of that night on the mountain when Karl Hausbaden had trained his gun on her. For a few horrible moments, Joseph had thought he would certainly pull the trigger.

He suspected that it had been in that moment that he had truly realised just how much he loved Holly.

He went into the kitchen with his mother to help make coffee and tea, leaving Holly to be fussed over by his sisters-in-law and the other women from church.

His mum smiled gratefully as he passed her the sugar bowl. "Thank you, son. How are you? You seem quiet."

He hesitated. "I'm fine," he reassured. "Just thinking about everything."

"It's certainly been a lot to take in these past few weeks," she said sympathetically. She looked at him. "Have you asked Holly out for dinner yet?"

"What? No," he replied quickly.

"You should. I see how she looks at you."

"You're just trying to match make, Mum." Joseph grinned, but he felt the flutter of excitement in his stomach at the thought that his mother might be right.

"Don't give me that, Joseph Carlton," she said in a mock stern tone. "Now that Max and Rob are settled, I'm not on the same urgent quest for grandchildren as I once was, but I do know a spark when I see one, and it's there any time you and Holly are in the same room."

Joseph sat at the kitchen table, momentarily forgetting all about the drinks. "Do you really think so? But what can I do? She'll be going back to Melbourne, and we'll both be too busy for a long-distance relationship. That's assuming she even wants one."

His mother smiled indulgently. "Have I taught you boys

nothing? If God wills it, then He will make a way. I have no doubt that you and Holly came together for a reason. You have to put this in God's hands, son, just as you have with your vocation."

He sighed. His mother was right, as always.

"Okay, you're right," he said, echoing his own thoughts. "But where do I start?"

"By finishing that tea," she said. "And then, while you're giving Holly hers, ask her out for dinner. If you don't ask, my love, then you'll never know, will you?"

He could hardly argue with that logic.

A WHILE LATER, after the other guests had left, the Carlton family and Holly were sitting on his mother's verandah watching the evening sun and enjoying the gentle breeze coming down from the mountain.

"We'd better get Polly back to bed," a very pregnant Junia announced. She and Max rose and said their goodbyes.

Then Rob yawned loudly and Emma pushed to her feet. "We'd better be going, too," she said.

"I'm just so busy," Rob grumbled. "I've had a ton of paperwork to file and reports to read in the aftermath of all this. And journalists keep ringing up for quotes, which I just don't have time for."

Holly winced. "I'm sorry," she said quietly. "Because of my coverage, it's still front-page news."

"Not at all," Rob said charitably. "It was a great story and the general public needs to know about Pure Light. I just wish journalists weren't so pushy in getting their stories."

Holly ducked her head guiltily, but Rob didn't seem to notice. Instead, he and Emma said their goodbyes. Then his mum started clearing up, bustling off behind the pair and leaving Joseph and Holly alone on the verandah. He knew his mother well enough to know that it was no mistake.

He cleared his throat. "I've got something I want to ask you." His heart beat a crescendo. *Why was it so hard to ask her out on a date?* Because she might say no, and he couldn't bear it if she did. But there was no guarantee she would agree.

"Go on," she said. He was sure hope flickered in her eyes, giving him hope.

"The thing is," he started, "I've been wondering if you'd like to go for dinner."

She nodded happily. "Oh yes. I'd love to go out for dinner with you guys. Though I don't know if a restaurant can beat your mum's cooking."

He groaned inwardly. She'd misunderstood. "Not with all of us," he corrected, his pulse flickering wildly in his throat. "I mean, with me. Just me and you…like a date."

Her eyes widened and then she blinked rapidly.

Joseph held his breath until a shy smile grew on her face and she said, "I would absolutely love to go on a date with you."

∼

A FEW MILES AWAY, sitting on the side of the mountain overlooking Eastbrooke, Sally stared down at the town. She hated the place, and the people in it. Heathens who weren't fit to lick her brother's boots.

Her poor brother…

In her mind, Karl had become the victim of persecution, jailed by the authorities in an attempt to suppress the truth. She had to do everything in her power to get him out; he would be counting on her.

Failing that, she at least had to seek revenge.

If she hated the people in the town below her in general, she hated the Carltons even more.

But she hated Holly Davidson the most.

Sally had a flight to catch in a few days' time. She would rejoin their father, Johannes, regroup, and see what was in store for her next. Freeing Karl would be a priority.

The way she saw it, if Holly Davidson wasn't around, there'd be one less witness against Karl. There was Makayla, of course, but their father would deal with his wayward niece.

Sally had been ordered to take no further action. Holly would be dealt with at the right time, but Sally wasn't happy with that. Karl needed her help now. And she wanted her reckoning with the woman who had brought all their carefully made plans crashing down around their ears. Her father and brother would thank her afterwards.

Because right now, she knew they blamed *her* for introducing Holly to them in the first place. She was desperate to get back into her family's good books. Getting rid of Holly Davidson would achieve just that.

As she gazed down on the town, she allowed herself a small smile as she thought of the knife in her backpack.

I'm coming for you, Holly.

CHAPTER 18

Holly lifted her gaze to the mountain standing like a benign giant watching over Eastbrooke and uttered a silent prayer of gratitude. Although memories of everything that had happened up at the commune still woke her occasionally during the night, she was intensely thankful for the breakthrough it had prompted in her life. She'd never felt so close to God, and getting baptised had been a wonderful experience. She loved being in Eastbrooke, and getting to know everyone better, especially the Carltons. She got on so well with Junia and Emma, that it felt they'd known each other for years, and Jean was like a second mother to her. She also loved helping out at the local paper, even if it was a lot smaller than what she was used to.

Then, of course, there was Joseph. They'd been spending quite a lot of time together, but because he hadn't hinted at anything permanent, like marriage, she wasn't sure where their relationship was headed. There was definitely a spark between them, wrought by their shared experience on the mountain, but was that all it was? Without knowing his heart, she couldn't be sure, and she was too afraid of rejection to ask.

Except now, she had decisions to make, and Joseph's intentions towards her factored into them.

Although she'd now achieved her dream of landing a big, national story, it didn't mean as much to her as she always thought it would. She was proud of her work and glad she'd been given the chance to expose a dangerous neo-Nazi group, but the fame and prestige aspect, now that it was on offer, meant nothing. That night when she'd been locked in the cabin had stripped away all pretence, and she now knew what was important in life.

Faith. Family and friends. Integrity.

And love.

She certainly had no intention of returning to the Post. Although William had suspected she was in danger, he'd encouraged her to stay for the sake of the story. That cutthroat world wasn't one she wanted to be a part of anymore. And yet it was still hard not to feel tempted to take one of the offers of reporting for a big national paper that she had received.

The Eastbrooke Telegraph had also made her an offer as Senior Editor. It was a high-level post, but with a small local paper. Did she really want to confine her skills to Eastbrooke?

There was another option, of course, and one that seemed ideal. She could take the Editor role while also doing some occasional freelance reporting for the bigger papers. She was regarded as something of a cult expert now, and with her proximity to Eli and Rob, she could even be the official reporter on the Hausbaden case. She was already being offered large sums of money for a follow up to her first piece.

It was the ideal answer to her dilemma, but something was holding her back from making a decision.

Joseph.

She glanced up at him as he walked next to her. They were both on a lunch break; he'd been at Max's retreat teaching the local youth group about Mountain Rescue, and so they'd met up for a walk in the sun. She cleared her throat, trying to pluck up the courage to start the conversation they needed to have.

"So," she began, "the Telegraph offered me a Senior Editor position."

He stopped walking and faced her. "That's amazing! Congratulations. Are you going to take it?"

She shrugged. "I don't know. It'd mean staying in Eastbrooke. I'd have to completely relocate and rent somewhere here. But I've also been offered a reporter position on The National."

Was she mistaken, or did a flash of disappointment cross his face before he adopted a neutral gaze? *Was* he disappointed? *Please tell me you want me to stay...* But she couldn't force the issue. It needed to come from him.

"You should take the reporting position, then," he said.

Crushed, she bit her bottom lip in dismay. "Really?" She willed him to say something else, to give her any indication that he didn't want her to leave.

He rubbed her forearms as he gazed into her eyes. "Yes, of course. It's always been your dream...there's nothing like that for you here."

She swallowed the urge to cry. Was this his way of telling her he didn't feel the way she did? He must realise she had strong feelings for him; perhaps this was his way of letting her down gently.

"I'd better get back," she said, her gaze dropping to her

shoes and wishing the ground would swallow her up. How could she have gotten this so wrong?

Smiling, he mumbled a goodbye and set off back towards the retreat while she turned and trudged along the track to the small office at the Telegraph, blinking away hot tears against the sting of rejection.

So caught up in her feelings, she didn't hear the rush of footsteps behind her as she passed the creek until it was too late.

She screamed as strong arms grabbed her and dragged her backwards, but then her scream died in her throat as the chill of steel pressed hard against her skin. Someone had a knife to her neck.

Even before her captor spoke in a soft but menacing tone, she instinctively knew who had hold of her.

Sally.

Sure enough, the woman whispered in her ear. "Hello, Holly. We meet again."

Holly swallowed as the knife pushed firmer against her throat. Another millimetre and it would sink into her skin. Her breaths grew faster and shallower as she tried to remain still. "Sally, please let me go. This isn't going to help. In fact, it will make everything worse."

Sally laughed, but there was no humour in the sound; it was a howl of rage and despair. "How could it be worse? Because of you, my brother is gone."

Holly couldn't help but feel a stab of sympathy for the woman. With Karl manipulating her since they were children, what chance had she ever had? "It doesn't have to be this way for you, Sally," she whispered, keeping as still as she could. "If you hand yourself in and tell the police how Karl has brainwashed you, they'll see that you're a victim. You could be free of him, forever."

There was a pause during which the pressure of the knife seemed to ease, but then Sally howled, a sound that was almost a sob, and she pressed the tip of the blade into her skin and Holly felt a trickle of blood down her neck. She closed her eyes.

Sally was going to kill her.

Holly began to pray silently, asking God to keep her family safe and well, her friends in Eastbrooke, and even Sally herself. "I forgive you, Sally," she murmured as she blinked back tears.

Suddenly, the knife was gone and so was the weight of Sally's arms around her. Holly spun around. Joseph had hold of the woman, had wrestled the knife from her grip, and had thrown it into the bushes.

Sally struggled, but within moments, she crumpled and dissolved into raw sobs.

As Holly's gaze found Joseph's, she saw the heart-rending tenderness in his eyes she'd been longing for. Joy like she not felt before bubbled inside her. "You came after me."

"Yes." He smiled. "To tell you what I should have told you before."

She held her breath, longing for him to kiss her. To hold her.

But then he grinned. "Before we get into that, do you think you could phone Rob?"

"Sure." She couldn't help but laugh.

AFTER ROB ARRESTED Sally and took her into custody, Joseph and Holly sat in his kitchen, drinking tea. His gaze kept turning to the band-aid on her neck. "I nearly lost you," he said for the fifth time.

She, however, felt perfectly calm. Rather than dwelling on

the attack, her thoughts kept turning to the words he'd spoken before she called the police. "Joseph," she said quietly, "what was it that you wanted to tell me?"

Blinking, he reached out across the table and took her hand, caressing her skin with his thumb while meeting her gaze. "I would never want to hold you back, Holly, which is why I encouraged you to take the reporter job in the city." His Adam's apple bobbed as he swallowed hard. "But the truth is, I would miss you *so* much... because... because... I've fallen in love with you. I have no idea if you feel the same, or if we could make it work long distance... but I couldn't let you leave without being honest with you."

Her heart sang as she squeezed his hand and smiled. "I've fallen in love with you, too. I just didn't know how to tell you, so I was hoping you'd ask me to stay when I told you about the job offers. I don't want to be a reporter in the city. If I've learned anything from this experience, it's that."

"But it's a fantastic opportunity."

"There are others." She told him about her idea of working and living in Eastbrooke while occasionally freelancing and reporting on similar cases. "It would be the best of both worlds. And I can stay in Eastbrooke—if you want me to."

Standing, he walked around the table, pulled her into his arms, and gazed into her eyes. "I can't think of anything I want more." He lifted a hand to her cheek and cupped her face. Her pulse skittered as his lips descended to meet hers. She responded by pressing her open lips to his, never dreaming that this moment would ever happen.

He took his time kissing her with warm, lingering kisses, the kind that left her in no doubt that he loved her as much as she loved him.

EPILOGUE

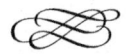

Six months later

Joseph smiled to himself, blinking back proud tears as Holly walked towards him. She wore a flowing white chiffon gown and held a bouquet of yellow roses, her favourite flower. Her hair was lightly curled but bounced on her shoulders. Behind her followed her bridesmaids. Junia, Emma, and Makayla were clad in the same delicate yellow as the roses, and in front, little Polly tottered along with a basket of daisies, eliciting murmurs of approval from the guests. They all made such a beautiful picture, but it was on Holly's face that Joseph's gaze was fixed.

He felt as though his heart would burst with love. The worship song that accompanied her up the aisle summed up his feelings, both for her and the Saviour who in His infinite wisdom had brought them together.

Oh, the overwhelming, never ending, reckless love of God

Oh, it chases me down, fights 'til I'm found, leaves the ninety-nine
And I couldn't earn it
I don't deserve it, still You give yourself away
Oh, the overwhelming, never ending, reckless love of God

The love he felt was so overwhelming, but it no longer felt reckless. In fact, he felt safer with Holly than he had ever felt before. She'd helped heal an aching in him that he hadn't even known was there; it was such freedom to be seen and loved by another person for who he was, not just as a Carlton brother, but as Joseph.

Of course, now he knew that his family had always loved him that way. He had just never allowed himself to receive it.

Taking Holly's hand with his family watching, he finally felt complete and knew that his dad would be smiling down on them.

As the song faded away and Pastor Peter went through their vows, Joseph was barely aware of the words as he lost himself in Holly's beautiful eyes.

Holly. His wife. When Peter announced them husband and wife, Joseph leaned down and kissed her deeply, hardly able to believe how blessed he was. He couldn't wait to share his life with this woman and to have a family of his own.

Their courtship had been swift as neither wanted to hold back on their feelings for each other. After everything that had happened on the mountain, they had both been certain that God had brought them together and their love was meant to be. He'd proposed just a few months into dating, and once his mother had gotten wind of their engagement, wedding arrangements hadn't taken long at all.

Now, they walked down the aisle hand in hand under a shower of confetti.

Holly squeezed his hand as she looked up at him. "I love you, Joseph," she murmured.

"I love you too, Holly." He grinned as he brushed her lips with his.

"Okay, you two," a heavily pregnant Emma laughed. "We've got photographs to take."

Joseph, Max, Rob and Eli all rolled their eyes as one. Not one of them liked photographs.

As they lined up, however, Joseph ensured that he got a few of just him and his brothers. The Carltons. All so similar, and yet each was unique.

He was a few months into Bible College now, and with every passing day, he knew that he had made the right decision. When the time came, he would miss Mountain Rescue, but he could no longer run away from his calling, and all three of his brothers supported him wholeheartedly.

"Let Mum in the picture now," Rob said, waving her over. "Then we'll get one with the bride and bridesmaids."

"Poor Uncle Eli," Polly piped up. "You're the only one on your own."

"That's okay," Eli laughed. "That's just how I like it."

Joseph glanced at his brother, wondering how much of his words were just bravado. Still living in Melbourne, devoting his life to hunting down what remained of the White League, Joseph was sure that Eli was lonely, even if he didn't admit it. Makayla had travelled back to Eastbrooke for the wedding, and Joseph hoped that as they both lived in Melbourne, they'd look out for each other. He worried about his little brother and wanted nothing more than for him to be happy.

Seeming to echo his thoughts, Max clapped Eli on the back.

"That won't last forever, little bro," he teased. "You're the last one of us to be single. If you don't find yourself a woman, no doubt Mum will!"

They all laughed as she shrugged, a grin on her face. "Time will tell," she said as Eli groaned. "God will provide."

"Indeed, He will," Joseph said softly, taking Holly's hand again and gazing into her eyes. "Indeed, He will."

HAVE MERCY ON ME, O God, according to Your unfailing love, according to Your great compassion, blot out my transgressions... Create in me a pure heart, O God, and renew a steadfast spirit within me. Do not cast me from Your presence or take your Holy Spirit from me. Restore to me the joy of Your salvation and grant me a willing spirit, to sustain me...The sacrifices of God are a broken spirit, a broken and contrite heart, O God, you will not despise.

FREED BY HIS LOVE

PROLOGUE

Unease over leaving Makayla behind churned inside Eli Carlton. In his hurry to call the incident in, he hadn't been thinking clearly. Why hadn't the agent called it in himself?

As he sped towards town, he shifted in his seat, gut clenching. Things shouldn't go this way. How many times had that niggling in his gut taunted him since the start of this undercover mission?

Something wasn't right.

He tightened his grip on the steering wheel. He'd learned long ago not to ignore his instincts—especially in matters of life and death.

What had the agent said after he'd told the man not to let Makayla out of his sight? *"Oh, believe me, I won't."*

A shiver shot up his spine. Something hadn't been right about the response.

Go back, a little voice whispered.

Eli's pulse accelerated as he yanked the wheel and did a U-ey. At any other time, he'd have credited his instincts for this feeling, but this was something far bigger. Like a whisper from God.

"Makayla, I'm coming," he called out before grabbing his radio. "Rob, I won't be coming in. I need to go back. Just send the team." He didn't wait for an answer, hanging up.

The last time he'd talked to God, it had been closer to cursing at the heavens than a prayer, but he spoke to Him now. *God, something's not right. If You're there, please protect Makayla until I get there. I know this is out of my hands. I can't do it alone. Please help, please...*

A remarkable sense of reassurance settled over him, calming the raging fear, sustaining him until he arrived back at the bed and breakfast where he and Makayla were hiding, pretending to be newlyweds.

He sucked in a sharp breath. There. The agent prodded Makayla to a van. Eli's hands went cold. The man had a gun pressed between her shoulder blades, the muzzle buried and hidden in her long silky hair.

Forcing himself to move cautiously, Eli slipped out of the car and made his way towards the van. He trained his Glock on the man, breathing deeply to keep calm. *God, this could go so wrong. I need Your help. Please guide my actions. Please protect Makayla.*

"Hold it right there." He approached the van in a crouching run, weapon held steady.

Soft, recently dyed platinum-blonde hair swirled around Makayla Hausbaden as she spun her head to look at him, her pale skin paler than usual. She mouthed his name as if afraid to speak aloud.

When the agent yanked her against him as a shield and slid the gun to her neck, Eli's stomach lurched. Chin high, back straight, she swallowed hard, every bit of her posture unyielding despite the danger.

"You get to choose how this plays out." Years of training helped Eli keep his voice even. "I've already called for backup. If they arrive and find you've harmed her, there's going to be a hefty price to pay. Cooperate, and you might get out of this easier. What do you choose?"

The imposter glared at him. "What kind of choice is that? Clearly, you don't know Johannes' men. We don't give up easily."

In the past, this remark would have enraged Eli. Instead, calm prevailed in his soul. "Johannes is a dangerous man to be caught up with. Association with him already puts you in a perilous spot with the law. I'd think carefully about resisting, especially once backup arrives."

The man shook his head and took a step towards the van, dragging Makayla backwards with him. "I'm taking her with me. Try and stop me, and I'll shoot."

"No."

At Makayla's voice, the imposter froze. He tilted his head towards her, jabbing the gun harder against her slim neck. "What do you mean no?"

"No," she repeated, her voice strong. "I won't go with you."

Huh. Eli brought his other hand up, steadying the weapon Weaver style. As diabolical as Johannes was, he'd prefer to have his niece delivered in one piece. Makayla must be relying on that. Eli, however, wasn't willing to take the chance.

"You don't get a choice, missy." The man hauled her another step towards the van. "Let's go. And you, Carlton, stay back."

Eli's throat closed when another heavily armed mercenary emerged from the van. One shouldn't go against two men without backup, but he didn't have a choice. His warning shot fired into the air.

Makayla screamed as the man dragged her towards the van while firing his weapon. Too frantic to be precise, his shots missed their mark.

When it became clear he wasn't going to give up, Eli shot him in the leg.

The man howled and clutched at the wound, spinning towards Eli, lowering his weapon just that fraction they needed. With him distracted, Makayla darted towards Eli.

Another shot rang out, this time from the other man's gun.

Makayla stumbled forward, and a strangled cry ripped from Eli's throat. "No!"

Screeching sirens penetrated the whooshing in his ears, but it was distant and unimportant as he gathered her into his arms, growing cold while blood trickled down her neck.

She'd been shot in the head.

Tears sprang to his eyes, and his heart clenched. *Lord, please, no.*

Law enforcement personnel swarmed them, but Eli saw only Makayla's face, now alarmingly pale.

"You're going to be all right, Makayla," he whispered, his voice breaking. "Hold on. Help is coming."

As he held her, he knew it—he loved this woman. He couldn't lose her now.

CHAPTER 1

Three weeks earlier...

Weddings in Eastbrooke were always momentous affairs. In such a close-knit community, just about everyone made the guest list. Eli Carlton stood back with an absent smile as the bride and groom posed for the last photos commemorating their special day.

Laughter vibrated around him as folks fellowshipped and celebrated. Kids ran back and forth on the lawn while families milled around the refreshment table laden with lemonade and freshly baked cookies.

Eli's brother gave his bride another kiss on the lips, playfully dipping her backwards for the picture. Joseph was the third of the four Carlton brothers to be married, leaving Eli as the only single sibling. Although he had the love of his family and good friends, he couldn't help feeling left out. Of course, he would never show this. When his brothers teased him about being the only one left to walk down the aisle, he'd dismissed them. How else could he maintain his self-sufficient front?

Working in the counterterrorism unit in Melbourne, he didn't lack responsibility or purpose in his life. No one could deny that his work kept him busy. Then there was his deep-rooted desire to apprehend the man who'd killed his father years ago. Not just the murderer. He twisted his grip into fists at the thought of the white supremacist group, the White League, that continued to wreak havoc on Eastbrooke. Someone needed to take them down.

So plenty in his life kept him occupied. And yet, all afternoon, he hadn't been able to stop staring at Makayla, the young woman two of his brothers had recently rescued from the terrifying clutches of Pure Light, a cult offshoot of the White League.

He drained the last of the lemonade from his plastic cup, wishing it held something stronger. Not that he drank alcohol often. But right now, he could do with a stiff drink. *You're just feeling left behind since you're here without a date, that's all.*

But it wasn't so simple. Ever since Makayla escaped the cult led by the family who was supposed to protect her, she kept invading his thoughts.

His heart broke every time he recalled the anguish on her face the first time he'd seen her. She'd been trying to overcome the trauma she'd experienced, and he'd felt a surge of protectiveness. And something else he was afraid to name…

"All right, let's get a photo with everyone now, the whole crew!" the cameraman hollered.

Max, his eldest brother, clapped Eli on the back and nodded towards the flowery trellis serving as the backdrop. "Come on, bro." He then waved to Makayla standing off to the side, alone. She had such big grey eyes. They always

CHAPTER 1

seemed to be looking at everything with... *wonderment*, as if she couldn't believe such a normal life were possible. "You too, Makayla, come on."

Those peachy lips that had at first seemed afraid to smile twitched into the beginnings of such an expression as she moved forward readily, her yellow bridesmaid's dress casting an angelic glow on her, her smile downright distracting. The way she'd regained the confidence the cult's brainwashing had stolen from her was nothing short of a miracle.

However, after spending time with Eli's family, she'd moved to Melbourne and into a safe house where she'd undertaken a deradicalisation program while helping the counterterrorism department with their enquiries. It seemed each day she further regained her joy and sense of purpose.

As happy as he was for his brother and new sister-in-law, Eli scuffled over to the group, dragging his feet before the final round of photos. He slipped in beside Makayla while doing his best to keep the butterflies dancing in his stomach under control. He was an expert who analysed the most brutal members of society. How was it, then, that a petite young woman with a gentle demeanour and enormous eyes could send his heart into such a state of disarray?

As he stepped in alongside the other bridesmaids and groomsmen, her floral perfume teased his senses. *It's just the smell of the roses, nothing more.* But just when he thought he had his emotions under control, she tossed a smile over her shoulder, her russet hair slipping over her shoulder with it, and his heart went tumbling over itself, even though nothing was mildly flirtatious about the look.

"Okay, on three!" the cameraman directed. "One. Two..."

Eli summoned a smile, aware of only one thing—the woman beside him driving him nuts.

When Joseph and Holly got into their car and drove away

to cheers and clanking cans dangling from the back bumper, relief loosened Eli's taut muscles. Sure, the reception had been fun, but maybe now he could return to his comfort zone.

After helping take down the tables and clean up, he made his escape towards his truck.

"I'm going to stay and mingle with the guests," his mother announced, beaming from the excitement. "See you at home?"

As much as he treasured time with his family, he let his shoulders droop. So it wouldn't be a full escape to Melbourne where his interactions with Makayla would have the protective layer of a professional setting. How had he forgotten he'd agreed to stay the night in Eastbrooke and leave tomorrow rather than set out directly after the festivities? He forced a smile and did his best to shake the melancholy. "Sure. I'll have a hot chocolate waiting for you."

She squeezed his shoulder and smiled before she dashed off.

∼

A LITTLE WHILE LATER, Eli scooted his chair back as Rob, his second eldest brother, joined him on the front porch of their family home. "Mum needn't have worried about the wedding's success." Rob eased into a wicker chair opposite Eli and crossed his legs. "The whole thing went off without a hitch. How often do you think that would happen?"

Eli gave a small chuckle before sipping his hot chocolate. "Not often." Except, Makayla's mere presence and its effect on him had been a *huge* hitch. At least, no one else noticed.

He inhaled and studied the burnt-orange horizon as the sun slipped behind the mountain towering over the town. To outsiders, Eastbrooke was a vast wilderness miles from civilisation. But to him and his brothers, it was home, and the open land grounded them. After growing up here, he revelled in his element and saw the beauty in it. However, he remained aware of the dangerous roughness within—namely, the White League.

As their mother bustled around in the kitchen preparing another round of hot chocolate, Rob leaned closer, his voice dropping to the serious tone he used as the chief of police here. "Any developments on the Hausbadens?"

Untangling the League felt never-ending, but the details of the Hausbaden family behind its inception were becoming clearer. Eli swirled the hot chocolate left in his mug, stirring up the settling cocoa. Releasing a heavy breath, he shifted his gaze back to Rob. "We know for certain Johannes was the original leader."

Years of controlling his emotions allowed him to keep his anger hidden, but the rage against his father's killer simmered deep inside him, sending heat now coursing through his blood. Was Johannes directly responsible? Eli's grip tightened on the cup, clenching so hard he almost feared to break it. He forced it to loosen with the same patience he kept his expression neutral. But he wouldn't stop until he knew and brought whoever it was to justice.

A possum with a baby clinging to its back skittered along the top of the side fence, the streetlight illuminating its outline. It stopped and sniffed the air, its nose twitching before it scooted up a grevillea tree and hid amongst the branches.

"That brings us one step closer to subduing the lot of them." Rob stretched his long legs out before him, crossing them at the ankles as relaxed as if they were still discussing the wedding. His boot heels rocked against the wooden porch. "Knowing who's behind the cult is a huge milestone."

No one should have gone through the emotional harm the cult's warped ideologies caused Makayla. Eli's anger burned with even more ferocity, and his chest began to heave. Raised in a Christian family, he was well aware the cult's beliefs did not align with those taught in the Bible.

His mother and brothers had accepted Jesus as their Lord and Saviour and were passionate about their faith. Eli remembered asking the Lord into his heart once as well.

But that was before Dad was killed.

Faith in someone he couldn't see had felt futile after that. Since then, he'd clung to the belief that, if he wanted someone to pay for their father's murder, he'd have to handle it himself.

"Revenge isn't the way, little brother."

Eli narrowed his eyes. "Who said anything about revenge?"

Rob sat back, his boot heels rocking again, the sound somehow hollow. "You don't like to admit it, but I know you almost as well as you know yourself. Not much you can hide from me."

Eli set his mug aside and rested his elbows on his knees, his back hunched. "There's a time and a place for retribution. We're talking about the man who took Dad from us, not to mention what happened to Makayla."

Despite the gravity, a knowing look crossed Rob's face. Eli groaned. He had to keep himself in check. He hadn't the faintest idea how to deal with these stirrings for Makayla. No way could he let others speculate on them. "Anyone in our situation would be indignant."

"I agree." Rob crossed his legs. "But in most cases, anyone involved wouldn't be allowed to be part of the investigation."

Bristling, Eli scrubbed a hand over his face. "We've already discussed this."

Rob raised his hands. "But I've always been concerned about you being so involved."

Eli arched a brow. "You're afraid I'll do something stupid?"

When his brother nodded, Eli's gut twisted. Not being allowed to continue now that they were getting close would be no less than torture.

"You're stellar at what you do, little brother. But you're also hot-headed."

Eli pursed his lips. "Out with it. Do you think I should be off the case?"

Spreading his hands, palms up, Rob huffed. "No. I simply want you to put the idea of revenge aside so you can do your job with a clear head."

Whew! Eli slouched back against the wicker chair. "I'll do my best."

It was a promise. He'd do *whatever* it took to find the man he'd been hunting and make him pay.

"You boys ready for seconds?" their mother called from the kitchen.

"Sure, Mum, I could use another cup." Rob stood and clapped Eli on the shoulder. "You do your job, Eli, and let God do His."

Eli exhaled and made no move to follow his brother. *Let God do His job? Had God been doing His job when Dad was murdered?*

He ran a restless hand through his hair as hate writhed inside him. Not hatred at God, exactly. More against the White League, but if God had done His job, maybe Eli wouldn't have had to grow up without a dad. George Carlton might have been present to watch his third son get married.

And maybe he could have offered advice on matters of the heart…

A moth fluttering around the porch light caught Eli's attention. The bulb's soft glow reminded him of Makayla's bridesmaid dress… how gorgeous and feminine she'd looked. Would he ever be in a place where he was worthy of her? After being rescued from the cult, she'd devoted her life to Christ. She'd invited him to the church she'd become a part of in Melbourne once. When he declined in favour of putting in extra hours on the case, she hadn't pressed. He appreciated that. She must know all too well the damage an imposed faith could cause.

He shook his head. Although he was drawn to her, a chasm would exist between them as long as he pushed God away. But he wasn't ready to welcome the Lord back into his life. Not yet, anyway.

CHAPTER 2

If only there was a light so she could find her way through the darkness, but fumbling in the dark in search of an electrical switch was pointless. Illumination, something Makayla had taken for granted in the real world, was a precious commodity within the commune. It was rationed, the same as all other comforts. Including independence.

She shivered. Just a tiny glimmer of light would have brought comfort. She yearned for that comfort now as much as she had on her first night in the commune.

Stumbling through the gloom, she groped for the cabin door, her breaths coming fast as panic clawed in. She had to get out. It felt darker than usual. *Where* was the doorknob? There! She turned it, but it didn't budge. She twisted harder before she yanked it, her pulse jumping.

It still didn't open. She whirled around, her chest heaving. "Holly..."

Holly had been her only beacon of hope since Makayla's arrival here. In fact, she had no idea why the woman, who didn't seem to fit, was there, but Makayla sure was glad of her company.

"Holly!" she yelled louder.

No response.

Where was she? Why wasn't she answering?

Makayla crumpled to the ground. She was on her own. Locked in. Forgotten. Gut-wrenching sobs overtook her as she wrapped her arms around her body and shivered.

"Help," she whimpered. "Somebody, help..."

Sitting bolt-upright in bed, she gasped for breath and stared at a shaft of pale moonlight beyond the window. Drawing her knees to her chest, she hugged them and panted. She wasn't up there in the mountains, in that cabin. She was in Jean Carlton's home in Eastbrooke, and she was safe.

Her breaths slowed. Reaching for the throw blanket at the foot of the bed, she snugged it around her shoulders and settled against the headboard. When her heart's wild pounding subsided, she switched on the lamp and took her Bible from the nightstand, flipping it open to one of the many verses she'd marked and kept for when times such as this threatened the peace she'd found in her faith.

Proverbs 18:10 was first. 'The name of the Lord is a strong tower; the righteous man runs into it and is safe.' Exhaling, she lifted her gaze to the window. Pure Light had promised many things—community, daily food, and even safety. But of all the emotions she'd felt during her time there, a sense of safety was not one of them.

Her cousins, Sally and Karl, had convinced her being with them was in her best interests and they were there to look out for her. But the doctrine they based their beliefs on was sorely misguided. For a long time, she hadn't known what was so wrong with it, even as she'd been convinced their motives were far from pure.

Now she knew the source of that unsettledness. The Holy Spirit had been guiding her heart, whispering to her conscience that there was a better way—God's *true* way. Jesus. *He* was the way, the truth, and the life.

Her eyes slid shut, her prayer leaving her lips in a whisper. "Lord, thank You for pulling me to safety and that I never have to be shut away in darkness again. Thank You for bringing me into a community that honours You and for folks like the Carltons who truly have my best interests at heart."

When Eli's face came unbidden to her mind, her heart flip-flopped. He was the only member of the family who didn't have a deep-rooted faith in Christ. The moment she'd met him, she'd sensed an undeniable struggle in his soul. Once she heard how the Carltons' father had been taken by violence, she understood why he struggled. She prayed daily for him to find the rest she found every day in the Lord. Healing from the brainwashing wasn't accomplished overnight, and the mending of Eli's shattered heart wouldn't be either. But she could feel the Holy Spirit working inside her every day, drawing her closer each time she reached out for help. God would take care of Eli in his struggle as well—if he let Him.

Opening her eyes, she flipped her slippery hair away from her face and turned to another marked passage. Deuteronomy 31:6 flooded her soul with another wave of reassurance. 'Be strong and courageous. Do not fear or be in dread of them, for it is the Lord your God who goes with you. He will not leave you or forsake you.'

After her experience, she was convinced of the truth of these words. No matter what was happening—and no matter how difficult it was to understand—God had a plan and a purpose for her life. Even as she'd struggled against the cult and the havoc it wreaked with her, He'd been there, holding her life in the palm of His hand.

"He holds your life too, Eli," she murmured into the quiet. Though she knew no Christian was 'beneath' another as each was a treasured child of God the moment he or she accepted Jesus as their Saviour, she set the Bible aside and tucked her chin against her upraised knees, pressing them tight to the aching in her heart. How could she help feeling underqualified to guide Eli towards the Lord? She still had so much to learn. Eli knew this better than anyone as he held a protector role in her life. They'd become quite close during her time undergoing deradicalisation in Melbourne.

She sighed, turning her chin so her cheek rested against her knees. She felt something for him. However, weaving together hopes for a man who didn't share her newfound faith was inadvisable. She could support him and be a friend, but she'd best guard her heart. They were both in fragile places with their faith, and she couldn't let anything interfere with their spiritual journeys. They were both in God's capable hands.

Laying back on her pillow, she prayed for him until she drifted back to sleep.

CHAPTER 3

*J*ohannes poured another cup of gritty black coffee. Taking a long sip of the strong brew, he stared out the cabin window at a Swiss mountain—which one, he couldn't remember and didn't care. Until recently, he'd been in Melbourne, close enough to Eastbrooke to control the White League's operations, but far enough away to remain inconspicuous. The authorities were closing in, and it irked him. First, the mountain drug bust, then that reporter, Holly, infiltrating Pure Light. Both compromised his and his son's business workings—*severely*. They needed to tread lightly to escape the Carltons.

A low growl issued from his throat. That family had been nothing but trouble from the start. He slugged another gulp of the brutal coffee. He'd done away with George Carlton before he'd known those mongrel boys were any threat, but the man's sons remained a pain in his backside, and now in his son, Karl's as well.

Hence, Switzerland. He snickered. How easy it was to outmanoeuvre those who thought they were in control.

A call coming in pulled his gaze from the window and the snow-covered Alps. Settling into a solid oak armchair, he answered the video call from Guy, his right-hand man back in Melbourne.

"What have you got?" Johannes drummed his fingers on the rustic wooden table. "We need a solid plan. Something foolproof to shake off the law for good. We have to if we don't want our operation to go up in flames."

Guy chuckled as he ran a rag over the Colt M1911 that was as much a part of him as his appendages. "Flames. Aren't the righteous saved from the flames?"

The quip fell flat, and he raised his hands in surrender. "Sorry, bad joke."

Johannes levelled him with a glare. He was in no mood to be sidetracked.

Setting his gun aside, Guy leaned forward. "Infiltrating the media will be our surest way. A smear campaign against the cops. Undermine their authority."

Already shaking his head, Johannes speared Guy with his steely gaze. "It's not enough. We need something more."

Guy quirked an eyebrow. "I wasn't finished."

A huff jumped up Johannes' chest. He slapped the table, making his laptop jump as well. "I should hope not. Go on."

"A platform of distrust through social media could pave the way for the League to take political control."

Hmm. That was better. Johannes sipped his coffee, tasting a bit of success in its gritty reality. "I could see that being beneficial."

Guy snorted. "Beneficial's an understatement. Mark my words."

Guy was by no means perfect. It was hard for a lackey to be perfect all the time, especially in this business. The tough calls they made left plenty of room for misjudgment.

But Guy had seen a thing or two, and Johannes respected him.

"With a foothold within politics, we'll be seen as a legitimate entity rather than one chased by the authorities." Guy grinned, revealing a gold tooth.

Corrupt dealings were Johannes' primary merchandise, apart from white supremacy, of course. Although he didn't set much store by 'faith', Pure Light had embodied the idea of continuing the elite, white race. Men and women within the cult married each other and were encouraged to produce multiple offspring to keep the line going. As long as the line from Pure Light continued, the White League would continue. The two entities worked in conjunction, and Johannes would guard against their destruction. No. Matter. What. It. Took.

"All right. Put everything you've suggested into motion." His phone buzzed, displaying the number of the prison incarcerating Karl. "I've got to go." He shut down their video connection, then answered the call. "Do you have any news?"

Little point in asking how his son was doing. Real men ended up behind bars at one point or another. Whining about it didn't get anything done. Their energy needed to be on furthering the League.

After a shuffling on the other end, Karl spoke, his voice barely above a whisper. "Makayla's safe house has been located."

Warm satisfaction uncoiled in Johannes' gut, energising him more than the wretched coffee. Savouring it, he sank back in his chair. "You have some of our people keeping an eye on her?"

"I do." Karl cleared his throat. "But... something else. She's under the protection of Eli Carlton."

"What?" Johannes jolted upright, slamming his knee

against the table, and cursed under his breath. "I might have known they'd choose one of the brothers to watch over her. Those Carltons…" He let out several more curses.

"He watches her like an emu guarding its chicks, my source says," Karl continued.

"He's a guard," Johannes snapped. "That's what they do."

Great, yet another obstacle the Carltons presented. They'd mastered the art of thwarting the League's plans. "Do whatever needs to be done to bring her in."

"I'm on it. That little traitor…" Karl's curses sang into Johannes' ears, his son's equal hatred soothing him. "But there's more to it."

Johannes' brows drew together. He took a few deep breaths as he shifted into a more authoritative position in his chair in preparation. Didn't matter what it was. He could handle it—he *would* handle it. "Well, go on. What is it?"

After more shuffling on the other end in the background, a prison guard told Karl to wrap it up. Johannes stiffened. Though prison was a hazard of the job, having his son behind bars with people telling him what to do grated. He should be helping to retrieve Makayla.

"She has information that will put us in jeopardy," Karl whispered. "If we don't catch her, we're all in trouble."

Before Johannes could press further, the call ended. He slammed his phone down and stared at the wall. What information did that drongo sheila have?

He couldn't wait until his son's next phone call to find out. He called Guy back. "Who of our group would be best at invading a safe house? It's time for my niece to return to the fold."

CHAPTER 4

When Max and Junia extended the invitation for Eli and Makayla to remain a few days longer in Eastbrooke, they accepted. Due to his current role as her protector, Eli had flexibility and no need to rush back as long as she was within his sight.

Did she even know how much danger she was in? Whenever he quizzed her, she replied that God was looking out for her. Which was a weird thing to say because *he*, Eli Carlton, was the one fulfilling that role.

He pulled up in front of the family home behind Max and Junia's car. Dusk was setting in, but an orange tinge lingered on the horizon, silhouetting the mountain towering over the town. He sat in the car and stared at it.

Staying longer in Eastbrooke felt almost like a holiday, but being constantly alert, watching out for Makayla, and searching for clues to his father's killer, kept him far from relaxed. Still, none of that caused his restlessness.

That was Makayla herself.

Every word she uttered, every move she made, distracted

him. All she had to do was walk into a room, and he could not look away from her. Her smile lit up the room like the rising sun. When she walked past him, all he could think about was how she would fit perfectly under his arm. When she spoke, the sincerity in her voice enthralled him. Face it, she was the most entrancing woman he'd ever met.

When his mother suggested the family get together for a spaghetti dinner and games night, his apprehension skyrocketed. Most of the time he was around Makayla, his family wasn't there. Could he keep his feelings hidden in such a homey and familiar setting, surrounded by people who knew him better than anyone else on earth? He doubted it, but he had no choice.

HE CLIMBED out of the car, grabbing the paper bag holding the carton of ice cream he'd been asked to bring, and loped up the stairs two at a time, the wood thudding under his boots, and stilled. He swiped a hand over his hair, the short strands prickling against his palm, and drew deep breaths, reluctant to go inside despite the melting ice cream. He needed to gather his thoughts and emotions that could so easily betray him with one swift glance from Makayla.

He shifted his grip on the now-soggy paper bag. The ice cream was going to drop through the bottom soon if he didn't get it inside. When Makayla had come to Melbourne after Joseph and Rob rescued her and Holly from Pure Light, Eli volunteered to look out for her. It made sense since he was based there, and other than her family in the cult, she didn't have close relations. Everyone needed a support system, especially someone who had undergone such trauma. Although she was under no immediate threat since both her cousins were in jail, they deemed she still needed some level of protection from others in the League. Her uncle Johannes, for one. She knew more about the League than she thought she did, and Eli hoped that, without even knowing, she might lead him to his father's killer.

But thinking of her as only a family friend or a means to an end had become... difficult. The more he saw of her, the more she caused his heart to stir. Unsure what to do with these emotions or even how to label them, he kept them to himself. Or at least, he tried to.

"Eli, is that you out there?" his mother called through the open window.

"Yes, Mum." Inhaling deeply, he opened the door. Voices of his family floated through the air. His mouth went dry when Makayla's laughter rose above the commotion. She'd travelled there with Max, Junia, and Polly, their little daughter, while he spent the day at the station.

His mother breezed into the hallway, clicking her tongue. "What were you doing standing out there on the porch letting the ice cream melt?"

He sent her the smile that helped him charm his way out of trouble. "I was taking in the view. It's a beautiful evening." It wasn't a lie.

She kissed him on the cheek and claimed the ice cream. "It won't be if our vanilla ice cream for the blackberry pie is reduced to milkshake consistency. Hang your coat and come into the living room."

He had little choice but to follow her orders as she headed into the kitchen. Even after the mental preparation to see Makayla, he hadn't been prepared for how his heart surged as he sighted her sitting amongst his family, her face alight while she played with Polly. They already had Candyland out on the floor, and Makayla looked at ease, as if she belonged and always had.

"We thought you'd never show up," Joseph chided, tossing an arm around Eli's shoulders. No missing the glow in his eyes. Marriage clearly agreed with him. Some bridegrooms would've been put out by not setting off on a honeymoon trip, but Holly and Joseph had opted to wait a couple of months for when they had more time. Joseph had just begun his coursework in seminary while Holly was establishing herself as a freelance journalist. Coupled with his continued work on the Eastbrooke Mountain Rescue Team, a lot was going on in their lives. Neither seemed to mind.

Seated on the couch sipping lemonade, Rob and Emma crooned over Isaac, the newest Carlton clan member.

"Ready for some good, old-fashioned competition?" Holly tapped the stack of games on the coffee table.

Eli forced himself not to look when he felt Makayla's gaze on him. "I sure am."

Wow. Listen to that. His voice sounded so normal.

"Dinner first," his mother called from the kitchen. "It's ready. Come and get it."

No one had to be asked twice.

When Makayla took a seat beside him at the long oak table, he groaned. How would he survive an entire meal with her so close?

Once they were all seated, his mother smiled at Joseph. "Would our pastor-to-be like to say grace?"

Joseph returned her smile. "I'd be honoured."

Although Eli had sat at this very table and joined in the saying of grace for years, he felt particularly left out today when Makayla bowed her head along with his family. He was the only one for which this routine didn't serve as a personal moment of connection with God. Even amidst his conflicted emotions towards the Lord, he started to wish he could share in the meaning of the prayer in the same way the others did. But too much had happened for him to do that... too much had been taken away....

"Heavenly Father," Joseph prayed, "thank You for bringing our family together for another meal around this table. It's such a blessing. Thank You for keeping us all under Your protection when we're apart. We don't take Your provision for granted."

Eli shifted in his seat. *How* could everyone around him feel the Lord's protection over them daily? *Seriously, guys, where was God's protective hand when Dad needed it?*

Although the question entered his mind regularly, having it pop into his head while his brother was thanking God for His provision felt incongruous, and bitterness chilled his core. When Joseph wrapped up the prayer and spaghetti and salad bowls were passed around, Eli licked his bottom lip and managed to quell his anger.

Disturbed by his brother's prayer, he forgot Makayla's presence until she handed him the salad bowl. "How are you, Eli?"

He cleared his throat. "I'm well. How are you?"

Had she any idea what her huge eyes and innocent face were doing to him?

"Good." She shook his mother's homemade lemon and honey vinaigrette onto her salad. "I'm always grateful to be here with your family. It'd been a long time since I experienced this kind of camaraderie. I didn't realise how much I'd missed it."

Everything bitterness had turned hard and cold melted, and warmth welled inside him. Her parents had been killed in a car crash when she was eighteen and heading off to University. Not long after, right when she was vulnerable and needing support, Sally and Karl had pulled her into Pure

Light under the guise of helping her. The very thought angered him.

"I'm sorry you didn't have more time with your parents." This—*this*—he could relate to. "It's hard losing one parent. I can't imagine losing both."

Her smile wobbled at its edges, those peachy lips sliding flat. "It's difficult for sure."

"What about the rest of your family? Apart from, you know…" Ugh. How could he be such a dill? When he was around her, what happened to the confident guy who knew what he wanted to say? Who was this awkward imposter in his chair letting words he didn't intend tumble from his mouth?

"Besides, Sally and Karl, you mean?" she supplied, shielding him from further embarrassment. Without an answer, she continued. "It's sad. There was a feud between my family members for… well, I don't remember a time when there wasn't a feud. For that reason, my parents rarely talked with my other relatives. I don't even know them."

Eli's brow lowered. "What was the feud about?"

She shrugged as she accepted the spaghetti bowl from Holly on her other side. "My parents didn't talk about it, so I don't know. Sometimes I wonder if things would've been different had I had support from the rest of my family."

"You mean you might not have joined the cult."

She nodded. "I'm not questioning the way God chose to work it all out, but I do wonder.…"

The endearing blush that overtook her face when she realised she'd become lost in her thoughts made Eli's throat thick. He wanted to reach out and squeeze her hand. Assure her she was safe. That she was amongst people who cared.

"I'm grateful your family has embraced me and I get to

come to events such as this." Ducking her head, she tucked a strand of hair behind her ear.

"I second that," Holly, who'd been listening in, piped up. "I never dreamed I would get to be part of a family like this."

Apparently, the whole table was listening in on the conversation. His mother's eyes shone. She smiled as she lifted her iced tea glass. "I say we propose a toast. To family."

Everyone lifted their glasses, clinking them together as they echoed her words.

As Eli exchanged a smile with Makayla before drinking from his glass, he wondered if she could see right through him. Could she see what having her here with his family was doing to his heart?

Rob's phone buzzed, drawing Eli from his contemplation. Since the family had demanding jobs, phones were never outlawed at the table. No one knew when they might be needed.

Rob pulled his phone out of his pocket and frowned.

"Who is it?" Their mother tilted her head at him, her brow wrinkling.

"Jerry." He pushed his chair back and stood. "Sorry, I've got to take this."

Jerry, Rob's partner long before Rob was promoted to chief of police, continued to be his right-hand man. He'd been involved in the League investigation from the start, working as hard as the Carlton brothers. A call from him on an evening he knew Rob would be with family was not a good sign.

Rob moved away from the table. Everyone, other than Polly, who continued chatting away in ignorant bliss, stopped eating.

Makayla's face was taut. Eli's heart twisted, and he slid his hands under the table, fisting them out of sight. Pure Light—

and indirectly, the White League—had caused her so much trauma. His resolve to put an end to the group strengthened.

"No… Are you serious?" Low but audible, Rob's words drifted into the dining room.

Eli stiffened, and a chill ran through him.

By the time Rob ended his conversation, Makayla had gone pale. "What's happened, Rob?"

Slipping his phone back into his pocket, he swung his serious gaze around the table before settling it on Makayla as he answered her. "The safe house in Melbourne's been attacked."

She gasped, and her eyes widened.

Holly placed a comforting hand on her shoulder.

Makayla swallowed hard. "What–what happened?"

Rob's gaze flicked to Eli. "Two men broke in and went straight for your room."

Her face paled further, and air whooshed from her lungs. "They've found me."

"Don't worry." Emma leaned forward and patted Makayla's arm. "You can stay with Rob and me as long as you need. Don't you think that's best, Rob?"

He nodded. "I do. At least until we know more details."

Makayla glanced back and forth between the pair. "Are you sure? I don't want to put you both in danger."

"Your safety is our priority." Rob's jaw hardened as his chin lifted. "That's what we need to think about. We're all in this together."

As he watched his brother's calm control, Eli's every protective instinct raged, and those hands, already fisted under the table, tightened so hard his knuckles might pop. He would not think of what would've happened if Makayla had been at the safe house. He would not.

She would have been captured. Or worse.

She was in danger, and he needed to take care of her.

"I'll be on watch, too."

She gave him a small, grateful smile. With her large eyes even bigger now, she looked almost on the verge of tears.

Finger by finger, he loosened his fists. He *would* get whoever was responsible. Why couldn't they leave her alone?

She knew too much. She was a threat to Hausbaden and his organisation—even if she didn't think so.

As Rob and the others went on to make further arrangements, all Eli could think about was keeping Makayla safe.

∼

When he answered the video phone, Johannes skipped the pleasantries. "Did you get her?"

"We got to her place, yes."

Of all the—What kind of answer was that? He waved a hand to speed Guy up. "And?"

"She wasn't there, boss."

His every muscle coiling tight, Johannes somehow kept from shaking the video screen. "You broke into her place when she wasn't there? How on earth did you make *that* mistake?"

"Sorry, boss." There was nothing else to say. Guy had failed.

"All right." Johannes rubbed a hand over his face. This was what happened when *both* his children were imprisoned. One could never trust help outside the family. "We know she's palsy-walsy with those Carltons. If she isn't at the safe house, she'll be with them. Find them, find her. Don't fail me."

"Yes, boss."

"Listen carefully." Johannes scooped up the laptop,

pressing his face close to the camera's eye. "Whatever it takes to get past those Carlton brothers, do it. They'll do anything to protect that piece of trash. Now it's time to play them at their own game. Kill them, if that's what's needed to get your hands on that little brat." He leaned even closer, his eyes burning. "Whatever it takes. Do you understand?"

"Absolutely."

CHAPTER 5

Baby Isaac grinned at Makayla from his car seat. Emma laughed as Makayla reached in to unhook him. "I'm pretty sure he's found his new favourite source of entertainment."

"He entertained me during the drive as well." Makayla chuckled. She'd been grateful for the distraction Emma and Rob's adorable little boy provided. When Emma invited her to do some shopping with her and Rob, Makayla had agreed to keep her mind off the raid.

She shivered. What would've happened if she hadn't been miles away with the Carltons? With a deep breath, she closed her eyes and focused on something the local pastor said in one of his sermons. 'When our anxious thoughts and feelings linger, so should we in the presence of our Great High Priest who understands every human emotion we've ever felt, even though He's the God of the Universe.'

Like other times those anxious thoughts crept in, she prayed and kept praying until her fears subsided and her peace returned. She'd escaped, but she wasn't free of the cult or the organisation behind it. And *her family members* were the ones after her. Would she ever be free of them?

She stepped aside as Eli closed his car door. She hadn't known he was joining them on the shopping trip until the last minute. She felt safe when he was near, but he, too, seemed on edge. That he didn't turn to the Lord for comfort grieved her. She sent up a silent prayer that, one day soon, he'd open his heart to God's love.

"All right, what's first on the list?" Rob hoisted Isaac's carrier into the crook of his arm.

Makayla smiled. How well being a father suited him. All the brothers had a reassuring, protective air, even Eli. Would he want a family someday?

"The department store," Emma replied. "We all need something from there."

"I don't," Eli protested, holding his hands out and doing a quick twirl.

Emma rolled her eyes. "Why do men put up such a fight when it comes to getting new shirts?"

He shrugged. "The old ones are comfortable. I don't see a reason for new ones."

"Trust me, you need them." His sister-in-law locked the car, then tossed a wink in Makayla's direction. "Besides, it never hurts to look your best."

Makayla's face heated. Had Emma noticed her fondness for Eli? She glanced at him to see his reaction but looked away when their gazes met.

He cleared his throat. "All right, my dear sister-in-law. Whatever you say goes. I'll get a new shirt."

Harsh lights and soft music greeted them as they stepped into the coolness beyond the automated doors. Posters hung above each department, their glossy likenesses beckoning customers to investigate their offerings. Makayla found it hard to be interested. Either the raid or Eli himself was distracting her. Every time his gaze met hers, her pulse quickened, and by the time they were in the baby section picking out new onesies, she had a feeling it was a combination of both.

As she inspected the baby shoes, clothes, and blankets, she tried to push away the unease. Rob had assured her staying with him and Emma would be her safest option. He was the police chief, after all. Still, something cold threaded up her spine. She'd suspected Karl would stop at nothing to get her back. Could he still be so effective while incarcerated? Gripping the baby shirt she was feigning interest in, she let the busy department store and garish lights fade from her consciousness.

Lord, when I asked You into my life, Your promise to never leave or forsake Your children became a truth in my life. This situation is not out of Your control. You've placed me where You want me to be, and I know You're watching out for me—for all of us, no matter what schemes Karl and the others might have. Thank You for Your protection, even now. Help me hand my fears and anxiety to You.

"Isaac doesn't need another footy sleeper, but this one with dinosaurs is so cute, I might have to get it." Emma held the item up to Rob.

"A boy can never have enough dinosaurs." Such fondness softened his gaze as he looked down at the infant slumbering in his carrier.

"You'd buy him everything in the store if you could," Emma teased. "I'm going to need to be careful, or this man is going to spoil our child, Makayla."

Makayla forced a smile. "He's so cute. It's hard not to want to buy him everything in sight."

Though praying had served as a good reminder about

Who was in control of the situation, her stomach tightened into painful knots as fear continued to twist at it.

She didn't realise her inner turmoil had reached her face until Eli arrived at her side, his brow knit. "Are you okay?"

Beginning to shiver, she wrapped her arms around herself. "I think I'll step outside for a minute. I need some air."

He took her elbow. "I'll go with you."

She eased away from his touch, further disoriented by the way his nearness made her heart flutter. "Thanks, but there's no need. I'll get a little air, and I'll come right back."

An uneasy furrow to his brow, he nodded.

She hurried away before he could change his mind. Outside, she slumped against the cement brick wall and sucked in a deep breath. Her pulse pounding in her head deafened her. She shut her eyes and leaned her head back, her hair snagging on the wall's rough edges, warm sunlight caressing her bare arms as if God sent it to soothe her.

Good. Her breathing became more even.

Just a few more minutes, a few more deep breaths, before she could rejoin the others.

A car engine and footsteps drew her eyes open. A man in a black sweatshirt stopped in front of her.

Probably just passing by.

Her heart rate kicked up again.

Just her paranoia. No reason to make a scene.

But… he *was* looking at her.

A scream started in her belly but died in her throat as he jammed a gun into her side and clamped a hand over her mouth. She rammed her elbows against him, hitting hard torso, then wrenched to one side, trying to shake away. But he held fast as if she hadn't moved.

Leaving the store without Eli was a dangerous mistake.

Clawing at the man, she struggled. Prayerful words flooded her head in desperate pleas. *God, please help me! Tell Eli to come.*

She bit at his hand, her heels pushing hard against the pavement to stop him from shoving her forward. Still, every moment brought her closer to the grey car he clearly intended on taking her away in. She was about to give up hope when his grip loosened. She tumbled to the ground, picked herself up, and scrambled away.

Reaching a safe distance, she looked back, and her eyes widened. Eli wrested the gun from the man while Rob struggled to secure him. He was putting up a good fight.

"Kidnapping in broad daylight, you're a gutsy one," Rob panted as the man continued to wrestle against him.

The man, whose dark beard and beady eyes made Makayla's stomach lurch, slammed a fist to Rob's stomach. "You'll regret this."

Eli already had his phone out and was speaking with someone.

She slumped against the wall, panting.

The moment he was off the phone, Eli was crouching by her side. He reached as if to touch her, then rubbed his hands on his thighs instead. "Are you all right?"

She nodded, her chest heaving. "I think so. It all happened so fast."

"He just came up and grabbed you?" Eli arched a brow.

She shuddered, feeling the man's hand on her mouth, his clamp on her middle. "Yes."

Rob and Eli exchanged a *look*.

She should have realised they'd look for her in Eastbrooke. Why had she put the family at risk?

Jerry and his guys came and took charge of the angry man.

Makayla shivered when he sent her a withering glare as they directed him into the back of a police car.

"Come on." Eli placed his arm around her, helping her away from the wall and ushering her towards the car park. "Let's get you to the car."

She drew comfort from his fiercely protective expression.

"I'll get Emma and the baby," Rob said. "We'll meet you at the car."

Makayla only managed a few steps before her knees buckled. She gripped the front of Eli's shirt as her body began to shake.

"You're in shock."

Even amidst the paralysing cold overtaking her body, she felt steadier when he pulled her closer and supported her.

"I'm sorry. I never should have let you go outside alone."

As regret twisted up his face, her heart broke. "It's not your fault. You didn't know they'd come for me right then."

His mouth set in a grim line. "I knew they were still after you, so I shouldn't have let you out of my sight. There was no excuse for me to put you in danger."

Without thinking, she took his hand. "Don't blame yourself. I'm fine. We're all fine, and the man's been caught."

He shook his head. "I should be the one comforting you, not the other way around."

She gave a wobbly smile. "It shook us all. Please don't blame yourself."

He cleared his throat, his gaze dropping to their intertwined fingers. "I don't usually make such careless mistakes."

She could only imagine how frustrating this must be after he'd been so vigilant for so long. She should have let him go with her. She squeezed his hand as they reached the car. "God had me in His care."

Shifting his weight, he glanced away, clearly uncomfortable, before meeting her gaze. "It's safe to say your cousin is determined to get you back. We need to figure out how to protect you better." Steady and calm, his voice held a steely determination. He would do things his way, without God.

Her heart sank.

CHAPTER 6

*E*li's hands balled into fists as he glared at the man through the interrogation room's one-way glass. The police station's midday bustle buzzed around him, but nothing could distract him from the man who had snatched Makayla.

The man sat there, ramrod straight, his bearded chin high, his severe, criminal-hardened face unmoving. A difficult one to crack, but Eli would make him talk. Standing there, fighting thoughts of someone dragging Makayla off made his desire to protect her that much stronger.

"Are you sure you can handle this?" Rob clamped a hand on his shoulder.

Deep breath in. Deep breath out. Eli faced him. "What are you talking about? I've completed countless interrogations."

Head tilted to one side, Rob eyed him. "Not in this type of situation."

In. Out. Expression neutral. "Don't say I'm too closely related to this case to be objective. We've already settled that. I'm staying on the case until we find Dad's killer."

His brother shook his head. "What I mean is you've never interrogated someone who tried to kidnap someone you care about."

"Doesn't mean I can't handle this." Eli held his gaze. "We all care about Makayla."

"We do." Rob lifted a brow. "But your heart's getting more involved than you care to admit."

No reason to respond to his brother's comment. Nothing would stop him from questioning the man. Eli cocked his head towards the interrogation room. "I think we should get down to business, don't you?"

Rob hesitated before he gave a nod. "Okay. Let's go."

When they entered the room, the would-be kidnapper leaned back in his chair and drummed his fingers on the metal table.

"I'm Chief Superintendent Robert Carlton, and this is Senior Sergeant Eli Carlton. We know your name's Guy Mangione."

The finger drumming stopped. His index finger poised above the table, then thudded down as he resumed drumming. "I know who you are."

"Great, then we can get right to it." Rob sat across from the shackled man.

There was a chair for Eli as well, but he opted to stand, his blood too hot to let him sit still. If Mangione knew who they were, he'd know the Carltons and the White League had a history. By apprehending this man, were they one step closer to finding who was responsible for murdering their father?

He folded his arms. "Did Karl Hausbaden commission you to kidnap Makayla?"

Mangione locked both hands behind his head and leaned back until he'd lifted the front legs of his chair off the cement floor. A smirk parted his moustache and beard and broke his hardened features. "Wrong, right out of the gate. I'm not working for Karl."

Eli's brow lowered, and he braced both hands on the table, bending so close he smelled the creep's hot breath. Ugh. "Who are you working for, then?"

"Someone much more powerful." Mangione dropped the front legs back on the floor and wagged a finger. "Someone a lot closer to what happened to the *other* member of your family who got too nosy."

Heat flared in Eli's chest. He slammed his fist on the table. "Who? Johannes?"

Rob was on his feet in a flash. Grabbing Eli's arm, he directed him towards the door. "Eli, let's step outside."

Eli struggled at first but complied. Having an altercation with his brother in front of this man wouldn't be professional. Once in the hall, he inhaled and folded his arms.

"I was afraid of this happening." Rob narrowed his eyes. "You didn't last two minutes before your emotions got the better of you. You have to be tactful during questioning. You're far too emotionally involved to do that right now."

Of all the... "I've *never* been too emotional to do my job."

Rob's steady gaze didn't waver. "There's no shame in being passionate. You're angry these men took Dad from us and are after Makayla, but you can't let your emotions get in the way of good policing. There's nothing wrong with stepping back and leaving this to others. It doesn't mean you care any less about Dad or Makayla or putting an end to the White League. We have to do what's best for the case's progress."

Eli rubbed the back of his neck, his taut muscles clenching up further. Rob was right. He hadn't kept his feelings under control. He'd get kicked off the case if he kept going.

Squaring his shoulders, he cleared his throat. "I'm sorry. It won't happen again. No more outbursts, I promise. Let's go back in."

Rob studied him for several seconds. "All right, but if it happens again, I won't hesitate to have you removed."

Eli stopped before the glass, eyeing the man within, and breathed in and out before facing Rob. What was wrong with him today? He prided himself on his years of controlling his emotions. "Understood, brother. Understood." He clapped him on the back. "Come on. Let's get this dude."

When they re-entered the room, Eli allowed Rob to take the lead. Despite his promise, he couldn't guarantee he wouldn't lose his cool again. Tension still smouldered inside him like a fire that hadn't been fully extinguished. He couldn't risk letting it burst into flames.

Displaying the same calm with which he approached every situation, Rob sat and surveyed Mangione. "We left off talking about who you're working for. If it wasn't Karl who sent you, who was it?"

Scoffing, Mangione rolled his eyes upwards and folded his beefy arms. "I don't have to tell you nothin'."

Nodding, Rob rested his arms on the table. "I'll make this simple. You can go to prison like Karl and await trial, not knowing whether you'll ever roam free again. Or you can help us with the information we need, and we can see about cutting you a deal. The choice is yours."

Mangione glanced at Eli before his gaze returned to Rob. "The information I have is worth more. I'll only tell you if you get me off the hook altogether."

Shaking his head, Rob chuckled. "I can't promise that. Only that we'll cut you a deal."

Mangione lifted his shackled hands. "Then we have nothing to talk about."

"Guess you're right." Rob stood. "I'll tell my deputy to lock you up."

Eli knew his brother well and wasn't surprised when his tactics elicited a reaction.

"Okay, okay. Wait," Mangione said.

Rob turned, his brow rising. "Changed your mind?"

A growl issued from Mangione's throat. "I'll tell you what you want to know. But I'm not going to prison."

Rob shrugged. "Tell us what you know, and we'll see what we can do. No promises. Refuse to talk, and you'll be locked away for sure."

Eli's heart pounded. They were so close to the information they needed.

Finally, Mangione spoke. "I don't work for Karl. I work for his old man, Johannes."

A shiver shot up Eli's spine. They'd known Pure Light and the White League were closely intertwined, but having it confirmed that Makayla's hunter was the group's legendary leader chilled his core.

"Why does he want Makayla?" Rob asked. "Karl seems to be the religious one, and she was a member of Pure Light, not the White League."

"She's his niece." Mangione's lips twisted into a mocking smile.

Rob leaned back in his chair, tapping his fingers on the table. "We both know the Hausbadens aren't an affectionate family. Tell us why he's putting so much energy into tracking her down."

Mangione stared at him, the stubborn, hard expression returning.

Eli threw his hands in the air and leaned closer to the

creep. "Just remember whether or not we cut you a deal is dependent on how forthcoming you are about what you know. No information, no deal."

When Mangione speared him with his gaze, Eli glared right back, barely managing to keep his anger under control.

"She has information Johannes doesn't want to get out." Mangione waved a hand. "If she knows what's good for her, she'll keep quiet. But Johannes can't risk it."

Eli's throat went dry. He'd seen this happen far too many times. An innocent person caught in the crossfire because of information he or she had never wished to obtain and possibly didn't know they had. Now Makayla had been placed in this situation.

Rob edged forward in his chair. "Tell Johannes to call off the search for her."

Mangione almost choked on his laughter. "It wouldn't do any good. You should know better than anyone that Johannes doesn't take orders."

Lava-hot heat swept through Eli. Reacting now would only get him thrown off the case, but he wasn't finished with this man. Or Johannes. Clenching his fists, he silently addressed the man he was now convinced had murdered his father. *Mark my words, Johannes Hausbaden. I'm going to track you down and make you pay if it's the last thing I do.*

CHAPTER 7

Seated on Rob and Emma's couch, Makayla switched her gaze between Eli and Rob, her mouth falling open. "I... I don't know what to say."

The brothers studied her. They didn't believe her. A chill spread through her chest.

"You must know what he's referring to." Rob cut a hand through the air. "Guy Mangione pulled this out as his main bartering chip. There must be something to it."

Makayla shifted on the couch and exhaled a long breath. "If I knew what he was talking about, I'd tell you. I have no idea."

Rob shook his head and raked his fingers through his hair. "That doesn't make sense."

Sure, he wasn't trying to insult her. Still, her chest tightened at his insistence. "I don't know anything. If I did, don't you think I'd tell you?"

"She's right, Rob." Eli'd remained silent throughout the conversation, but now, the understanding in his expression caused her eyes to sting.

She let her tight shoulders inch down from her ears and kept her focus on him. *Thank You, God!*

Yes, she needed that. She needed someone to believe in her, support her, especially now with the attack still so fresh.

"Mangione might have said this to scare us," Eli remarked, his voice low. "And to scare Makayla. Remember what kind of men we're dealing with. People like him will say whatever serves them best."

Rob ran a hand over his jaw. His gaze swung back to her. "I'm sorry. I thought we'd gotten such a big scoop and what he'd told us would help us piece everything together."

She managed a small smile. "I understand. I appreciate everything you're doing, and I only wish I could do something to help." Her heart did a flip when she caught Eli watching her. Their gazes met and held. That he had her back assured her she'd be okay, but as much as she was telling herself that's all it was, she also knew she was developing feelings for him. Feelings she welcomed and sensed might be reciprocated. But the situation was growing more serious, and Eli and Rob needed clear heads. She couldn't let herself be a distraction for either of them, especially for Eli.

Rob pushed to his feet and paced, seemingly deep in thought. Finally, he stopped in front of Eli. "Regardless of any discrepancies in the information Guy Mangione gave us, I'm willing to bet he was serious about Johannes' determination to find Makayla."

"I agree." Eli rubbed between his eyes. "We can't ignore such a threat. We need to find a new safe house since Johannes' men can easily search all the Carlton households. She can't stay here."

A shiver ran up Makayla's spine. She was putting this family in harm's way. She didn't remark on it, however, as they'd only remind her their jobs often entailed danger and it wasn't her fault.

"We need somewhere inconspicuous." Eli tapped his cheek with a finger. "A place where even the property owners don't know she's in danger."

Rob paced to the fireplace. Snapping his fingers, he pointed in his brother's direction. "I've got it. The bed and breakfast on the outskirts of town. It's off the beaten track and is used by vacationers and honeymooners. It's small with only a few rooms."

Eli cocked his head. "That sounds unassuming enough."

Makayla frowned. "But if it's small and used for vacationers, wouldn't it look suspicious having a guard standing watch?"

Rob folded his arms, his brows furrowed. "Good point. Your protector will have to become part of the ruse."

"I'll be her guard."

"I thought you wanted to help track down Johannes?" Rob lifted a brow.

Conflicted emotions crossed Eli's countenance. She dropped her gaze to her hands to hide the inevitable redness of her cheeks. Was there... There *was* more to his determination to stay by her side than simply doing his job, wasn't there? Her heartbeat skittered into faster speed.

"Since I've been involved in her protection so far, it's best if I stick close to her."

Rob hesitated before giving a nod. "I can't think of anyone I'd trust more for the job."

Neither could she.

"We'll need to come up with a believable story about what we're doing there," Eli said.

"The place is too small to take up two rooms for an

extended time," Rob mused. When he spoke again, his voice was hesitant. "I have an idea, but I'm not sure you'll like it."

Makayla and Eli exchanged glances.

"What is it?" she asked.

Rob licked his lips. "Just hear me out, okay? What if you pretended to be honeymooners? Then Eli would be able to stay in the same room, and no one would realise he's your guard. Everyone would expect you to be together."

Honeymooners? Makayla's mouth fell open. She shifted uneasily on the couch. Her hands grew clammy despite the overhead fan flinging cool air on her. She didn't want to sound ungrateful, but this plan could be problematic. Could she trust Eli to honour her?

Ouch. How dare she think like that? The Carltons had been raised well. Just because his trust wasn't in the Lord didn't mean he was devoid of morals.

He must have been reading her mind because he said, "I promise nothing untoward will happen."

She blinked. "Oh, I wasn't…"

He raised a hand, stopping her with a gentle shake of his head. "I understand your reservations, which is why I want to reassure you this is all business."

Heat crept up her neck again. "I didn't mean to infer otherwise."

"There's no need to feel bad." Rob reached over and patted her knee. "None of this is ideal, and if you're uncomfortable, we can think of something else."

Keenly aware she'd just wished there was something she could do to help, she shook her head. "I trust you both. Tell me the plan."

Rob sat on a chair across from her. "We'll say you're visiting from Melbourne. You're newlyweds and wanted somewhere not too far from home for your honeymoon

CHAPTER 7 | 435

while still feeling like you're on vacation. You'll wear wedding bands and act like you're honeymooners." He watched them both closely. "I'm not suggesting you do anything that would make either of you feel awkward. You need to be convincing, though."

She had no trouble being friendly with Eli. But what would such a charade do to her heart? She'd need to be careful not to let her emotions run away with her. That slippery slope would be all too easy to tumble down with a man as handsome as Eli pretending to be her husband.

"We can handle it, Rob." She jutted up her chin. "I want to make things as easy as possible for you, so tell me what I need to do."

Rob gave a grateful nod. "Hopefully it won't be for long. Just until we track down Johannes. We'll work on the details."

She took a deep breath. "I'm thankful to have people like you looking out for me." She glanced at Eli, who quickly lowered his gaze, but not before she saw the vulnerability in his eyes. He wasn't as tough as he made out.

"I'll make the arrangements, and we'll get you moved in tomorrow." Rob pushed to his feet.

"You mean, we'll arrive for our honeymoon." Makayla chuckled in an attempt at lightness.

Rob chuckled as well. "Yes, for your honeymoon."

The moment their conversation ended, every ounce of strength drained from her body, leaving her fighting to keep her eyes open. "I think I'll head to bed."

"It's been a trying few days," Eli replied with understanding.

She headed towards the stairs but turned back before going up. "Thanks again for everything you're doing."

He regarded her, his gaze steady. "I'll be on watch tonight. Rest easy."

"Thank you." Her heart pounded as she made her way upstairs. As tired as she was, sleep would be anything but peaceful tonight with tangled thoughts of safe houses and honeymoon disguises, then Mangione, Johannes, Karl, and Eli Carlton weighing on her.

∽

THE FOLLOWING MORNING, Makayla wrapped a towel around her shoulders as Holly readied the platinum-blonde hair dye that would be part of her disguise.

"Just looking at this stuff makes me feel rebellious," Holly joked. "Isn't this what girls do when they want to rebel against their parents?"

Makayla laughed. "Yes, although I didn't feel the need to."

Holly's expression grew wry. "I did. I was into anything questionable, always putting myself out there, trying new things—getting into trouble."

Makayla tipped her head. "I sensed that when I first met you at the commune. It took a lot of courage to sneak into Pure Light as an undercover reporter." She exhaled. "Now, all of you are wrapped up in this mess."

Holly reached over and gripped her arm, the plastic glove she wore crinkling. "Don't talk like that. We're all in this together. Now, let's get to this hair dye, shall we?"

Though still not sold on the idea, Makayla nodded. She'd wondered if dying her hair was necessary. However, Rob, adamant that every precaution be taken, was quick to assure her it was best to 'disappear' as much as she could. She'd not dyed her hair before. She loved the natural russet she'd inherited from her mother, but on even a small chance to make it harder for her uncle's men, she'd do it.

Although nothing was fun about their reasons for dying her hair, a great deal of hilarity filled the process as they behaved like young girls experimenting with their hair for the first time.

But all mirth left Makayla when she saw her reflection. The finished product produced the desired effect. She looked so different. Not herself.

Holly placed her hands on her shoulders and caught her reflected gaze in the mirror. "Are you okay?"

Makayla nodded. "I'm just being silly. It took me by surprise, that's all."

Holly turned her and looked straight into her eyes. "Feelings are never silly. Tell me."

Makayla ran her fingers through her hair and shrugged. "I don't feel like myself. It's like I don't even know who I am anymore."

Tears pooled in her eyes.

"Oh, honey." Holly embraced her, pressing their cheeks together. "I know this is hard. I can't tell you how difficult it was for me to sneak into Pure Light and tell Karl and Sally I was someone I wasn't, then convince them I believed something I didn't." She stepped back and shook her head. "But it was *my* choice. In your case, you have no option but to assume a new identity. Your life depends on it."

Makayla wrapped her arms around herself. "I don't want to seem like I'm complaining. It could be so much worse, but it all seems surreal. Sometimes I feel like I'm watching someone else's life unfold."

"Anyone would experience a little of that if they were to walk in your shoes." Holly paused before leaning closer to

Makayla. "Can I tell you what helps me when I'm unsure of my identity?"

Always grateful for this woman's godly wisdom, Makayla nodded. "Yes, please."

"Well, 1 John 3 tells us we're children of God. And Colossians 3 verse 3 reminds us Christ died for us and we're now hidden in Him. He's our hiding place, no matter how conflicted we feel about our identity in this world. We can feel pulled in a million different directions, but God's view of us never changes. We can always trust that we're safe and known and loved by Him."

A weight lifted off Makayla's shoulders. "What a wonderful reminder." She gripped her friend's hands and smiled. "Thank you."

Holly tugged her in for another hug before surveying Makayla's hair. She reached out and fluffed it. "It's different, but blonde isn't a bad colour on you."

Makayla laughed and glanced in the mirror. "You think so?"

"Absolutely. It'll just take some getting used to, that's all."

Makayla wondered what Eli might think, but then pulled herself up. She couldn't let herself go down that path, although his opinion had come to matter more with each passing day despite her attempts to suppress her growing feelings.

Fortunately, Holly was too wrapped up in rummaging in her jewellery box to notice Makayla's inner conflict. She returned with a sterling silver ring. "You can't pass as newlyweds without one of these."

Makayla chuckled. "I guess you're right." She slipped the band onto her ring finger and stared at it as another thought crossed her mind. *What would it be like to wear Eli's wedding band for real?*

She shook the thought away. *Stop it. You know the danger of letting your thoughts go down this path.*

"Rob and Eli should be here soon. Why don't we go downstairs and wait for them over a cup of tea?"

Although Makayla agreed, her stomach churned. How could she protect her heart and keep her mind pure when she would be so close to Eli, day and night? Maybe this was a bad idea. But it had gone too far to back out now. *Lord, help me to keep my focus and trust on You at all times. Let my thoughts remain pure and pleasing in Your sight. And please help the team find Johannes, and keep them safe.*

By the time the men arrived and she and Eli needed to leave, she felt more at peace, although her heart ticked over as he stood at the door and their gazes met. He wore glasses, and his hair was darker and combed flat. He looked handsome and sophisticated, but although his outward appearance had changed, his brown eyes were warm and would have melted into hers if she hadn't averted her gaze.

CHAPTER 8

*E*li glanced at Makayla as he pulled up outside the bed and breakfast in the hired car Rob had organised. He'd expected her to be on edge. Maybe she was, but she appeared calm, while he, an anti-terrorist professional, felt utterly discomposed. "Are you ready for this?" He winced at the edge to his voice.

Nodding, she tossed a smile over her shoulder as she opened the door and climbed out.

He unloaded their bags from the boot. When she offered to carry her own, he objected. It was easier if his hands were full so he didn't have to decide whether he should hold her hand. Although, at some stage, he would have to, wouldn't he?

The quaint cottage with a thriving front garden and a picturesque lawn must seem ideal for real honeymooners. Shaking his head, he tried not to stomp up the steps. The proprietress smiled from the front desk when they entered the reception area. "Welcome! You must be Mr. and Mrs. Thornton."

Eli wasn't a stranger to assuming another identity for work purposes. However, having Makayla referred to as his wife would take some getting used to, and his voice faltered. "Ye–yes, Mrs. Langly. How are you?"

"Just fine," the grey-haired woman bubbled. She looked between them, her expression knowing, her blue eyes twinkling. "I've made sure the honeymoon suite is all ready for you lovebirds. Nothing but the best for newlyweds around here."

Makayla smiled sweetly. "Thank you. How kind."

How did she do that? Just slip right into the role. He stood back with the luggage as she fell into easy conversation with the woman who led them upstairs.

Meanwhile, his awkwardness was nearly as remarkable as the way his emotions had been conflicting with his work of late. He bumbled behind her, trying not to scratch the soft mint stairwell with toggles on the duffle bags. He needed to figure out what was going on since he had a job to do. And he couldn't let his heart get in the way. Not when Makayla's safety was at stake.

"You two have the best view in the whole house if you want my opinion." Mrs. Langly placed her hands on her plump hips as she nodded to the large picture window.

Eli placed the bags on the luggage holder before crossing the polished timber floor to look out. He swept aside the filmy curtain and braced a hand on the mint and rose wallpaper beside the window. The house where two agents would be staying was just visible through the trees.

"It's a great room, Mrs. Langly." Makayla offered her sincere smile.

The woman beamed. "So glad you like it. Dinner is served downstairs at six p.m. Unless you two would prefer to have a tray sent up here so you can be alone…?"

Makayla waved a hand. "No, that's all right. We'd love to join you. See you at six."

Once alone, she turned to face Eli. "I hope you didn't mind me saying we'd go for dinner. I thought it might seem more... natural."

Eli cleared his throat. "That's fine. You're doing a great job keeping up the...the front."

She shrugged, hesitating before reaching for her duffle bag. "I guess I'll get unpacked. I'll take the drawers on the left. You take the ones on the right?"

"Yeah, yeah, that's fine." Seriously, what was wrong with him? Now he was acting like a tongue-tied schoolboy! Why was this arrangement unsettling him so much? He reached for his bag, grateful to have a task. "I have to say, you're doing a lot better pulling off this disguise than I am."

Makayla angled her head, big eyes blinking at him. "You're having trouble with it?"

A mirthless chuckle rasped against his throat. "Just a little."

Her expression softened. "It's because of all the responsibility, that's all. I'm sure there's so much on your mind."

His heart overflowed with appreciation for her kindness. He accepted the cover and nodded. "I guess that's it."

Despite her words, he wouldn't be able to rely on her to make this disguise work forever. He needed to get his head in the game. He had a job to do.

∼

THE DAY PASSED. They'd each brought their own things to occupy their time. She'd brought a book and some crossword puzzles. He'd brought his notes from the case—notes he'd studied ad infinitum. Bent over them spread out on the antique desk, he tried to narrow his focus on the words as a soft breeze drifted the filmy curtains inward. There had to be some clue as to where Johannes was. He lifted his head, rubbing between his eyes, a headache starting.

He'd not known how difficult being in a room all day with Makayla would be. Her very presence distracted him, and he kept glancing at her. She was so breathtakingly gorgeous as she relaxed on the brocaded lounge, reading, the scent of her freshly washed platinum hair tickling his nostrils. Although he liked the colour, he preferred her natural russet. The warmer tones suited her better.

Finally, it was time to go downstairs for dinner. Man, her green dress showed off her trim figure—um, not that he was looking. Heading to the bedroom door behind her, he averted his gaze to the floor as he tucked his crisp, white shirt into his jeans. He shut the door behind himself. When he took her hand as they walked down the timber stairs, she smiled at him. They'd discussed how they should act in public, but he wasn't prepared for the way his heart raced at the touch of her skin. He swallowed hard. Protecting her might prove easier than protecting his heart.

Three other couples were already seated in the dining room. Thankfully, they each had their own tables and only had to nod and smile, not engage in small talk.

Mrs. Langly brought out a lovely meal on delicate bone china, and flavourful steam curled from roast chicken and vegetables with a thick, tempting gravy. Makayla couldn't finish the huge serving. He had no trouble, though he lingered over it, not wanting to leave the dining room. Eating helped fill the time and the awkward silences. Although every now and again, when they met each other's gazes and a blush crept up her cheeks, it almost felt like they *were* newlyweds.

Long after dinner, he sat alone by the bedroom window and peered out through the curtain. Although he wouldn't have been good company, it might have been better to have accepted Mrs. Langly's invitation for after-dinner coffee downstairs. If they had, he wouldn't have to sit in here with Makayla. She wasn't doing anything other than reading her Bible on the bed, but her presence disturbed him.

He watched her reflection on the glass window. She looked so peaceful and at ease. If only picking up the book she held would give him that same restfulness.

When she shut her eyes, her lips moving slightly, he found it impossible to look away. He studied her serene face until she opened her eyes again and looked straight at him, their gazes meeting on the window. He tore his away, embarrassed at being caught staring.

"Something wrong?" Her brow crumpled, and genuine concern tightened her voice.

"Nothing's wrong." He shook his head and faced her. "I was just wondering…"

She closed her Bible and settled against the headboard. "Wondering what?"

He swallowed hard. "Remember the other night when we were all eating together at Mum's table?"

Her brow scrunched a little more, but surely, that was confusion, not fear, as she nodded.

He ran a hand over his hair. It wasn't too late to keep quiet, but something spurred him on despite the vulnerability of doing so. "I looked around at everyone and realised each person believed the God they prayed to was there listening… and He cared. I wondered then what that was like. Just now, when I saw you praying, I asked myself that question again."

The open compassion on her face was almost more than

he could bear. His throat grew tight. Perhaps being this transparent with her wasn't wise.

"Trust in God isn't an easy thing." Her gaze moved beyond him to the window, her expression stilling. "When Karl and Sally brought me into Pure Light, trusting in the things they said about God, that He has a divine plan for us and so on, took so much effort."

Her lips twisted. Even in light of the heavy topic, Eli couldn't help thinking about how perfectly formed they were.

"As you know, the doctrine presented within the cult is far from Biblical." She waved a hand. "They said God had a purpose for each of us, to continue the line of white supremacy to preserve a superior race. I did believe initially, but it was hard to trust. They're two separate things."

She looked at him then, her gaze steady. "Later, when I came to know Christ as my personal Saviour and understood that He cared about me intimately, it didn't mean trust came easily."

Something loosened inside him. He almost took a step forward as he whispered, "Really?"

He'd always imagined everyone around him felt this magical peace that never went away, that something was wrong with him because he couldn't feel it, too.

"Really." She nodded. "I still pray daily that God will give my heart rest in Him. Just because I know He has my best interests in mind and I know I'm saved doesn't mean I don't struggle with trust."

Turning away, he braced his hands on the windowsill and stared out. It was easier than looking at her. "I find it hard to believe He cares when He's allowed such terrible things to happen. I don't understand, and that makes it hard for me to trust."

Silence hung in the air before the bed squeaked and Makayla joined him at the window.

Keenly aware of her petite frame beside him, he kept his gaze steady.

"I've asked myself those same questions." Her words fogged the glass below where the steam from his was fading. "I can't tell you how many times I've wondered why God allowed my parents to be taken away from me during the years I needed them most. I've questioned why He's allowed a misleading cult like Pure Light to convolute His Word and destroy so many peoples' lives." She angled her head upwards. "Do you want to know what I do when these questions won't leave me alone?"

He hesitated before nodding.

"I remember what the Bible says about God working all things together for good for those who love Him." She returned to the bed and grabbed her Bible, flipping through the pages as she came back. "This is what I was just reading. 'For My thoughts are not your thoughts, neither are your ways My ways,' declares the Lord. 'For as the heavens are higher than the earth, so My ways are higher than your ways and My thoughts than your thoughts.'" And then, another passage. This was just before Jesus was betrayed. Here, He knew what lay before Him as He said to His disciples, 'You don't understand now what I'm doing, but someday, you will.'"

She lifted her gaze to his. "God understands our human tendencies to question and to want to know *why*. One day we'll know why, but in the meantime, if we understand *Who* He is, we'll be able to trust that He does have everything under control and He does care about us but He sees a bigger picture than what we do."

Eli's heart twisted. He'd been angry at God for so long,

even blaming Him for his father's death, but Makayla's humbly spoken words struck a chord within him. He'd never allowed himself to think that perhaps God *did* care what happened to him. He'd always assumed He didn't because of what had been taken from him.

He barely managed to speak around the lump in his throat. "When trusting is hard, where do you start?"

Compassionate understanding softened her delicate features. "Where you can. God doesn't scold us for struggling. All we need say is 'Lord, I don't understand this, but please show me how to give it to You.' He'll do it, Eli. Our faith might waver at times, but when it does, we can get right back on our knees and talk to Him about it once again. He wants to hear from us—no matter what state we're in."

Suddenly exhausted, he let his shoulders sag. He'd been running nonstop for years, striving to make everything—revenge, justice, peace—happen all on his own. Had his efforts all been in vain? He looked at Makayla, amazed once again by the light radiating from her countenance. He wanted to share in this. But how?

"I want to believe." He pushed the words past the tightness in his throat and chest. "But..." How could he explain? "I'm afraid of being disappointed. What if...?"

"What if God doesn't come through?" she finished, her voice solemn.

He dropped his gaze to the floor and nodded.

Placing her hand on his shoulder, she turned him to face her. "Eli, look at me."

It took all his strength to meet her gaze. Once he did, the confidence in her eyes left him vulnerable and assured at the same time.

she spoke again, it was with renewed fervency. ne through. It might not always be in the way you want Him to, but it will always be for the best." Emotion spilled from her eyes. "I can see you're burdened. Jesus said, 'Come to Me, all you who are weary and burdened, and I will give you rest.'" She touched his cheek. "Stop carrying the burden on your own. You were never meant to shoulder it by yourself."

All he could hear was his pounding pulse. Could letting go of this hatred that had been eating at him for so long be so close, so accessible?

She pulled back her hand, blushing. "Sorry."

He shook his head. "Don't be sorry. I'm the one who should be sorry for dumping all that on you right now. But thanks for talking about it."

She breathed in slowly. "You'll find your way. Just be willing to open your heart to God and then let Him do His part."

Hadn't his brother said something similar? Straightening his shoulders, he managed a return smile. "Thank you."

An awkward silence followed before she chuckled. "So, about the sleeping arrangements…?"

He crossed to the wardrobe and produced a spare blanket and a pillow from the shelf inside. "I'll sleep on the couch, no problem."

Her brows scrunched. "Are you sure?"

"Absolutely."

She shrugged. "Okay."

He grabbed his washbag and headed towards the adjoining bathroom. Once the door was shut, he inhaled and leaned on the sink, struggling with what to do with these emotions. The irresistible desire to take what Makayla had said and run with it was strong. But after doing everything on his own for years, surrendering that also felt like an insurmountable feat.

He brushed his teeth and washed his face before changing into pyjama pants and a T-shirt. He nodded to Makayla as they traded places.

By the time she returned, he was settled on the couch but far from ready for sleep.

Her large flannel pyjamas swallowed up her slim frame. She'd probably picked nightclothes to disguise her form. Grateful for this, he laced his hands behind his head and peered at the slow ceiling fan. She was already terribly distracting without even trying.

"Ready for me to turn off the light?" she asked.

"Sure." He shifted his pillow in an attempt to get comfortable. He felt around the side table to make sure his pistol was within reach and glanced at the door, ensuring it was locked. "Good night."

"Good night," she replied.

He listened as she settled down in the bed before the room went silent. He'd just closed his eyes when she spoke. "Eli?"

"Yes?"

"Could I pray for you?"

The tightness in his throat once again threatened to choke him. At least the darkness concealed his turmoil. "Sure. I guess that would be all right."

"Great." She paused before she began. "Lord, I know You've been a part of our discussion tonight. You know our struggles better than either of us ever could."

She paused again for so long Eli thought the prayer was complete. When she did continue, the tenderness in her voice tugged at his heart and brought tears to his eyes.

"Be with Eli tonight. Bring comfort and peace to his thoughts. Show him You're there to share his burden. He's done so much for me and the rest of the family, Lord. He deserves a rest."

He swallowed hard, battling the threatening tears. How was it he could stand up to the worst of society, yet a single prayer could break through every one of his defences?

When he was sure he could speak without sounding tearful, he thanked her and listened to her say he was welcome.

Silence stretched between them as he was left alone with his thoughts. He turned her words over and over in his mind, wrestling with the idea of surrender until, eventually, sleep came.

CHAPTER 9

When Mrs. Langly told Makayla about a village church nearby, she was hesitant about mentioning it to Eli. He'd turned down her invitation to attend a church service before, but if she went alone, it might arouse suspicion. After all, they were meant to be acting like a happy, newlywed couple, not a bickering one.

After some deliberation, she asked him since the thought of not attending church made her heart sink, especially as they had no idea how much longer they'd need to stay. She was pleasantly surprised when he agreed.

"Sure, it could be good to go… all things considered."

It was dangerous to read too much into his response, but she couldn't help hoping their conversation the other night had planted a seed. Perhaps the prayers she'd been offering on his behalf since they met were being answered and his heart was opening to God's love.

Their first "newlywed" Sunday dawned clear and beautiful. The fresh air and bright blue sky had her in the best mood since her almost kidnapping. Plus, the prospect of being under one roof with other believers gave her remarkable energy.

She couldn't help admiring the pressed dress shirt Eli wore. He always looked handsome, but his church attire was dashing. She said a little prayer, knowing it would be difficult to keep her mind on the sermon when he looked the way he did. Especially with those glasses making him appear so mysterious and sophisticated.

Through breakfast, they managed to keep up their newlywed façade—it seemed to be getting easier with each day—before they set out on the short walk to church. There'd been no sign of any of Johannes' men, although that could change at any time. Eli appeared constantly alert, and even as they held hands and chatted, he was on duty.

Folks mingled out front as they approached. Their voices and chatter warmed Makayla. But as she glanced at Eli, her heart went out to her uncomfortable-looking escort. How long had it been since he'd attended a church service? Months? Years? She squeezed his hand. "Should we go in?"

He gave an unconvincing smile. "Sure."

Inside, they took a seat in one of the middle pews, and she tried not to keep peeping at him, even though it was strange to see this self-assured man look out of place. At least, he'd been willing to attend.

The pastor stepped to the pulpit. The middle-aged man with salt-and-pepper hair, Russel, as Mrs. Langly had told her, smiled at the congregation as he opened his Bible. "Aren't you a great-looking crowd today?"

Good-natured chuckles rippled through the sanctuary.

"I'm always grateful to share Sunday mornings with you all." He looked down at his Bible. "I don't claim to know what you've all been dealing with this week or what state you've arrived in today. However, may I be so bold as to suggest that, on some level, we're all here for the same reason? Any guesses as to what that reason might be?"

Pews creaked as the congregation made guesses.

Pastor Russel studied them before answering his own question. "Forgiveness."

Though she kept her gaze forward, Makayla sensed Eli tense beside her.

Lord, please open his heart. I know You've brought us both here today for a reason. Please speak to him today in the way only You can....

Pastor Russel leaned forward, resting his elbows on the pulpit. His casual posture made him appear like a grandfather figure about to impart wisdom rather than a pastor she'd never met.

"I'm guessing most of you, no matter how much time you've spent in church, have heard of the forgiveness God offers. You know, in our culture, the idea of people getting what they deserve is glorified, isn't it?"

Murmured agreement filled the room.

"The phrase 'an eye for an eye, a tooth for a tooth' is actually Biblical." Pastor Russel's gaze moved along them. "But it's important to note its context. Does anybody know where it appears?"

"Old Testament," a man in the front row called out.

Pastor Russel pointed at him. "Exactly. This was in a time when people's wrongdoings were penalised according to their crime. The phrase is still often quoted today, and our modern judicial systems still use this guiding principle when determining a penalty. Revenge and justification were—and are—the overriding objectives. Forgiveness rarely gets a look in." No longer bracing on his elbows, he stepped back from the pulpit.

"We're all wrongdoers, guilty before God. The Bible says

'all are sinners and fall short of God's glory.' He has every right to dole out the punishment we deserve, and yet, He loved us so much that He sent His perfect Son, Jesus, to die on the cross, paying the penalty for our sins. Just as God forgave us, we're also told to 'forgive those who trespass against us.'"

Makayla held her breath, feeling Eli growing increasingly uncomfortable. She wanted to reach out and grab his hand, to reassure him somehow. But she dare not smother him, so she resisted, continuing to pray he'd venture past his discomfort and allow the words to penetrate his soul.

"While we can't allow murderers and thieves to go free, if we harbour unforgiveness in our hearts, anger and bitterness will find root and grow. There's no need for personal vendettas, regardless of how wronged we might feel. Let the law—and God—do their work. Jesus said, 'Do not judge, and you will not be judged; and do not condemn, and you will not be condemned; pardon, and you will be pardoned.' A spirit of forgiveness will release you from a hard and bitter heart. I understand how difficult this can be, especially when you believe you're in the right, and yet, when Jesus hung on that cross, what did He say?" The pastor glanced at the wooden cross above the baptistery. "He said, 'Father, forgive them, for they do not know what they are doing.'"

Eli stood to his feet. Makayla didn't even have enough time to reach out to him before he was out of the pew and headed towards the exit.

Heart pounding, she followed him.

It didn't work, Lord. Her heart heavy, she hurried from the sanctuary. *I thought maybe today would be the day he'd come to understand and let go of the pent-up anger. God, was I wrong to suggest we come here?*

Once outside, she looked frantically around. Eli was leaning against a nearby oak, his back to her.

She sprinted to him, already planning out a speech about being glad he'd tried church and it being all right for them to head back to the bed and breakfast, but she stopped, stunned. Tears were streaming down his cheeks.

"Eli," she murmured, her heart breaking.

He turned his head away and swiped at his cheeks. "It was stuffy in there."

She braced a palm against the sturdy trunk. "I don't think that's why you're out here all alone. Are you all right?"

He cleared his throat. "Of course."

Gauging her words, she took a tentative step towards him. "I know you're used to being strong, but it's okay to not be."

Fresh tears filled his eyes.

Reaching out, she wrapped her arms around him.

He tensed, then accepted her embrace.

They remained that way until she pulled back and searched his face. "What was it the pastor said that affected you?"

He folded his arms and blinked. She could only imagine how embarrassed he felt about his candid display.

"That there's no need for personal vendettas, regardless of how wronged you might feel." He blew out a breath. "It was like he was talking directly to me."

Her heart kicked up a hopeful tempo. *He did hear You, Lord! Is this the breakthrough his family has been praying for? The one I've been praying for?*

"The idea of trusting God is hard." His rough voice seemed to catch in his throat. "But I've been allowing hate and bitterness to drive me. I want whoever killed Dad to pay, but I've let it get too personal. I can't handle carrying that hate anymore. It's destroying me."

Her heart aching for him, she rubbed his arm. "Remember how we talked about starting wherever you can?"

She smiled as he nodded. "The realisation you've just reached is the perfect place to start."

He sucked in a jagged breath. "I don't know if I can."

Praying for the right words, she went on. "Would you do something for me?"

When he met her gaze, he looked so vulnerable, and compassion surged through her.

"I'd do anything for you, Makayla."

Her eyes widened before she blinked. No. He couldn't mean that. He meant he'd do anything to protect her. "I know you would." She swallowed hard. "You've proven it over and over again. But what I'm asking you to do is for *you*. Would you try reading my Bible? Just a chapter a day or however much you feel able to read. If it doesn't help, fine. But give it a try because I believe the Lord speaks to our hearts when we seek Him. He meets those who search for Him. Will you do it?"

He searched her face. "Okay. I'll give it a try."

Relief whooshed out of her lungs, and she squeezed his arm. "God will meet you, Eli. Trust me."

He looked deep into her eyes, and before she could suggest they return to the bed and breakfast, he pulled her into his arms.

Her breaths came faster as she leaned into him. Unsure of what was happening, she said nothing. *Lord, please keep Eli in Your care and open His heart. And please protect mine....*

CHAPTER 10

Though he was never off his guard, Eli began to relax as the days went on. He found himself better able to trust the two additional guards looking out for them than feeling he had to be on high alert. Was this what it felt like to begin trusting God? There was a freedom to it he hadn't expected.

Just as Makayla asked him to, he'd been reading her Bible each day. Nothing had struck him with the force of the Sunday service, but he became more open to verses that simply used to be words on pages. Despite the subtlety, he'd begun to believe there was something to what Makayla had said—God met those who searched for Him.

Near the end of their first week, she suggested they take a walk. Enjoying the picturesque landscape sounded great. Besides, he was growing restless staying inside, hiding away, although being with her wasn't a chore.

While they strolled in companionable silence, her hand in his, warm air stirred her pale hair around her, carrying the sweet scent of the bottlebrush trees lining the path. Rainbow lorikeets screeched in the branches as they foraged for the nectar.

As her hair brushed his arm, he almost rubbed his thumb across the back of her hand. How their interactions had changed! Though his breakdown and demonstration had been uncomfortable, it had dissolved a wall between them. They understood each other now, lending a deeper compatibility.

A young couple with a toddler came towards them. The child broke away and chuckled as his father sprinted after him, sweeping him into his arms moments before he slipped down an embankment and into the creek below. So innocent. Much like Makayla. Although she was now more aware of the danger she was in.

Growing fonder of her, Eli nearly let remarks about his feelings slip. He'd caught himself, but remembering he couldn't afford to demonstrate anything beyond protectiveness until he finished his job was getting harder.

Her fingers rested so lightly in his, so comfortable, adding to his suspicion she might also be attempting to balance a growing attachment. She was a sweet woman by nature, making it difficult for him to tell. If she *was* developing feelings, she kept them in check remarkably well. He knew why. They were still divided in their beliefs. Although he was doing his best to seek God, keeping their distance was best until he was sure of his feelings towards the faith she held dear.

"It feels like we've been here for a long time, doesn't it?" she remarked as they approached a shady park.

"The days are starting to blur together," he agreed. "Though I must say, I've never had an assignment like this."

She tossed him one of her smiles that never failed to steal

his breath away. "I haven't been too much of a trial to you, then?"

"You're not a trial at all." A seriousness invaded his tone. He needed a subject change—fast. "We've done a good job pretending to be married, haven't we?"

She chuckled. "Does this mean I'm cut out for undercover work?"

He played along, brows rising. "I think, were you to enter the field, you'd be one of the best."

She laughed, turning her attention back to their surroundings. Her expression sobered.

"That's a serious face."

She shook her head. "I was thinking about Guy Mangione and the information he said I had."

Eli exhaled. "It sure would've been helpful if he'd given us more to work with." Knowing Makayla had been kept in the dark about most of the workings of Pure Light and the League, he'd refrained from questioning her during their time here. However, they'd grown close enough he could probe without being intrusive. "Are you sure you can't think of anything that would make you invaluable to your uncle? Anything at all?"

Her hand slid from his, and she twisted a strand of hair around one finger. "No. I mean, besides having lived among the cult members and knowing their ideologies, I can't think of any special information I gained."

He'd just opened his mouth to tell her it was all right and he believed her, when she halted.

"Oh my!" Her hand flew to her mouth.

He reached for her arm to balance her, her sudden paleness worrying him. "What is it?"

She stared at him with enlarged eyes. "I remembered something that might be important."

He nodded, his mouth going dry.

"I heard Karl and Sally talking once about a farm ranch in Switzerland. They whispered about it like it was some secretive location. I thought it strange for them to talk about a place so far away, but sometimes they disappeared for weeks on end."

Eli's heart raced. "That could be it… a destination of interest. A safety point, maybe?"

Her face had grown paler. "That's what I was thinking."

He grabbed her elbow, turning them back towards the bed and breakfast. "You might be better at undercover work than we thought," he teased, though his tone remained serious. "I have a feeling you're onto something."

"Do you think it'll help you find Johannes?"

"We can't know for sure, but it warrants a call to my unit in Melbourne. We need everything we can get right now, so there's no time to waste."

They'd almost reached the bed and breakfast when one of the agents watching out for them jogged up, stopping them. "You'll need to stay back."

Eli pushed Makayla behind him, shielding her. "Why? What's going on?"

"There's been an altercation at the house where Ben and I have been staying."

"What? Is he all right?" Eli blinked.

"He'll be okay, but he's been injured."

"Did the attacker get away?"

The agent nodded, his jaw taut. "But I'm sure they were Hausbaden's men. We need to call for backup. His reinforcements won't be far behind."

Eli hesitated. He didn't know this agent well, but he'd been assured the man knew the ins and outs. This wasn't a time to take chances.

"All right, I'll go and call for reinforcements. Stay with Makayla and don't let her out of your sight." He was already headed back towards the bed and breakfast.

"Oh, believe me, I won't," the agent called after him.

Eli didn't feel quite right about leaving her behind, even with a qualified agent, but he pushed that fear aside, chalking it up to his growing protectiveness. They had to get backup, or they could all be in trouble.

CHAPTER 11

The moment Eli sat down in one of the impersonal hospital waiting room chairs, he got right back up to continue pacing. He stopped to look at the clock. After being shot by the imposter at the bed and breakfast, Makayla had been in surgery for over an hour, and still, he'd heard nothing.

After the men who'd attempted to kidnap her had been apprehended, his family had joined him at the hospital. He'd accepted their company, then insisted they go on their way because there was much to do after what had just taken place. His mother and Holly refused to go, stating he shouldn't be alone at a time like this.

He appreciated their concern but would have preferred time alone to sort through his thoughts. After they ran out of things to talk about, he resumed pacing.

How could this have happened? He'd done everything to keep Makayla safe.

"Mr. Carlton?"

Eli spun on his heel and hurried to meet with the doctor, arriving at the same time as his mother and Holly.

"The surgery's over?"

The doctor nodded. "She pulled through the surgery."

Eli's heart plummeted. "But…?"

The doctor folded his arms. "The prognosis isn't good. We were lucky to get the bullet out, but we can't tell how much damage it did until she wakes up."

Damage? Bile rising to his mouth, Eli swallowed. "What kind of damage?"

His mother slipped an arm around his waist.

The doctor shifted his weight, his expression grave. "When a bullet enters the head in the way this one did, there's a chance there'll be lasting repercussions including possible memory or motor function… impairments. We won't know until she's conscious and we're able to assess her condition."

With his world spinning, it was a miracle Eli remained on his feet. "When will she wake up?"

The doctor shrugged. "Maybe in an hour, maybe in a week." With a wince, he laid a hand on Eli's shoulder. "Welcome to the waiting game, son. I'm sorry I don't have better news for you."

Eli inhaled, fighting to stay calm. "It's all right."

"Do you know who her next of kin is?"

Was that a fist squeezing his insides? He pressed a hand against it. "She doesn't have family. I'll be her contact."

The doctor patted his shoulder and nodded to his mother and Holly. "We're doing everything we can."

Eli stared at the back of the doctor's long, white coat as he strode down the sterile hallway. Then Eli dropped into the waiting room chair and covered his face with his hands. Lava-like heat exploded within him.

How could You, God? I asked for Your help. I tried to trust You, and this is what I get.

HANDS FISTING, he rocked back and forth before he grabbed his phone. If God wouldn't take care of this, he would.

Excusing himself, he walked outside and dialled a connection in the anti-terrorism unit. "Mike? I need you to do some research. The Hausbaden case."

"Sure. Hey, I heard what happened. Just tell me what you need. I'll do anything."

Eli's free hand balled into another fist. "I need you to look up large plots of land in Switzerland. Farm ranches. Look into who owns them and let me know if any look shady. Johannes and his people are utilising one as a stronghold—find it."

"You're kidding."

Eli rubbed the back of his neck. "I wish I were."

"I'll get right on this, Eli."

"I appreciate it. Keep me updated."

He rejoined his mother and Holly inside, but before he could sit back down, a scrub-clad nurse approached. "Mr. Carlton? The doctor's cleared Makayla for one visitor. She's not responsive, and you'll have to keep it brief. But you're welcome to go to her."

Half in anticipation, half in dread, with his heart jumping inside his chest, he nodded his gratitude. "Thank you."

He did his best to prepare as he strode towards Makayla's room, but his heart broke at the sight of her. Limp and frail, her small form almost blended into the hospital bed. Oxygen tubing pumped life into her while the lifelessness of her face beneath her head bandaging caused a cold pit to form in his stomach.

He stepped closer. "Makayla, I'm so sorry." But his throat closed over the words, and she probably wouldn't have understood the choked sound if she'd heard him.

Almost afraid to touch her, he crossed his arms and tucked his hands inward to keep from reaching out. Surely, with her so fragile, even the slightest disturbance might cause her to break. Every bit of him tense as if he could fight this battle for her, he stood there for the longest time.

Then he reached out and stroked her cheek. The softest skin he'd ever felt, plush like velvet, grazed his fingertips. He'd wondered for a long time what it would be like to caress her beautiful face. He'd never dreamed it would happen at a moment like this.

He drew his hand back and sank into the chair by the bed, watching her, willing her to wake up. "Please, Makayla, it can't end like this. I won't let it."

When she remained unresponsive, knots tightened things inside him, and fearsome heat burning against the entire situation welled up. *God, how could You? She didn't do anything wrong.*

He pushed to his feet. He couldn't sit around watching her fight for her life. He'd find Johannes and finish this.

He didn't have long to wait for a call back from headquarters. He'd just exited the hospital when his phone rang.

THE FARM RETREAT had been located. He grilled Mike about every aspect. The discoveries they'd made about its inhabitants—their irregular visits, their keeping to themselves, their odd clothing—matched Karl and Sally.

By the time Eli reached the bed and breakfast, he'd booked a flight to Switzerland. It would depart at five a.m., but he wouldn't sleep tonight, anyway.

He threw a few sets of clothes and toiletries into a duffle before slipping his Glock in alongside. Going off on his own without notifying anyone was against protocol, not to mention unsafe, but Makayla didn't deserve to be fighting for her life in a hospital room. It was time for Johannes to pay.

CHAPTER 12

The flight to Switzerland was anything but restful. But at least, without phone access during the trip, he wasn't flooded with worried messages. He ground his teeth, willing the plane to travel faster. He needed to obtain a lead before they raised the alarm at his absence.

Beyond the window, a blanket of clouds spread beneath the aircraft as the sky lightened. He rubbed his forehead, forcing the tension from his muscles. Maybe his actions could be considered reckless, but he couldn't sit around, waiting, while the man responsible was on the loose.

Rather than going straight to a hotel upon arrival, he jumped into a rental car and turned towards the mountains and the ranch. He'd have to control himself since he wanted nothing more than to pounce on the place and arrest whoever inhabited it. But that would only lead to trouble. Plus, while doing this rogue, he had to be even more strategic.

Two hours later, his heart hammered as he manoeuvred his rented Ford along the winding mountain road. With the ranch so isolated, it was little mystery how it had managed to remain a secret.

The Alps rising around him offered no distraction. People came for honeymoons and vacations to glimpse them, but he'd come for one thing only—Johannes. If this was a dead end, he'd keep looking. He would finish this. Whatever it took to make the man pay for this second blow he'd inflicted on the Carlton family.

By the time a rustic log cabin appeared in the distance, enough hate to shoot the first person he saw pulsed through Eli. He parked far enough away to keep his car hidden and conceal his presence for as long as possible. He forced himself to pause and take a deep breath as he opened the locked case he'd transported the gun in and strapped on his weapon belt. This was it. He couldn't afford to mess up.

Ice-cold air cooled his cheeks as he clicked the car door shut, eased his gun from its holster, and scanned the property, then sprinted from tree to tree as he approached the cabin, patches of hardened snow crunching under his feet. He hunkered under a sweeping cedar, adrenaline pumping, and sent one final glance around before crouching to the building. There, he pressed his back against the wall as he listened for signs of habitation.

Birds chirped.

Wind rustled.

A plane droned high above.

Nothing sounded within.

Inhaling, he leaned in to glance through a nearby window.

No one.

Glancing around to ensure he was still alone, he slipped around the corner to the wraparound front porch. Expecting to break in, he stilled when his hand turned the unlocked doorknob. Heart thudding, he lowered his gun, gripped it with both hands, and slipped inside.

His eyes adjusted to his dim surroundings. With every piece of furniture made of solid oak, nothing offered creature comforts. So this must be used as a hideout.

He edged towards the door leading to the cabin's one bedroom. Rumpled sheets had slid off one side of a cot. A water bottle overshadowed a grimy ashtray on the bedside table. Smoke lingered in the air. Someone had been here—recently.

With precious few moments to ascertain the inhabitants' new location, he strode to the desk near the fireplace. Moving the gun to his left hand, he pulled out a stack of maps from the drawer. Red pen marks snaked out numerous routes. Kind of strange that they were paper maps in this computer era, but the cult abstained from modern technology. These must belong to the Pure Light leaders so they could track the White League's missions and smuggling routes.

Eli's palms began to sweat. The maps indicated they were supporting the White League's diabolical efforts.

He was about to slip the maps into his coat pocket when the cock of a gun broke the silence. A shiver shot up his spine as a voice spoke from the doorway. "And what do you think you're doing?"

His heart pounding, Eli locked eyes with Johannes himself. He'd never come face to face with the man, but he'd seen enough pictures.

From Johannes' look of recognition he, too, had done his homework. "Well, well, if it isn't a member of the Carlton brood."

Eli raised his gun and aimed back at Johannes. "In the flesh."

Johannes shook his head, laughing, the reaction chillingly out of place during their standoff. "I don't think you want to be doing that."

Eli's pulse raced. All sense of reason was slipping away, but he didn't care. He'd waited years to put a bullet in this man. "Oh, I think I do."

Footsteps came from the back door. His chest tightened. Johannes' sneer grew as a second gunman inched forward, his weapon trained on Eli.

Everything in Eli rebelled against reality. *How* had he been so absorbed in the maps he'd missed both men's approach?

Johannes twitched his gun. "You shouldn't have come here. When your old man meddled with us, it didn't end well, did it? Now, you're about to have the same ending."

A heavy weight dragged Eli down. He'd been so sure setting off on his own was the best way to get the job done, but how wrong had he been? With no one watching his back, he'd put himself in an impossible situation.

Isolated—with no backup.

Cornered—with nowhere to turn.

Lost—with no one knowing his whereabouts.

He'd ruined his chance to execute justice. Nauseous, he swallowed down the rising bile. His hatred and desire for revenge had landed him here. He *was* a hot-head, just as Rob had said.

I'm sorry, Dad. I'm sorry, Makayla.

"You're cornered." Johannes stalked closer. "Nothing's stopping me from putting a bullet in you right now, so I suggest you put your gun down."

Eli's gaze flickered towards Johannes' comrade. Unwavering, the man peered back. With no other choice, Eli set his gun on the desk behind him and raised his hands.

Johannes nodded to his crony. "Tie him up."

Emotionless, Eli stood there as the man secured his hands behind his back, then shoved him towards the windowless bedroom. He'd failed his father. And Makayla. Her sweet face lingered in his mind as his captor shut the bedroom door, plunging him into darkness.

CHAPTER 13

A machine's persistent beeping pulled Makayla from sleep. Her eyelids felt heavy. Managing to drag them open, she stared at the white ceiling. Where was she?

Her finger twitched, and something tickled her arm. Huh. An IV drip was flowing into her vein. Her throat closed as a tangle of memories flooded back. Rob and Eli… The man grabbing her, the gun pressing into her back, her running, then searing pain…

God, I thought I was going to die. But You saved me. Thank You.

"Makayla?"

Somehow, she turned her head towards the voice. *Rob…* She managed a weak smile. "Hi."

He leaned forward, his brow furrowed. "How are you feeling?"

"Tired."

"No surprise there. You've been through a lot these past three days."

Three days? She blinked. "I've been asleep for three days?"

"You've been out ever since you went into surgery."

She winced, registering the pain at the back of her neck. "My head hurts."

He laid a gentle hand on her arm. "I wouldn't move around too much right now. Head injuries are dangerous, and you sustained a bad one." His eyes moistened. "The doctor wasn't sure you were going to make it."

She blinked again. "Really?"

"At the very least, he expected some brain damage." His grip tightened a fraction, and his voice shook. "But here you are, talking to me. It's a miracle."

Head injury. Surgery. Three days. The words pounded with the pulsing in her head. But her eyelids began to droop. She opened them with a start. "Where's Eli? Is he all right?"

Rob's face twisted.

Cold curled in her stomach. "Rob, what is it?"

"He wasn't hurt." He patted her hand, quick to reassure her. "But... he's missing."

Missing? Her brows scrunched. The whooshing in her head made it hard to think, to remember. Someone had been trying to get her into a van. Had they taken *him*? "What do you mean?"

"After you got out of surgery, he left without a word to anyone. Knowing my baby brother, it has something to do with the case."

The cold welled inside her. "It's all my fault. If it hadn't been for me—"

Rob shook his head. "There's no point in thinking that way. Eli does what he wants, and you know that."

She did, all too well. The chill froze into something solid and settled over her. She'd thought he was learning how to entrust God with the pain Johannes inflicted, but now...

Lord, please protect Eli. I don't know what I'll do if he gets hurt because of me.

"Don't worry. We'll find him," Rob assured. "You rest now. I'm going to let the doctor know you're awake." He gave her hand a gentle squeeze. "And I'll phone the family right away. We've all been praying for you."

"Give them my love…" But as exhaustion crowded in, she wasn't sure whether she'd spoken aloud or not. She was half-asleep before he left the room. Eli's face lingered in her mind until she drifted off.

∞

WHEN MAKAYLA WOKE AGAIN, she felt rested but disoriented. The stark hospital surroundings made it impossible to distinguish the time of day. But, with a slight lull in the hall, it might be evening.

A figure by the bed moved into her vision. "Good evening, sleepyhead."

"Hello." Makayla smiled at Jean as she tried to push herself up. "What time is it?"

"Nearing eight p.m. They're about to tell visitors to skedaddle, so I'm glad you woke up before I left. It's such a joy to see those pretty eyes of yours open again."

Emotion twisted in Makayla's chest. Jean looked endlessly motherly in her crocheted sweater, the scent of rose perfume lingering around her, tenderness softening her expression.

Makayla pushed back tears. "Thank you. Is there any news of Eli?"

"Not yet." Letting out a heavy sigh, Jean shifted in the seat. "That boy's tenacity has gotten him places, but it's also gotten him into trouble. Most of the time, he makes it through, but the White League isn't a force to be taken lightly. They've never been kind to the Carltons."

With emotions twisting her chest, Makayla fought the urge to scream, but Jean... "How are you staying so calm when he could be in so much danger?"

Jean shrugged. "It's taken a lot of practice, but having a husband and sons all involved in dangerous work has been good training. I've learned to place all my concerns in God's hands. The situation with Eli is out of our control, so we have no choice but to entrust his safety to the Lord."

She was right, of course. Makayla drew in deep breaths, working on her heart. "It's just so hard," she murmured. "I feel like he wouldn't be in this situation if it weren't for me. He's determined to make Johannes pay for what happened to your husband and this isn't about me, but I can't help feeling partially responsible."

Jean's eyes narrowed. "You're wrong, you know."

Makayla's brow knit. "What do you mean? About what?"

Smiling, Jean reached for her hand and squeezed it. "You're wrong about it not being about you. I know my sons better than anyone, and I've never seen Eli this way."

Makayla angled her head. "What way?"

"In love."

Air rushed from her lungs. "In love? With me?"

Jean laughed. "Yes, with *you*. Is that so hard to believe?"

Averting her gaze, Makayla let out a tight chuckle. "I guess not. It's just... we're in such different places in our lives." She took a moment before continuing. "I do feel for him, but I don't want to be a distraction while he's searching for God."

Still holding Makayla's hand, Jean rubbed her thumb across the back of it. "I've seen that, Makayla."

Makayla turned her fingers to return her friend's clasp.

Knowing she'd been so transparent disconcerted her, but speaking freely about her feelings was a relief. "I thought he was starting to reach out for God, but this rash decision makes me fear I was wrong."

Jean shook her head. "Rome wasn't built in a day, and neither is a person's relationship with God. Trusting isn't going to come easily to Eli—no matter what. Just because he's chosen to handle this situation in his old manner doesn't mean those seeds haven't taken root. All we can do is pray he'll think back on those seeds wherever he is. No situation we get ourselves into can bar God from getting through to the deepest parts of our hearts."

"I have to admit I've been doing more worrying than praying on his behalf," Makayla confessed.

Jean's hand tightened once again on hers. "It's not too late to change that. Why don't we pray for him right now?"

"That would be great." Makayla managed a small smile as her throat closed over. She might have been incapable of speaking, but her heart clung to Jean's every word as they lifted Eli up in prayer.

CHAPTER 14

When hours began to tick by, Eli stopped trying to decipher the time of day or night—or how long he'd remain locked in the bedroom, bound and helpless. This wasn't how he'd expected this mission to end.

He'd failed.

His chest tightened until breathing became difficult. During his time with Makayla in the bed and breakfast, he'd felt his heart softening towards the things of God, felt trust working its way back into his life.

"God, how did I end up here?" He voiced the question in quiet desperation, the weight of it all pressing so heavily on his shoulders he wasn't sure he could take it any longer.

He drew his knees to his chest. Tears sprang to his eyes, not out of fear for his own life or of never being found. They were mourning that he'd resorted to this rage-driven solution. He'd fallen prey to his demons once again. He longed to be by Makayla's side, gaining strength from her calm confidence in the Lord. He'd started to believe there was something to this confidence, yet he'd acted rashly and taken things into his own hands again. Would he never learn?

He dropped to his knees.

I'm sorry, Lord. Doing things my way has never worked. Throughout all these years, all it's done is create more hatred inside of me. You placed Makayla in my life to show me that I need to trust Someone outside of myself if I'm ever going to feel closure. I ignored this lesson and went off on my own again. Please forgive me.

As he sucked in a breath, the calmness he'd experienced during his recent Bible readings seeped back in, comforting his troubled heart. After allowing peace to take hold, all he had left was concern over Makayla's well-being.

Had she survived? Would he ever even know? How could he bear it if she hadn't or if she'd sustained permanent damage? *Lord, please heal her. Please...*

The lock rattled, and the door pushed open. His stomach twisted as Johannes himself blocked the doorway, light spilling in around his big frame. What was he still doing here? Why hadn't he killed him?

"Right where I left you." In singsong cadence, the words taunted Eli.

At another time, he might have answered with a scathing remark, thinking it the best way to stand up for himself. However, this time, he remained silent.

"Nothing to say?" Johannes braced a shoulder against the doorjamb. "Realising how stupid coming here alone was, are you?" He clicked his tongue. "Rumour is you're the rash one of the family. You must've gotten that from your old man. He didn't know when to stop, either."

As much as hearing this man speak of his dad grated, the indignation he would've felt remained absent. Even

Johannes' sneer did nothing to disrupt the calm claiming him.

"My dad did what he thought was right." How foreign his voice sounded! Eli shifted on his knees, the wooden floorboards cutting into them. "And I did what I thought was right. But this is bigger than you or me. Even you know that deep down."

A flash of something—uncertainty?—crossed this so-called supreme leader's face before the mockery settled back into the lines it had long carved. "You're talking nonsense. But whatever you need to tell yourself to gain peace in your last hours is fine."

Johannes' words were a scare tactic. He wanted Eli to become desperate and do something stupid. He wanted to incite a reaction. Eli had been reacting for years, and it had gotten him here. He wouldn't take the bait.

"Do what you want to, Johannes. God will have His way in the end." Where those words came from, Eli had no idea, but as they crossed his lips, he *believed* them.

Johannes scoffed. "You'd better pray to God then, because He's the only one able to save you now."

With that, he turned away and slammed the door before once again locking Eli in.

Instead of falling back into despair, Eli prayed.

Lord, whatever Your plan is in all of this, help me to follow Your way. Mine hasn't worked, and I'm ready to try Yours.

In his half-sleep, Eli dreamed his brothers had come to rescue him.

That was why Johannes hung around. He was waiting for Eli's brothers to come. He thought he could finish them all.

~

THE CABIN'S front door banged open. Eli sat bolt-upright.

Had they come?

His heart pounded. Dread curled in his stomach.

Johannes would kill them all.

A man swore. "Who are you, barging in like this?"

"International anti-terrorist unit," another man's voice answered. "Hands up where I can see them."

Eli scooted to the door and pressed in closer, the tension draining from his every muscle as relief swelled inside him. Not his brothers.

Another round of curses issued from Johannes' mouth.

"It's over, Hausbaden. You're coming with us."

Despite being cornered, Johannes released a chuckle. "Think again, sonny."

The man ignored him. "Where's Carlton?"

Eli's heart hammered. They knew he was here. *Thank You, Lord. I don't deserve this, but thank You.*

He wanted to shout that he was alive, make his presence known, but overcome with emotion, he couldn't speak.

"Carlton's dead," Johannes spat.

"*Eli* Carlton," the man clarified. "We know he's here, so there's no point playing games."

A shot sounded.

The door flung inwards. Eli scooted backwards as an unknown man stepped inside. "Carlton?"

He nodded. "Yes."

The man made quick work of freeing Eli's hands and feet. He helped Eli stand and supported him as they left the room.

Freedom had never felt so good. He'd never take it for granted again.

Johannes' face contorted. "This isn't over, Carlton."

"It is," Eli's rescuer replied. "Turn around and face the wall, Hausbaden. You're under arrest."

As he was turning, other men burst through the back door, weapons raised.

"Looks like we're at an impasse, boys." Johannes' grin widened. "I'm sure you're well aware my men won't hesitate to shoot, so you have an important decision to make. Do as we say—or die, here and now. That includes you, Carlton."

A gunshot rang out. Utter chaos ensued.

Eli's instincts and training warred as fiercely as the fighting teams. Everything in his nature demanded he join the fight, but his well-trained mind registered that he was weak and unarmed. So, when one of the unit members ushered him from the cabin, he went without a fight.

"Get into the car," the man ordered. "And stay there."

At any other time, a unit member would have stayed with a recovered hostage, but since every man was needed, he was expected to look after himself.

He climbed into one of the cars, his chest heaving as the scuffle continued. Although grateful to be free, he closed his eyes as a sense of helplessness returned. He should be in there, helping, not hiding away.

He'd just gripped the handle to open the door and get out when the passenger window shattered. Shards of glass tickled his arms as he covered his head with them. When he lifted it, Johannes stood there.

"You came to get me." Johannes twitched his gun again, using it to beckon Eli. "Get out and fight."

Somehow, he'd managed to slip through the mayhem and was set on finishing Eli the way he had his father. The League's leader had ignored caution and acted in rage.

This was the moment Eli had dreamed of. He climbed out, ready to fight despite his disadvantage, adrenaline surging through him.

Johannes stepped back and aimed, his thin lips parting.

He pulled the trigger. But as his hand jerked, the shot went wide.

Eli lunged forward, knocked the revolver from his hand, and locked Johannes' hands behind his back.

Johannes growled as Eli pinned him to the ground and pressed the gun into his back. "You Carltons think you can get away with anything," he spat. "You're going to pay for this just like your dad did."

"No, Johannes, you're the one who's going to pay up." Eli stared at the .38 in his hand. The weapon, though not his own, fit so well in his grip, the vendetta so long a part of him. His finger caressed the trigger. Just one little squeeze. That's all it would take to end this. He'd sworn once that, if the chance to kill Johannes presented itself, he'd take it without hesitation. So why couldn't he bring himself to fire the gun now?

Even as Johannes struggled against his hold, something in Eli reached out to God.

It was never Your plan for me to get revenge, was it, Lord? All along, You wanted to teach me how to entrust all outcomes to You. Even if I were to shoot him now, would I feel fulfilled? No. Justice belongs to You.

"Carlton!"

Three members of the anti-terrorist unit were racing towards him. Within moments, they'd taken hold of Johannes.

"We're lucky you're a trained agent," the agent at Eli's side remarked. "I don't know how he slipped through, but your training saved you just now. You're a Carlton, all right."

A bittersweet sensation washed over Eli. "You knew my dad?"

A twitch jerked the agent's jaw. "I did. He would be proud of you, Eli."

As Johannes was cuffed and secured in a squad car, a myriad of emotions surged through Eli.

It was over.

His father's killer had been captured.

But was it too late for Makayla?

The agent's phone rang. The man answered and then held it out. "It's your brother, Rob."

Eli blinked and took the phone. He swallowed the lump in his throat. "Hey, Rob."

"Thank God you're all right. We've all been so worried about you and praying nonstop."

Eli chuckled. "I've been doing a fair amount of that myself." Now that he had the chance to ask after Makayla, he was almost afraid to. "How... how's Makayla?"

"It's a miracle." Tender joy softened his brother's voice. "She woke up, and she's going to be fine."

Eli's knees buckled as relief coursed through him. "No brain damage?"

"None at all. God protected her in the most amazing way."

Eli leaned against the squad car, a choked sob escaping. "That's wonderful."

"She's been asking about you."

His collapsing body jerked to attention. "She has?"

Hope buoyed him, although his shoulders sagged. How could he face her after going rogue? She'd be so disappointed.

"Yes, she has."

"Does she know where I went?"

"It didn't take long for her to guess. That's how the antiterrorism unit knew where to look for Johannes. And for you."

Of course. Eli drew in a deep breath, pushing out the

words that needed to be said. "I'm sorry for worrying you. Going off without telling anyone wasn't right."

Rob laughed. "It's not like we don't know how you work, little brother."

"I know." Eli shifted his weight, switching the phone to the other ear. "But I'm seeing now how wrongly I've handled so many things. Will you forgive me?"

"Of course." Rob's voice sounded as thick as Eli's felt. "We're just grateful you're safe."

Eli glanced at the agent beside him. "The man who owns this phone, did you know he knew Dad?"

"Yeah," Rob answered. "I wish Dad had lived to see this day. You did well, little brother."

"Thanks." Eli rubbed his tired eyes. It. Was. Over. "See you at home."

Home. No place had ever sounded so good.

CHAPTER 15

Makayla peered in the mirror for the hundredth time. If only there was some way to spruce up the knitted top she'd pulled over her hospital gown. Sighing, she fluffed her hair, taking care to avoid the bandage, but it looked no different to how it was two minutes earlier. At least they hadn't had to shave more than a patch in the back—or so they told her. She hadn't seen what was left in the back under the bandage. But she should have asked Jean to bring some better shampoo. The stuff at the hospital wasn't doing her dyed locks any good.

She forced herself to lower the mirror.

Stop it. He knows you had surgery and almost died. He's not expecting you to look like a pageant queen.

Butterflies erupted in her stomach whenever she thought of Eli. As eager as he'd been to come home, he'd stayed in Switzerland to get things with Johannes' arrest squared away. Although she'd focused on recovering, the last days had dragged. Sure, she'd been told he was fine, but the danger he'd put himself into made her shiver. She wouldn't relax until she saw him.

Then there was the matter of his faith. Despite the good outcome, she couldn't ignore those disappointed twinges over how he'd rushed off on his own, putting his life at risk. But then, everyone made mistakes. Who was she to judge?

She leaned back against the pillows, forcing taut muscles to relax. No matter how many times she told herself to act natural, she jolted up each time footsteps sounded in the hall.

When his deep voice resounded outside her room, her pulse quickened. He was here! Moments later, he stepped into the room, and their gazes met.

"Eli. I'm so glad you're back." Her chest heaved as she took in the sight of him.

"Makayla," he murmured her name, the tender tones causing her stomach to flip. Her heart pounded as he approached, his gaze intense, his stride purposeful.

"I was afraid I'd never see you again." He reached as though to touch her face, then jerked his hand back, and fisted it.

She'd been just as afraid of the same thing. And yet... "God was watching over us both."

"Yes, but I shouldn't have gone off on my own." He blew out a breath, scowling at the window. "I was... so *angry*.... Impatient, I reverted to my natural desire to take matters into my hands."

She touched his arm, drawing his gaze back to her. "I know."

His eyes narrowed. "You're not disappointed in me?"

No reason to deny it. She shrugged. "A little."

He ran a hand over his hair. "When I learned you might not wake up, this burning desire to make Johannes pay raged through me. I forgot about the quiet I'd let into my soul during our time at the bed and breakfast and at church when I sensed God speaking to my heart. I forgot it *all* in my haste to find Johannes. It took being locked in a room, bound and helpless, for me to realise I'd let my demons get the best of me again. When I couldn't do anything, I did the most important thing I've ever done in my life—I sat there in the dark and begged for God's forgiveness...."

Her heart aching for him, she gripped his arm tighter. Tears threatened, but she warded them off. He'd been through so much. Now, it was her turn to be strong. "Eli, any humble plea for God's forgiveness will be answered. God heard you."

"I know." He nodded. "I was prepared to die in that cabin. I'd made peace with God and knew He'd forgiven me for my waywardness. I didn't expect to escape. Yet He saw fit to save me. I don't know how long Johannes would have waited for my brothers before he killed me, but I believe the anti-terrorist unit arrived just in time. They could have so easily been unable to find me before it was too late."

"God obviously has plans for you." Awe over His timing and provision filled her, warming her heart and soul. "He really is good."

"He absolutely is." Smiling, Eli nodded towards the chair beside the bed. "May I sit?"

She laughed and released his arm. "Of course." She studied him while he settled onto the plastic chair, his aftershave teasing her senses.

His brow lowered as they shared a pleasant silence. Then he lifted his gaze. "Makayla, these crazy past few days... I–I think it was the wake-up call I needed."

"Wake-up call for what?" A tumble of hopeful thoughts and feelings assailed her. She angled her head.

He interlaced his fingers, dropping his gaze to them. "To

get my life right with God. To not waste a single moment trying to manage things in my own strength. Doing that only leads to dead ends and emptiness." He spread his fingers. "I've fought God for so long, but you helped me to see that He could be trusted—even with the most painful things in my life. You have no idea what you've done for me."

Her heart tumbled over itself. She blinked. "I didn't do anything. God had a plan, and I allowed Him to take the reins. But the truth is you saved my life." Unable to hold back any longer, she stroked his cheek, savouring the roughness of his whiskers beneath her fingertips.

His eyes softened as he covered her hand with his. "I know you're still in recovery and have been through a lot, but can I get something off my chest?"

"Yes, of course." Her heart pounded as their gazes held and the complete openness in his eyes revealed his heart.

He cleared his throat. "When you got shot, I held you in my arms and wondered if that was the end. No more chances to talk to you, to hear you laugh… to be with you." He swallowed hard, moving her hand from his cheek and pressing a kiss to her palm. "I realised then how much I felt for you. How much I love you."

Her mouth dropped open. *He loves me?*

"I'm not nearly good enough for you, but—"

She interrupted him with two fingers to his lips. "Don't say that. God is still at work in both our lives."

He clasped her hands. "I still have a long way to go, but after everything that happened, I had to tell you."

"I…" The words swelled up her chest, emerging on a whisper. "I love you too, Eli."

He leaned towards her, capturing her lips with his own, ever so gently. His sweet, undemanding touch made her forget everything—the shooting, the cult and its leader, and even the hospital room.

When they broke apart, he enfolded her into his arms. She sank into his embrace, savouring the strength and warmth of his chest as her heart swelled. *Thank You, God, for this... for bringing us together at last... for bringing Eli home to You... for everything.*

CHAPTER 16

When a knock sounded on her apartment door, Makayla set the pitcher of iced tea she'd prepared on the small table. As excited as she was to see Eli, she stalled, one hand on the chilled glass as a shiver threaded through her. She swiped at a bead of condensation, parts of her cold and sweaty like the pitcher over what Eli might be feeling this evening.

The three months since Johannes' apprehension had been good, despite the difficult news Eli received soon after arriving back from Switzerland. His decision to go off on his own to hunt down Johannes had come under serious observation. After a great deal of deliberation, the anti-terrorism unit had placed him on suspension for actions considered insubordinate and dangerous.

While, to the entire unit and beyond, Eli was being hailed as a hero for bringing down the White League almost single-handedly, he'd been aware there would be consequences for his actions. But that didn't make the news any easier.

The unit afforded him proper respect by keeping the suspension quiet to preserve his stellar reputation. During that time, he'd decided to withdraw from law enforcement altogether. He'd assured his surprised family that he'd prayed and was following God's guidance.

Through this life-changing decision, Makayla rejoiced knowing that, no matter how difficult the past few months had been, they'd brought Eli closer to the Lord. She could see it in his eyes and hear it in his voice. He spoke with such peace now, a calm she hadn't witnessed in him before. Although Jean wanted him safe, she voiced concern about what he was giving up. Makayla, however, was convinced he was making the right decision. God had brought him back to Himself and had a plan for his life—a plan He would reveal in His own time.

THIS MORNING, Eli had gone to clean out his locker and say goodbye, concluding his time with the unit. As right as the decision felt, having the hunt for Johannes end with his departure from the career he'd devoted his life to would be difficult. She'd need to be sensitive to that, even as excitement over her own news thrummed through her. Since completing the deradicalisation program and recovering from her latest ordeal, she felt surer than ever about what the future held for her. She couldn't wait to share her idea with Eli.

But first, she'd have to open the door. Shaking her head at her hesitation, she crossed the space and flung it open. "Hey." She braced herself on the door.

His smile warmed her as thoroughly as it had the day she knew she loved him.

"Hey, yourself." He bent in and brushed his lips against hers.

New shivers coursed through her, but she cupped a hand to his cheek, drawing him back enough to see his face. "How did it go today? Are you okay?"

He nodded and took her in his arms. "Yes, I'm good."

With his tightening arms around her, she leaned against him and sighed out any remaining worries. "I was praying for you all day."

"Thank you. That means a lot. I feel at peace about leaving."

They held each other until she took his hand and pulled him towards the kitchen. "Dinner's ready. I hope you're hungry."

"Starving." He winked. "I could eat an ox, but whatever you're cooking smells great."

She chuckled. "It's just a chicken pie."

As she slid the pie from the oven, her stomach churned. It was time to tell him. During the past months, Eli had been supportive of her as she, too, grew in Christ, but what would he think of her current idea?

Praying for the right words, she carried the pie to the table and sat across from him. After giving thanks, he served her a section and then himself and dug right in. Enticing smells begged her to taste her work, but she wouldn't dare eat with such knots in her stomach.

"Eli, I have something to tell you."

His utensils clattered against the plate as he paused, his brow creasing. "Sounds serious." His gaze held hers. "I'm all ears."

She took a deep breath, unprepared to explain her ideas.

Clearly noting her struggle, he set aside his fork and reached for her hand. "Is everything okay?"

She nodded, letting out a silly laugh. "I'm just trying to find the right words."

"Just tell it like it is." He squeezed her hand. "I'm listening."

"All right." She swallowed hard and held his gaze. "I want to start a program for vulnerable youths who are at risk of being dragged into cult life." All she could hear was the pounding of her heart as she studied him. What would he think? Would he consider she was aiming too high? She had no formal training in things like this.

Letting out a low whistle, he stared at her. "Wow. What made you decide that?"

She leaned closer, turning her hand to return his clasp. "You know how lost I felt after my parents died and Karl and Sally took me in?"

He gave a nod, his gaze steady.

"I want to stop vulnerable young people from the same fate I suffered. Cults promise a sense of community and belonging. But that fades, and before you know it, you're trapped. I wish someone had reached out and shown me a better way. God's way. I believe I can use my painful experiences to guide others. Imagine it!" An excited laugh escaped. "The struggle I experienced during those years—everything that happened—could help others. I feel that God is waiting to use those experiences for His glory." Still holding his hand, she sat back and expelled a deep breath. "What do you think?"

His eyes shone. "I think it's a wonderful idea."

"You do?" Why did her voice squeak? It sounded like she was doubting him.

He stood and came around the table. Kneeling in front of her, he grasped both her hands, his eyes glowing. "I do. I can't imagine anyone better equipped for the task. God has placed a mission on your heart, Makayla. You must follow it."

She freed a hand to brush a tear from her cheek. "Thank you. Having your support means more to me than anything."

Their gazes held steady before he gave a small smile. "It might be hard for you to believe, but I've also been thinking about how to use what I've been through for God's glory."

Sliding her hand back into his, she shook her head. "That's not hard to believe at all. God's been working in your life, too."

He peered down at their hands, his thumbs moving absently over the backs of hers. "Letting go of being a cop isn't easy, but I feel God pulling me towards something else. After what you said, I think I know what." His chin lifted, and a sheen of purpose glazed his eyes. "It might sound crazy, but how would you feel about having a partner help you start this program?"

A gasp rushed from her lips even as her eyes widened. "You're serious?"

His hand came up and cupped her cheek. "As serious as I've ever been about anything."

"Oh, Eli. God aligned our visions and put us in a place where we can pursue them together. It's so like Him to work things out in ways we could never have pictured. I can't think of anyone I'd rather have by my side than you."

"I was hoping you'd say that."

Her eyes widened further when he reached into his pocket and produced a small black box. "It's a time of transition for us both," he said, his eyes gentle. "But I know one thing. God brought you into my life at the perfect time. The way I see it, the fact that He cleared our paths to make room for this program you envision is further confirmation of what I already knew. I love you, and I want to spend the rest of my life with you. Makayla, will you marry me?"

Tears flowed down her cheeks, blurring her vision of the diamond ring he held. Speechless, she couldn't possibly find the words to express her joy.

He chuckled. "Do I get an answer?"

Oops! Grinning, she looked into his beloved face before throwing her arms around his neck. "Yes! The answer is yes!"

EPILOGUE

One year later...

Eli forced himself to sit on the hospital waiting room chair only to spring back up. He'd made it through the first four hours of Makayla's labour. But then, he'd become so emotional that he'd had to step out of her room for some air. One look at his pale face had his mother insisting he remain at a distance for the duration of the birth. Holly was with Makayla now, and he had to admit she was a far more stable and comforting presence.

"I've taken down white supremacists and battled terrorism," he muttered as he paced. "How is it I can't support my wife through labour?"

His mother chuckled. "Many men have a hard time with the birthing process. Having to step out is nothing to be ashamed of. Your dad stepped out many times during the birth of each of you boys."

Her words comforted him before he went right back to

thinking of Makayla. He stopped feet in front of his mother. "When will it be over?"

She patted his arm. "The doctor will be out as soon as your child is here. Don't worry, son."

As if on cue, the doctor appeared. Eli's heart slammed against his ribcage. "It's over?"

Compassionate and knowing, the doctor's smile settled him. "It's over, Mr Carlton. Go and meet your son."

Eli didn't need to be asked twice. He made it to Makayla's room in record time. As exhausted as she looked, he'd never seen her face so aglow.

"Did he tell you, Eli?" she asked. "We have a son."

Eli rushed to her bedside, a love more powerful than he could ever have imagined flooding through him at the sight of their newborn child. He settled down next to Makayla and reached out to stroke the baby's velvety-soft head.

"He's perfect, Makayla. You did amazing, my darling." He bent lower and kissed her lips.

She beamed while stroking the baby's tiny fingers.

"We never did settle on a name," Eli said.

She grinned. "I did during labour."

Really? He hadn't been able to think of anything other than trying to breathe. "Are you going to enlighten me?"

Her eyes softened. "George."

His throat closed. "Really?"

"Yes." She gripped his hand. "I never met your dad, but I know he'd be so proud of both you and our son. His legacy must continue."

Contentment and gratitude steadied him as he gazed at their sleeping child.

Thank You, Lord. Your love has freed and blessed me in ways unimaginable. Your goodness is beyond measure, Your loving-

kindness is everlasting, and Your faithfulness is to all generations. Amen.

∽

NOTE FROM THE AUTHOR

I HOPE you enjoyed **The Heroes of Eastbrooke Series** and were blessed by it.

If so, would you please take a moment to leave a review? Honest reviews of my books help bring them to the attention of other readers just like yourself, and mean the world to me! .Thank you in advance!

Now, please enjoy a bonus chapter of 'The Shadows Series", a story readers describe as an "amazing, heartfelt, but gritty, story".

BLESSINGS,

Juliette

∽

The Shadows Series books 1-5 preview...
Chapter 1
North East England 1981

MARRYING DANIEL O'CONNOR WAS A RISK, no two ways about it. Lizzy still didn't know why she'd agreed to marry him, but tomorrow at midday, come what may, she would be saying "I do".

Although impetuous, she was also loyal, and while her actions were highly irregular, she *would* see it through, and she *would* be a good wife to Daniel, regardless of what anyone thought. And she'd prove her father wrong.

She would also ask God to bless their marriage, even though Daniel didn't yet share her beliefs.

The past week had been busy, keeping her mind off tomorrow, and now she had to collect Sal, her best and most loyalist of friends, from the station. Lizzy glanced at her watch and tapped her fingers on the steering wheel as the traffic stalled in front of her.

"Come on, you lot! I don't want to be late. Move!" She thumped the wheel, and then sped around the car in front that had completely stopped and was going nowhere.

The train pulled into the station just as she entered the car park. She zipped into a spot someone had just vacated, jumped out of the car, slammed the door, and sprinted to the entrance, taking the stairs two at a time. People of all sizes and shapes were already piling out of the train onto the platform, but Sal's carrot red hair stood out amongst the crowd, making her easy to spot.

"Sal!" Lizzy waved and called out, not worried in the slightest what the people around her would think. Running down the stairs against the general flow of traffic, she bumped into anyone who wasn't fast enough to get out of her way, and almost knocked Sal off her feet when, finally reaching her, she threw her arms around her best friend with uncontrolled abandon.

"I'm so glad you could make it, Sal. It's great to see you!" Lizzy whirled her around and hugged her again.

"Wow Liz! It's great to see you too, but it's only been

three months!" Sal drew her eyebrows together and tilted her head slightly, curiosity loitering in her smile as she searched Lizzy's face. "Are you okay?"

Lizzy pulled back, annoyed at Sal's perception. "Of course I'm okay. What makes you think I'm not?"

"Oh, you just seem a little on edge."

Lizzy's eyes narrowed and her lips flattened into a thin line as she picked up Sal's dark brown carry all.

"I'm fine."

"Okay then." Sal glanced at Lizzy from the corner of her eye before tucking her arm through the crook of Lizzy's elbow as they walked back along the platform. "I still can't believe you moved all the way up here. Couldn't you have gone somewhere just a little closer?"

"You know why I did." Lizzy breathed in deeply. "Oh, but Sal, I do miss home." Lizzy fought back the sudden tears that pricked her eyes, and then turned her head to Sal, a forced smile planted on her face. "But enough of that. Tell me everything that's been happening."

All the way to the car, the girls chatted like two long lost friends, and Lizzy's mind was taken off the events of the morrow yet again.

The traffic hadn't lessened, and as she pulled out of the car park, Lizzy turned on the wipers. *A wet day. Great. That's all I need.*

She slammed on the brakes as a car pulled out in front of her, and blasted the horn while she shouted at the driver, a futile exercise, but it made her feel better. Her nerves were a little on edge.

"You haven't told your parents yet, have you?"

Lizzy bristled and held the steering wheel a little tighter. *Why did Sal have to bring my parents up?* She shook her head without looking at Sal.

"Don't you think you should?"

Lizzy clenched her jaw. *Why can't she let things be? Maybe asking her to come was a mistake.* But Sal was her best friend.

She put her foot down to beat the lights that had just changed to amber. "No. And I don't feel bad about it. They'd never agree to me marrying him, so I'm just going to do it. I know they'll be angry when they find out, but it'll be too late to do anything about it then. They shouldn't have been so horrible to him."

"Are you sure you know what you're doing, Liz? Have you prayed about it?"

Sal's eyes bored into her. Lizzy wasn't game to look. *Maybe I should tell her how I'm really feeling.* But if she knew the truth, Lizzy was sure that Sal would try her best to stop her from marrying Daniel, and it wasn't worth the risk. Having set her path, Lizzy was determined to stick to it. She'd actually contemplated calling it off a few times over the past couple of weeks, but the prospect of being alone again made her banish those thoughts immediately. It had to be better to be with someone than to be lonely.

Lizzy took a deep breath and calmed herself. "Yes, I've prayed about it. And yes, I do love him. I know what I'm doing, Sal, even if you think I don't." She slowed down to take the next corner. "He's a bit of a lad, so different to Mathew, but I love him. He makes me laugh and smile. I feel happy when I'm with him." She turned her head and glanced at Sal. "I know what you're thinking, and you might be right. I probably am marrying him on the rebound, but you know what? I don't care. I can't handle being on my own any longer." She wiped the tears from her eyes and hoped Sal hadn't seen them.

Sal looked at her intently. "I hope you'll be happy, Liz. I really do."

They sat quietly the rest of the way to Lizzy's apartment on the outskirts of town. The street lights had come on early, and the drizzle had increased to light rain. The windscreen wipers were doing their thing, and their squeak reminded Lizzy she needed to get new blades.

"This is it. Home sweet home." Lizzy pointed to the block of apartments on the left as she reversed into a small gap on the narrow street lined with cars. Four storeys high, and spanning half a block, the complex's only redeeming feature was the garden that ran between the brown brick walls and the footpath. "It's better on the inside," she said as she saw the look on Sal's face.

"I would hope so!" Sal raised her eyebrows. "A bit of a come down, Liz. "Are you going to live here once you're married?"

"For a while. It really is much better on the inside." Lizzy opened the car door and climbed out. She zipped her jacket and covered her head with its hood before grabbing Sal's bags out of the boot and directing her up the flight of stairs. Opening the door to the apartment, she held her breath as she waited for Sal's reaction.

"Wow, Liz! You weren't wrong! This really is nice!" Sal entered the living room and fell onto the new sofa Lizzy had picked up recently at a sale. "You always did have an eye for nice things."

"Thanks Sal." Lizzy's face expanded into a broad grin. "I'll just put these in your room and then make us a drink."

Lizzy placed Sal's bags in the spare room, and then busied herself making a cup of tea. She glanced at the clock. Daniel would be here any minute.

~

"Liz! I know you told me he was good looking, but you didn't tell me how much!"

"Shh! He'll hear you!"

"Okay, I'll just sit here and drool."

"He is pretty cute, I have to agree." Lizzy laughed and glanced over to where Daniel was standing at the bar, and her heart warmed. Maybe she did love him after all.

"Here you go, my lovelies! Two shandies with flair!" Daniel placed the glasses on the table and winked at Sal.

"Daniel! You shouldn't do that! What will she think!" Lizzy said with a laugh in her voice.

"Oh, go on," he said in his best Irish accent. "I was just having a bit o' fun!"

"It's okay, Liz." Sal patted Lizzy's leg and then looked up, a warm smile on her face. "Thank you, kind sir."

"My pleasure." He bowed, and then took his seat beside Lizzy. He placed his arm around her shoulders, and pulled her close. She didn't resist, instead, she snuggled closer.

"Good of you to come up for the wedding, Sal," Daniel said. "Lizzy's told me a lot about you."

"Has she just?" Sal glanced at Lizzy with a glint of mischief in her eye. "And what exactly has she been saying?"

"Oh, only good things," Daniel replied.

"I'm pleased to hear that!" Sal said.

"And what has she told you about me?" Daniel raised his eyebrows.

Sal hesitated and stole a glance at Lizzy before replying. "Only good things!"

Both girls burst out in laughter at Sal's attempt to copy his accent. Lizzy sat up and smiled at Daniel. As their eyes met, a tingle of excitement ran through her body. Cheeky he might be, but he was also lovable. And he was going to be her husband.

"Come on you two! You'll have enough time for that tomorrow!" Sal said.

Lizzy turned her head and grinned at Sal. "Yes, you're right. Let's order, shall we?"

As Lizzy laughed and reminisced with Sal over dinner, her heart lightened and her anxiety over her forthcoming wedding lessened. For a while at least.

When she climbed into bed a few hours later, however, her active mind kept her awake. Did she really know what she was doing?

Chapter 2

Lizzy woke early from her restless sleep and peeked out the window. The sun was nowhere to be seen, just thick black cloud hovering in the sky, just like the cloud that hovered in her heart.

She propped her pillows behind her and sat up. She reached for her Bible, but could only stare at the cover. What if she read something she didn't want to hear? No, she couldn't risk that. Closing her eyes, Lizzy tried to pray, but instead, she drifted off to sleep.

She woke with a start when Sal placed a cup of tea on the dresser beside her bed some time later. Sal sat down and took her hand.

"Hey."

"Hey yourself." Lizzy looked at her friend and smiled warmly. The knot in her stomach she didn't know was there loosened. No need for words. They knew each other so well after all they'd been through. Her heart lifted knowing Sal was here to support her on this day. Lizzy wished she could talk honestly, but probably had no need. Sal knew.

"Come on, kiddo. We need to get you ready for your big day." Sal stood and opened the curtains. "I think that man of yours is champing at the bit to marry you."

Lizzy laughed at the thought. How many times had he suggested they run off and get married at Gretna Green? And how many times had she told him they were almost doing the same thing, anyway?

She straightened herself and sipped her tea. This was it. She would go ahead with the wedding, right or wrong. She lifted her head and her eyes met Sal's. "Okay, kiddo, let's get this show on the road."

THE HOUR or so she and Sal spent at the beauty salon having their hair and make-up done had been relaxing, but now they were back at the apartment, and the time had come to get ready.

"Do you want something to eat before we begin?" Sal called out as she put the kettle on. "I think I'll have a cup of tea and some toast."

"Mmm, maybe not." Lizzy rubbed her stomach. "I don't know I could eat anything."

Sal looked at her tenderly. "Are you sure you're okay?"

Lizzy paused for a moment and took a breath. "Yes, I'm fine. It's just hard to believe it's all happening." She smiled at Sal and reached for the cross hanging around her neck. "I'll go fetch my dress."

She'd chosen a simple dress to get married in. After all, it was a morning wedding at the Register Office. A full blown wedding gown would have been over the top.

"Come on, let me do that." Sal placed her tea and toast on the table and took over from Lizzy.

Maybe she could have done it herself, but Lizzy's hands were shaking, and she was having trouble doing up the little buttons on the front of the bodice. As she stood there while

Sal battled with each tiny button, she was aware of the clock ticking. *Not much longer now...*

"There you go! Let me look at you." Sal stepped back and Lizzy turned around slowly. "Beautiful!"

"Thank you, Sal." Lizzy looked at herself in the mirror. Maybe she did look beautiful today. Well, almost. Beside Sal she often felt very plain, but today, with her hair done nicely and her make-up done properly, and wearing the dress the shop attendant had insisted suited her perfectly, maybe she did look beautiful.

THE TAXI ARRIVED and Lizzy and Sal walked carefully down the stairs and climbed into the back seat. The rain that had been threatening still held off, and although the sky was still grey, small patches of blue were visible in the distance. Maybe the sun would beat its way through the clouds and shine down on this day after all. She could always hope.

"Are you nervous?" Sal asked as the taxi made its way along the streets towards the town centre.

Lizzy looked down at her hands before replying. "A little."

"I'm not surprised. It's not too late, you know." Tears formed in Lizzy's eyes at Sal's gentle, caring tone. Sal reached out and squeezed Lizzy's hand. "You don't have to go through with it, you know."

Lizzy looked out the window, forcing her tears to stop. It wouldn't do to turn up at her wedding with red eyes and mascara blackening her cheeks. She pulled a tissue out of her purse and dabbed her eyes.

With the flow of tears stopped, she took control of herself, and turned back and looked at Sal. "I'm okay. I know it's not what I wanted, but Daniel loves me, and I do love him. It's just last minute nerves, that's all."

"Okay then." Sal squeezed her hand again. "If ever you need to talk, you know where I am."

THE TAXI PULLED up outside the Guildhall. On a sunny day, the dark coloured sandstone building would have looked more appealing, but on this dreary winter's day, it looked cold and unwelcoming. A sudden gust of wind hit as they alighted from the cab. Lizzy shivered and pulled her coat tighter.

"This is a beautiful old building, Liz," Sal said as they entered the foyer. Looking around at the plush furnishings and artwork, Lizzy had to agree it was indeed a much nicer building inside than out.

Sal's gaze settled on Lizzy. She stepped closer and tucked a piece of hair that had been blown in the wind back into place. "Are you sure you're okay, Liz? Last chance."

Lizzy stood steadily and reached for Sal's hand. "Yes, I'm sure. Let's go find everyone."

They found the small room that had been allocated for the ceremony without any problem. Before they entered, Lizzy stopped and inhaled deeply. For a moment, she wanted a crystal ball. Was she doing the right thing? Was she really ready for this? Neither she nor anyone else had one, so she held her head high and entered the room with Sal beside her.

THE FIRST PERSON she saw was Daniel. Always the life of the party, today he was no different. The fears of her heart melted away when he winked at her. She looked into those cheeky blue eyes and saw the man who had swept her off her feet only months before.

She'd first laid eyes on him at his cousin Nessa's thirtieth birthday party. A fine autumn evening, Lizzy had been looking forward to getting out after being house bound with all her school work. Nessa had befriended her at church, and was keen for her to make some friends. This was the perfect opportunity, she'd said.

The party began with cocktails in Nessa's garden. Lizzy wore a long Indian type skirt and felt almost bohemian. She stood with Nessa, chatting to a couple of girls she'd just been introduced to, when Nessa called a dark haired young man over to join the group.

"Everyone, this is my cousin Daniel from Belfast. Daniel, this is Susan, Lizzy and Brianna."

"Pleasure to meet you lovely ladies." He bowed with a flourish, and then asked if he could get the girls a drink.

"Thanks, but I'm okay at the moment," Brianna replied. Lizzy just shook her head and laughed. She'd never heard such an intriguing accent before. She thought it suited him. He was far too attractive to just sound normal.

"How long have you been here?" Susan asked.

"Oh, going on two weeks now. Bonny place."

"You really think so?" Brianna asked. "I've always thought it was rather a boring backwater type town, myself."

"I guess it's what you compare it with. I think it's grand. There's the river, and the sea not far away, and the pubs. A lot of pubs." He cocked one eyebrow and grinned. "Are you girls from here?" He looked at each of the girls in turn, but his cheeky eyes caught Lizzy's and she was mesmerized by them for a fleeting second.

She let out a huge breath when Susan answered first, because it took her a moment or two to gather herself. Susan and Brianna had both replied, so now it was her turn. She didn't want to tell him she was from the south, but Lizzy figured he'd know as soon as she opened her mouth.

"Oh, we've got a posh one here." His eyes sparkled and then he winked at her.

"I'm not really." Lizzy lifted her chin to a haughty angle and glared at him. "My family might be, but I'm not. I'm just an ordinary person, doing an ordinary job."

"Posh **and** fiery! And what job might that be?"

"I'm a teacher." She looked him straight in the eye.

"That's a grand job. Teachers are the backbone of our society, don't you agree?" Susan and Brianna both nodded. They appeared to be fascinated by this gregarious, cheeky man, but it was Lizzy he was interested in, so it turned out. He took her arm when dinner was announced, and led her to a table where they dined together and engaged in friendly banter for the next hour or so.

When the music started, he led her to the floor, and literally swept her off her feet.

"You dance very well, Elizabeth," he whispered in her ear, causing her pulse to race. Being from a 'posh' family, she certainly knew how to dance, but she'd never danced like this before. What would Mother think if she could see her now? Casting that thought aside, Lizzy decided to enjoy the moment. Perhaps he was holding her just a little too close, but she didn't push him away.

Lizzy didn't know what he saw in her. She was plain, nowhere near as attractive as either Susan or Brianna, but he was taken with her, and she with him. Maybe her rebellious spirit had attracted him. Whatever it was, they spent the rest of the evening together, and when it came time to leave, he asked if he could see her again. She didn't hesitate. She was ready for this. *Maybe at last I can forget Mathew.*

. . .

"LIZZY! There you are! And what a treat for sore eyes, might I say!" Daniel strode towards her and was about to wrap his arms around her when his mate, Johnno, stepped between them.

"Uh, uh - none of that yet. Wait until you've tied the knot, man."

"Get outta here, Johnno. Can't I give my lady a peck on the cheek?"

"Wait until you're legally wed. It's bad luck if you kiss her beforehand."

"Says who?"

"Says me."

"Okay then. Well, let's get this show on the road, and then I can kiss her all I want - right?" He looked at Johnno, and then at Lizzy. "Lizzy, you ready?"

"Yes Daniel, let's do this." She smiled at him. How handsome he looked in his pin striped suit. He loved wearing nice clothes, but the suit made him look suave and sophisticated. A thrill of excitement ran through Lizzy's body at the thought of being alone with this man later in the day.

Only ten people were present, plus the officiating celebrant. Daniel, Lizzy, Sal, Daniel's cousin Nessa and her husband Riley, Daniel's mate John, Lizzy's fellow teachers, Janine and Robert, and her friends from church, Colin and Linda. Colin had agreed to give her away.

"Colin, let's go." She hooked her arm in his as Daniel and Johnno took their places beside the celebrant. Sal led the way, and stood to the side when she reached the front. Lizzy walked the whole ten metres with her eyes glued on Daniel's. Colin's hand on hers helped to steady her pounding heart, and she tried not to think of anything apart from marrying Daniel, but in those fleeting moments, images of Mathew and her parents flitted through her mind. *Oh God, not now. I can't deal with it. Later. I promise. Later.*

Colin placed her arm in Daniel's when they reached the front, and gave her a reassuring squeeze before taking his place beside Linda. She heard very little of the ceremony. Like an out of body experience, happening to someone else. Not to Elizabeth Walton-Smythe of Wiveliscombe Manor in Taunton Deane.

The familiar words pulled her out of her trance, and back to the here and now. She'd heard the words many times before at the endless weddings of distant relatives she'd been forced to attend, but now it was her turn.

"Do you, Elizabeth Anne Walton-Smythe, take Daniel Rorey O'Connor to be your lawful husband, to have and to hold from this day forward, for better, for worse, for richer, for poorer, in sickness and health, until death do you part?"

She looked at Daniel and saw the sparkle in his eyes. She took a deep breath.

"I do."

DANIEL GOT his way at last, and kissed her long and hard in front of everyone. She felt her cheeks flush, and pushed him away gently. He stole one more brief kiss before he turned her around and pumped his arm in the air.

Someone wolf whistled. She thought it was Johnno, and then everyone clapped. She saw the smiles on Sal's and Nessa's faces. It was real. It had really happened. She was now Mrs Elizabeth O'Connor.

THE WEDDING BREAKFAST was a noisy occasion. Daniel was in his element, and Lizzy could tell he was happy. He kept hugging and kissing her, and whispering words in her ear that made her blush. She knew it wouldn't be long before he'd want to leave, but to be honest, she wasn't in that much of a hurry now the time had come.

Sal sat on the other side of her, looking stunning in her green suit. Lizzy reached out and squeezed her hand.

"I wish you could stay longer, Sal." Lizzy's eyes teared up a little, and she quickly wiped them away, hoping Sal hadn't noticed.

"Oh sweetie, we'll catch up again soon enough." Sal returned her squeeze and smiled tenderly, almost causing Lizzy's tears to break free.

"I wish I could have come up earlier. Such a bother, this work business!" Sal's laugh lightened the moment, and Lizzy breathed easier.

"I agree. At least we've got a week off now. We'll have to catch up again soon, Sal. I don't know I can bear not seeing you."

"Come on, Liz. You've got Daniel to keep you company now." Lizzy caught Sal's eyes, and in that instant, what she'd done hit her like a ton of bricks. She was now married, for better or for worse, to Daniel O'Connor.

Chapter 3

Daniel and Lizzy left soon after. Daniel had planned their honeymoon, and all he'd told her was not to bring much. That wasn't very helpful, so she'd packed for almost all possibilities, just in case. As it turned out, she really didn't need much at all, as they stayed in their hotel room most of the following week.

He was a skillful lover, tender and kind, and their first week together was bliss. Lizzy had never imagined that married life could be so wonderful. Her mother had never spoken to her about what happened behind closed doors.

The limited information she had as they began their marriage had been gleaned from the odd magazine and hushed whispers amongst her circle of friends at University. Never in her wildest dreams had she thought she could be so close to another human being.

They ventured out once or twice to get some fresh air, but the chill wind of the north east coast soon drove them back inside into the warmth of each other's arms.

The week passed all too quickly, and before long they headed back into town to start their real life together.

Not once had she thought of Mathew.

"Come on Daniel, I'm going to be late!" Lizzy grabbed her coat off the hook and opened the door. "I'll go without you," she called out playfully.

"Coming! Just give me a minute."

She looked back inside and saw him tying his shoe laces. His hair was rumpled and his shirt still undone, and as he stood, the sight of his bare chest made her insides quiver. She almost forgot she was in a hurry.

"I'm sorry, Lizzy. I'll be right there." He raced into the bathroom and she soon heard water splashing, and thought with dread about the mess he was making. Living with a man was certainly different to sharing a flat with a girlfriend, but it did have its benefits. Her mind started to replay their lovemaking of the previous night whilst she stood at the door waiting for him. Daniel had completely won her over with his constant tenderness and eagerness to love her at any hour of the day or night. It was no wonder he slept in.

"Well come on then, what are you waiting for?" He snatched a quick kiss as he flew past her.

EPILOGUE

Lizzy locked the door and ran down the steps, catching him as he reached the car.

She threw him the keys.

"You'd better drive today. I might be a bit late finishing this afternoon."

They climbed into the car, and took off towards Hull Elementary. She looked at her watch. They might just make it. The traffic seemed to be getting worse every day, but maybe it was because they were late every day. She'd never been late to school when she was single, but now, most mornings the bell was ringing as she jumped out of the car and sprinted to her classroom in an effort to beat the children.

Lizzy's preparation was suffering. How long would it be before she was spoken to about it? She muddled her way through each day, but she wasn't doing the best she could. Now Kids' Club was starting up again. Why had she agreed to it? Lizzy raced, yet again, into the classroom just ahead of the children.

"Good morning class." Lizzy stood with her hands on her hips, taking a number of slow, deep breaths, and surveyed the class of eight year olds standing before her.

"Good morning Mrs O'Connor." Her heart jumped as she once again heard the name. Still not used to it, every time Lizzy heard it, she thought of Daniel. A mental image of him pushing a trolley at the hospital flitted through her mind. It was the perfect job for him. He lit up anxious people's lives every day with his wit and humour, and he could whistle and sing as much as he wanted. The faintest of smiles played on her lips at the thought.

"Take a seat, class." She opened the folder on her desk and glanced inside. Normally she would have asked them to sit quietly, but this morning she let them talk amongst themselves for a few moments while she planned the day.

DANIEL ARRIVED BEFORE KIDS' Club had wrapped up. He leaned on the door frame of the activities room as she sat in front of the children, strumming her guitar whilst they sang a song she'd just taught them. His arms were folded, and the twinkle in his eyes suggested he was enjoying himself.

The children gave her a strange look when she stumbled over some words and played the wrong chord. *Drat him for having this effect on me.* She tried to concentrate on the job at hand, all the while aware of him taunting her from the back of the room.

At the end of the song, the children turned around when they heard clapping. Lizzy shook her head as he came closer.

"That was lovely, children, and Mrs O'Connor."

She knocked the music stand over in her hurry to get up. "Children," Lizzy sighed and straightened her skirt. "this is Mr O'Connor. Say good afternoon."

"Good afternoon, Mr O'Connor," they all said in a sing song chant.

"And good afternoon to you, too," he replied in a similar fashion, making the children laugh.

"What are you doing?" she whispered sharply.

"Just thought I'd come and meet some of your little protegees. That's alright, isn't it?"

"Not really." She turned her back so the children couldn't hear. "Best if you wait outside in the car. We're finishing up now." She leaned closer. "I could get into trouble with you here."

"Okay, I'll go. Don't stress your pretty little head. Bye

children. Nice to meet you." He waved as he walked back the way he came.

"Nice to meet you, too," they all called out.

"Miss, he sounds funny," a little blond haired girl said after he'd gone. They all laughed again.

"He's Irish, that's why," Lizzy said, quickly tidying up and dismissing the children.

THE PARENTS WERE all waiting outside, and once the children were handed over safely, Lizzy headed for the car. She'd calmed down a little by the time she reached it, but she still gave Daniel a good talking to.

"You just can't do that. You can't walk into a classroom full of children and take over." She folded her arms and glared at him.

"There there, Lizzy. I'm sorry. I just couldn't help it. I heard your sweet voice and the guitar music and it drew me in. I won't do it again, I promise." The twinkle in his eyes got her again. How did he manage it? Every time they had a disagreement, he'd sweet talk her and apologise; she'd forgive him, and then she'd end up in his arms.

It was hard to be angry with Daniel O'Connor for long.

The following day, two things happened that rocked their almost perfect world.

TO CONTINUE READING, **order your copy of The Shadows Series Omnibus here: www.julietteduncanbookstore.com/products/the-shadows-series-omnibus**

OTHER BOOKS BY JULIETTE DUNCAN

Find all of Juliette Duncan's books on her website: www.juliette-duncanbookstore.com

Beneath the Southern Cross: The Dawn of a Sunburned Land Series

Love's Unwavering Hope

A young woman forging a new life, an unscrupulous wealthy suitor, and a farmer fighting for her heart...

Love's Rebellious Spirit

She's abandoned her life of privilege. He's young and rash, but determined to provide for his headstrong bride, even if it leads them into the untamed heart of Australia...

Love's Distant Dream (coming soon)

From dust to destiny: an epic journey of love, loss, and legacy...

A Sunburned Land Series

A mature-age romance series

Slow Road to Love

A divorced reporter on a remote assignment. An alluring cattleman who captures her heart...

Slow Path to Peace

With their lives stripped bare, can Serena and David find peace?

Slow Ride Home

He's a cowboy who lives his life with abandon. She's spirited and fiercely independent...

Slow Dance at Dusk

A death, a wedding, and a change of plans...

Slow Trek to Triumph

A road trip, a new romance, and a new start…

Christmas at Goddard Downs

A Christmas celebration, an engagement in doubt…

True Love Series

Tender Love

Tested Love

Tormented Love

Triumphant Love

Precious Love Series

Forever Cherished

Forever Faithful

Forever His

Water's Edge Series

When I Met You

A barmaid searching for purpose, a youth pastor searching for love

Because of You

When dreams are shattered, can hope be re-found?

With You Beside Me

A doctor on a mission, a young woman wrestling with God, and an illness that touches the entire town.

All I Want is You

A young widow trusting God with her future.

A handsome property developer who could be the answer to her prayers…

It Was Always You

She was in love with her dead sister's boyfriend. He treats her like his kid sister.

My Heart Belongs to You

A jilted romance author and a free-spirited surfer, both searching for something more...

I'm Loving You

A young widow with an ADHD son. A new pastor with a troubled family background...

Finding You Under the Mistletoe

A beloved small-town doctor and a charming diner owner...

The Shadows Series

A jilted teacher, a charming Irishman, & the chance to escape their pasts & start again.

Lingering Shadows

Facing the Shadows

Beyond the Shadows

Secrets and Sacrifice

A Highland Christmas

A Time For Everything Series

A mature-age Christian Romance series

A Time to Treasure

She lost her husband and misses him dearly. He lost his wife but is ready to move on. Will a chance meeting in a foreign city change their lives forever?

A Time to Care

They've tied the knot, but will their love last the distance?

A Time to Abide

When grief hovers like a cloud, will the sun ever shine again for Wendy?

A Time to Rejoice

He's never forgiven himself for the accident that killed his mother.

Can he find forgiveness and true love?

Transformed by Love Christian Romance Series

Because We Loved

Because We Forgave

Because We Dreamed

Because We Believed

Because We Cared

Billionaires with Heart Series

Her Kind-Hearted Billionaire

A reluctant billionaire, a grieving young woman, and the trip *that changes their lives forever...*

Her Generous Billionaire

A grieving billionaire, a devoted solo mother, and a woman determined to sabotage their relationship...

Her Disgraced Billionaire

A billionaire in jail, a nurse who cares, and the challenge that changes their lives forever...

Her Compassionate Billionaire

A widowed billionaire with three young children. A replacement nanny who helps change his life...

The Potter's House Books...

Stories of hope, redemption, and second chances.

The Homecoming

Can she surrender a life of fame and fortune to find true love?

Unchained

Imprisoned by greed — redeemed by love.

Blessings of Love

She's going on mission to help others. He's going to win her heart.

The Hope We Share

Can the Master Potter work in Rachel and Andrew's hearts and give them a second chance at love?

The Love Abounds

Can the Master Potter work in Megan's heart and save her marriage?

Love's Healing Touch

A doctor in need of healing. A nurse in need of love.

Melody of Love

She's fleeing an abusive relationship, he's grieving his wife's death…

Whispers of Hope

He's struggling to accept his new normal. She's losing her patience…

Promise of Peace

She's disillusioned and troubled. He has a secret…

Heroes Of Eastbrooke Christian Romance Suspense Series

Safe in His Arms

Some say he's hiding. He says he's surviving.

Under His Watch

He'll stop at nothing to protect those he loves. Nothing.

Within His Sight

She'll stop at nothing to get a story. He'll scale the highest mountain to rescue her.

Freed by His Love

He's driven and determined. She's broken and scared.

Stand Alone Books

Leave Before He Kills You

When his face grew angry, I knew he could murder…

The Preacher's Son

Her grandmother told her to never kiss a preacher's son, but now she's married to one…

Promises of Love

A marriage proposal accepted in haste… a love she can't deny…

The Madeleine Richards Series (Pre-Teen/Middle-Grade Series)

Rebellion in Riversleigh

Trouble in Town

Problems in Paradise

ABOUT THE AUTHOR

Juliette Duncan is passionate about writing true to life Christian romances that will touch her readers' hearts and make a difference in their lives. Drawing on her own often challenging real-life experiences, Juliette writes deeply emotional stories that highlight God's amazing love and faithfulness, for which she's eternally grateful. Juliette lives on the beautiful Sunshine Coast of Queensland, Australia, and she and her husband have five adult children and eleven grandchildren. When not writing, Juliette and her husband love exploring the great outdoors.

Connect with Juliette:

Email: author@julietteduncan.com

Website: www.julietteduncan.com

Juliette's bookstore: www.julietteduncanbookstore.com

Facebook: www.facebook.com/JulietteDuncanAuthor

BookBub: www.bookbub.com/authors/juliette-duncan

Printed in Great Britain
by Amazon